The Wizard's Edict

Thomas Ian Doyle

To the women who gave notes, edits
& endless encouragement:

Mazz, Kasi, Nicky, Gabrielle & Mum

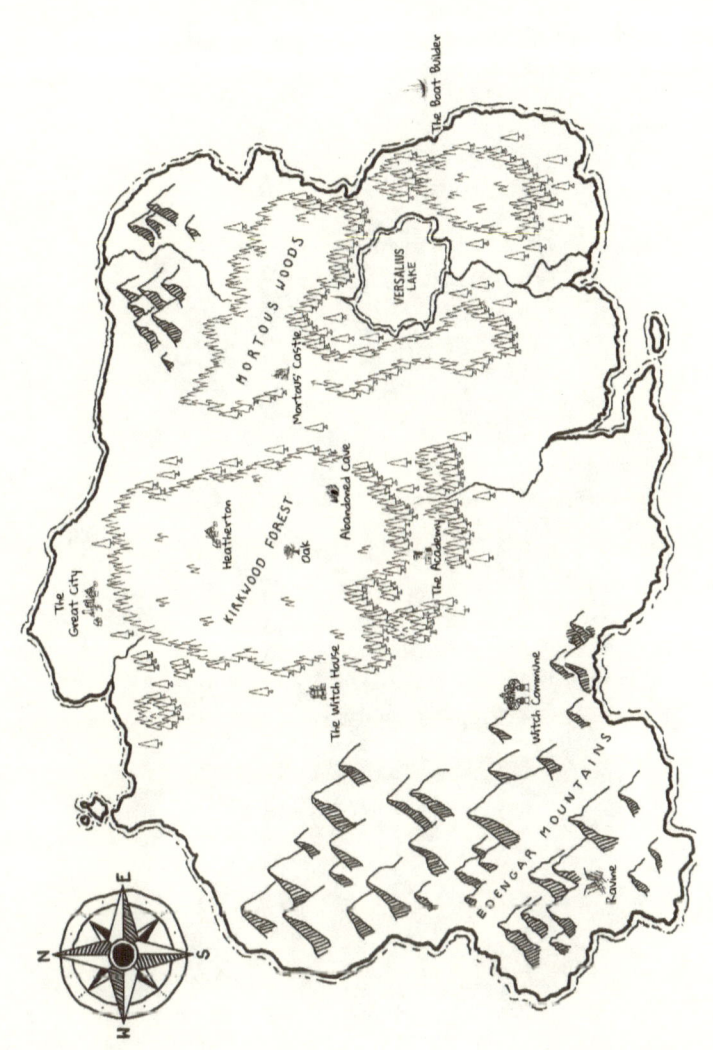

NALDY
The Wizard's Edict
Thomas Ian Doyle

Book Three

Chapter One

A PUBLIC INVITATION

Rupert had made up his mind. Without hesitation, he dived headfirst from the small rowboat into the lake.

On impact, Rupert's bones felt as if they had instantly frozen. He glanced behind him and saw the underside of the rowboat, pleased to see it gliding away.

Holding his breath, he felt himself being drawn further and further beneath the lake's surface. The water itself seemed to be pulling him.

Then, through the murky dark blue, came a glittering yellow light. As he was forced closer to the source, Rupert made out the naked body of the Great Fairy Queen. Her long blue hair floated majestically, and her large, glass-like wings were outstretched. She held out her arms, welcoming him.

Rupert panicked. He tried to swim in the opposite direction, desperately wanting to return to the surface. He was taken closer and closer to the imposing Fairy Queen. Soon, their faces were inches apart.

'You belong to the lake now,' said the Fairy Queen

in her husky voice. A smirk played on her pink lips as her delicate hands grasped his shoulders and pulled him deeper into the darkness below.

The Fairy Queen remained close to him, a calm expression on her alluring face.

Rupert spluttered, his lungs almost empty of air and his chest heavy from the pressure.

'Your life is mine,' she said sweetly. 'Here, you will rest forever.'

Down and down, together, they went.

'Where did you find such plump berries?' asked a man's voice casually. He recognised the voice—it was his younger cousin's. 'Did you use the magic of the Devante?'

Naldy's eyes snapped open. She glanced at Ralph across the table carved from rock, adjusting her posture to sit upright instead of slumped in her dining chair.

'Did you just take a nap?' Ralph asked, blinking at her over his empty plate, which had been licked clean.

Naldy cast her eyes at the untouched slice of blueberry pie in front of her. She realised she must have nodded off while they were eating dessert.

'I'm sorry, Ralph,' Naldy replied, picking up her fork and taking a small bite of the pie she had baked earlier that day. It was to celebrate their last evening in the furnished cave together. 'I didn't realise I was so tired. What did you ask me?'

'Where the blueberries came from,' answered Ralph. 'They're the most delicious. They must have been created with the Corium.'

'I picked the blueberries near the river—it was quite a walk.'

'What were you dreaming about?' he asked curiously.

'I can't even remember,' said Naldy, looking at her plate.

The same unnerving visions of Rupert had invaded her sleep almost every night since they'd settled in the spacious cave four months ago. Naldy hadn't confided in Ralph about the recurring nightmares of Rupert's death, afraid of upsetting him.

'Why don't you come south with me for a bit?' asked Ralph, leaning back in his green wingback chair. 'Professor Piggett has extended yet another invitation. The Academy is extremely comfortable.'

Naldy smiled at him before glancing around the cave. It had been furnished cosily using the magic of the Corium. Given its size, they suspected it had once been home to a dragon when such creatures still roamed the Kirkwood Forest. From their recent adventures, Naldy and Ralph knew the last living dragons now resided deep in the mountains of Edengar.

'You've done a lot of work on it,' said Ralph, noticing her taking in the cave. 'Although I'm heading south, it doesn't mean you have to leave too.'

'It's time for us both to move on,' replied Naldy. She hoped that leaving the cave might end the unsettling nightmares. 'This place was always meant to be temporary, just to ensure Maverick hadn't followed us. I think I'd like to head directly to Edengar. I don't want to distract you from your study of witches.'

'Wizards,' Ralph corrected her, the candlelight glinting from his emerald earring. 'I've decided to shift my focus to the study of wizardry. Well, I won't be visiting you, not if you really do settle in Edengar.'

'I found it peaceful,' said Naldy, recalling the gurgling river flanked by tall rock walls where the dragon caves were situated. 'I'll build a stone house, go for long walks along the riverbank, and plant the most beautiful flowers on Odorf's grave. I will have a big garden with turnips, pumpkins, and other vegetables. There'll be a bridge made of large slabs of rock crossing the river. I think I'll be happy there.'

'If the dragons don't eat you,' said Ralph.

A fluttering noise came from the shadowy corner of the cave. Naldy was familiar with the sound, but Ralph seemed nervous.

'It's just Smookers,' said Naldy, 'and he has brought something in with him.'

To confirm Naldy's suspicions, Smookers slinked from a darkened corner with a small, brown, helpless bat in his mouth. The defenceless creature was flapping its damaged wings in a failed attempt at escaping. The cat dropped the bat on a nearby woollen rug. The poor thing tried desperately to fly away, but its wings were too mangled to carry its weight. Smookers proceeded to swat at the little animal.

'You naughty cat,' called Naldy, standing to shoo him out of the way. 'We should have left you with Betty.'

They had collected Smookers on their return journey from Arkus Day from their old friend, Betty, who resided in Heatherton. Upon seeing them, Betty's face had become a river of tears. The news that Rupert had not made it back with them had hurt her deeply.

'I've told you many times, Smookers,' said Naldy with a pinched tone, 'stop hunting things for sport.'

Smookers lifted his tail and stole out of the room. Naldy bent to lift the poor, damaged creature from the ground. The trembling bat clung to her fingers, breathing heavily. She concentrated on the animal, casting the healing spell—*Sanitatem Restituere*.

The bat leapt from her hands and took off towards the cave's entrance, fluttering its black wings. Naldy could see Ralph watching with a hint of jealousy—she knew using magic to help save the bat's life had made him think of Rupert.

'You know I can't, Ralph,' said Naldy softly.

'You *can*,' returned Ralph, meeting her hazel eyes. 'What you really mean is that you *won't*.'

'We've been over this.'

'Yes, but your mother might have been wrong, Naldy,' Ralph replied sternly. 'Tarren didn't know Rupert. *You* knew him. He would want to come back.'

'I could bring everybody back,' said Naldy,

reaching over the table to collect Ralph's empty plate. She went to the cave's kitchen, where part of the black rock had been carved and polished into a sizable benchtop and sink. A grand chandelier filled with tapered candles was suspended above. 'I could bring back my parents, and Oak, and even Odorf.'

'You can. So why don't you?'

'You know why,' stated Naldy, placing Ralph's plate in the stone basin.

'We'd both be dead if Rupert hadn't sacrificed himself. The *Banned Spell of Death* prevents resurrecting those who are unknown to the one casting the spell. But you knew him, Naldy. You don't need to break the *Banned Spell* to use the Corium's magic to revive him.'

'Don't ask me how, but although it's not a *Banned Spell,* something within me knows it is a spell that shouldn't be used.'

Two tulip-shaped crystal glasses and a decanter filled with brandy floated down from the nearby pantry, summoned by Ralph.

'It's our last evening together,' he said, taking the decanter from the air. 'Let's not argue. I'm sorry, Naldy. Let's enjoy some brandy.'

'You can have the rest of my slice. I'm not going to finish it.'

'Really?' asked Ralph excitedly, pulling Naldy's slice of pie closer to him. 'Let's celebrate saving the Corium. Magic has been rescued from permanent destruction.'

'Well,' said Naldy, returning to her chair. 'There

are still Devante hunters, including Maverick, who won't stop seeking the magic.'

'These Devante hunters you speak of,' said Ralph. 'They are all out busy looking for books or leagons. Is that what's been troubling you lately?'

'Except Maverick,' she said, frowning. 'He is still searching for me. I've no doubt about that.'

'I don't think so,' said Ralph. 'He doesn't know you're Tarren's daughter, and he doesn't know that when she passed, the magic of the Corium was transferred to you. If Maverick was still looking for us, we'd know about it by now. Besides, the wizard has no Devante, not even the Aurum. You have the last surviving Devante. We should toast to that.'

Naldy lifted her glass and half-heartedly clinked it with Ralph's. What he said was true, but she couldn't shake the feeling that Maverick remained more powerful despite lacking the advantage of a Devante.

After Ralph finished Naldy's slice of pie, she bid him goodnight before heading to her sleeping quarters, an indoor tent fashioned from draped golden fabric. Once inside, she settled on the edge of the mahogany bed. The candle on the bedside table gently flickered. She would be sad to part with Ralph —they had spent so much time together—but Naldy knew they couldn't stay in the cave forever. She knew the time had finally come for them to go their separate ways. Naldy blew out the candle and lay on the linen sheets. She kept her eyes open, scared that if she closed them, she'd be taken back into the disturbing nightmare. Weariness settled over her, and she couldn't help but drift to sleep.

Naldy awoke the next day with her body cold and the sheets damp. Unsurprisingly, Rupert had plagued her sleep. She lifted her tired body from the bed and tried to push the image of the old rowboat from her mind.

After bathing and dressing, Naldy found Ralph at the kitchen table sipping brew. Ralph had pulled back the screen at the cave's entrance to let the sun stream in.

'Help yourself, there's plenty,' he said as Naldy settled into the chair opposite him.

'Thank you,' said Naldy, pouring herself some brew. 'I have a surprise for you.'

'For me?' said Ralph, smiling.

'Yes, I was going to give it to you last night, but I forgot,' she said, passing him a package wrapped in brown paper. 'Here.'

Ralph eagerly unwrapped it, and tears welled in his eyes when he saw its contents.

'My magic carpet,' said Ralph, stunned. He unfurled the brilliant blue carpet, its coarse fabric elegantly stitched and its glossy material catching the light. 'But, Naldy, how did you...'

'The Corium, of course,' she replied, trying to mask the emotion blooming in her voice. 'I did my best to replicate the one Maverick stole from you.'

'It's perfect,' said Ralph, running his hands over it. 'Truly perfect. I can't thank you enough.'

'It's enchanted—like your old magical carpet,'

said Naldy. 'So it will fit nicely inside your pocket.'

'I didn't get you anything,' said Ralph shamefully.

'You've done plenty for me, Ralph,' said Naldy. 'You accompanied me through Edengar, the Mortous Woods, and even Arkus Day. I wanted to thank you.'

After breakfast, they gathered the things they would take, packing them into rucksacks. Then, they made their way outside, where the sun peeked through the gaps of the tall pines surrounding them. Smookers was splayed out, lazily chewing the petals of a yellow dandelion. Naldy pulled the screen shut across the cave's entrance—from this side, the screen was fashioned to resemble hanging watergrass.

'You must walk with me for a bit,' said Ralph, throwing a comforting arm around her. 'We are both heading south, and I'd like to let my brew settle before we fly.'

Naldy collected her broomstick leaning on the exterior wall of the cave. They set off into the forest, Smookers lazily strolling behind them.

'Something doesn't feel right,' said Naldy, cautiously glancing around as a soft breeze billowed through her black travelling cloak.

'Of course it doesn't,' said Ralph matter-of-factly. 'The sun is shining. Birds are chirping. It's a perfect day—and we are parting ways. After everything.'

They walked together for almost an hour before Naldy stopped to face him. 'Are you ready to say goodbye?'

They looked at each other fondly.

'You'll have to take off first,' said Ralph. 'I think I'll continue on foot for a bit. Perhaps the whole way if the weather holds out.'

Naldy threw her arms around him, hugging Ralph tightly with her head on his shoulder. Her vision clouded with tears.

'We will see each other again,' said Ralph. 'We will.'

Over Ralph's shoulder, through her watery eyes, Naldy noticed a poster nailed to a nearby pine.

'What is that?' she asked, letting go of Ralph.

'Please, don't hesitate,' said Ralph, sounding on the verge of sobbing, 'fly away, or we'll never part ways.'

'It's Maverick,' said Naldy, approaching the poster.

'Maverick?'

The poster depicted a skilfully done sketch of the wizard, dressed smartly in a black cloak and with one hand perched on his black cane. His countenance and posture were dignified.

A NEW ERA BEGINS
A public invitation
Join the new head of The Establishment
and chairman of the board, Maverick
Gadswell, as he unveils The Establishment's
plans for a more promising future.
Date: *First day in October*
Time: *Sundown*
Place: *The Grand Steps of The Bleckdale*

Witchery Museum, The Great City

'Head of The Establishment?' said Ralph, outraged. 'Maverick? But what happened to Sallandra?'

'I'm not sure,' said Naldy. 'We should go to find out.'

'We really have been living under a rock,' said Ralph, ripping the poster from the tree and scrunching it up. 'I'm glad we are going in the opposite direction.'

'Ralph,' said Naldy, taking the scrunched poster from his hands. 'I think we ought to attend.'

'To watch Maverick unveil his plans?' said Ralph, raising a strawberry-blonde eyebrow. 'Whatever for? It'll be some half-witted proposal, and it's the opposite way to The Academy and to Edengar.'

'It's the first day in October,' said Naldy. 'What are the chances that we should come across this invitation today?'

'Naldy, I'm not going to The Great City because of coincidence,' he said, snatching the poster which she'd begun to unfold. A spark of magic set it alight, and it burnt until nothing remained but smoke. 'And neither should you, especially if Maverick will be there.'

'I'm a stubborn witch, Ralph, and I've made up my mind.' She climbed onto her broom and hovered in mid-air. 'There's no obligation for you to come with me. Professor Piggett will be waiting for you.'

Smookers jumped onto the tail end of Naldy's

broom and snuggled into the twigs.

'You won't make a slight detour south to The Academy with me, but you'll make a great diversion to The Great City up north.'

'I need to know what he is up to. If we don't leave now, we'll never make it by sundown.'

'Oh, okay, fine,' said Ralph, retrieving his carpet from his cloak pocket. He shook it out to unravel it before climbing on. 'Someone needs to make sure you don't do anything foolish. But after Maverick's grand unveiling, I want one of those pink drinks from *The Mortismor.*'

Naldy smirked, pleased he had agreed to accompany her. They shot above the green pines of Kirkwood Forest. The sky was clear and brilliant blue.

'We should arrive just in time,' called Naldy, her black hair blowing.

It was excellent weather for flying. The sun warmed their faces, and the cool air was sweet with the fresh smell of pine. Smookers slept soundly at the rear of the broom.

As the afternoon approached, they passed over Heatherton.

'I wish we had time to stop in and visit Betty,' said Ralph, peering over the edge of his blue carpet at the quaint town. 'But we'll miss Maverick's grand occasion if we do.'

'Perhaps on our way back,' suggested Naldy, leaning forward to increase her speed.

A few hours later, they could see the tall stone

buildings of The Great City framed by a pale purple sunset. Naldy knew they needed to be quick if they were to arrive in time for the event. They landed in an empty alley on the city's outskirts. Ralph stretched his limbs, pleased his feet were on solid ground again. He stuffed his carpet deep into his cloak pocket, and it magically shrunk to fit inside. Although the narrow alley was quiet, they could hear the distant sound of a large crowd.

'We better hurry,' said Naldy.

'We don't have disguises,' said Ralph anxiously. 'If anyone recognises us, we'll end up in The Great City's prison.'

She knew he was right. They had once stolen artefacts from the museum, and it would be foolish to risk being seen. She reached out her hand and ran it over Ralph's clothes. His plain travelling cloak transformed into a floral pattern, and his strawberry-blonde hair turned a jet black. Ralph caught his appearance in the reflection of a nearby window.

'Naldy,' said Ralph, outraged, tugging at his hair. 'You'd better be able to change it back.'

'I'm the Corium, Ralph,' said Naldy as her garments changed into a navy tartan. 'We don't want to be recognised. I think you might still need something more.'

Naldy held a hand up to Ralph's eyes, and a pair of silver square reading glasses appeared on his face. She then touched her own long black hair, which shortened to shoulder length and gradually changed to ash blonde.

'That'll have to do,' said Naldy, walking along the cobbled alleyway carrying her broomstick. 'We don't have time. The last rays of the sun are already vanishing.'

Ralph followed her, with Smookers trailing behind. They turned into a busy road where the street lamps had been lit. There were many people, most heading towards the Bleckdale Witchery Museum. Horses and carts lined the streets, caught in a traffic jam.

'It seems everybody wants to know what Maverick is up to,' said Naldy, watching passengers alight from the carts stuck in traffic to continue their journey on foot.

'Tightening his ugly grip on power, obviously,' said Ralph. 'He doesn't have possession of any Devante, so it seems he has turned his efforts into securing Sallandra's job.'

'I can't believe the crowds,' said Naldy, with her broom in one hand. 'Quickly now, we don't want to miss it.'

'Wait,' said Ralph, stopping and taking her hand. 'I need you to promise me you're not going to try and…'

'Try and what, Ralph?'

'Maverick mightn't have possession of any Devante,' continued Ralph. 'But I don't want anything to happen to you. You won't try and duel with him, will you?'

Before Naldy could answer him, a stony-faced

woman began shouting at them.

'You filthy witch!' cried the woman, her face scrunched in anger and her clenched fist waving at them. 'Your lot have always thought you were better than the rest of us. But not tonight. Tonight, your lot will pay!'

Naldy and Ralph quickly crossed the street. Smookers hissed at the woman before following them. Passersby stared as they fled the woman's shouting.

'What was all that about?' asked Ralph, dumbfounded.

'I don't know,' said Naldy. 'But I don't like it.'

A passing elderly man, relying on an old wooden walking stick, placed a gentle hand on Naldy's shoulder. He had been tottering in the opposite direction to the rest of the crowd.

'If you're going that way, dear,' croaked the wrinkled man, 'I'd suggest leaving the broomstick behind. This is a terrible night for witches. Terrible.'

'What do you mean?' asked Naldy, looking into the old man's worried eyes.

'It was long before my time,' said the man, a deep sadness in his voice, 'but my grandfather used to tell me stories of dark times long ago. It seems dark days are upon us tonight, and history will repeat itself.'

'Repeat itself?' said Naldy.

'The last burning at the stake was during those dreadful years. None have happened since. Tonight, the night sky will be filled again with smoke and sorrow.'

'They're burning a witch?' asked Ralph, horrified. 'Tonight? On the museum steps?'

'A wizard,' corrected the old man. 'They are burning a wizard. I suggest you fly away on that broomstick and in the opposite direction.'

'But who are they burning?' asked Naldy as the old man shuffled away.

'They are burning Sallandra.'

—Chapter Two—

THE HUNT BEGINS

Curious faces stared at the stone museum steps where Maverick stood, formidably dressed in a regal green garment. He was framed by the grand wooden doors of The Bleckdale Witchery Museum. The wide cobbled street below him was crowded with onlookers. The sky was dark, the moon and stars obscured by clouds, and the flames of the streetlights cast an ominous yellow glow over the spectators.

Naldy and Ralph had ditched the broom before making their way to the main street, weaving through the restless audience until they were positioned outside a familiar bistro, *The Mortismor*. Its doors were wide open, and the staff nervously gathered in the doorway, watching Maverick's address.

'Tonight, history will be made,' declared Maverick, his voice echoing over the crowd. 'And justice will be delivered.'

'We needn't have bothered with the disguises,' said Ralph to Naldy. 'I've never seen so many people gathered in one place before.'

'Will they really burn her?' said Naldy, peering over the tops of the many heads.

'It looks that way,' said Ralph.

Halfway up the steps, a tall wooden pole had been erected, surrounded by planks of wood and piles of straw. Secured to the pole, with her hands fastened behind her back, stood Sallandra. The wizard's angular face was framed by her long black hair, her expression fearless and steely.

The city guards, who had once answered Sallandra's commands, stood dressed in blue military blazers and porkpie hats, lining the steps and awaiting Maverick's orders.

'As your new head of The Establishment,' declared Maverick boldly, 'it is my priority to ensure honesty is restored to governance and that our law-abiding citizens are protected.'

'I have to stop him,' whispered Naldy to herself. 'I can do it.'

'I know you're the Corium, Naldy,' said Ralph tensely. 'But you cannot risk taking on this many people.'

'I can invent any spell, Ralph,' said Naldy, anger building inside her. 'This isn't right. I won't stand by and let them burn Sallandra.'

'Before you,' bellowed Maverick as he descended the stone steps, 'is a familiar face. I'm sure you all recognise your previous leader. The wizard has kept a dark, horrible secret from you—one that has put your safety in jeopardy.'

The crowd whispered fervently, shifting

uncomfortably.

'The Establishment's duty is to maintain strict control and regulation of magic.'

The spectators applauded nervously. Maverick held up his black cane, and the crowd fell silent. The tension was palpable on each onlooker's concerned face.

'The previous administration has failed you. There is a witch or wizard out there who has the ability to produce any spell—a dark sorcerer.'

The crowd murmured in discomfort, unsure what to make of Maverick's statement.

'We should go,' said Ralph uneasily. 'I don't think we are safe here.'

Naldy did not move. This was the man who had ended her mother's life—the man who had killed Odorf and Oak and burnt down the Witch House. Rupert might still be alive if they hadn't needed to race Maverick to Arkus Day.

'I have to stop him, Ralph,' said Naldy, 'and this time for good.'

'Please, don't do anything foolish,' said Ralph, concerned.

Maverick was making his way closer to Sallandra, fastened to the stake. She kept her gaze forward, avoiding his eyes.

'The traitor before you,' called Maverick, 'has known all along that there is a rogue witch or wizard amongst us. They call this person the Corium.'

Naldy felt her heart pounding heavily in her chest. With every word that Maverick uttered, she became more enraged. Ralph squeezed her arm.

'Traitor!' echoed a shrill voice from the crowd as someone threw what appeared to be a shoe at Sallandra.

'Before the wizard faces her punishment,' said Maverick, 'I will deliver a plan designed to protect us from uncontrolled magic. Designed to see this dangerous power captured and contained. Designed to keep us all safe.'

The spectators erupted into their loudest applause yet, some shouting more abuse while others threw small stones at Sallandra.

Glints of white began to fall from the sky, and at first, Naldy thought it was snow. She quickly realised it was small sheets of white parchment tumbling from the darkness above. The crowd cheered, catching the falling parchment. Naldy bent and picked one up from the ground. On one side of the paper, in a black regal font, were the words: *The Establishment's Edicts.*

'Edict Twenty-Two,' read Ralph from the reverse side of the parchment he had caught, 'no witch or wizard shall engage in travel by broomstick or any other enchanted object without first obtaining a licence from The Establishment.'

Ralph glanced at Naldy with horror on his face. She noticed that the majority of the crowd appeared pleased by the edicts. There were only a few other crestfallen faces.

'What does yours say?' asked Ralph.

'Edict Nine,' read Naldy, a lump forming in her

throat, 'magical individuals may possess only one copy of The Establishment's revised compendium of approved spells. All other spellbooks must be destroyed.'

'These edicts,' said Maverick, outstretching his arms to the crowd, 'will be posted in every town and village throughout the Kirkwood Forest and will come into effect at sunrise.'

As Naldy studied Maverick's pale face, taking in his black slicked-back hair and his composed posture, she felt an overwhelming desire to put an end to the wizard's existence.

Ralph gasped as he read another of the edicts that had tumbled from above.

'What is it?' asked Naldy.

'I think we should get out of here,' said Ralph timidly. Naldy snatched the small, square, thick parchment from him.

'Edict One,' read Naldy, 'the entity known as the Corium must be apprehended and killed. Individuals who assist in the capture of the Corium will be rewarded by The Establishment.'

Her expression must have exposed her inner thoughts, as Ralph turned to Naldy with an empathetic look.

'You can't kill him, Naldy,' he said.

'No one will know it's me,' she whispered resolutely. 'I'm the Corium. I have to put an end to this madness.'

Naldy focused all her energy on casting a spell to make Maverick fall. She wanted him to slip and hit his head on the stone steps. She wanted the wizard to pay for all of the lives he had unjustly taken.

Maverick's feet didn't budge.

'It's not working,' said Naldy, frustrated.

'What's not working?' asked Ralph.

'My magic,' said Naldy, closing her eyes and trying again.

Nothing happened. A cold smirk spread across Maverick's face.

'My magic isn't working, Ralph,' said Naldy, clenching her fists. 'I've spent the last few months creating anything I have wanted. Now, the thing I most want—it won't happen.'

She redirected her focus, willing the guards to topple over. Instantly, every one of them lining the steps lost their balance and landed on their bottoms. The crowd was startled into silence.

The guards were helping each other to their feet, their fearful eyes darting towards Maverick for reassurance. Maverick took several confident strides down a few more steps.

'Do not fear,' he said, addressing the stunned onlookers. 'The one possessing the power known as the Corium must be here with us.'

An anxiety rippled through the crowd.

'You have nothing to be afraid of while I am your leader. I have a message for the one who comes carrying such dark magic. Whoever you are, we will hunt you, and you will burn. Together, Edict One will be our paramount objective.'

Maverick's words quelled the crowd's anxiety.

'Sallandra,' called Maverick, pointing his cane at her. 'Do you have any final words for the people you have kept this secret from?'

'I have served the people faithfully,' said Sallandra stonily. 'You are a wizard, Maverick, and it is you who deceives those gathered here today.'

'Yes, like yourself, Sallandra, I am also a wizard,' agreed Maverick coolly. The end of his cane ignited with an orange flame. Maverick moved closer to Sallandra. 'But unlike you, I will use my power to protect the people, not to keep dark secrets from them.'

'We have to do something, Ralph,' implored Naldy.

Maverick lowered his cane, and the orange fire ignited the piles of straw. Sallandra did not try to move or make a sound as the flames wrapped themselves around her body. She stood remarkably still, staring unwaveringly ahead.

Naldy concentrated on the fire. Willing the flames to extinguish themselves. Her eyes were squinted and focused—but the fire did not diminish. The flames continued to engulf Sallandra.

'It's not working,' said Naldy anxiously, salty tears catching in her mouth. 'I can't do it.'

Those at the front of the crowd hurled more small rocks at Sallandra. The flames had grown, and her face was now concealed by the violent orange blaze. Maverick leant on his cane, a smirk on his face as he watched her body burn.

'Naldy, look,' said Ralph, tugging at the sleeve of

her cloak.

Naldy turned to see a familiar grey-haired woman approaching, holding Smookers in her arms.

Chapter Three

BEYOND THE CURTAIN

There was a troubled expression on the woman's wrinkled face as she approached.

'If it weren't for Smookers,' said Betty, meeting Naldy with her kind grey stare, 'I wouldn't have recognised you both. A sad day to be reunited.'

Naldy flung her arms around the old woman, and emotion engulfed her. She sobbed into Betty's shoulder. Smookers meowed consolingly, wedged between their chests.

'This way now,' said Betty, passing Smookers to Ralph and gently taking Naldy's arm. 'Let us get away from this crowd.'

Naldy's tears had drawn unwanted attention, and Betty appeared eager to escape prying eyes. The old woman pushed through the throng and led them inside the luxurious dwelling adjacent to *The Mortismor*. The extravagant foyer was familiar to them, as they had stayed there with Betty once before when they'd spent weeks searching the museum for a reference to Audry.

'You secured a room at *The Golden Opulent?*' asked Ralph.

They passed a porter on the staircase, clad in his red cloak uniform, complete with its rich gold trim.

'Can I bring you anything, Miss Hexogg?' asked the handsome porter.

'I think the lamb, with some potatoes and bread,' instructed Betty kindly, 'and a carafe of your finest brew, please, Syvia.'

'Of course,' replied the porter. 'It will be up shortly.'

'You didn't bother with a disguise then?' asked Ralph once the porter was out of earshot.

'In case you hadn't noticed,' she replied, mounting the final step of the varnished staircase, 'more than half of Kirkwood has flocked to The Great City for tonight's spectacle. The crowd is the greatest disguise one could have. Although I must commend you on your efforts—far superior to the Pezileon wigs we once fashioned for our trip to The Bleckdale Witchery Museum. The Corium's magic, I'm guessing?'

Betty stopped when they reached the entrance to the same suite they'd stayed in on their previous visit.

'Do you both have accommodation reserved elsewhere?' asked Betty, searching for the room key in her cloak pocket.

Ralph and Naldy exchanged a concerned look.

'Do not worry, you can stay here with me,' said Betty, rummaging in another pocket. 'I booked this suite because I recalled it overlooked the museum steps. Every room in The Great City was booked weeks ago. Ah, here's the key.'

Betty opened the door to the spacious suite, complete with its own elegant open kitchenette adjoining the living area. They had a clear view of the crowd and the museum steps through the ceiling-high window. Below, the flames were still burning high around the stake, and Maverick was addressing the crowd. The windows were made of thick glass, and the wizard's speech was muffled from inside the suite. Betty made her way over to the window and pulled the heavy olive-green velvet curtains closed.

'That's enough of that,' said Betty before taking a seat on the room's grand sofa. Smookers curled up comfortably next to her. 'Come and sit. Our meal should be up shortly.'

'Shouldn't we open a window,' suggested Naldy, making her way to the curtains. 'We should listen to what he is saying.'

'Maverick?' said Betty, reaching into her pockets and retrieving sixty-odd small bits of parchment. She sprinkled them messily onto the low marble table in front of the sofa. 'This nonsense is what he is harping on about.'

Naldy peeked through a gap in the curtain. The crowd below seemed captivated by Maverick's speech.

'Come away from the window,' said Betty sternly, 'there is much for us to discuss.'

'Maverick can't get away with what he has done, can he?' asked Ralph nervously, sitting in one of the armchairs facing Betty.

'You tried to stop him,' said Betty, her grey eyes glancing at Naldy.

'And failed,' replied Naldy miserably, reluctantly making her way to the sofa and perching her bottom next to Smookers. 'The magic worked on the guards. But for some reason, not on Maverick.'

'Which can only mean one thing,' said Betty casually.

'What thing is that?' asked Ralph.

'He has created a spell using the Devante to protect himself.'

'But how?' asked Ralph. 'He doesn't have a Devante.'

'Not presently,' affirmed Betty. 'But many have passed through his hands.'

'I hold the magic of the highest-ranking Devante,' said Naldy irritably. 'I should have been able to extinguish his flames, at least.'

There was a soft knock at the door.

'Come in, Syvia,' called Betty.

The door opened, and the tall porter entered, carrying three silver-covered trays and a large carafe of honey-coloured brew.

'Thank you, place it on these papers here,' said Betty. Syvia did as instructed, setting the serving ware on the low table before them.

Before Syvia could collect dinnerware from the suite's kitchenette, crockery and silver utensils glided across the room towards the table—Betty or Ralph must have summoned them.

'We can manage from here,' said Betty, passing the porter a few currents, 'thank you kindly.'

The porter bowed politely, and he left the room.

'Syvia can be trusted,' informed Betty. 'But I think we shouldn't discuss the Corium in his presence.'

'Do you think I could have my hair back?' asked Ralph, noticing his jet-black hair in the reflection of a silver cloche covering one of the trays.

'If I can even manage it,' said Naldy irritably.

'Of course, you can manage it,' said Betty, lifting the cloche on the juicy cut of lamb. 'You can also manage to undo Maverick's protection, Naldy. You are, after all, the Corium.'

Betty removed the two remaining silver-domed covers, revealing crispy, buttered potatoes and warm, crusty sourdough bread.

Naldy undid their disguises; Ralph's black hair returned to its strawberry-blonde state, and Naldy's grew and darkened.

'Oh,' said Ralph, touching his nose, 'it feels strange without the glasses now.'

'You're telling me I could have saved Sallandra?' asked Naldy as Betty filled their crystal glasses with brew. 'I simply needed to have undone his protection charm?'

'Yes, back when he had possession of the Devante, it seems Maverick cast a protection spell on himself to prevent anyone from interfering with his magic. However, you are the Corium, Naldy, and the Devante's power not only allows you to create spells but also to undo them.'

'He won't be able to cast the charm again,' said Ralph, loading his plate with food. 'He doesn't have a Devante.'

'We have him cornered then,' said Naldy. 'Good. I'll use the Corium to put an end to his evil. The wizard deserves to die.'

Betty placed her glass of brew on the table and squinted at Naldy with a curious expression.

'You don't agree,' said Naldy, registering Betty's disapproval. 'He should die for what he has done—and not for tonight's actions alone.'

'I do not believe it wise to take the wizard's life,' said Betty, loading food onto Naldy's empty plate. 'He may not be acting alone. Death may not mean the end of what he has begun.'

'It is Maverick's fault Rupert is gone,' said Ralph, raising his voice.

'And Oak,' added Naldy, 'the Witch House and all the Devante and Odorf and...'

Naldy ignored the plate of food Betty had served. She stood, returning to the window. Pulling back the curtain a little, Naldy could see the flames still burning on the museum steps.

'He murdered my mother,' she said softly, taking in the crowd below listening to Maverick's speech. 'I want him dead.'

Naldy felt her heart beating heavily as she closed her eyes tightly. She had never undone a spell before and had only created a few simple things using the powers of the Corium. Yet, something instinctual within her understood that all she needed to do was focus on reversing Maverick's protection charm—and it would be done.

She felt her body plunging, as if falling. She realised she'd been transported to a large, darkened meeting room with a long wooden table. She was still standing upright. The moonlight shone through a nearby window, initially providing the only light source in the room, but then there was another light—a bright glowing amber. Was she dreaming? Had undoing Maverick's protection charm caused her to be knocked unconscious?

Naldy spun to see Getergrin smiling nervously, bouncing on the balls of his feet. Her first instinct was to raise her palms in self-defence, but Getergrin appeared not to notice her. The round man didn't even flinch. He seemed preoccupied with staring at an amber light hovering above him. Maverick stood nearby, his cane in one hand, having conjured the amber spell. Naldy's heart skipped a beat. Clutched in Maverick's other bony hand was her family's red spellbook—Rubrum!

This had to be a dream, thought Naldy. *How could it be real? Rubrum had been destroyed by Maverick a long time ago.*

The bright amber light slowly lowered itself towards the large red spellbook in Maverick's hands. It was unmistakably her family's spellbook—somehow, it still existed.

'Stop,' cried Naldy, but neither Maverick nor Getergrin seemed to hear her.

She reached out her hands, but they went

through the book as if she had become a ghost. The light entered the book. Naldy felt her whole body lurch forward, and the scene vanished.

She found herself transported to a cosy cottage. An old woman with curly red hair, greying in places and tied in a messy bun, was seated at a wooden table with a warm cup of brew before her. There was a second empty cup at the opposite end of the table. The woman appeared to be waiting for someone.

Her eyes flickered towards the darkened window as the fireplace crackled peacefully. Naldy heard the door open, and Maverick entered.

'What have you done with Rubrum?' exclaimed Naldy, her palms raised.

Neither Maverick nor the woman took notice of her.

'I thought you may come tonight,' stated the woman calmly. 'I had a feeling, so I made us some of your favourite brew from Edengar.'

'That's very kind of you, Audry,' said Maverick evenly.

Audry reached for the brewpot. She leant her weary body over the table to fill the second cup.

Naldy's heart beat faster. She had only heard the name Audry once before, in Betty's kitchen, when the Devante had given them a clue as to the location of the Corium. The anagram 'Ask Audry' had led Betty, Ralph, and Naldy to the museum, where they'd spent weeks searching for any mention of the name. They had found one mention, written on a burnt tapestry connected to the name Hannah.

'Come, sit now,' said Audry politely. 'I know the journey here is long.'

'You were difficult to find,' said Maverick as Audry sipped her brew.

'I believe I am the last?' she said, delicately placing down her cup.

'I've always admired your ability to remain calm in dire situations, Audry.'

'It saddens me to see you've lost your way as the years have passed, Maverick. There was so much promise in the beginning.'

Maverick took the seat opposite Audry, and he sipped the brew she had made.

'You've always made a good brew.'

'Thank you.' She turned to face the window. 'I have enjoyed this corner of the forest. It has always been a peaceful place.'

'I suppose you'll want to know why?' said Maverick, wincing slightly as if his thoughts were painful. 'The others begged me to tell them why I'm determined to see magic destroyed. I suppose you will ask the same question. But I won't answer. I did not tell them, and I won't tell you, for it is not your business.'

'I know why, Maverick,' said Audry gently. 'I have only pity for you.'

'You needn't waste your emotions on me,' scolded the wizard bitterly.

'It is not the *why* I am interested in knowing, but *how*.'

'That's enough,' said Maverick, one hand

clenched tightly around his black cane.

'You felt betrayed,' continued Audry delicately. 'If others knew the truth, I think they too would pity you.'

'I said enough!' snapped Maverick.

Audry refilled her cup. Maverick looked hurt or perhaps frightened by Audry's words.

'If you've murdered Lampard,' she said softly, 'then, yes, I am the last who knows of your secret.'

'You will not survive because you pity me,' said Maverick, rising to his feet and pointing his cane at Audry. She bravely stared past his cane, meeting his gaze without a hint of fear on her wrinkled face.

'Your secret may follow me to the grave,' said Audry calmly, 'but many others still in the Society uphold the oath to protect magic. They may never understand the true reason you are hell-bent on seeing it destroyed, Maverick. But they will stop you, nonetheless. Cutting the tongue off your secret will not help you win this fight.'

Could it be the same Audry connected on the tapestry with Hannah? Then again, how could it be? Naldy would have had to have journeyed into the past.

As she had the thought, her eyes snapped open. She found herself back in the suite with Betty and Ralph, standing by the window as if she hadn't moved.

'What happened?' she asked.

'Happened?' repeated Ralph, confused.

'I went somewhere.' She hesitated, noticing

Maverick through the gap in the curtains, positioned below on the museum's steps—he had paused mid-speech. 'I saw Maverick. He was with a woman named Audry.'

'Audry?' repeated Ralph.

'Yes, it felt like I went back in time. I saw Rubrum. Maverick was destroying it. And then Audry— she mentioned Maverick had some secret. I think Maverick was going to kill her.'

'You didn't go anywhere, Naldy,' said Ralph, troubled. 'You've been stood by the window.'

Naldy was at too great a distance to fully make out the wizard's expression, but she sensed that Maverick was suddenly worried. He hastily announced something to the crowd before retreating up the steps and through the museum's grand wooden doors.

Naldy wasn't entirely sure what had happened, but deep within her, she knew one thing for certain —Maverick's protection charm had been reversed.

'What did you see?' asked Betty curiously, watching Naldy intently from the sofa.

Chapter Four

SOUND OF THE SPELLBOOKS

The wizard's quick address and swift retreat had produced unease in the crowd, many of whom began to depart, trampling over the white edicts as they dispersed. The guards remained stolidly on the steps.

'What was it that you saw?' repeated Betty with concern.

'Maverick was holding my family spellbook,' said Naldy. 'Then, I was suddenly transported to a cottage.'

'Not in the vision you had,' said Betty. 'Just now, outside the curtains.'

'Maverick,' said Naldy softly, returning to the sofa. 'He seemed anxious, and then he fled into the museum.'

'Audry,' wondered Ralph. 'Do you think it was the same Audry we once discovered on the tapestry?'

'I had the same thought,' said Naldy. 'Audry knew something about Maverick that he didn't want others to know. What's the matter, Betty?'

'There is someone I need to send a lucurn candle to,' said Betty, standing. She seemed troubled.

'He may have answers. He knows much about the Devante. I best send it now, before Edict Thirty-Three comes into effect.'

'What is Edict Thirty-Three?' asked Ralph.

Betty picked up her goblet and rummaged around in some of the small white papers resting underneath.

'Ah, here,' said Betty, passing Ralph one of Maverick's edicts before heading down the hallway, presumably to send the message.

'Edict Thirty-Three,' read Ralph aloud. 'All communications transmitted via lucurn candle will be strictly monitored. The sending or receiving of unregistered messages is prohibited.'

'I know how we can end this,' said Naldy. She took a deep breath. 'He cannot live.'

'You want to break the *Banned Spell of Death*?' asked Ralph, eyeing Naldy with an unsettled expression.

'We must be done with him, Ralph. Even though we cannot see where the coward is hiding, breaking the *Banned Spell* will allow me to take his life and end this madness.'

'Naldy,' sighed Ralph gently. 'I can't imagine dealing death to be an easy thing. As much as I detest Maverick, I don't think it's within me to deal the final blow myself.'

'He has taken the lives of so many. We should have done it a long time ago.'

Ralph did not reply but tossed Maverick's paper edict, which fluttered down to join the others on the table.

She needed to do it—before the flicker of courage she felt disappeared. Ralph was staring at her pityingly, and Naldy turned her head away towards the closed green velvet curtains. She recalled the pain Maverick had caused them. She recalled all the deaths. Believing he deserved the same fate, Naldy tried to will the *Banned Spell of Death* to break. But as she focused her thoughts on breaking it, she knew her will was only half in it.

'I cannot break it,' she said, tears welling up.

'Because you are wiser,' said Betty, re-entering the room.

'I am the Corium,' said Naldy. 'I have the power to end it, but I can't conjure the strength.'

'It is not solely your responsibility, Naldy,' said Betty, returning to her seat. 'Dealing death is no easy task. Besides, taking Maverick's life may worsen the wickedness he has started. Maverick may not be acting alone; he could have people waiting in the wings to take his place. We must identify who supports him. Death may eventually play a part, but first, we must find out more.'

'I fear if I do not kill him, more innocent people will die.'

'We must play the long game and learn more about his intentions. You've managed to undo his protection charm, Naldy, and that has clearly worried him. He has taken refuge inside the museum, which might mean he will expedite his plans, whatever they may be. We have no time to waste.'

'Are we to go to war with the Establishment?' asked Ralph nervously.

'We may have no other choice,' said Betty, passing Naldy her untouched plate of food and nodding as an instruction to eat. 'First, we must find out how large his supporter base is.'

'People surely won't allow a return to the dark ages,' remarked Ralph, helping himself to more lamb and potatoes. 'He cannot get away with burning witches and wizards—and these silly edicts—being killed for owning unapproved spellbooks or flying on broomsticks without registration.'

Betty drew in her wrinkled cheeks and released a soft, pitying sigh.

'But how did this happen?' continued Ralph through a mouthful of food. 'How did Maverick become head of The Establishment? And how is everybody cheering him on while he cold-bloodedly murders Sallandra.'

'He has made them believe Sallandra was a liar,' said Betty. 'I've no doubt she knew about the Corium—many people do—but Maverick has created a narrative where the Corium is dangerous and Sallandra has kept the information from them. Look outside that window: Maverick has gained the people's trust. He has ignited a fear within them, and if we were to murder Maverick, it would not extinguish that fear. It may even intensify it. We must act cautiously. We have quite a task ahead of us.'

'Where do we begin?' asked Naldy. 'If not with killing.'

'We begin by protecting the Corium,' said Betty softly, eyeing Naldy. 'Protecting you.'

'You needn't worry about my protection. I've decided to make for the ravine in Edengar. I will be safe there.'

'You cannot return to Edengar,' said Betty solemnly.

'Why not?'

'Maverick may return to the ravine. I'd be surprised if he doesn't.'

'But why would he ever go back there?' asked Naldy.

'The dragons, my dear.'

Naldy sighed. She had neglected to remember that dragon properties were highly valuable—and magical! Now that Maverick no longer had possession of a Devante, he would perhaps consider returning to Edengar to collect some rare magic.

'If I cannot go to Edengar,' said Naldy, 'I'll make for Arkus Day. Maverick won't expect me to go there.'

'He might not,' said Ralph, 'but there are many people who believe the Corium resides in Arkus Day, and now Maverick has unleashed the secret of the Corium, more people may try and seek it there.'

'Well, if I cannot go to Edengar,' said Naldy frustratedly, 'or to Arkus Day, then where am I to go?'

'For now,' said Betty, selecting a slice of the sourdough bread, 'we must finish our dinner and go to bed. You are safe here for the night.'

'Safe!' exclaimed Naldy, ignoring her dinner and standing to peek through the curtains again. 'Maverick has declared war on every witch and wizard. I don't know how you can both sit there, eating so calmly? He won't stop until he finds me.'

The crowd outside had thinned, and the cobbled street below was littered with the little white parchments—Maverick's edicts—which, from the window, looked like snowflakes.

'Perhaps Mortous could help us?' suggested Ralph. 'The Society have dedicated their lives to protecting the Corium.'

Betty shifted uncomfortably in her chair.

'What is it?' asked Ralph. 'You don't believe Mortous will be able to help?'

'I have been to see Mortous,' said Betty, as Naldy turned from the window to face her. 'You may both recall that the Society closely watched Maverick's movements. They knew the moment he set foot in the Mortous Woods.'

'If they are keeping an eye on him,' said Ralph, waving his fork around, 'they can help us keep track of his whereabouts. While we keep Naldy safe.'

'I confided in Mortous,' said Betty rigidly. 'I told him you had become the Corium, Naldy. I asked for his assistance in keeping you protected.'

'And what did he say?' asked Naldy, framed by the window's olive-green curtains.

'There are some in the Society that I do not trust. I made it clear that I would not disclose your location. I asked Mortous if the Society would keep us informed of Maverick's movements.'

'He refused,' said Ralph, discerning the answer from Betty's tense expression.

'If I joined the Society, he declared that all of its secrets would be entrusted with me in time.'

'Then you must join,' said Ralph passionately. 'They've asked you many times, Betty. If we know Maverick's next move, we'll have a better chance of keeping Naldy safe. You must put your stubbornness aside.'

'Alas,' said Betty, leaning back in her chair and pursing her lips. 'I will be expected to drink Veserum with each moon cycle.'

'You'll do it?' said Ralph.

'Yes, I intend to join. I have already informed Mortous. But doing so will not help us for many months. The Society is known to withhold information from new members, and it may be some time before they share its secrets with me.'

There was a loud bang outside the window. Ralph jumped in fright, sending his plate to the floor, where it broke.

Naldy pulled back the curtain and peered into the street below, the room filling with the reflection of a flickering orange light.

'What was that?' asked Ralph anxiously as Betty rushed to the window. Ralph had no desire to get close and remained seated.

'They are burning books,' said Naldy, staring at the street below.

Most of the spectators had departed, but a few stood around an enormous bonfire set up at the bottom of the steps in the middle of the road. The guards emerged from the museum's grand wooden doors with enormous armfuls of books. They tossed them into the flames, made their way back up the steps to enter the museum, and returned to the fire with more.

There was another enormous bang as the flames of the bonfire erupted in a brief explosion of orange flame. The blaze quickly returned to its original size.

'What on—' said Ralph, who had spilt brew all over his clothes.

'Spellbooks,' said Betty sadly. 'Some of them are refusing to go quietly.'

'I have to stop them,' said Naldy.

'You must wait,' said Betty seriously, holding up a warning hand.

'I'm the Corium,' she said. 'I have to do something. We don't have time to wait—we can't sit here and let the guards destroy all those spellbooks.'

'She must save them,' agreed Ralph, using a few of the paper edicts to soak up the spilt liquid from his clothes.

'Naldy, my dear,' said Betty in a delicate tone. 'I fear Maverick wants you to act. For if you do, he'll know you're nearby, watching.'

'Are you suggesting we just let him destroy them?' she remarked irritably.

Betty didn't respond, and Naldy knew the old woman was right. After undoing Maverick's protection charm, perhaps the wizard had sent out guards carrying armfuls of books to lure her into saving them. It could be a test to see if she was still in the city.

'Naldy, I might need your help,' said Ralph, whose clothes were soaked in brew. 'I can fix the broken plate myself, but I'm not sure what to do with these wet clothes.'

Naldy turned from the window and came to seat herself opposite Ralph. The plate repaired itself, returning to his lap as if it had never been broken. Ralph's brew-soaked clothes began to dry as the liquid evaporated.

'Thanks,' he said, loading more food onto the repaired plate.

A deafening pop vibrated the entire building, and Ralph clutched his chest in fright.

'Even the Devante don't make such blasting sounds when burnt,' said Ralph, holding the plate steady on both his knees.

'The Bleckdale Witchery Museum,' said Betty, 'is home to some of the oldest spellbooks. Many that survived The Great Witch Hunt were donated to the museum to be conserved. Only the most ancient spellbooks will make such a sad sound. It seems Maverick is determined to see them all destroyed.'

'Will it take long for Mortous to trust you?' asked Naldy, trying not to think about the spellbooks.

'I have resisted joining for so many years, and some members of the Society may be hesitant to share their secrets. But one thing is certain—I must find a reason to refuse disclosing your location, as I do not trust all of them.'

'Currently, we don't have a location to disclose,' said Naldy. 'It seems I have nowhere safe to go.'

'I have sent a message to someone I believe we can trust,' said Betty. 'They may be able to help us with that problem.'

'Who are they?' asked Ralph.

'I do not want to get our hopes up,' she said. 'Let us wait until we receive a reply, and then I will tell you more.'

'I might go to bed,' said Naldy. 'I am tired after today and think I'd like to be alone.'

Another loud bang split the air.

'How are we going to get any sleep,' grumbled Ralph, 'with Maverick roasting the contents of the museum?'

'I will see you both in the morning,' said Naldy, lifting herself from the sofa.

'Take your plate of food with you,' said Betty in a stern motherly tone.

Although Naldy had no appetite, she picked up her plate and made her way along the suite's hall.

Smookers padded after her, jumping onto the large bed and sprawling out, purring softly. Naldy sat on top of the red wool bedspread, petting his head.

Another thunderous boom broke the quiet. Smookers lifted his head irritably, briefly glancing at Naldy with a pleading look, as if calling on her to do something about the noise.

'I can't use the Corium to stop it, Smookers,' said Naldy sadly. 'It'll draw too much attention. We'll have to be careful how we use it from now on.'

Smookers flopped his head onto the covers, purring no more.

—Chapter Five—

DISLOYALTY AND DEVOTION

Naldy woke with a jolt. Her sheets were drenched in sweat. The morning sun shone brightly through the bedroom's large windows, as she had forgotten to close the curtains. She rubbed her eyes and lifted her body from the damp bedding, trying to shake off another unsettling nightmare about Rupert.

She went to the lavish ensuite to shower, wanting to wash away the sweat. Although the warm running water was relaxing, her thoughts kept returning to the recurring nightmare and the vision of Maverick and Audry from the evening before. Both experiences felt strikingly lifelike, and Naldy wondered why she was suffering these vivid visions—was it guilt? Or was there something more to them? One thing Naldy was sure of: the two felt eerily similar.

After dressing, Naldy found Betty and Ralph sitting in the main living area. The heavy green curtains were still closed, blocking out the morning light. The flames of the small gas lamps flickered, casting long shadows over the room. Pastries and fruits were laid out on the marble table for breakfast.

'Brew?' asked Betty kindly as Naldy sat opposite Ralph.

'It's quite dark in here,' remarked Naldy, helping herself to a golden pastry.

'Yes, we should open up the curtains,' Betty agreed, lifting her body from the sofa. 'Did you sleep well?'

'I've been having nightmares,' Naldy said tensely. She had avoided disclosing the unsettling visions, not wanting to make Ralph uncomfortable; however, she felt it was time to confide in the others. 'About Rupert. I thought maybe they would stop, but now that I've had my first night away from the cave, they seem to be getting worse.'

Betty returned a concerned expression as she pulled back the curtains, letting the sun stream in, before pottering around the room to switch off the gas lamps. Naldy blinked as she adjusted to the light. Through the window, she could see the blackened cinders on the steps where Sallandra had stood the previous night, steely and resolute. In the middle of the broad street were the remains of the bonfire, congesting the traffic. From the size of the pile of embers and ash, it was evident that many books from the museum had been destroyed. The carriages were bottlenecked as they struggled to navigate around the obstruction.

As Betty returned to the sofa, Naldy noticed a grey tinge beneath her eyes as if she hadn't slept much. There was tension in the room.

'What's happened?' asked Naldy, putting her pastry down.

Betty and Ralph shared a nervous glance.

'What has Maverick done now?' asked Naldy. 'I knew I should have broken the *Banned Spell of Death*. I should have ended it last night.'

'Ralph,' prompted Betty, calling on him to speak.

'It is about your nightmares, Naldy,' he said, taking a deep breath. 'You see, I know the reason why you have been having them.'

Naldy leant forward in her chair. Ralph bit his lip uneasily.

'You know about the nightmares?' she asked.

'I'm worried that if I tell you,' Ralph began, swallowing hard, 'you'll never forgive me.'

Naldy could feel her heartbeat quickening in her chest. Ralph's eyes had filled with watery tears.

'What is it?' pressed Naldy, urging Ralph to continue. 'Does it have something to do with the Corium?'

'I've been trying to bring him back,' muttered Ralph, his face scrunched in guilt.

She didn't need Ralph to admit whom he'd been trying to resurrect—Naldy knew it was his cousin, and she now understood why vivid images of Rupert had repeatedly interrupted her sleep.

'Like the visions I had last night of Maverick and Audry,' she said quietly. 'The nightmares were too vivid to simply be night terrors.'

Tears trickled down Ralph's cheeks.

'You've been trying to use my powers while I've

been sleeping.'

'You were never going to agree to bring him back,' he said quietly. 'I know he would want to come back. Each night, I tried to use the magic of the Corium, but it never seemed to work.'

'I discovered him,' said Betty. 'In your sleep, Naldy, you appeared to be thwarting his attempts.'

'I'm glad you helped to stop him,' said Naldy.

Ralph glanced at Betty, urging her to speak.

'There is much for us to discuss,' Betty conceded, shifting uncomfortably under his gaze. 'Ralph has never cast a spell using the Devante's power. He could not achieve it alone.'

'Alone?'

Betty fussed with the white paper edicts, still messily scattered across the low table from the evening before.

'Are you going to tell her, or am I?' asked Ralph.

'You brought him back,' said Naldy, glancing around the suite as if expecting to see Rupert's charming, white-toothed smile. 'Did you bring him back? Tell me.'

'He went to stretch his legs,' said Betty softly.

Naldy's heart quickened as joy filled her chest— Rupert was alive. She stood, moved to the window, and peered out, hoping to catch a glimpse of him. But there was no sign of him in the congested street below, and the surge of joy she'd felt moments before was replaced by disappointment.

'He'll be back shortly,' explained Betty.

Disappointment gave way to something stronger

as she met Ralph's sheepish gaze—anger swelled inside her. How could her friends have betrayed her like this, using her powers while she slept?

'We knew you would not have agreed if we—' began Ralph, but Naldy cut him off.

'—You decided to bring him back from death! Why didn't you ask me?'

'I did ask you,' said Ralph, suddenly impassioned. 'I've been asking you for months, and every time you have refused.'

'And you,' said Naldy, turning to Betty with cold eyes. 'You've always been opposed to reviving the dead.'

'There is much for us to explain,' said Betty.

'I won't hear it,' said Naldy. She was too angry to look at them. 'I need some air.'

'You shouldn't go outside without a disguise,' said Ralph.

'I won't listen to you,' shouted Naldy, already halfway to the door. 'I won't trust a word either of you ever say again.'

As Naldy passed through the suite's door and descended the dwelling's staircase, her mind reeled with outrage. How could the two people she trusted most be so brazenly disloyal? Her heart felt bruised, as if it had been struck.

'Can I help you with anything?' asked Syvia as Naldy passed through the sleek entrance hall.

Naldy feared that if she stopped to reply, she would be overwhelmed by emotion, so she continued into the crisp morning air without a word. She made her way down the cobblestone street, the morning sun reflecting off the pavement. Although the roads were bustling with activity as townspeople went about their day, Naldy couldn't help but feel alone. She felt foolish for ever trusting Ralph, and Betty's behaviour bewildered her—the old woman had always stoutly disapproved of meddling with the dead.

Naldy didn't stop until she stepped on a half-burnt page from a spellbook that had survived the bonfire. She lifted her foot, and it fluttered across the ground in the morning breeze.

It was the worst day ever. Maverick had declared a witch hunt with the intention of capturing her, and her two friends had betrayed her. She had no desire to return to the dwelling and considered making her way into the Kirkwood Forest—until she realised Smookers was still in the suite and she'd have to go back.

'I knew you'd make it to Arkus Day,' said a familiar voice, clutching the page Naldy's foot had landed on.

She glanced up and saw the broad-shouldered man who had been invading her sleep, standing only a few metres away. Was this moment real? Naldy feared that if she moved to hug Rupert, he would dissolve into nothing, just another vision.

'It's me,' said Rupert, the corner of his lips curling into a half-smile.

'Oh, Rupert,' she cried, throwing her arms tightly around him. His body was warm, and she was relieved blood was flowing through him. 'I wanted to bring you back, I did! I wanted to, Rupert, but I... is it really you? Is it?'

'I'm here,' said Rupert, letting out a sound—a half laugh, half sob. 'It's good to be back.'

'I can't believe it,' said Naldy, pulling back from the tight embrace but still gripping his shoulders.

'There is so much we need to catch up on,' said Rupert. The smile on his face vanished as his tone grew serious. 'And there is still so much for us to do. We should head back to *The Golden Opulent*.'

'It really is you.'

'Firstly, you shouldn't be out here. It's unsafe. Secondly, there's much to be done, and we've no time to waste.'

Naldy noticed Rupert's gaze had drifted to the large mound of black ash blocking the road.

'Betty and Ralph have already told me what has happened,' said Rupert, taking her hand as they began returning to the dwelling. Naldy felt like she was dreaming again. 'There is much for us to tell you.'

When they re-entered the suite, Ralph and Betty were sitting by the window, deep in a tense conversation. Smookers was curled up on Ralph's lap. Upon seeing them, all of Naldy's anger seemed to dissipate. How could she have ever thought that bringing back her friends and family was a bad thing? Why hadn't she listened to Ralph?

'I'll make us a fresh batch of brew,' said Betty, standing to fill the cauldron by hand.

'I was wrong,' Naldy admitted, making her way further into the suite, 'and I'm sorry I got so cross with you both.'

'You have every right to be upset,' murmured Betty, entering the suite's open kitchenette and adding bark to a cauldron. 'We should have sought your permission before using the Corium's magic. Our judgment was clouded by the situation.'

'You don't need to apologise,' said Naldy, her eyes fixed on Rupert. She was afraid that if she glanced away, he would disappear.

'They do,' said Rupert. 'They should never have used your magic without you knowing.'

'It doesn't matter,' remarked Naldy, her delight at being with Rupert outweighing any prior resentment. 'But look at you, Rupert—you're not a shell of your former self. It's you, just as you always were.'

'The magic of the Corium,' said Betty, stirring the cauldron with a ladle, 'is unlike any other magic.'

'You have been telling me for months we should bring everyone back,' said Naldy. 'You're right, Ralph, we should. We should have done so a long time ago.'

Betty made her way to the sofa, leaving the cauldron to stir itself.

'The instinct you had,' said Betty seriously, 'is a wise one, to let the departed be at peace. Bringing people back to this world upsets the balance of things.'

'What are you saying?' asked Naldy agitatedly. 'I

should not bring those I love back to this world? They have all given their lives to this quest! How can you mean that when you have brought Rupert back? Rupert is happy to be here, aren't you?'

Rupert smiled but turned it into a half-frown when he noticed Betty's pursed lips and stern expression.

'I will not stop you,' remarked the old woman calmly. 'Nor can anyone here. You may use your power as you see fit. But you must ask yourself— would you like to be pulled from your eternal rest?'

'If you feel that way, why have you brought him back?'

A tray laden with a brewpot and cups floated down to the table, and Betty set about serving the floral-smelling liquid. Rupert joined Ralph and Betty, sitting beside his cousin, but Naldy was too restless to sit.

'Come have some brew,' said Betty.

'I don't want brew,' snapped Naldy. 'I want to know why you think bringing Rupert back from death is reasonable, but you believe I shouldn't bother reviving anybody else.'

'When I found Ralph trying to use your power, Naldy,' began Betty. 'Well, I was quite vexed with him. I gave him a stern telling off; I'm surprised we didn't wake you. We came in here and sat by this window, the firelight from outside casting its yellow and orange light across the room as books and books were being destroyed. A great deal of history and valuable knowledge was lost to the fire last night.'

'I'm the Corium,' said Naldy enlivened. 'I can bring them back. We can bring back everyone and everything that Maverick has destroyed. Perhaps even the Devante?'

'The Devante cannot be revived,' said Betty. 'Not even with the Corium.'

'Well, the spellbooks and history books he burnt last night,' said Naldy, 'I can at least use the magic to bring those back, and my parents, and Odorf, and…'

Naldy trailed off into silence. None of the others appeared to show any excitement. If anything, they looked troubled.

'That's exactly what Maverick wants you to do, Naldy,' said Betty. 'He is waiting for you to perform magic and draw attention to yourself. You must take my warning seriously. He wants you to use the Corium. If he doesn't notice you doing it— never mind—because last night he enlisted all of Kirkwood to be his eyes.'

'But you brought Rupert back,' said Naldy, scrunching her forehead.

'Reviving the dead can be a risky business,' remarked Betty. 'I believe within yourself you know that to be true.'

Naldy felt aggrieved by Betty's hypocritical advice. Betty sighed, taking a sip of her brew before continuing.

'My dear, I'm not telling you to never perform magic. But when you do, it would be wise to stick to the most ordinary spells.'

'You want me to avoid using the Corium's power?

That won't stop Maverick hunting me. And if you think it wise to stick to ordinary spells, why on earth has Rupert been resurrected?'

'Because Maverick has started a war,' said Ralph, his fingers nervously tapping his cup. 'Time is not on our side. We need a way to know his movements.'

'To keep you safe,' added Betty.

'You brought Rupert back to find out the Society's secrets,' said Naldy, knowing it to be true.

'Although I also plan on joining,' said Betty, crossing her legs and leaning back, 'it could be many months before the Society trusts me with their secrets. However, Rupert has been a member for some time, so it was important to resurrect him.'

'I am pleased to be resurrected,' said Rupert, grinning at them. 'I wish we were in better times, but I am ready to fight, and we will all come out of this on the other side.'

Betty seemed unconvinced by Rupert's words but still returned an affectionate smile.

'So, we are all off to Mortous's castle in the woods,' said Naldy, thinking fondly of the banquets Mortous had shared with them on their previous visits.

'Rupert and Betty are,' said Ralph. 'You and I are heading south.'

'South? To the witch commune?'

'To The Academy,' said Ralph.

'But why aren't we going with Betty and Rupert?' asked Naldy, longing to enjoy another of Mortous's lavish feasts.

'As I've said before,' replied Betty, 'I do not

trust all members of the Society. You must be kept somewhere safe, Naldy.'

'If we go with them,' added Ralph, the morning sun glinting from his emerald earring, 'it will delay the Society divulging their secrets. It's best only members go.'

'But why The Academy?' asked Naldy, glancing at the others who were seated.

'Professor Deslong Piggett,' began Betty, 'is a dear old friend of mine. He taught me much about the Devante when I was considerably younger. He can be trusted.'

'Won't it be a target for Maverick, though?' asked Naldy apprehensively. 'He just spent an evening destroying all the books in the museum. The Academy sounds like the sort of place Maverick might want to destroy next.'

'I believe Maverick will overlook The Academy, for it is very far south. Although Deslong himself is a witch, the students themselves are non-magical.'

'Professor Deslong Piggett is a witch?' blurted Ralph in disbelief. 'Whatever do you mean? I've never seen him perform magic.'

'He is more patient than a Creleaville flower,' said Betty, smirking. 'He keeps much to himself.'

'He must be patient,' added Rupert, 'for Creleaville flowers only bloom once every century. Their roots stretch far beneath the ground.'

Naldy noticed Rupert's silver seagull pin fastened to the breast of his cloak.

'Are we talking about the same Deslong Piggett?'

asked Ralph sceptically. 'The one I began my studies with on witches. The same professor who has invited me back to now complete a paper on wizards? How could he be magical? He talks of magic as if it is this rare thing he's only seen on the odd occasion.'

'Yes, that is him,' said Betty, chuckling. 'Deslong has always known how precarious magic's survival is. He has mastered being discreet, and mark my words, if the worst were to befall us all, Professor Deslong Piggett would be the last witch standing.'

'I have just been to the Tebellos,' said Rupert, gesturing for Naldy to drink her brew. 'He will be expecting you both before sunrise.'

'You mean we'll be leaving tonight?' asked Naldy, taking a seat beside Rupert. 'But we haven't had enough time together. Surely, we can spend a few more weeks here.'

'Time,' said Betty, pursing her lips, 'is something we already have too little of. If it weren't for Maverick's edicts, I would have us leaving now. The Establishment have already made arrests—people who took to the sky this morning. There'll be another burning tonight.'

'Arrested for what?' asked Naldy, concerned.

'Arrested for flying,' said Ralph, his shoulders slumping wearily. 'Many came to the city to hear Maverick's speech. A lot of them were witches and wizards, and most were keen to leave at first light, but the guards were waiting on the steps—we could see them across the street. The moment they spotted a broom in the air, they flew up on their own broomsticks to arrest them. We couldn't bear to watch, so we closed the curtains.'

'And they plan on burning them?' asked Naldy, astounded.

'A warning to all,' said Betty gravely, 'to take the edicts seriously.'

'How many did they capture?'

'About a dozen,' replied Betty, sadly. 'Most people quickly understood the danger of what was happening, and they abandoned their broomsticks and hurried off on foot. There hasn't been a broom in the air since. I sent Rupert to collect two abandoned broomsticks and safely gave them to Syvia. But we must wait for the cover of darkness.'

'But how can they get away with this?' asked Naldy, outraged. She could feel anger bubbling inside her again.

'Fear is a powerful thing,' said Betty softly.

'Any messages sent from the Tebellos must be registered,' said Ralph, his voice bitter. 'Edict Thirty-Three. That's why we sent Rupert to see if Deslong had replied. They seem more relaxed with those who don't have magical abilities.'

'The Tebellos was practically empty,' said Rupert. 'It seems every use of magic is being monitored.'

'But if they're monitoring the Tebellos,' said Naldy worried, 'you shouldn't have risked sending or receiving any messages.'

'The message was sent last night,' said Betty, 'using a lucurn candle before the edicts came into effect. We sent Rupert to collect the reply from the Tebellos this morning to be safe. There was some risk, but we were careful.'

'Oh, that reminds me,' said Rupert. 'Deslong's response also expressed that he could assist with the visions.'

'Good, I thought he might be able to help,' said Betty, clapping her hands together. 'The professor knows much about the Devante. He should be able to provide some answers, Naldy, as to why you saw Maverick when you broke the protection charm last night.'

'So that's it?' said Naldy, standing. 'I'm to be locked away at some academy. I don't want to hide, Betty. I want to fight.'

'*Your* protection is our greatest priority,' she replied. 'The time for fighting may come, but until then, you must remain safe.'

'Safe?' said Naldy, glancing at the museum through the window. 'I'm the most powerful witch around, and I'm being sent away to some academy to sit about. I could take Maverick down right now with the magic within me.'

'And Maverick may quickly be replaced with someone else,' said Betty.

'I could take on any replacement, too,' added Naldy.

'At some point, killing Maverick may be the answer,' said Betty, concerned. 'But right now, the focus must be on understanding his plans. We must work out who is supporting him. Maverick has gained the people's trust by taking advantage of their fear. They are afraid of the power you have, Naldy. Inflaming their fear is not the answer to peace.'

'He is the one burning people,' said Naldy, raising her voice in frustration. 'They should fear him, not me.'

'Maverick has convinced the public the burnings are keeping them safe,' said Betty. She looked at Naldy with motherly warmth. 'Now, our priority must be to keep *you* safe. Until we know more.'

Naldy slumped back into the sofa. It had been an exhausting morning, and despite holding the coveted power of the Corium, she felt a sense of powerlessness.

'So that's it,' said Naldy. 'I'm being sent away to The Academy with nothing to do but to twiddle my thumbs.'

A moment of silence passed over the four of them. Naldy thought the air in the room felt hotter. She had already spent months hiding away in the cave with Ralph, and after only one day since emerging, she was being sent away for more hiding.

'I will order us a feast for lunch,' said Betty, her old knees struggling to lift her body from the sofa. 'Let's see if Syvia can bring us something special. It has been some time since we have been able to enjoy each other's company. Let us have a nice meal together to celebrate having Rupert here with us again.'

Chapter Six

WHEN DARKNESS COMES

Golden shafts of light from the late afternoon sun shone across the low table. Though they had finished eating hours ago, Betty had ordered so much food that the leftovers still looked as if they hadn't even begun lunch. Trays laden with meats, fruits, bread, and sauces remained laid out in an impressive spread. Their bellies were full, but they occasionally nibbled on the leftovers while enjoying each other's conversation.

'It's been a strangely relaxing afternoon,' said Naldy. 'It is nice being here together again.'

'I wish I could be standing alongside Betty when you reach Mortous's castle,' added Ralph, slumped comfortably on the sofa. 'I'd love to see his face when Betty finally joins the Seagull Society.'

'I suppose I won't be able to refuse drinking Veserum.'

'Yes, you'll live forever,' said Naldy, picking up another thin shaving of roast beef with a toothpick.

Across the road, the grand wooden doors of the museum opened, and several guards dressed in blue uniforms carried long wooden poles down to the centre of the stone steps. The stakes were erected in a single line, but the poor prisoners had yet to be brought out.

'How many are there?' asked Rupert gloomily.

'Fourteen stakes,' replied Ralph timidly.

'Will they really burn more people?' asked Naldy, dropping the roast beef back onto its tray. 'For what? Flying on a broomstick without signing some silly registration form. A rule that Maverick invented overnight.'

A small crowd had begun gathering at the foot of the museum steps.

'We have to do something,' Naldy continued, clenching her fists. 'I cannot just sit up here and watch Maverick burn fourteen innocent people.'

'We must not stop him, Naldy,' said Betty.

'Maverick no longer has his protection charm, and I'll be able to extinguish any flame he lights. When he brings out the prisoners, I will free them.'

'That's precisely what he wants you to do, dear,' she replied with grim thoughtfulness. 'He is tempting you to act, Naldy. He'll have the entire city locked down and every room searched. Tonight's barbaric show is for you. He expects you to act. He expects nothing less of you.'

Naldy feared Betty was right. Yet the thought of doing nothing was unbearable. Watching the spellbooks burn had been difficult enough, but sitting idly by while he burnt witches was too much to bear. The old woman must have sensed Naldy's resolve to do something, as she narrowed her wrinkled eyes before continuing in a despairing tone.

'The city is much quieter tonight.' She fiddled with the edge of the napkin on her lap. 'Almost every witch and wizard fled after last night's dreadful event. They'd have left on foot if they didn't get away on a broomstick. Maverick is not ignorant. He knows how powerful the magic of the Corium is. Mark my words—he'll be prepared. We must not risk it.'

'What are you saying?' asked Naldy, increasingly irritated with Betty. 'You believe we should let Maverick murder them?'

'We cannot risk Maverick getting hold of the Corium,' said Ralph, his fingers playing with his emerald earring.

'Listen to yourselves,' said Naldy, outraged. 'We can't sit here and do nothing. These are innocent people. I have the power to stop him.'

'Betty's right,' said Rupert, his blue eyes fixed on the floor. 'If we stop the burnings, he'll know we are in the city.'

'If you are captured, Naldy,' began Betty, the lines on her face softening as she spoke, 'things will become far worse for many more people. We must carefully plan our retaliation.'

Naldy went to the window, taking in the fourteen stakes ominously lining the museum steps. Her heart felt heavy as if a lead weight had been attached. How could she lock herself in the dwelling's suite while Maverick murdered innocent witches and wizards below? How could she do nothing when she held the power to intervene? Naldy's stomach churned as she looked out at the townspeople gathering below—there was anticipation amongst them as they eagerly waited for the public burnings to begin. She pulled the thick curtains closed. The room was shrouded in darkness.

'Let's set out before it begins,' said Naldy, her voice cracked as she spoke. 'I don't want to be here longer than we need to be.'

'That's settled then,' said Betty, warmth in her expression. 'Once night falls, we will fly towards Kirkwood Forest.'

'Maverick wants you to believe you have a choice,' said Ralph, joining her by the curtains as the lamps in the room flickered to life. 'There isn't one. Not really.'

The four of them waited quietly with sombre faces. Smookers settled in Rupert's lap, making himself comfortable. When they heard the muffled sound of the crowd cheering, they all knew Maverick had arrived.

'That marks our time to leave,' said Naldy, tearfully.

'A few more moments,' replied Betty, remaining in her chair.

'You said we would depart once Maverick arrived.'

'And we will, yes,' assured Betty unhurried, 'I am just waiting for—'

Before the old woman could finish her sentence,

there was a light knock on the door.

'That must be Syvia,' said Betty, lifting her tired body from the sofa. 'Now we can leave.'

Betty opened the door to the suite, and Syvia stood there holding two brooms in his burly arms.

'Thank you, Syvia,' said Betty, taking the broomsticks and passing them to Rupert. 'Your hospitality has been excellent, as always. We've left a generous gratuity on the table for your service.'

'The gas lights on the rooftop have been turned off,' said Syvia, nodding courteously at Betty. 'Take the stairs to the top, but please be careful, won't you?'

'I hope we will be back again,' she said, clasping Syvia's hands. They shared a sad parting look, as if they understood they may not see each other again. 'And in much better times.'

Betty led them into the corridor and up a wooden staircase until they reached another long hall lined with a braided green rug. Smookers sauntered behind them as they passed by many cedar doors displaying brass room numbers. When they reached the end of the hall, they climbed a final staircase leading to the roof. As Syvia had mentioned, the gas lamps on the rooftop had been turned off.

'We best not linger,' said Betty. 'The moon provides a brighter light than I'd hoped for.'

Naldy ignored Maverick's voice, drifting upwards on the night air. His speech was interspersed with deafening praise from the crowd.

'How long will I need to remain at The Academy?'

asked Naldy.

Betty hesitated, averting her gaze.

'You must have some estimate,' said Naldy irritably.

'It could be months, Naldy,' said Betty, her voice weighted with seriousness. 'The more we learn about Maverick from the Society, the more chance we have of crafting a plan to stop him.'

'Take a look over the edge there,' said Naldy. 'We can't let this go on for months.'

'We should get going,' said Rupert nervously, passing one of the brooms to Betty.

'I'm sure it needn't be said,' urged Betty, lifting a leg over the broom, 'but you mustn't send any communication through the Tebellos or by any other means. We will come to The Academy when the time is right.'

Rupert handed the other broom to Naldy, and she climbed on.

'I have my carpet,' said Ralph, reaching into his pocket.

'Best you travel together,' insisted Betty. 'The less enchanted objects in the sky, the better. We will turn east at Heatherton. It would be foolish to stop, for we do not know how wide Maverick's edicts have spread. We must say our goodbyes here.'

Ralph mounted the broom behind Naldy, and Smookers nestled into the broom's twigs.

'I wish we didn't need to part so soon,' said Rupert, climbing on behind Betty, 'or at all. Do be careful, both of you.'

Betty gave Naldy and Ralph a tender smile before directing her broom upwards. Naldy followed, rising above the buildings of The Great City.

Maverick's voice filled the air, making Naldy shudder, but she kept her gaze on Betty. She felt guilty about leaving and had to fight the instinct to direct her broom towards the museum.

'Leaving is the right choice,' said Ralph in her ear. 'Don't worry, we will be back, and we will stop him.'

The tall pines of the forest were soon below them.

'Nobody has followed us,' said Ralph as chilly air whooshed past.

Naldy secretly wished someone had, for her irritation was still bubbling—she felt a duel would be the perfect way to release it.

They approached Heatherton quicker than Naldy would have liked, and Betty gave little more than a nod before veering east towards the Mortous Woods.

'Surely Maverick's edicts haven't reached as far as Heatherton,' said Naldy, watching Betty and Rupert disappear into the distant night sky. 'It would have been nice if we could have spent one last night together in the comfort of Betty's home.'

'Betty said it was best not to stop,' reminded Ralph.

'I'm not stopping,' replied Naldy, leaning forward on the broomstick to accelerate their speed. 'I'm just expressing that it would have been nice.'

As they left the twinkling lights of Heatherton behind them, Naldy couldn't help but feel dispirited.

It seemed to her that while Betty and Rupert were advancing the mission to stop Maverick, she was being sent away with Ralph to languish at some old academy.

It was the early hours of the morning when they landed in the windy southern part of Kirkwood Forest. Clouds were now above them, blocking the moon from view. The trees had a slight lean northward due to years of exposure to the harsh weather coming from the south.

'It's much smaller than I imagined,' said Naldy, pulling her travelling cloak tightly around her body as they crossed a large clearing where the small castle stood.

'We best get indoors before we blow away,' said Ralph, quickening his pace.

Naldy had expected something grander, but The Academy was smaller than the Witch House. The stone building had only one sizeable cylindrical turret connected to a square section that had been weathered by the southerly winds.

'The edge of Kirkwood is just beyond those trees,' said Ralph. 'It seems always to be windy here.'

The wooden door leading into the castle's turret creaked open before they could knock. A slender man, who appeared to be around sixty with an oblong face and grey stubble, held the door open.

'You must both be tired,' said the man, his short grey hair sticking up from the wind. 'Come in, quickly. Let's get you out of this bitter night and get you both warm.'

Inside the turret, the large circular entry hall was adorned with silver sconces. As the man took their travelling cloaks, his bright green eyes—kind and reminiscent of Betty's—scanned Naldy with curiosity. He wore a brown travelling cloak, as if he had recently been out walking. He hung their cloaks, along with his own, on pegs beside the door.

'Yes, your cat has the right idea,' said the man, smiling at Smookers, who had bounded up the staircase. 'My name is Professor Deslong Piggett, and you must be Naldy—it's a pleasure. Your beds are made up for you, and there's some hot food ready in your rooms, which the beautiful cat has already sniffed out.'

Next to the stone staircase, on the far side of the circular room, a grand set of ornate double doors led further into the castle's lower floor.

'I'm so pleased to be back,' chimed Ralph, beaming.

'It is a pleasure to have you here again,' said the Professor, taking Naldy's broomstick and hanging it on the holder beside their cloaks. 'Come, let me show you to your rooms. You must be weary after your flight from The Great City. The sun will rise in but a few hours. Let us see you fed and rested. Later, there will be plenty of time for much discussion.'

Naldy was pleased Professor Piggett was prioritising their rest, as she was eager for the comfort of a warm bed.

'Do you travel with the beautiful creature, Ralph?' asked Deslong, mounting the spiral stairs.

'Smookers travels with me,' said Naldy, following behind.

'It seems Smookers has decided on the Little Eagle room higher in the turret,' said the Professor. 'Ralph, you will take the Gold room here.'

Naldy was taken aback by the simplicity of the candlelit bedroom. She had expected the grandeur of Mortous's castle, but the interior was surprisingly humble. The walls, floor, and roof were all fashioned from the same hefty old stone blocks as the exterior. The furnishings were modest: a large four-poster bed, a burgundy wing chair, and a gold-patterned wool rug.

'I'll sleep well,' said Ralph, settling onto the comfortable bed near the welcoming fireplace. 'I'll see you both at breakfast.'

They bid goodnight to Ralph before continuing further up the winding staircase.

'Professor?' asked Naldy. 'Betty said you might be able to help me understand the visions I had of Maverick, Audry, and Rubrum.'

'There shall be plenty of time tomorrow,' said Deslong as they reached Naldy's quarters. 'However, such matters are best discussed after a good rest.'

Deslong smiled before continuing up the staircase.

Naldy's room was almost identical to Ralph's, but instead of a gold-coloured rug, the floor covering was fashioned from interlaced eagle feathers.

Smookers sat splayed in front of the fireplace, where a rich-smelling stew bubbled in a black cauldron. Naldy ladled the meal into two bowls, placing one on the floor for Smookers. The food was hearty and comforting after the long flight.

When Naldy's head hit the pillow, she began to think of Rupert and Betty. She imagined them being welcomed with a lavish feast in Mortous's dining room, and she longed to be with them.

Smookers jumped onto the bed, nestling beside her feet.

'I suppose there's nothing we can do, Smookers,' said Naldy as the wind whistled outside. 'We must hide out here and leave the rest to Betty and Rupert. It seems our future rests in everybody else's hands.'

Smookers yawned widely before closing his eyes and purring softly.

Chapter Seven

PROFESSOR IN THE SOUTH

When Naldy woke the following day, it was already ten o'clock, and the fire in the grate had reduced to dying embers. Outside the castle, the wind was relentless, blowing strong and howling.

Ralph was not in his room, so she descended to the circular entrance hall. Behind the ornate double doors, she could hear Ralph and Professor Deslong Piggett's voices. Drawn by the sound of their conversation, she made her way across a stone corridor to a humble kitchen, where she was greeted by her friend's smile.

'Morning,' said Ralph happily.

'I do hope you had a good night's rest,' said Deslong, standing to prepare a bowl of porridge with wild berries and a drizzle of honey.

The stone room had one small window, which let in very little light. To compensate for the lack of illumination, the candles were burning.

'I slept well, thank you,' said Naldy, joining Ralph in one of the four rickety wooden chairs.

'There's hot brew in the centre of the table,' said

Deslong. 'I understand you must feel—perhaps a little abandoned—your friends are off to learn more about Maverick, and you've been banished to this windy corner of the world.'

'I'm thankful for your hospitality,' said Naldy as Deslong set down a large bowl of porridge.

'Ralph and I were discussing the papers he wishes to begin,' said the Professor, taking his seat at the table. 'He will venture into the complex study of wizards.'

'It should keep me busy,' affirmed Ralph. 'We may have some time to wait until the Society fully trust Betty and Rupert.'

'I've no doubt,' said Deslong. 'Now, we must find something to occupy your time, Naldy.'

'I don't need a distraction,' asserted Naldy. 'I want to find a way to see Maverick defeated.'

'Perhaps Maverick ought to be your topic of study,' said Deslong.

'Maverick?'

'If you want to stop him,' continued Deslong. 'It would be beneficial if you first understood him and his intentions.'

'His intention is to eradicate magic,' said Naldy, setting her spoon on the table.

'Maverick has a long history,' said Deslong, folding his hands on the table. 'Very long.'

'Do you mean what I think you mean?' asked Ralph, an eyebrow raised.

'Well,' continued the Professor, 'if you mean Maverick drinks Veserum with each moon cycle—

like myself—then yes.'

'Maverick drinks Veserum?' repeated Naldy, shocked.

'The wizard has been coveting the Corium since its invention,' said Deslong. 'He has lived a long life.'

'And you drink the potion also?' asked Ralph in disbelief, still struggling to grasp the reality that the Professor he'd known for some time was a witch. 'But where do you get Veserum from? It requires dragon's blood to produce it.'

'I am a member of the Seagull Society,' replied Deslong. 'Veserum is delivered to all members.'

Naldy nearly choked on her mouthful of hot porridge.

'You,' said Ralph, staring at the Professor with distrust.

'Yes, I can see it is a lot to process,' said Deslong, smiling warmly at them. 'Once you have finished breakfast, let us head into the library, and I will tell you more.'

'I've finished,' said Naldy, taking one last spoonful of the oats.

'Very well,' said the Professor, eyeing her mouth still full of porridge. 'Come this way.'

Deslong led them along the stone passageway towards the entrance hall.

'The library is through here,' Ralph said, gesturing as Deslong passed a door leading from the passage.

'That is not the library I wish to show you,' said Deslong, continuing along.

'Do you trust him?' whispered Naldy to Ralph.

'I thought I did,' replied Ralph. 'Betty seems to trust him.'

'Yes, but Betty didn't mention anything about Deslong being a member of the Society.'

'Perhaps she doesn't know.'

When they reached the circular entrance hall, Deslong pulled a sconce attached to the wall, causing the floor in the centre of the room to open up and reveal stone stairs leading downward.

'What's down there?' asked Ralph, his eyes darting from the hole in the floor to the Professor.

'Below is where it all began,' said Deslong, a gleam of fond memories flashing across his face.

Naldy felt oddly drawn to the trapdoor. She had a strong desire to descend the stairs.

'Who are you?' Ralph shouted.

Naldy drew her focus from the trapdoor and watched as Ralph raised his palms towards the calm, grey-haired professor.

'What have you done with Professor Deslong Piggett?' cried Ralph, his voice echoing from the castle's stone. He glowered at his old teacher with distrust, as if he no longer knew the man.

'I understand your confusion, for you have known me for some time, Ralph,' said Deslong, unperturbed. 'There are many parts of my history you have not yet been privileged to learn.'

'If you're a member of the Society,' said Naldy, raising her own palms, 'you must know Maverick's whereabouts. We know the Society have kept track of his movements.'

'He is in The Great City,' said Deslong, 'but that is no secret. The Society knows some of what he is planning, but I cannot disclose what we know, for I have sworn an oath to the Seagull Society. But you are safe here.'

'Maverick must be stopped,' insisted Naldy.

'You are the Corium, Naldy. You can end his life or find out anything you want with a simple spell, but I caution you against it, for it would not be wise. The *Banned Spells* were invented for good reasons. Betty and Rupert will, in time, be trusted with the Society's secrets. Until then, are we to duel, or will you lower your palms so we can proceed with our first lesson?'

'Lesson?' asked Naldy.

'There is much history that is not strictly Society knowledge, and I am at liberty to disclose it to you.'

They, somewhat reluctantly, dropped their palms.

'Let us begin,' said Deslong as the wind howled around the castle. 'Before we descend to the library, may I ask you to undo a spell.'

'What spell?' asked Naldy.

'One that prevents people from venturing below,' said Deslong, pointing to the trapdoor, 'unless they were present when the magic was cast. You should be able to undo it quite easily with the magic of the Corium.'

'What happens,' asked Ralph nervously, 'if we go down and this spell is not undone?'

'Better I don't tell you that,' muttered Deslong.

Naldy concentrated her energy on undoing the magic protecting the trapdoor.

She felt her body lurch forward, then found herself standing outdoors in a large ravine. The sunlight warmed her skin. As her eyes adjusted to the glare, Naldy realised she was in Edengar. Everything around her was just as she remembered it: the large rock walls flanking the gurgling river, the fresh air, and the snow-capped mountains in the distance. But how did she get here? Had the Professor tricked her? How had she suddenly been transported to Edengar?

Naldy started to worry about Ralph being left behind at The Academy, but no sooner had she thought of him than she was distracted by an intense whoosh of flame from nearby. Turning, she saw an enormous reddish-brown dragon standing beside the river, breathing a fierce, fiery breath. The huge beast mesmerised her with its majestic stance as it breathed fire. She thought about running to safety, but the creature's beauty stopped her, and she couldn't look away from the dragon.

It took Naldy a moment to realise the beast's searing flame was directed at a tall man nearby —whom she recognised as Maverick. The wizard was holding out his Imporiom, a bright green spell deflecting the dragon's flame. Getergrin cowered nervously behind the wizard.

As the dragon stopped to draw breath, Maverick skilfully directed his cane towards the graceful creature, producing an electric black light. The beast was too slow, and Maverick's spell pierced the dragon's stomach. It let out a harrowing bellow as reddish-blue blood oozed from the injured beast.

'No,' shouted Naldy desperately. 'Please, don't hurt him.'

It was too late. The dragon's legs could no longer support its weight, and it landed on its stomach beside the river.

She found herself falling again—transported to a small, grimy room. On one side of the room was an unmade single bed with unwashed, crumpled linen marked by sweat stains. There was a small fireplace and a scuffed round table with two mismatched wooden chairs. Through the dusty window, Naldy could see the room was on the second floor and overlooked a neglected, muddy town.

Maverick was seated at the table in front of the stone fireplace.

'What do you want?' asked Naldy, her palms raised.

Maverick did not respond, and as Naldy drew nearer, she realised the wizard could not see or hear her. The wizard's hair was oily and hung forward messily. His appearance was grubbier than Naldy had ever seen him. There was something else that was different about him, but Naldy couldn't pinpoint it.

A knock at the door startled both Naldy and Maverick.

'What is this week's excuse?' called a shrill voice

from outside the room.

Maverick reluctantly made his way to the door. In a failed attempt, he tried to neaten his hair with his hand before unlocking it.

'His Highness has risen,' said a shabby older woman, bowing sarcastically. 'The lodging fee is overdue.'

'You haven't put a stop to the noise,' said Maverick, glancing at the ceiling.

'The noises are in your head,' replied the woman, rolling her eyes. 'If you don't have board by the end of next week, you'll have to move on.'

'You cannot expect me to pay,' said Maverick, 'not when the obnoxious ringing from the floor above keeps me up at night.'

'I will not fall for your tricks,' said the woman stubbornly. 'There is no high-pitched vibration coming from overhead. I've told you, there is no floor, and only the attic is above. It is filled with useless junk that previous lodgers have left behind.'

'I am not making it up,' said Maverick. 'The sound comes late at night.'

'You are the sole lodger in this dwelling complaining of such a noise. This is your last warning. You are out if you don't have the board in full by the end of next week. No more excuses.'

The woman lumbered down the hall, and Naldy was surprised Maverick had tolerated her rudeness. Then, just as Maverick had described it, high-pitched ringing could be heard from the attic overhead. On hearing the sound, Naldy immediately realised what was different about Maverick—he was not carrying his black cane.

Irritated by the noise, Maverick dashed out into the hall. Naldy followed him up an unsteady wooden staircase until they approached a wooden door leading into the attic. The door was locked, but Maverick forced it open with his shoulder. Inside, the room was dark and crowded with dust-covered objects.

Maverick entered the room without hesitation, pushing himself past old forgotten trinkets and abandoned broken furniture until he reached the corner. A black cane was leaning up against the old stone walls. Naldy watched as Maverick curiously picked up his Imporiom, and the ringing stopped.

Then, her body lurched forward, and she found herself standing in The Academy's circular entrance hall, opposite Deslong and next to Ralph.

'How long was I gone for?' questioned Naldy, her forehead feeling clammy. 'Did I travel by magic, or was it some sort of dream?'

'Dream?' asked Ralph, with a puzzled expression. 'Are you certain you undid the spell on the trapdoor? Is it safe to go down?'

'You have not travelled anywhere, Naldy,' said Deslong. 'Although it may have felt as if you did. No time has passed, and neither have you been dreaming. You have witnessed a glimpse into the past of the person who invented the spell you have just undone.'

'But I saw Maverick,' said Naldy, confused.

'While he did not cast the spell placed on this trapdoor,' replied the Professor, 'Maverick was the original inventor of the spell.'

'Maverick?' asked Naldy.

'He invented it many years ago,' said Deslong, approaching the stairs in the floor. 'You see, Naldy, undoing a spell using the magic of the Devante will take you briefly into the past of the person who initially created that spell.'

'That's why I saw my family's spellbook, Rubrum,' said Naldy, recalling how the image of Maverick holding it had come to her mind when she had undone his protection charm at *The Golden Opulent*. 'And why I saw Maverick with Audry.'

'Why did she see Rupert, though?' asked Ralph, looking guiltily at his feet. 'She had nightmares of him when I tried to use the magic to bring him back. We weren't undoing an invented spell. We were bringing him back to life.'

'But you were undoing a death,' said Deslong, as the wind whistled past the castle's arched windows.

'So if we undo a spell using the Devante,' said Ralph, 'we will see a memory into the person's past?'

'We believe Mason may have introduced the quirk into the Devante's creation. We never quite worked out who was responsible, and we tried to remove it, but we were unsuccessful.'

'Mason?' asked Ralph. 'Do you mean the Boat Builder?'

'Do you mean that you also helped to invent the Devante?' asked Naldy, picking up on his use of the word 'we.'

'Hannah Hale did not produce the Devante single-handedly,' said Deslong. 'Although she is the witch most commonly associated with its creation.'

'How could Mason and you have helped invent the Devante?' asked Naldy. 'That would make you both centuries old.'

'Veserum,' said Deslong.

Ralph raised both eyebrows in astonishment.

'You have both found yourselves caught up in a story that began long ago. A story with a long history. Let us descend the stairs, and I will share what I can with you.'

Chapter Eight

THE REIGN OF TITUS

Deslong was the first to descend the grey stone-block stairs. Curious to learn more, Naldy and Ralph made their way after him into a small underground library with a low ceiling. Rows of dusty old books lined the room, and well-worn armchairs appeared inviting from various little reading nooks.

'I never knew this was underneath here,' said Ralph, astonished. 'I've spent many months at The Academy—why have you never shown me?'

'As I said earlier,' replied Deslong, 'it has been enchanted so that only Society members may enter.'

'There are so many old books,' said Ralph enthusiastically.

'And plenty of time to read them later,' said the Professor, leading them across the room. 'Come this way.'

When they reached the wall of books at the far end of the room, Deslong dusted the titles with his fingers as if he were looking for a particular volume.

'Ah, here it is,' said the Professor, tilting a book titled *The Invention of all Invention*.

As Deslong let go of the spine, a secret door in the bookshelf opened. The room beyond the library had a much higher ceiling, and at the far end of the cluttered chamber stood a great fireplace—the largest Naldy had ever seen—with a comforting blaze crackling away. She peered around the cluttered room, reminded of the Witch House. There were many strange objects: a vase filled with beautiful feathers, a marble bust of a man, a large gilded harp, several cauldrons, and many other curious things.

'This is where the magic of the Devante was created,' said Deslong in a sentimental tone. 'This very chamber.'

Naldy was drawn to the centre, where an old cauldron surrounded by delicate glass jars of red liquid rested on a large stone benchtop.

'Odorf,' remarked Naldy, reminded of the woman who had led them through the Edengar Mountains.

'And look,' said Ralph, pointing to the vase of green feathers, 'piglinn feathers.'

'Yes,' said Deslong, nodding, 'they were some of her things.'

'Are you saying Odorf helped to invent the Devante, too?' asked Naldy. Glancing around the room, she felt like she'd stepped back in time.

'Come, there's a sofa by the fireplace. Let us sit, and I will make us some brew.'

'I don't need brew,' said Naldy irritably. 'I want some answers.'

'Yes, I will give you all the answers you desire,'

said Deslong. 'But first, let us settle by the fire and satisfy our thirst. History cannot be told truthfully in one simple sentence.'

As they navigated the odd items on the way to the fireplace, Naldy felt fortunate to be in the same place where the Devante had been forged many years ago—but it also aroused a sadness within her. She was reminded of all the Devante they had failed to save. She held the power of the last one.

As they drew closer to the fireplace, Naldy was surprised that, despite the fire's size, the flames weren't overly hot—they were the perfect temperature.

'The same fire has been burning since we began,' said Deslong as Naldy and Ralph settled into the cushions of the long burgundy sofa in front of the hearth. He peered into a small cauldron, checking that it was satisfactory for the brew. 'The flame never goes out. Ancient magic that no longer exists. If the fire were to be extinguished, I'd have no idea how to reignite the *Forever Flame*.'

'Naldy could relight it,' said Ralph. 'Using the Corium.'

'Yes, I suppose she could,' said the Professor, reaching up to a shelf stacked with round glass jars containing different types of brews, each labelled with a scrawl of black ink. 'This one is from the north of the Mortous Woods. A sweet bark. Courtesy of Mortous Flint.'

'Are you going to tell us Mortous helped create the Devante, too?' quipped Ralph, rolling his eyes.

Deslong nodded.

'It's the Society members, isn't it?' commented Naldy, watching Deslong scoop bark into the empty cauldron. 'You all helped Hannah to create the Devante?'

'The Seagull Society has changed over the years,' replied Deslong, pouring a large glass flagon of clear liquid into the cauldron. 'Water from the highest mountains of Edengar. The finest you can use for the brew's base.'

'My cousin Rupert is a member,' said Ralph. 'Surely, he would have been told about the Seagull Society *inventing* the Devante.'

'New members, like your cousin,' said Deslong, placing the small cauldron onto the iron hook that dangled over the flames, 'have occasionally been invited as the years have passed. Most are not told the Society's history.'

'So it's true?' asked Ralph as the Professor took a seat next to him.

'Yes, the founding members helped create the Devante. It's no secret that the Seagull Society has always been interested in advancing magic.'

'Who were the founding members?' asked Naldy.

'There were eight of us in the beginning,' said Deslong.

'Yourself,' said Naldy, listing them on her fingers. 'Mason, Odorf, Mortous, Hannah. I can't list anymore.'

'There was Grace,' said Deslong. 'She is still alive. There was Audry, but she has sadly passed away.'

'That's the woman I saw in Maverick's memory,' added Naldy. 'He was going to kill her.'

'I believe he was successful,' said Deslong. 'She disappeared years ago after Hannah's death. We will get to Audry. First, let us start at the beginning.'

'Wait,' said Naldy. 'We've listed seven founding members. We're missing one.'

'Of course,' said Deslong. 'There was also Maverick.'

'Maverick?' repeated Ralph, shocked.

'But how could Maverick be a founding member?' questioned Naldy, her heart beating heavily. 'The Society has pledged to protect magic, haven't you?'

Naldy felt frightened of Professor Deslong Piggett. She wondered if he had invited them to stay at The Academy so he could steal the power of the Corium. Had he led them to the underground chamber to corner them?

'You needn't be afraid,' said Deslong calmly. 'I am not in league with Maverick. But I will not deny you the truth; the wizard was there in the beginning.'

'If Maverick helped create the Devante,' asked Naldy, 'won't he know about this place?'

'I believe Maverick will think this place is secure,' said the Professor. 'Although Maverick did not cast the spell on the trapdoor above—the one you have just undone, Naldy—he was present when it was cast on the entrance. He is the one who invented the spell and gave it to Hannah Hale to cast. We were all present. This is the last place Maverick will expect the Corium to be—hidden where the magic was first created.'

'I don't understand,' said Ralph as Deslong stood to look for cups. 'Why would Maverick want to destroy something he helped to invent?'

'A very good question to ask,' said the Professor, opening a cupboard stacked with mismatched crockery. 'But it's best we start at the beginning.'

'With Naldy's great-great-grandmother?' asked Ralph.

'Hannah Hale certainly played a pivotal role,' said Deslong, spinning to face them. 'But our story does not start with the famed witch.'

'Where does it begin?' asked Naldy.

'With The Academy,' said Deslong, selecting three cups and placing them onto a low cart, which he wheeled over, ready for when the brew finished boiling. 'For hundreds of years, this place was humming with inquisitive minds. It was a bigger castle back in those days. People came to study from all corners: witches, wizards, and even townsfolk arrived from Kirkwood, the Northern plains, and also from Edengar. All in the pursuit of furthering magic. New spells and potions were being invented, and this castle was where people would come to share their discoveries.

'During this time, great witches governed the city of Bleckdale—as you know, it is now called The Great City. Spellbooks were written here in the castle turrets and sent to Bleckdale to be printed and widely distributed. The Establishment of the day was controlled mostly by witches and a few wizards. They encouraged and rewarded the pursuit of magic. But that was all changed by a young man named Titus.'

The cauldron reached a boil, and Deslong became distracted, turning to attend to the brew.

'Let me serve the brew,' said Ralph, standing to take the ladle from the Professor. 'You continue on. I want to know who this Titus fellow was?'

'It needs another minute, I think,' observed Deslong, lowering himself onto the sofa. 'Take it off the heat and let it stew a moment.'

'Please, continue on, Professor,' urged Ralph. 'Who is this Titus?'

'Titus's story has a sad beginning but an even sadder ending. His father, Grigory, was the head of The Establishment and a celebrated witch. His mother, Abagail, died giving birth to him—he was an only child. Grigory disliked his son for two reasons: first, because his spouse, Abagail, had died in childbirth; second, Titus was born without any magical ability.'

'You said his father, Grigory, was a witch,' marvelled Naldy, shocked.

'His mother, too,' said Deslong. 'Both families had long histories of being well-respected because of their aptitude for magic. Nobody had ever heard of such a tragic thing happening. Since then, such a phenomenon has not been known to occur again. Yet, here was Titus, a child born to magical parents but bereft of power.'

'That's horrible,' said Naldy.

'It devastated his father, Grigory,' said Deslong. 'He was deeply embarrassed by it. The brew should be ready to serve now, Ralph.'

'What happened to him?' asked Ralph, ladling the brew into the cups.

'Poor young Titus,' replied Deslong with a sad tone. 'He convinced himself that maybe, one day, he'd become a wizard.'

'But you cannot simply decide to be a wizard,' said Ralph, chuckling. 'An Imporiom must choose you.'

'Right you are,' said Deslong. 'An extraordinarily rare thing to happen. Titus was desperate to please his father and knew that without magical abilities, Grigory would never truly accept him.'

'It's difficult to imagine a world,' said Naldy, staring into the fire, 'where witches and wizards were the ruling class.'

'Witches and wizards still govern today,' said Deslong, surprised by Naldy's comment.

'Yes, Sallandra was a wizard,' said Naldy, 'and Maverick, a wizard, is now head of The Establishment, but—'

'—But neither has helped to protect magic,' interrupted Ralph. 'They seem more concerned with protecting those who don't have it.'

'In the old days,' said Deslong, the reflection of the fire flickering in his eyes, 'magic was highly valued and celebrated. Which brings us back to Titus, the man who changed that.'

'But how did he change it?' asked Ralph before

taking a sip from his cup. 'Oh my, Professor, this brew! It really is delicious.'

'The Academy,' said Deslong, pleased, 'was not only interested in furthering spells and potions, but also other certain artistic pursuits. Brew-making was Mortous's specialty. He developed this particular combination.'

'How did The Establishment go from respecting magic to burning it?' asked Naldy, trying to bring them back on topic.

'Titus had an astonishing gift,' said Deslong before pausing to take a sip from his own cup. 'Oh, the brew is very good. Thank you, Ralph. Now, where was I?'

'Naldy, you must try the brew,' insisted Ralph. 'It's the best I've tasted.'

Naldy took a small sip. The brew was superb, with a delicate, floral note. Though she enjoyed the flavour, she was eager to steer the conversation back to Titus.

'It's good, yes,' said Naldy. 'Titus had a gift that wasn't magical?'

'Yes, Titus was an extremely sociable character. He was known for being able to charm anybody. He was one of the first people without magical ability to be granted a position within The Establishment, and he achieved this at the very young age of fourteen.'

Deslong paused for a brief moment. His forehead was creased as if he struggled to find the right words.

'Well, go on,' said Naldy. 'You can't stop there.

What happened next?'

'It's remarkable,' said Deslong, with a pained expression, 'that one boy's desire to be loved by his father could set in motion all the suffering that came next.'

Naldy and Ralph didn't speak but patiently waited for the Professor to continue. Deslong stared into the fire, his eyes containing a deep sadness.

'Titus had befriended many prominent people in The Establishment,' the Professor continued. 'He became well regarded. He was only fourteen years old when he ordered a witch to be burnt at the stake.'

'But who?' asked Naldy, feeling shivers all over her body. 'And how, when he was so young and had no magical ability?'

'Many townspeople privately disliked the influence that magical folk had,' said Deslong. 'Some were jealous, while others were simply afraid of the rate at which magic was advancing. Titus used this fear in people to justify the first burning. He announced himself as the new head of The Establishment and declared that he would ensure magic would be strictly regulated. He would protect everybody.'

'Sounds like someone we know,' said Ralph, squinting as he gave a rigid shake of his head.

'But why did the others in The Establishment allow it?' asked Naldy, feeling outraged. 'Weren't they all magical themselves? Why did they listen to Titus?'

'Never underestimate the power of popularity,'

said Deslong. 'When young Titus was rejected by his father, he focused on earning the respect of many influential individuals. He had the gift of charming people. They admired him and thought he had vision. Titus promised them status in his *new* Establishment. He even changed the name of Bleckdale to The Great City.'

'Yes, but why did he burn a witch?' asked Ralph, sitting forward.

'The witch that Titus sentenced to death was no ordinary witch,' said Deslong darkly. 'The witch was Grigory.'

'His father?' said Ralph, stunned.

'He claimed Grigory had allowed magic to go unregulated. People saw this brutal act as a sign of Titus's commitment to the people. They could not see it for what it really was—bloody murder.'

'He burnt his own father at the stake?' said Naldy, feeling sick at the thought.

'Then he burnt others,' said Deslong. 'The Great Witch Hunt began. Anybody who opposed or questioned his regulations was killed. The Establishment devised a list of approved spells, and all others were to be destroyed. Many wonderful books are now lost. But not just books—Titus ordered any witch or wizard found practising or owning unapproved spells to be burnt. Soon, The Academy was attacked, and most of the old professors were murdered. Only this small section of the castle survived.'

'It's so horrible,' said Ralph meekly. 'We can't let

Maverick repeat history. He is imitating Titus.'

'I'm afraid it does seem that way,' said Deslong uncomfortably. 'It is a horrible method that worked for Titus in the past, and Maverick seems to have adopted it today.'

'How did The Great Witch Hunt end?' asked Naldy.

'Ah,' said Deslong, standing to pick up the ladle resting in the cauldron. 'Let us fill our cups with more brew before we continue on. This is where your great-great grandmother's heroic story really begins, Naldy.'

Chapter Nine

THE HALE LINE

Naldy stared into the wavering flames as Deslong refilled their cups.

'I still cannot believe the Devante were created in this room,' said Naldy, in awe.

'Where were we?' asked Deslong, returning to his seat on the comfortable sofa.

'The Great Witch Hunt had begun,' said Ralph.

'Yes, young Titus had seized control of all of Kirkwood. That is when your grandmother, Hannah, assembled an unlikely team of eight witches and wizards from all corners of the land. We pledged to protect magic. Our goal was to create spellbooks that allowed the invention of any spell. It was slow work, let me tell you.'

'But you succeeded,' said Ralph.

'Eventually, yes,' said the Professor. 'But let's not jump ahead. You see, we had set ourselves an impossible task—nothing like it had ever been accomplished. We faced many setbacks along the way and many failures. Titus's rule stretched far across Kirkwood. Many witches and wizards were killed, and much magic was lost. Just as hope was fading, we had a marvellous breakthrough.'

'The Devante,' said Ralph.

'Not quite yet,' said Deslong, smiling. 'Veserum. Odorf single-handedly had created the potion. It granted us the gift of time. We thought it might take us many more centuries to create the spellbooks. The invention of Veserum filled us all with a new sense of optimism.'

'Were you all living at The Academy then?' asked Naldy.

'In what was left of it, yes. As I had said, this castle was once much larger before Titus ordered it to be destroyed. We knew rebuilding would be foolish, so this chamber underground had been made for us to work in.'

'What an exciting time,' said Ralph.

'Exciting?' said Deslong, with a sour expression. 'Living during The Great Witch Hunt was terrible. I doubt Maverick's rule will match it.'

'The Devante,' murmured Naldy, 'it must have been created not long after the invention of Veserum?'

'That's right,' said Deslong. 'The invention of Veserum filled us with hope and gave us renewed energy to continue our work. Soon, we had achieved our greatest ambitions. Seven Devante were created.'

'Seven?' asked Ralph.

'Yes, in the beginning, there were only seven,' replied Deslong. 'You see, the Corium had not yet been invented, nor had...'

The Professor stopped.

'Nor had what?' asked Ralph.

'The *Banned Spells*,' said Deslong hesitantly.

'No *Banned Spells?*' asked Naldy.

'Our imagination was the limit,' said Deslong, a trace of anxiety etched on his face. 'Each of us, except Odorf, was given a Devante to protect.'

'Why not Odorf?' asked Ralph.

'Odorf refused,' said the Professor. 'It is why only seven were made. She became sceptical of the Devante's power and thought nothing good could come of it. She returned to Edengar.'

'After all the work she had done?' asked Naldy.

'Odorf decided Veserum would be delivered to each member with every moon cycle. She hoped the shipments would be a reminder of the Society's pledge. We could have cast a spell using the Devante to keep us alive forever, but we each agreed on consuming the potion.'

'Which Devante were you given?' asked Ralph curiously.

'I was given the Aurantiaco,' said Deslong fondly, his eyes sparkling. 'We all went our separate ways. Hannah and Audry resided on the edge of the forest, west of Kirkwood. Mortous returned to the woods, and the others moved on. But Maverick, who had been entrusted with the Aurum, well, he disappeared.'

'Disappeared?' repeated Ralph, his voice cracked as he spoke. 'What do you mean by disappeared?'

'None of us knew where he went. Then, the most

curious thing happened. The Aurum fell into Titus's hands—his head, I should say—for its glorious gold metal had been fashioned into a stunning crown.'

'Of course,' said Ralph irritably. 'Maverick must have given it to Titus.'

'Perhaps,' said Deslong, 'but it was well known that Titus possessed no magical ability—he could not use the Aurum. At the time, we believed Maverick had been burnt at the stake.'

'Maverick has proven that he wants magic destroyed,' said Naldy. 'Just as much as Titus. He must have given it to him.'

'Some thought Maverick had willingly gifted Titus the Devante, while others believed Titus acquired it by chance.'

'I think he gave it to him,' said Ralph intensely. 'After all we've seen, Maverick has proven he doesn't care for the Devante's survival. To date, he has destroyed every single Devante—he even tried to eradicate the Corium, but it came to Naldy because of the bloodline.'

'In any case,' said Deslong, 'the mystery of how Titus ended up with the Aurum remains unsolved. Then, many years later, long after Titus had been killed—Maverick unexpectedly returned. He gained influence within The Establishment and became mayor of various towns.'

'So his Veserum shipments continued to be sent?' asked Naldy.

'I suppose they did,' said Deslong. 'There is a large supply of Veserum hidden somewhere, and the gulls deliver the potion to each Society member.'

'Have you spoken with him?' asked Ralph. 'Or has anyone in the Society, since he returned?'

'It is getting on,' said Deslong, standing and approaching the shelf with brew. He reached up and selected one of the jars. 'We should go upstairs, and I'll prepare lunch for us. This smoked ashwood brew will go wonderfully with the roasted pheasant.'

The Professor opened his mouth in alarm as a silver tray appeared on the sofa cushion. The large tray held a golden, crispy-skinned pheasant, roasted potatoes, and steamed greens. Naldy smiled, impressed by the meal she'd conjured using the Corium's power.

'It's been a long time since I've witnessed magic like that,' said the Professor, expressing both wonder and fear.

'I'll make us a fresh cauldron,' said Ralph, standing to take the jar from Deslong. 'I want to know if you've spoken with Maverick since he returned?'

The Professor nervously lowered himself onto the sofa, appearing hesitant to speak.

'Have you not asked him where he disappeared to?' asked Naldy.

'We are not on speaking terms,' said Deslong. 'When Maverick suddenly appeared again, it was obvious to us all that he had been disloyal.'

'But what about the Aurum?' asked Naldy, summoning a knife from thin air to begin carving the juicy meat. 'And the other Devante? If they were each placed in a Society member's care, how did they end up with my family and the Hexoggs?'

'And what happened to Titus?' added Ralph, emptying a flagon of clear water into the cauldron. 'You say he had been killed, but how?'

'Titus had developed a taste for the dreadful burnings,' said Deslong, frowning. 'He would sit on his throne on the steps of his palace—now known as the Bleckdale Witchery Museum—with his exquisite golden crown atop his head. He would hold a silver cup of wine, fat jewels draped around his neck, and always a smirk on his face, as he watched the innocent die at the stake. Titus would hold a burning every evening. Thousands of innocent people were killed.'

'How was he finally stopped?' asked Naldy. 'Did you use the Devante to overthrow him?'

'Let me get us some plates,' said Deslong, standing.

'I'll fetch them,' said Ralph, who had finished preparing the brew and had hung the cauldron above the *Forever Flame.*

Before the Professor or Ralph could retrieve plates, Naldy summoned crockery and cutlery from nothing but air.

'It stops my breath,' said Deslong, his long fingers clutching his chest, 'to witness such astounding magic again.'

'Shall we serve ourselves?' said Ralph, picking up a plate and some silver serving spoons.

'The Society set out to create the Devante,'

pressed Naldy, turning to the Professor, 'to stop Titus, hadn't you? To save magic?'

'This pheasant looks wonderfully succulent,' said Deslong, waiting patiently for Ralph to finish loading his plate.

Naldy could sense the Professor resisting answering her questions. Before trying again, she waited until they had all settled on the sofa, their meals and brew resting on their laps on silver trays.

'Did nobody try to use the power of the Devante to stop Titus?' asked Naldy.

'It was complicated,' replied Deslong. He took a large mouthful of greens so that his mouth was too full of food to elaborate, but Naldy waited patiently for him to finish chewing and swallowing. 'I'll admit, Naldy, we made a mistake. Perhaps Odorf had been right. We feared Titus and the influence he had.'

'Well, who finally stopped him, then?' asked Ralph through a mouthful of potatoes.

'Hannah Hale,' said Deslong. 'But first, she betrayed us.'

'What do you mean?' asked Naldy.

'In secret,' continued Deslong, placing his silverware onto his metal tray, 'Hannah decided to create the Corium. The Devante was made behind our backs. A Devante that could control the others. Some believed it was Hannah's plan all along— to take advantage of our knowledge of magic and betray us once the Devante had been invented.'

'Why would she betray you all?' asked Naldy,

feeling somewhat nauseated. 'You had all worked together.'

'Up until that point, we had,' continued Deslong. 'Other members of the Society believed Hannah created the Corium because we had failed to demonstrate our desire to protect magic, as we'd pledged. I'll admit it, we had been somewhat selfish —hiding in our own corners of the world—but we were afraid of our Devante being destroyed if we tried to bring down Titus. We had already seen the Aurum fall into his hands. And Maverick had always been a highly skilled wizard.'

Naldy took a bite of her pheasant. She felt disappointed that the Society hadn't attempted to defeat Titus. Had Maverick perhaps tried to defeat him and failed?

'Of course, Hannah did not work alone,' said Deslong, squinting thoughtfully. 'She had a relationship with another woman who was also a member.'

'Audry,' said Naldy, recalling the burnt tapestry they'd once discovered at The Bleckdale Witchery Museum, where the name Hannah had been connected to the name Audry.

'Yes,' confirmed the Professor, 'that brings us to Audry.'

'But Betty was convinced Hannah Hale never had a spouse or children,' said Ralph.

'That is how history tells it,' said Deslong. 'But history is not always recorded accurately. The two were deeply in love, and together, using their exceptional knowledge of magic, they bore two daughters.'

'One of which was given the burden of the Corium,' said Naldy.

'They knew the highest-ranking Devante could not be an object, for they had seen how easily objects could end up in the wrong hands. After the Corium was created, they used its power to track us down and to steal our Devante.'

'They stole the Devante from you?' asked Naldy, shocked. 'After everything you'd done together to help create them.'

'Yes,' replied Deslong. 'Some are said to have relinquished theirs willingly. Most did not hand them over without a fight. But we had little chance of winning against the power of the Corium and the arrival of the *Banned Spells*.'

'But why did they take them from you?' asked Ralph.

'Hannah believed we could not be trusted,' said Deslong. 'She accused us of being power-hungry. The thing we had worked together on was taken from us.'

'What happened then?' asked Naldy.

'Some in the Society, having felt deceived, searched for this highest-ranking Devante. Many believed it to be another book, while rumours also spread that the magic was entrusted to a creature. At the time, we were not aware that the magic of the Corium resided in a child. Whispers of the existence of the Devante spread throughout Kirkwood. The number of burnings, particularly of spellbooks, increased. Rumour spread that there was a dark sorcerer.'

'How did Hannah overthrow Titus and his golden crown?' asked Ralph.

'The Aurum was the last to be retrieved,' said the Professor, lifting the tray from his lap and placing it onto the trolley. 'Hannah died reclaiming it, and history remembers her for that.'

'She had possession of all of the Devante,' said Naldy, shifting irritably, 'and Titus still managed to kill her?'

'She underestimated Titus,' said Deslong. 'But Titus also underestimated the impact Hannah's death would have on his reign. After the boy sentenced Hannah to death, people believed the feared sorcerer had been killed, and they grew tired of his nightly burnings. Titus soon lost his influence. The Establishment sentenced Titus to the same fate that befell his father, and he was burnt at the stake on the steps of the Bleckdale Witchery Museum.'

'He deserved it,' said Ralph sharply. 'After all of the people he had murdered.'

'What happened to the Devante?' asked Naldy. 'You said Hannah and Audry stole them from the members of the Seagull Society. What did they do with them?'

'We found this out much later,' began Deslong. 'They had designed the magic of the highest-ranking Devante to be transferred to the first female when the bearer died. They divided the other seven Devante between their two daughters and insisted the books be bequeathed to the eldest female descendant.'

'Betty,' said Naldy, sitting upright, her chest fluttering. 'Her mother had possession of four Devante, and they were given to Betty and Barbra when they were children.'

'Yes,' said Deslong, smiling warmly. 'This might surprise you, Naldy, but our dear old Betty is your first cousin twice removed.'

Naldy took a deep breath, her heart pounding heavily. She struggled to believe the information Deslong had just imparted.

'But how can I be related to Betty?' Naldy raised her voice in disbelief. 'And if I am, why did Betty never say anything to me?'

'I suppose that makes you related to Barbra too,' added Ralph, scrunching his nose.

'Now that Audry is gone,' said Deslong calmly, staring into the fire, 'I believe I may be the only one alive who knows that you are both descendants of Hannah and Audry.'

'First cousins?' asked Naldy, shaking her head as she tried to piece together the lineage that connected them. It was truly difficult to believe.

'Twice removed,' said Deslong. 'Hannah and Audry bore two children together, whom they named Corium and Hexogg. Hexogg, even as a baby, was always known as H.'

Naldy thought of the 'H' embossed into the inner

covers of the Devante. She realised the mark must have been an inscription to mark the book's owner. She had only ever seen it in Betty's fake copy of the Aurantiaco.

'Corium and Hexogg were siblings,' continued the Professor. 'Hexogg gave birth to Betty and Barbra. Sadly, Hexogg died in childbirth. It was not wise for the children to embrace the family name of Hale—not after Hannah was sentenced to death—so the children were given their mother's first name as their last: Betty and Barbra Hexogg. Of course, it was your family's lineage, Naldy, that has been burdened with the responsibility of the Corium.'

'And on Naldy's side then?' asked Ralph, his brow furrowed as he too struggled to piece together the family history.

'Hannah and Audry brought Corium into existence. Corium gave birth to Naldy's great-grandmother, Emery, who then gave birth to Naldy's mother, Tarren.'

'I'm still struggling to grasp the relation,' said Ralph, narrowing his eyes.

'Here,' said Naldy, thrusting a palm towards the *Forever Flame.*

Smoke drifted from the fire, arranging itself into smoky strands to form a family tree in mid-air:

```
              ┌─Corium — Emery — Tarren — Naldy
Hannah + Audry
              └─Hexogg (H) — Betty & Barbra
```

'So neither Betty nor Barbra know?' asked Naldy,

wondering what their old friend would make of the news.

'They do not,' said Deslong as the family tree of smoke dispersed. 'Neither of them is aware they are related to Hannah and Audry. They certainly do not know that you, Naldy, are also related—albeit distantly.'

'I understand Hale would have been a dangerous surname to adopt,' said Naldy. 'Betty and Barbra were named after their mother, Hexogg. But where did my last name, Elahline, come from?'

'The first half, read backwards, spells Hale,' explained Deslong.

'The Hale Line,' said Ralph. 'Does Maverick know all this? Do all the members of the Society know?'

'I don't believe they do,' said Deslong, warming his hands with the *Forever Flame*. 'It is a history few are concerned with, and even fewer have knowledge of.'

'You say Maverick contributed to the Devante's creation,' said Naldy, feeling a bubbling anger as she said his name.

'He did, yes,' said Deslong, nodding. 'Maverick contributed a great deal.'

'Then why would he give the Aurum to Titus—and just disappear—only to show up hundreds of years later with a mission to destroy magic?'

'I believe there were some in the Society,' said Deslong, a heaviness in his tone, 'who may have understood why Maverick desires the Devante's destruction. But Maverick has killed those who knew his secret, and I fear there is nobody left alive who can answer your question, Naldy, except perhaps Maverick himself.'

'From the memory I saw,' said Naldy, 'I think Audry knew.'

'Let us head back upstairs,' said Deslong, lifting himself from the sofa. 'Our heads are full to the brim with enough history for one day.'

Deslong wove through the clutter, heading for the secret door leading back into the library. Naldy and Ralph remained on the sofa. She was too stunned by all the information to move.

'I still can't believe Betty and Barbra are your cousins,' said Ralph. 'I'd never have guessed.'

'First cousins twice removed,' said Naldy, laughing briefly. She sank into the sofa, feeling defeated. 'We've learnt much about the history of the Devante, Ralph, but I don't see how it helps us against Maverick. Nor does it bring us any closer to understanding his motives.'

'Come,' said Ralph, standing and offering a hand to Naldy, helping her up from the sofa. 'I know it doesn't give off much heat, but it still feels stuffy down here with that *Forever Flame.* Let's go outside for a walk and get some air.'

Chapter Ten

HOME AMID THE SOUTHERN WIND

Three windy months elapsed without news from Betty or Rupert, and despite Ralph's constant assurances that they were both fine, Naldy couldn't help but feel a sense of dread.

'They can't send a lucurn candle,' Ralph had repeatedly said. 'It's better if we don't hear from them. Besides, I'm sure Mortous is looking after them both.'

'It's been so long,' Naldy had always replied. 'I just wish we could be doing more.'

The days started to blur together, and she grew bored of The Academy and increasingly restless with the endless waiting. Every morning, after finishing breakfast, Deslong would refer to the newspaper to read aloud the list of names of those condemned to be burnt at the stake that evening. Ralph would then seclude himself in the underground library to spend the day perusing spellbooks while Deslong kept himself busy reviewing papers sent in from student scholars. Naldy often found herself alone, slumped in an alcove by a window, staring at the trees outside as they yielded to the relentless wind. She spent hours thinking about Maverick and was itching to do more to stop him. Lunch was often eaten separately, but when they gathered for dinner, Deslong and Ralph spent most of the time discussing the art of witchcraft and wizardry. Little, if anything, was said about Maverick. Afterwards, Naldy would collapse onto her bed at night, defeated by another wasted day of waiting.

Ralph sometimes accompanied Naldy on a walk before secluding himself in the underground library. Wrapping their travelling cloaks tightly around their bodies, collars turned upwards, they would brace the ruthlessly biting gales.

'Why doesn't Professor Piggett ever join us?' asked Naldy. 'It feels as if he's avoiding us.'

'The Professor is busy with his students' work. You have spent hardly any time in the quarters underground since he showed us, Naldy. I'm confident most of the books predate The Great Witch Hunt. You should join me after our walk.'

It was true that Naldy had barely ventured into the chambers below the castle. She was reminded too much of the Witch House, and the place evoked memories of her mother and of Odorf. She didn't want to be distracted by painful memories—she wanted to focus on how she could defeat Maverick.

'I think we're leaving too much up to Betty and Rupert,' said Naldy.

'Once the Society trusts them,' replied Ralph, stopping to consider the grey clouds above, 'they'll better understand Maverick's next move. They told us it could take some time.'

'Deslong *is* a member of the Society,' said Naldy, exasperated. 'Not just any member, a founding member. He should know Maverick's next move. He also hasn't taught us anything more about him since we first arrived. He must know plenty, considering they invented the Devante together.'

'He is bound by the Society's oath,' said Ralph, his strawberry-blonde hair tussling wildly with the wind. 'The Society isn't what it used to be.'

'We can't sit about while more burnings are happening, Ralph. We need to be doing more than hiding. It feels somewhat foolish we are lying low in a place Maverick is familiar with, even if it was a long time ago since he was last here.'

'We should head back,' said Ralph, nodding at the gathering clouds overhead, 'or we'll get caught in the rain.'

'I keep thinking about what Deslong said about Hannah sacrificing herself. The Great Witch Hunt ended because people believed the feared sorcerer —Hannah Hale—was killed. Sometimes, I think the only way to end what Maverick has started is to turn myself in. He's made me—the Corium—the feared sorcerer.'

'You can't surrender, Naldy,' said Ralph, his voice low with quiet affection. 'First, Hannah wasn't the one who possessed the Corium's magic. She gifted it to her daughter.'

'Burdened, you mean.'

'Secondly, Titus wouldn't have been able to use it even if she had carried the power. If you turn yourself in, Naldy, Maverick would have free reign of the highest-ranking Devante. Unlike Titus, he can cast magic.'

'I just don't see how we win this fight,' said Naldy, as drops of water splashed on their cloaks. 'Even if Betty and Rupert are successful, how does knowing Maverick's plan really help us?'

'It helps us to keep you safe,' said Ralph, wrapping his arm around her shoulders. 'Now, come on, let's get back before we're both drenched.'

When they returned to the castle, Ralph made his way down to the underground library to study more books. Naldy found herself alone in an alcove once more, watching the rain patter diagonally against the window. Her thoughts kept returning to the powers of the Corium, particularly the *Banned Spells*. She had to resist the temptation to break the *Banned Spell of Death*, reminding herself that Betty had cautioned her against it—they must wait to learn more.

Naldy hadn't noticed Smookers entering the room. Hours must have passed with her sitting by the window, for although the dark rainclouds still concealed the sun, the light had slowly faded.

'Deslong knows something,' said Naldy softly as Smookers rubbed himself against her leg. 'I can't shake the feeling he knows more. If only I could get him to talk about anything other than his students' work during dinner.'

Smookers leapt onto the window ledge and settled against the glass, his black furry head resting on his outstretched paws.

'I could break the *Banned Spell of Knowledge* and force the information from Professor Piggett,' said Naldy as Smookers yawned. 'I know you don't care, Smookers, but it matters. We may be safe here for now, but it won't be long before Maverick's edicts extend all the way south. I've never broken a *Banned Spell,* and Betty seemed to think it would be foolish. If only there was another way.'

Naldy sat upright. An idea had come to her. She made her way out of the alcove and towards the circular entrance hall. The trapdoor in the floor was open, and Naldy knew Ralph would still be below, busy reading. She made her way outside, where the rain was still falling heavily. Finding a clear patch of grass, Naldy held out her arms, palms facing downward.

A grand pavilion tent made of exquisite golden fabric rose from the ground around her. Antique chairs appeared around a large round table, and dangling majestically from the ceiling, an emerald chandelier with long red tapered candles emerged. An impressive banquet materialised on the table: roasted meats, well-seasoned garden vegetables, and stone-baked slices of bread with herb dips.

She felt proud of the magic she'd performed and was certain Deslong would be impressed by it. As she admired the opulence of the setting, rain splashed against her cloak. Though she was standing beneath the tent, the wind was so strong that the downpour still reached her.

'Well, that won't do,' said Naldy, focusing her inner power on the weather.

The rain and wind ceased, and the grey clouds dispersed, revealing a golden setting sun.

'This is sure to please him,' said Naldy to herself —but moments after uttering the words, she caught sight of something moving in the nearby trees. Now that the branches had stopped swaying, she noticed a figure retreating into the forest wearing a grey cloak and carrying a broomstick. The person glanced back over their shoulder, and Naldy momentarily glimpsed the figure's face. She was a middle-aged woman with short brunette hair and a disgruntled expression. Naldy had the strange feeling that the woman had been watching her.

'I knew it was you,' shouted the Professor irritably, his black travelling cloak billowing behind him as he approached from the castle.

Naldy tried to glimpse the woman in the forest again, but she was gone. The Professor continued plodding across the lawn with a sour-faced expression.

'Look what you have done! You must be careful, Naldy!'

'I thought we could enjoy dinner outdoors,' called Naldy, surprised by the Professor's bad temper. 'I wanted to thank you for letting me stay.'

'It is not just Maverick you need to be afraid of,' said Deslong as he reached her, breathing heavily from exertion, his forehead creased with anxiety. 'Others also seek the Corium's power. Let us hope nobody has noticed the sudden change in weather.'

'I'm sorry,' said Naldy, frustrated that her plan had backfired. She had thought the Professor would be impressed by the magic. 'It was only the weather south that I changed—I can change it back.'

'Don't change it back,' said Deslong abruptly. 'It is done now, and let us hope anyone who witnessed the marvel didn't think it was the work of a witch but simply Mother Nature's doing. The last thing we need is for The Establishment guards to come by and escort you back to The Great City.'

'There was a woman with a broom,' said Naldy, feeling horrible. 'In the trees, just now. I think she may have seen it. I'm so sorry. I just wanted to thank you for your hospitality.'

'Nonsense,' said the Professor, sitting in one of the chairs to catch his breath. 'You didn't want to thank me, you wanted to impress me.'

'Impress you?' asked Naldy, surprised the Professor had guessed her plan.

'You know I'm concealing something from you. You wanted to charm me with dinner, isn't that so?'

'You admit you are hiding something then?' asked Naldy, narrowing her hazel eyes.

'I am impressed,' said Deslong, taking a moment to admire the grandeur of the pavilion. 'Mightily impressed by the magic. But you needn't have gone to all the effort—a simple spell to gift yourself charm would have sufficed and would have been far less pronounced.'

'What about the woman?'

'We are not the only ones in this corner of the forest,' said Deslong. 'Let us hope she keeps the marvel of the spell she witnessed to herself. If she was a witch, she likely will. There is nothing we can do about that now.'

Naldy felt foolish but was quickly distracted by Ralph, crossing the lawn with an armful of books. The light was fading fast, and twilight was beginning to set in.

'Are we having dinner out here then?' asked Ralph, his eyes scanned eagerly over the food as he approached. He glanced at the clear sky. 'The work of the Corium, I'm guessing. The air here is never still.'

'Naldy has prepared us a feast,' said Deslong, gesturing to one of the ornate chairs. 'A spread lavish enough to rival even Mortous's hospitality. Let us sit, for the time has come to share more of the Devante's history with you.'

Ralph, who had already begun sampling the food, promptly took his seat. Naldy remained standing.

'You admit you have been keeping something from us?' asked Naldy, irritated by Deslong's relaxed demeanour.

'I have been waiting for the right moment to share more with you,' said Deslong, picking up the silver serving spoons. 'The Devante have a complicated history. Good food and drink are the perfect setting for us to discuss it further.'

Ralph's hand, reaching for a crusty bread roll,

stopped midway, and his mouth opened in surprise. Naldy had caused the food and drink on the table to vanish.

'I don't trust you,' said Naldy as Deslong smiled at her patiently. 'I don't want you to tell us half the story. I want you to tell us everything.'

'You are the Corium, Naldy,' said Deslong, calmly returning the serving spoons to the table. 'You carry a great deal of power, but you also bear a great burden. I don't deny that there is more to tell, but I have hesitated to add to the burden and have been waiting for the right time.'

'Can we eat while discussing things?' asked Ralph, looking disappointedly at the empty silverware.

Naldy restored the feast and took her seat, unfolding a linen napkin onto her lap. Ralph quickly loaded his plate with food, afraid Naldy would make it vanish again.

'I believe you carry a list of the Devante,' said Deslong, rubbing his grey stubble.

'What do you need the list for?' asked Naldy, reaching into her pockets to see if she had it with her. She failed to find it. 'There is nothing on it apart from the Corium. The Devante disappear from the list once they have been destroyed.'

'May I?' asked Deslong, holding his hand out to Naldy.

'I don't have it,' said Naldy, turning to Ralph, who was busy savouring a mouthful of pickled courgette. 'I think it may be in your cloak pocket, Ralph. If it's not, we may have discarded it.'

Ralph reached deep into his pocket, where he found the parchment. He passed it to Naldy, who unfurled it.

'See,' said Naldy, tossing the list to the Professor. 'We failed to save the others, and there's your proof.'

The Professor scanned the paper. Naldy struggled to interpret Deslong's stony expression.

'There are two names on this list,' said Deslong matter-of-factly as he helped himself to a serving of the courgettes that Ralph was relishing.

'Two,' said Naldy, folding her arms. 'There is only the Corium.'

'Take a second look,' said the Professor, passing her the parchment.

Naldy scrutinised the front and reverse, but underneath the 'H', Naldy could only see the Corium listed on the paper. Then, the realisation struck her.

'Hexogg was known as H,' said Naldy.

'Quite right,' said Deslong.

'What are you getting at?' asked Ralph, putting his utensils down and dabbing his mouth with the edge of his napkin. 'That both of Hannah's children, Corium and H, were gifted the power of the Devante?'

'I always thought the H stood for Hale,' said Naldy. 'But it stands for Hexogg, doesn't it?'

'But, Professor,' questioned Ralph, leaning forward. 'I thought you said Hannah and Audry set out to make one higher-ranking Devante to rule the others?'

'I fear that if I am to divulge what I know,' the Professor continued, 'it will add to your already full plate of burdens.'

'I am the Corium,' said Naldy coolly, as the brewpot lifted itself from the table, filling their cups. 'You can volunteer the information, or I will find a way to extract it from you. We want to know the truth.'

Deslong chuckled, amused by Naldy's unexpected threat.

'You may laugh,' said Naldy seriously, 'but Maverick is out there burning innocent people, and I take this to be an extremely urgent matter.'

'You need not question my commitment to the Devante,' said Deslong calmly. 'I helped to create the magic. I will tell you what you wish to know, but I fear it will only trouble you.'

'It's the children,' said Naldy, her heart rate increasing. 'How far apart in age were H and Corium?'

'Four—' began Deslong, but he swallowed the rest of his sentence.

'Four years?' asked Ralph.

'Minutes,' said Naldy. 'H and Corium were born four minutes apart, weren't they?'

'But that would make them...' said Ralph before Deslong interrupted him—

'Twins,' said the Professor. 'Hannah and Audry had two daughters, H and Corium, who were twins.'

'Do you believe the magic was split between H and Corium?' asked Ralph, his forehead wrinkled with concern. 'Do you think the H on the list is another surviving Devante?'

'I am certain that it is,' said Deslong. 'The magic they created was divided between their two daughters, Corium and H.'

'But wouldn't that mean that Betty and Barbra are now Devante?' asked Ralph, too stunned by the information to continue with his dinner. 'You said they are both the children of Hexogg. Was the magic passed down to them when H died?'

'But how could it have been?' asked Naldy. 'Both are skilled witches, but neither Betty nor Barbra has shown any sign of possessing extraordinary magical ability.'

'It is my belief that the magic of H has been fractured,' said Deslong, his attention fixed on the trees growing darker in the distance. 'Importantly, H's children—Betty and Barbra—were also twins. I believe that each carries a portion of the Devante's power, but this further split has caused the magic of H to become dormant. When one of them passes, I believe the magic will transfer to the surviving sister—and become whole again. The H on this list proves Hexogg's magic is still alive, even if it remains inactive for now.'

Neither Ralph nor Naldy responded. Although darkness now surrounded them, the pavilion was still glittering with the light from Naldy's grand chandelier.

'This changes everything,' said Ralph, using his fork to play with his food. 'I wish you had waited until we reached dessert to bombard us with all this history. I seemed to have lost my appetite.'

'Does either of them know?' asked Naldy.

'I don't believe so,' said Deslong. 'Neither Betty nor Barbra is even aware that they are the descendants of Hannah and Audry. They have both proven careless with the Devante they were entrusted with as children. The magic was always designed to be passed to the first female when the bearer died. But you see, H died in labour before either twin was birthed. The children, Betty and Barbra, were lucky to be saved.'

'Does anybody else know?' asked Naldy.

'They must,' said Ralph, 'surely people noticed Hannah and Audry had children. Two of them!'

'Hannah and Audry moved into the Witch House on the edge of the forest and kept to themselves. They lived quite a solitary life. To keep the children safe, they were careful who they confided in.'

'Are the Corium and H equal then?' asked Ralph curiously. 'In power, I mean?'

'We cannot be certain,' said Deslong, gazing at his dainty plate as he bit his lip. 'Maverick has previously used the Corium's magic to briefly undo the *Banned Spell of Death* when he channelled its power through Naldy's mother, Tarren. But it is known that H was born before Corium by a few minutes, making Hexogg the eldest daughter. Though it is believed that only the highest-ranking Devante can break the *Banned Spells,* I think the two may be equal in power—and both capable of doing so.'

'We must tell Betty,' said Naldy, lifting her angular jaw. 'She's joined the Society, she'll be consuming Veserum, and she'll outlive her sister. If Maverick finds out, Betty will be hunted. We should not keep that information from her.'

Deslong busied himself with the food, loading his plate with roasted meats.

'She ought to know,' continued Naldy.

'I think if Betty knew,' said Deslong, averting his gaze, 'she would have second thoughts about drinking Veserum. The responsibility of the Devante is not a light load to carry, as I'm sure you know.'

'Second thoughts?' echoed Naldy, trying to catch Deslong's attention.

'If she knew that the Devante's magic lies dormant within her,' said Deslong, resting his hands on the table. He blinked several times, as if the mere thought distressed him. 'I know her well. She would refuse to drink Veserum. Betty would see it as an unfair advantage over her sister. She must never know the weight she is to carry.'

'Betty ought to know what's at stake,' said Naldy, leaning back into her chair. 'We must tell her.'

'You must not,' urged Deslong abruptly, rising to his feet. Naldy and Ralph were surprised by the Professor's firmness.

'She will find out eventually,' said Naldy. 'When her sister dies.'

'You mustn't tell her,' said Deslong sharply. Moments ago, the Professor had refused to meet her eyes, but now his gaze bored into Naldy with unsettling intensity. 'Betty will want to leave things to chance. The stakes are too high to let chance decide who inherits the magic of H.'

The Professor took his hands from the linen tablecloth and fastened the centre button on his travelling cloak.

'Now, if you'll excuse me,' continued Deslong more calmly, 'I have papers I must read before bed. Thank you for the wonderful dinner.'

Deslong made his way across the dark lawn towards the small castle. Neither spoke until the upper windows in the turret were glistening with candlelight.

'Are we having dessert?' asked Ralph.

'We barely finished our dinner,' said Naldy, scowling. 'How can you be thinking of sugar after everything we just heard, Ralph?'

'Deslong has a point,' he replied, settling for a buttered bread roll. 'If Betty knew why the Professor wanted her to join the Seagull Society—so that she outlives her sister and ends up with H's power— she'd refuse Veserum. It's better our dear old Betty becomes the guardian of the Devante. Imagine if Barbra were to end up with it.'

'I don't believe he has told us everything,' said Naldy thoughtfully. She could see the shadow of Deslong playing on the sheers of the turret's upper level as he settled by the window to read papers. 'Even after all the Professor has disclosed, I still cannot help but feel there is something else he is withholding from us.'

'You're being paranoid,' said Ralph, tilting his head. 'Professor Piggett has told us that a second Devante exists and lays dormant, split between Betty and Barbra. He has told us plenty.'

'But I don't believe he has told us everything.'

'He took an oath to protect the Devante,' argued Ralph. 'He is right that Betty is the superior candidate to guard the magic of H. They need to make certain Betty outlives her sister. Maybe he is keeping information from us for our protection. Just like he wants to keep certain information from Betty for her protection. You don't trust him?'

'All the Devante have been destroyed except two, Ralph.'

'Your point?'

'Where was Professor Deslong Piggett when we were fighting Maverick in Edengar?' asked Naldy, sighing. 'We've sent Betty and Rupert to the Seagull Society so that they can learn about Maverick's next move. Deslong and Mortous are *already* members of the Society, so why aren't they out there fighting him?'

'They are,' said Ralph.

'Well, why aren't they telling us his next move?' said Naldy fiercely. 'They appear overly concerned with keeping Betty and myself alive but are reluctant to tell us what's happening.'

'I think you should contact Betty,' said Ralph gently. 'Then you can see she's okay and safe—and probably well-fed, thanks to Mortous's banquets. I think it will help to put your mind at ease.'

'You know I can't contact her,' said Naldy stroppily. 'Maverick is monitoring communication sent from the Tebellos.'

'Naldy,' said Ralph, smirking. 'You are the Corium. You don't need the Tebellos to send or receive a lucurn candle.'

Naldy couldn't help but return the smile, her cheeks flushing. She felt a little silly for not realising earlier that she could, of course, send communication to Betty and Rupert without requiring magical candles from the Tebellos. She could send communication Maverick was unable to intercept.

A sticky date pudding with a ramekin of custard appeared before Ralph, and his eyes widened with joy. Naldy had summoned it to distract from her fleeting embarrassment.

A red tapered candle floated down from the suspended chandelier and rested in the centre of the table.

'I'm not sure where to start,' said Naldy. 'It's been so long since we've seen them, and I can't think what to say.'

'Here, let me,' said Ralph, leaning over the table and taking hold of the candle. He whispered some words before blowing out the flame.

'What message did you send?' asked Naldy.

'I said it was me, Ralph, and that I was here with you,' he explained, holding his spoon over the untouched pudding. 'I mentioned we'd made it safely to The Academy and asked, if they had any news, to please send it through this channel. Oh, and I said that we missed them and that I'm no longer jealous of their feasts because Naldy's now a master of cookery. Aren't you going to create some pudding for yourself?'

'They'll need to blow out a candle to receive the message,' said Naldy. 'I doubt I'll sleep until we receive a reply from them. They can use any candle to respond. I've used the Corium to ensure it doesn't have to be a lucurn candle. Do you think it'll take long to hear from them?'

Before Ralph could reply, the unlit red tapered candle flickered to life. Its yellow flame danced mesmerisingly in the night air.

'They've responded,' said Naldy, feeling relief.

Naldy leant forward and blew out the candle. The smoke curled upwards and fashioned itself into only one word—a word that chilled Naldy's bones.

Fly.

Chapter Eleven

A CALL TO FLY

Naldy could no longer see the Professor's shadow against the sheer curtains of the candlelit upper windows of the turret.

'What does she mean, *Fly?*' asked Ralph, staring at the red tapered candle as if he was searching for more words in its grey curling smoke.

'She means to run,' said Naldy, standing. 'I need to fetch Smookers.'

'You're scaring me,' said Ralph, his expression pinched. 'Betty didn't say run, Naldy.'

'Something is not right,' she replied tersely, beckoning Ralph to stand. 'I'll fetch Smookers, and we need to go.'

'But go where?' Ralph asked, leaning forward in his chair. 'And why are we to leave in such a hurry? I think we ought to ask Betty to clarify.'

'Judging by her short reply,' said Naldy, 'we don't have time to linger.'

Before Ralph could stand, the castle's front doors opened, and Deslong marched across the lawn towards them. The night sky was still clear of clouds, thanks to Naldy's spell keeping the weather at bay.

'Naldy,' called Deslong, taking wider strides with each step. 'Ralph, you must both come indoors.'

'What's happening?' called Ralph.

'Come into the castle, and I can explain everything,' replied Deslong, the moonlight reflecting from his travelling cloak as he approached.

Naldy wasn't sure whether to trust him, and Betty's message had put her on high alert. She went to move to Ralph's side of the table, but as she did, the shatter of broken glass resounded through the air. A quick silver spell had collided with the chandelier suspended from the pavilion, and Naldy was sure she had meant to be its intended target.

'Where did that come from?' asked Naldy, grabbing Ralph's arm and pulling him underneath the table.

'The Professor,' said Ralph, his face pale. 'I don't understand why he's attacking us.'

They heard the whizzing of another spell tear through the tent's golden fabric.

'Has he gone mad?' said Ralph, his eyes wide with shock.

'There is no point in you hiding,' called Deslong's voice. 'It'll be better for you both if you come out, and we can discuss this.'

'Somehow, I think he knows we have communicated with Betty,' concluded Naldy.

'You cannot run. We have you surrounded.'

Naldy could hear the whooshing of flames. The

broken chandelier must have set the table alight, and she knew they could not stay underneath it much longer.

'Listen, Ralph,' said Naldy, squeezing his arm. 'I'm the Corium. This is not a fight Deslong can win. I want you to stay back, and I'll—'

'He created the magic,' interrupted Ralph, his voice cracking with fear. 'It sounds like he is not alone either. We're not ready for a fight, Naldy.'

'You're right,' she agreed. 'Betty said to run.'

'No,' replied Ralph, pulling out the majestic blue magic carpet Naldy had created from his pocket. 'She said to fly.'

'Come out,' demanded Deslong. 'You will not be harmed.'

'You're right, Ralph,' said Naldy, holding out both hands, palms facing up. 'But we should split up.'

Between her fingers, a mahogany broomstick appeared. The fire crackled louder on the table above them, and Naldy felt the heat rising. There was little time.

'I do not wish to harm you,' came Deslong's voice. 'You are leaving me with no choice. You have until the count of three... One.'

'Meet at the old dragon cave, where we spent the last few months,' said Naldy, lifting a leg over the broom. 'I'll go right, you go left.'

'Two,' called Deslong, his voice loud and strong.

'I'm going to bring back the wind,' said Naldy, 'so brace yourself.'

'Two point five,' called Deslong in a strained but

clear voice.

Ralph laid the magic carpet out and perched himself on top, gripping the carpet's corners.

'Your time's up,' called Deslong. 'Three.'

The wind howled. Naldy shot upwards on her broom. The roaring gust strengthened the fire's power, and although Naldy didn't turn to watch the grand pavilion being consumed by flames, she knew it had expanded—judging by the brilliant flash of orange that lit up the surrounding trees.

Naldy gripped the broomstick's smooth wood, keeping her face bent low towards the handle. She focused all her effort on gaining speed and putting distance between herself and The Academy. Although she was flying against the wind, this was the fastest she had ever flown. The branches below whizzed past, becoming mere blurs in her vision.

She thought of Ralph, hoping he'd escaped. Naldy had always suspected Deslong to be hiding something, and now she was sure that he'd been keeping his desire to possess the Corium from them. She wished she'd been more careful.

A cloaked figure, poised atop a grey broomstick, was hovering ahead. Naldy was travelling at too fast a speed to safely veer around them. She knew she'd topple from her broomstick if she attempted to swerve. Naldy had no option but to lean back and pull the tip of her broom, trying to decrease her speed.

Thankfully, she stopped less than two metres from the cloaked flier, and Naldy was surprised to recognise the woman's face.

'Who are you?' asked Naldy, taking in the face of the disgruntled figure who had watched her earlier that evening from the trees.

'Grace,' said the woman with a sneer. 'Pleasure to be acquainted.'

'Grace?' asked Naldy, recognising the name as one of the founding members of the Seagull Society from Deslong's history lessons. 'The Grace?'

'I've wanted to meet you for some time,' replied the woman dryly.

Naldy heard others approaching and she swung her broom around. She found herself surrounded. Three other people on broomsticks had encircled her. She slowly recognised their faces. Deslong was one of the fliers. Naldy was surprised to see Mason beside him. The Boat Builder's expression was tense beneath his wiry beard, but she felt somewhat calmer on seeing him.

Naldy turned, noticing Mortous atop a redwood broom. His round face was flushed pink and sweaty from flying.

'I shouldn't have run,' said Naldy, immediately feeling foolish for convincing Ralph to fly away—he was probably well on his way to the empty dragon cave in the Kirkwood Forest.

Deslong squinted over Naldy's shoulder at Mortous, his lips pursed.

'What are we waiting for?' asked Deslong in a sour tone. 'It's best we get on with it. We can no longer keep her here.'

A blinding flash of white light erupted.

Naldy dipped in and out of consciousness. She lay on her back, her body resting on a firm wooden surface.

She recognised Mortous's voice. 'We should wait for him,' he said quickly, his voice filled with tension. 'This has not been done before.'

'If she wakes, Mortous,' replied Deslong darkly, 'we may not be able to protect ourselves.'

'She is squirming,' Naldy heard Grace's grating warning.

'She will not wake,' said Mortous. 'You needn't worry. The spell is strong. Let us wait and be patient.'

The room was dark, and the candles in the low-hanging chandelier above her were cold and unlit. A lone candle on the table beside her cast the only light —a faint, flickering glow.

She had seen the elaborate chandelier before but couldn't recall where.

A shuffle of movement came from beside her, and she briefly met Mortous's dark eyes before another flash erupted nearby.

The next thing Naldy could feel was the plush upholstered pillow supporting her head.

'You're awake?' said Betty.

But how could it be Betty's voice? Was she imagining it? Had she also imagined Mortous and Mason perched on their broomsticks surrounding her? Perhaps she had fallen asleep, and someone was using the magic of the Corium. It was the sole explanation Naldy could think of as to why one moment she was flying and the next she found herself resting on a sofa.

'I am sorry to see you here,' said Betty softly.

Naldy leant on her elbows to prop herself up, surprised to find that it was daylight. She was in a large stone room with a big empty fireplace. The grate held cold ashes. One set of shutters had been opened, letting in chilly air. Through the window, Naldy could see the thick trees of the Mortous Woods stretching into the distance. She immediately understood where she was, for Naldy had been in this same room once before—having consumed Veserum for the first time while seated on the sofa she was now lying on.

'I was flying,' said Naldy as Betty perched herself on the sofa.

Betty's appearance shocked Naldy. The old woman had grey circles underneath her eyes, and her grey hair was bristly, as if it had not been washed for some time. Her clothes were creased and marked by stains. Had it not been for Betty's calm voice, Naldy might have suspected the woman to be her twin sister, Barbra.

'What am I doing here?' asked Naldy, sure she wasn't dreaming because of the pinching headache.

'I should never have sent you to Deslong Piggett's castle,' said Betty, placing a remorseful hand on Naldy's knee.

'Can we close the window?' asked Naldy, pulling the thin blanket around her body. 'It is cold in here.'

'What happened to Ralph?' asked Betty, ignoring Naldy's question. 'Was he with you?'

'I don't think so,' said Naldy quietly. 'We were chased. We went separate ways.'

'That's some good news, at least,' said Betty, her eyes watering with relief.

'I might need a bath before breakfast,' said Naldy, rubbing her aching temples. 'I don't mean to sound rude, but you look as if you may need to wash too.'

'There's a pan in the corner if you need the bathroom,' said Betty, 'but they will only allow you to bathe on Sundays. As for breakfast, it should be up shortly.'

'Only once, weekly?' asked Naldy, forcing herself to stand.

Betty had a pained expression. She appeared to be searching for the right words. Naldy shuffled towards the fireplace and started loading cut wood onto the grate.

'Weekly, if they remember,' disclosed Betty, leaning back to rest more comfortably in the sofa's cushions. 'You shouldn't light the fire.'

'It's freezing in here,' she remarked, lifting another log onto the cold ashes.

'If they haven't lit a blaze in the dining room below,' said Betty quietly, 'their conversations travel up the flue. The air from the open window helps the sound to carry.'

'Whose conversations?' asked Naldy, leaning into the unlit fireplace and straining her ears.

'The Seagull Society,' replied Betty.

'I hear a crackling,' said Naldy. 'And the thumping of my head.'

'You may light it then,' said Betty disappointedly, 'they must have lit the fire below. It is a cold morning, I suppose.'

Naldy turned to Betty, her face etched with concern as she waited for an explanation.

'It is as you expect,' replied Betty, turning both palms upwards, gesturing to the room. 'They've locked us in here. My movements have been restricted to this room since our arrival months ago —apart from most Sundays when I am locked inside the bathroom and permitted to wash.'

'I don't understand,' said Naldy, trying to recall what had happened. 'I was encircled. Deslong pursued me. Then I saw Mortous and Mason. The last thing I remember is a flash of light.'

'The people that chased you,' said Betty in a bitter tone, 'are Seagull Society members. They are working alongside Maverick.'

'With Maverick? The Society?'

'It's difficult to accept, I know. Mortous had me locked up the moment Rupert and I arrived.'

'Where is Rupert?' probed Naldy, concerned. 'They didn't harm him, did they?'

'Oh no,' she said, shaking her head. 'Rupert is a proud member of the Seagull Society.'

'Whatever does that mean?' asked Naldy.

'Rupert will be of no help to us,' said Betty with an aggrieved expression. 'I should never have brought him back to life.'

'Oh, Betty, don't say that,' said Naldy sadly. Her chest felt like it was tightening. 'Where is he? Did he escape?'

'Escape?' scoffed Betty. 'He is working alongside them.'

'Rupert came here to help protect the Corium. I am certain I didn't see him encircling me on any of the broomsticks.'

'Well, for starters, he is not magical and cannot fly,' she said. 'But more importantly, I can confirm your speculations that Rupert was not chasing you —on broom or on foot—because he was guarding that very door. I have pleaded with him to help me on many occasions, but he will not. No, I fear it is too late for Rupert. The Society has him in their clutches.'

'Maybe he could not unlock the door?' suggested Naldy, trying to shrug off the growing despair.

'Rupert was in the room when I received your message,' said Betty. 'I had to act fast. I had a brief moment to reply to you before he carried every candle from the room and informed the others that I had instructed you to fly.'

'How did they get to us so quickly?' pondered Naldy, continuing to place wood into the grate. 'The Mortous woods is some way from The Academy.'

'The Society members have been guarding The Academy since you arrived, Naldy. They have been waiting.'

'What do you mean waiting?' she asked.

'Biding their time,' said Betty rigidly. 'They are

keeping me alive, you see. They are waiting for my sister to die so that the Devante's magic, H, is transferred to me.'

'How do you know about H?' asked Naldy, shocked.

'The sound travels up the flue,' said Betty, twiddling the white pearl pendant that hung on a gold chain around her neck. Naldy recalled that the pearl would turn black when Betty's twin sister, Barbra, died.

'I'm going to get us out of here,' said Naldy. 'I have the magic of the Corium. We will go out the window. I'll create some broomsticks for us.'

'You won't be able to use magic while in this room,' said Betty softly. 'They have cast a spell to prevent any witchcraft or wizardry.'

'I have the power of the Corium,' said Naldy. 'I can undo the restriction on magic. Why are you looking at me like that, Betty? *Comburite.*'

No flame emerged in the fireplace.

'Oh, Naldy, my dear,' said Betty, as tears trickled down the old woman's cheeks.

'Sundays when they take us to bathe,' said Naldy, lifting herself from the stone floor, 'I will undo the restriction when they escort me.'

Betty tried to wipe her tears away with the back of her fingers, but the woman's face was still wet when her hands returned to her lap. Sunlight streamed in through the one window with its shutters open, reflecting Betty's smudged tears.

'I am still the Corium,' said Naldy, squaring her

shoulders.

'The Society created the magic,' said Betty softly. 'They have taken the power from you, my darling girl. They have previously tried to extract the power of H from me, but while it is split and dormant, it seems they are unable to.'

'They can't have,' said Naldy, wincing as she spoke. 'You cannot take the Corium's power. It is a bloodline. It is part of the Hale Line.'

'It is unclear to me why they did not take it from you sooner,' said Betty. 'They seem to have been waiting for something. I believe they had the ability. I have picked up bits of their conversations over the past few months.'

'But if they've taken the Corium's power,' said Naldy, anxiety beginning to overwhelm her, 'will I still be able to perform witchcraft? Or did all my magic get ripped out with the Corium? Oh, Betty, please tell me I am still a witch?'

'I do not know,' said Betty quietly. 'We will only find out if we are ever to be rid of this prison. Neither of us can cast spells while we are trapped within the walls of their enchantment.'

Naldy reached into her cloak to remove the list of Devante. She was relieved to find the Corium and H still written on the parchment.

'Oh, Betty,' said Naldy, slumping onto the sofa beside her. 'If they have the Corium, as you say they do, Maverick can extinguish magic everywhere. How are we to know they haven't already destroyed it?'

'I suppose we won't know,' replied Betty, 'until we are outside this room. But it is encouraging that the Devante are still on the list.'

'I don't understand why the Society would want to help Maverick. Haven't they sworn to protect magic?'

Before Betty could answer, a metal key turned in the door, and Mortous entered, dressed in a purple shirt with floral embellishments. He carried a wide tray laden with a delicious spread of breakfast items. After entering, he kicked the door shut with his foot.

'It is a shame you cannot join us in the dining room,' said Mortous, placing the heavy tray on the floor before the cold grate.

He brushed back his thin, balding hair—it had fallen out of place when he bent to set down the tray. Turning to the unburnt wood in the fireplace, he scowled. Then, a warm blaze erupted in the hearth.

'Although you cannot join us below,' said Mortous, smiling at them, 'I wouldn't dare welcome you without a proper breakfast. There's a little bit of everything: golden flaky pastry, bread, cheeses, honeyed nuts, eggs three ways, a selection of brews, and my favourite plum preserve. A precious phial of Veserum for you both, too.'

'Let us go,' muttered Naldy. 'You have what you want.'

'What was that, Naldy, dear?' asked Mortous. His tone was surprisingly cheerful, as if he were unaware they were imprisoned.

'I said to let us go,' warned Naldy firmly. 'You have

betrayed us.'

'Betrayed you,' repeated Mortous, offended by the accusation. 'The Society is working to create a better world, and it is a pity you had to become embroiled in all of this. But do not worry—we are working extremely hard to have it over with as quickly as possible. Though it is chilly outside, it is a glorious day, and now that the fire is roaring, we should open the rest of the shutters.'

Mortous strolled over to the windows, pushing open the wooden shutters that Betty had not yet unlatched.

'Look at that wonderful sunshine,' said Mortous, standing by the window with his hands perched on his plump hips. He peered out at the tops of the thick tangle of trees stretching into the distance. 'It's lovely, that crisp morning air. Now that we have two of you sharing a room, I will prioritise arranging a few more furnishings for your quarters. I do apologise, Betty. It should have been organised much sooner. I have been quite preoccupied down south, and I've proven to be a terrible host. It is quite unforgivable, making you sleep on the sofa.'

'Unforgivable,' repeated Naldy, standing and facing the witch. 'You've abducted us. That is what's unforgivable. You must let us go and return the Corium's magic. It does not belong to you. It is mine.'

'*Your* magic,' said Mortous, a smirk playing on his lips. 'The Devante were created by members of the Society. It belongs more to us than it does to you.'

'My family created it,' said Naldy. 'You must give

it back.'

'You're awfully quiet this morning, Betty,' said Mortous, ignoring Naldy. 'You're looking worse for wear. I will try to arrange for daily baths, but you must forgive me. Our schedule has been full, and we have been stretched for dear time.'

'Why are you keeping me alive?' asked Naldy, picking up one of the cups of brew from Mortous's tray and taking a sip. 'And why have you waited until now to extract the Corium's magic? You have known where I was this whole time, so why have you only removed it now?'

Mortous was unsettled by Naldy's questions and wasted no time walking towards the door.

'I know why you want Betty kept alive,' continued Naldy, stopping him in his tracks. 'You're waiting for Barbra to die so you can collect another Devante. Barbra's half will transfer to Betty, and the magic of H will be whole again—its power restored. Then you can steal that, too.'

'I did caution Deslong against bothering you with all that history,' said Mortous, standing by the door. 'He cannot help himself. You needn't concern your minds with all of that. I hope this can all be over soon.'

'Why have you brought me back here?' asked Naldy. 'You've taken the Corium's magic from me, so why have you locked me up? Why haven't you killed me?'

'I hope you both enjoy your breakfast,' said Mortous, and he hurried from the room.

'I cannot talk to him,' said Betty, pain in her voice. She picked up a warm cup of brew from the tray and took a sip. 'I can barely look at him. I really did believe we were friends. I'll tell you, they won't keep me alive with Veserum. I have been emptying the little phials out the window when they leave the room.'

'It doesn't matter,' said Naldy, helping herself to a lemon pastry. 'They know you too well.'

'What do you mean?' asked Betty.

'They must know you have been tipping it out the window,' said Naldy. 'There is Veserum mixed in with the brew.'

Betty was surprised, and she pursed her lips tightly.

'It is what that peppery sweet taste is,' said Naldy.

'To think,' pondered Betty, staring into her cup, 'I have been thoroughly enjoying the brew's flavour, and all this time, I've been consuming dragon's blood.'

'Why are they working alongside Maverick? And if they knew where I was, why didn't they take the Corium sooner?'

'Questions I do not have the answers to.'

'And if they already have possession of the Corium,' said Naldy, biting into her pastry and pacing anxiously, 'why are they also after H? They can break the *Banned Spells* with the Corium, Betty. Maverick has achieved it once before. Why do they need either of us?'

'I suppose they are keeping me alive to make sure

they obtain the magic of H. To ensure it doesn't fall into someone else's hands. I have no clue why they are keeping you alive now that they have extracted the Devante's power.'

'We need to find a way out of here,' said Naldy.

'Yes,' agreed Betty, 'but first, let's finish our breakfast.'

The two ate the generous spread in silence. Naldy spent the time contemplating ways they might escape.

Shortly after finishing their meal, Mortous returned. He was accompanied by a procession of bulky ornate furnishings, which he directed into the room with his palms. Mortous commanded two hefty king beds to settle at the chamber's far end, and he positioned a regal black and gold room divider between them. There was a large mahogany chest of drawers, a leather reading chair, a woollen rug, and even floral window drapes.

Betty ignored Mortous, turning coldly away from him.

'How long are we going to remain locked up?' asked Naldy once the furnishings were in place.

'That's a little better,' admitted Mortous, dabbing a silk handkerchief at the beads of sweat glistening on his pink forehead.

'You know Maverick's aim is to destroy magic, don't you?' probed Naldy. 'Why are you helping him? Have you already destroyed it?'

Mortous left the room in a hurry before Naldy could ask any further questions. She heard the key turning in the lock.

'Well, that at least settles some of our unanswered questions,' said Betty, allowing herself to smile at the sight of the king bed now that Mortous had departed.

'What questions are settled?' asked Naldy. 'Mortous scurried away before answering any of them.'

'Magic still exists,' said Betty. 'We should have seen it earlier—now that I think of it—because Mortous used magic to light the fireplace when he delivered breakfast. And he has just now used it to bring in the furnishings. Magic has not yet been destroyed, even if we cannot presently cast it from within the confines of this enchantment.'

Naldy knew Mortous must have been carrying some sort of magical object that allowed him to perform spells while in the room. She had seen magic like this before; the Bleckdale Witchery Museum guards had carried magical stones. If Mortous had also been carrying a magical stone, it had not been dangling on a belt like the stones the museum guards possessed, it had been stuffed deep inside his pockets and kept well out of their reach.

'You don't seem happy that we have proof magic hasn't been eradicated,' said Betty, glancing sideways at Naldy.

'Happy,' repeated Naldy, crossing her arms, 'they've taken the Corium's power, and the Society is working alongside Maverick. They've locked us both up, and we still have no idea why they are bothering to hold me hostage. There's little to be happy about.'

'There is still hope,' said Betty gently.

'Is there?' said Naldy, her eyes welling with tears. 'Things have never seemed this hopeless.'

Betty took Naldy's hand in both of hers.

'Ralph is still out there,' said Betty, squeezing Naldy's fingers. 'And we will do what we can while trapped here.'

—Chapter Twelve—

HIS BETRAYAL & HER SACRIFICE

The floral curtains, bedding, and rug were made of such durable fabric that no matter how much energy Naldy and Betty expended, the material could not be torn.

'Well,' said Betty, 'we won't be rappelling down Mortous's castle.'

'What if we tied them all together?' suggested Naldy, despite knowing there wouldn't be enough material to reach the bottom unless they managed to tear it into longer strips.

'It won't do,' said Betty, running a hand through her unkempt grey hair. 'Mortous is a clever witch, and he has been strategic with what he has left us with.'

'We could try the butter knife again?' suggested Naldy, sitting on the edge of the king bed.

'It will be no good,' she replied, hanging the curtains back over the window. 'Ralph may be our only chance. We must hope that he comes for us. In the meantime, I think our energy will be best spent trying to find out as much as possible about the Society's plans.'

Once the fire died, they did not relight it. Despite the sunshine, the weather remained chilly, so they rugged themselves up in the blankets that Mortous had left them and spent the evening beside the unlit fire, listening for any sign of conversation taking place. All they could hear when they stuck their heads into the cold grate was the crackling from the fire in the dining room below.

The following day brought slightly warmer weather. Naldy woke early after a restless night. She did not wake Betty, who was peacefully sleeping, but made her way to the empty fireplace and settled on the cold tiled floor wrapped in a blanket. Placing her head into the fireplace, she was thrilled to hear voices travelling on the whistling air moving up the flue—the fire had been left to die overnight.

'He does not understand,' came a familiar voice. Naldy recognised it as Deslong's, and he sounded irritated.

'I think you made the right choice, Professor,' replied the Boat Builder's calming tone.

'Tell that to Mortous,' said Deslong. 'He thinks I disclosed too much—and you know how he holds a grudge. He is polite enough, but his disappointment with me is palpable. You'll notice it when he returns from his garden and joins us for breakfast.'

'You had no choice,' said Mason. 'You had to tell the girl something. She held the power of the Corium.'

'Exactly,' agreed Deslong. 'Had I not revealed enough, she would have used one of the *Banned*

Spells to extract everything we know—and, oh my, that would be far worse. I needed to provide enough information, so she trusted me and refrained from using any magic. But Mortous thinks I went too far.'

A key in the door startled Naldy, and she quickly pretended to be loading wood into the grate.

'Rupert,' said Naldy, beaming as the tall figure with tousled strawberry-blonde hair entered the room. His muscular shoulders were squared and held high. 'It's you. How you scared me.'

'Put these on,' said Rupert coldly, tossing Naldy a pair of thick black leather handcuffs.

'What have they done to you?' asked Naldy, unsettled by Rupert's aloof demeanour.

'Stand up,' said Rupert, his expression stony.

'Do you not recognise me, Rupert?' asked Naldy, standing and moving to approach him. 'You came here to help protect the magic. Do you not remember?'

'You will put them on,' commanded Rupert, 'and you will do it without causing a fuss.'

'It's me,' said Naldy, feeling crushed by Rupert's unfeeling attitude. 'Have they put some sort of hex on you?'

'I am under no hex,' said Rupert. 'And if you want to bathe this week, I suggest you do as you're told.'

Betty stirred, sitting upright in the king bed and rubbing her wrinkled eyelids.

'Is it bath day, Rupert?' asked Betty sleepily.

'Getergrin will be up to escort you soon, Betty,' replied Rupert, his gaze still fixed on Naldy. 'I'm to escort her today.'

Naldy slipped the leather cuffs onto her wrists, and Rupert held the door open. When Naldy was out in the dark hallway, she considered running. Turning her head, she found Rupert close behind her and realised she wouldn't get far with the handcuffs restricting her movement. They were soon standing before the door leading to the guest bathroom. A wooden chair was propped against the stone wall next to the bathroom's entrance, and a newly fitted lock was attached to the door's exterior.

'You have twenty minutes,' said Rupert, sitting on the chair.

'Aren't you going to uncuff me?' asked Naldy, holding out her restrained wrists.

Rupert simply nodded sternly towards the bathroom. Naldy sighed as she entered the lavish chamber, hearing the lock click behind her. A large bath had already been filled with hot, soapy water. She knew there would be no point in trying to remove her nightgown while handcuffed, so she climbed into the tub with it still on. Although the water was soothing, she struggled to fully relax, restricted by the leather restraints.

'I suppose I still have my magic then,' said Naldy, loud enough that Rupert would hear. 'I'm certain you wouldn't have bothered to handcuff me and latch the door if you had taken all my powers. They've taken just the Corium from me, then?'

There was no reply from outside.

'We brought you back to life,' she continued, 'so

that you could help us defeat Maverick, and instead, you've joined him.'

'You didn't bring me back to life,' came Rupert's voice from outside the door. 'You held the power to resurrect me, Naldy, but you chose not to. Ralph and Betty were the ones to bring me back.'

'The Seagull Society has brainwashed you,' she said. 'They've turned you against us. You know that Maverick plans to use the power to destroy magic.'

'I am not brainwashed,' said Rupert, almost laughing. 'The Society created the Devante, Naldy, and they will use it to change the world.'

'Change the world?' repeated Naldy, sitting upright in the tub. 'Maverick has declared war against anyone possessing magical abilities. He wants to kill witches and wizards, and you are helping him, Rupert.'

'Maverick is not who you think he is. If you keep talking, bath time will be over.'

'I know he has destroyed every Devante that has passed through his hands.'

'Magic is a dangerous thing,' said Rupert. Naldy heard him shifting uncomfortably in the chair outside the door. 'The Devante's power should not be trusted in the hands of just anyone. We are the rightful guardians of such potent magic.'

'Guardians?' disputed Naldy, exasperated, pressing her fingers to her forehead. 'You sacrificed your life so that you could save the Devante. So that you could save me. Now you're holding me captive and helping the people who want to see it destroyed.

Please, I need your help, Rupert.'

'You don't know what it's like,' said Rupert darkly. 'To live in a world where some are granted the privilege to perform magic, while the rest of us must live in fear. The Devante is a dangerous power, and it is the Society's responsibility to keep magic under control.'

'They are burning witches, Rupert. You are allowing them to murder innocent people.'

'Bath time is over,' said Rupert, as the lock clicked and the bathroom door swung open. Rupert picked up a towel and held it out. 'Get out, or I'll have to force you.'

Naldy stood, taking the towel from him. The restrictions of the handcuffs made it difficult for her to wring out her wet nightgown before wrapping the towel around her body with some effort. She went with Rupert back to the chamber serving as their prison cell. There was no sign of Betty in the room, and Naldy supposed she had been escorted by Getergrin to take her bath.

'I don't recognise you,' Naldy told Rupert as he removed the leather handcuffs from her wrists. 'You've been resurrected, but you are not the same person you were before you jumped into that lake.'

'You think what you are doing is important,' contended Rupert, his blue eyes reflecting the morning sun streaming through the open shutters. 'But you are wrong, Naldy. The Society is working to equalise and to protect everybody.'

He turned and left, locking the door behind him.

Once Naldy had changed out of the wet nightgown, she settled on the floor in front of the fireplace. When she stuck her head into the opening, she was pleased to hear voices still floating up from the room below.

'I don't see why I have to remain behind,' came a husky woman's voice—she recognised it as Grace's. 'Or why any of us should need to risk travelling such a distance with the burden and responsibility of the Corium. Maverick ought to make the journey here.'

'Someone must ensure the prisoners are fed and kept alive,' replied the Boat Builder.

'Why is it to be me?' grumbled the woman. 'I would like to spend some time in The Great City. Why can't the boy be the one to stay behind?'

Naldy heard a third person enter the dining room below.

'Well, do not wait for little old me,' said Mortous, chuckling. 'Your food will turn cold. My apologies, the Kettering flowers require a strict watering regime.'

'Breakfast smells superb,' she said.

'Why, thank you, Grace,' replied Mortous, as Naldy heard the scrape of a dining chair, indicating Mortous had seated himself. 'Had I known the weather would be so glorious this morning, I would have served us breakfast on the terrace. Where is the Professor?'

'He has finished eating,' said Mason. 'He has papers to attend to.'

'For   someone   with   extensive   scholarly

knowledge,' said Mortous, 'he seems to struggle with prioritising.'

'Is the boy joining us?' asked Grace. 'I have not seen him this morning.'

'He is on bathroom duty,' said Mortous, nibbling something juicy. 'As is Getergrin. Two captives to care for now.'

'I do not like the plump man and his floral waistcoats,' said Grace sourly.

'Oh, do not tease Getergrin for being rotund,' said Mortous. 'I, myself, am a round man. It is a sign that one has enjoyed themselves.'

'A little much, perhaps,' replied Grace. 'I won't welcome him into the Society. We have already accommodated Rupert, who possesses no power. I suppose he has at least proven himself knowledgeable regarding the native flora of these parts. What does Getergrin offer?'

'Maverick is fond of him,' said Mason. 'He has proven himself to be loyal.'

'We are all loyal,' said Grace in an exasperated tone. 'What does Maverick see in him?'

'He has made himself incredibly useful,' added Mortous. 'He has earned much influence within the ranks of The Establishment.'

'We are the ones that now control The Establishment,' said Grace.

'He is upstairs,' Mason chimed, 'ensuring our guests are bathed and fed—'

'The Corium's magic has been extracted from the girl,' snapped Grace. 'I don't see why we are keeping her alive.'

'It is temporary,' said the Boat Builder. 'Removing it from Naldy was risky enough. The Corium's power may only survive if the girl is living.'

'I think we are being overly cautious,' replied Grace huskily.

'We must be cautious,' said Mortous, sounding as if he were sucking on the pip from a plum. 'The Corium was created by Hannah—and as we all know too well, she cannot be trusted, even in her death. At any rate, Maverick has ordered us to wait until it is delivered to him. Then we can decide what to do with the girl. The plans to set out this afternoon have been made.'

'I am to stay here and feed the prisoners,' groaned Grace. 'Pass the birchwood brew, would you, Mason?'

Naldy started as the door to the chamber opened. She was lucky Betty entered the room first, giving her just enough time to remove her head from the unlit fireplace before Getergrin entered. Betty had dressed in the bathroom and now seemed much more like her old self after washing.

'I see they've provided you with some comforts,' mumbled Getergrin, almost to himself.

Betty held out her wrists, which were strapped into leather handcuffs, just as Naldy's had been. Getergrin begrudgingly unfastened them and shuffled from the room, as if afraid their powers might return despite Mortous's enchantment.

'They haven't lit the fire in the dining room below,' said Naldy quietly. 'I think I might know why they have kept me alive.'

Betty approached, taking a seat on the sofa.

'Maverick does not yet have the magic of the Corium,' continued Naldy. 'The Society plans on taking it to him this evening. They believe the magic may only survive if I am living.'

'How curious,' said Betty, rubbing her wrists where the cuffs had been. 'It seems you have interfered with their plans by running away from The Academy. I've no doubt Maverick would have wanted to be there for the extraction.'

'We cannot allow him to get his hands on its power,' said Naldy.

'We must find a way out,' said Betty with a serious tone.

'What if...' she trailed off.

'Death, Naldy,' said Betty, 'is not the solution. If the power of the Corium no longer existed, there would still be the magic of H.'

A key turned in the lock, grabbing their attention, and the Boat Builder entered, holding a tray with their breakfast. Naldy's heart sank upon seeing him. She couldn't bear to see the face of someone else she had once trusted who had also betrayed them. She felt deeply hurt.

'You're a traitor,' said Naldy, avoiding meeting his eyes. 'You are helping Maverick carry out his wicked plans.'

'I have brought you breakfast,' said Mason. 'Where would you like it?'

'On the sofa, please,' said Betty.

The Boat Builder came nearer and gently placed the tray beside Betty.

'Why are you helping him?' asked Naldy, standing. 'You pledged to protect magic.'

Mason looked at her. Beneath his wiry beard, there was a sadness in his expression.

'Magic is a dangerous thing,' replied Mason, his cheek twitching briefly. 'Particularly when in the wrong hands. We must do what we can to protect it.'

'I do not want to see you,' said Naldy bitterly.

'I understand you are disappointed,' said Mason gently. Naldy thought she saw tears welling in his eyes. 'I am sorry I did not come to say hello sooner, but I have been busy, and I was assigned breakfast duty only today.'

Naldy faced away from him, peering out the open window to the tangled trees. She did not want the Boat Builder to see her pain.

'I must get on,' said Mason, making for the door. 'A few of us will be heading to The Great City for business with The Establishment, and we must depart soon.'

'Why was I taken to The Academy?' asked Naldy. 'Why did you not lock me up sooner?'

'The plum jam is particularly delicious today,' replied the Boat Builder. 'It pairs well with the rye bread. I recommend you try it.'

'I know they'll kill me,' said Naldy, turning to face him. 'Once Maverick has the Corium.'

'They were not sure the magic would survive if extracted from you,' said Mason. 'You held the power of the highest-ranking Devante, Naldy. The enchantments in this room would not work on you. They needed to keep you alive but could not keep you locked up. So, instead, they kept you at The Academy under close watch. Once you tried to run, they had no choice but to attempt to extract the magic, for if they had left it inside you, you'd hold enough power to escape any prison they placed you in. Lucky for them, extracting the magic from you has worked.'

'You keep saying they,' remarked Naldy. 'But you are one of them.'

The Boat Builder's entire countenance was tight with tension—as if he were cross and holding something back. His neck muscles strained, and he seemed to force himself out of the room. When the door snapped shut behind him, Naldy felt her chest grow heavy, as though hopelessness were pressing on her. Betty placed a consoling hand on her arm.

'I feel I've lost everyone I trusted,' said Naldy sadly.

'I know it seems as if everyone has turned against us,' replied Betty gently, 'but I am still here, and Ralph is out there, somewhere.'

'What if they have already caught him?' asked Naldy. 'How would we ever know?'

'You would have heard them talking about it downstairs,' said Betty. 'I do not believe they are concerned with Ralph. They are too preoccupied with the Devante.'

Betty helped herself to some fruit. Naldy didn't

feel hungry, so she continued staring aimlessly out the open window.

'You must eat something, my dear,' said Betty.

'I have no appetite.'

'I will make you some bread with jam,' said Betty, dipping a knife into the ramekin filled with the sticky plum jam. Betty's eyes squinted curiously as her knife clunked against something solid. Naldy watched as she stuck her fingers into the jam, and pulled out a small key coated in the sugary preserve.

'Look at that,' said Betty. 'It seems we do have some friends here, after all.'

'You think Mason placed it there?' asked Naldy, her heart racing with excitement at the sight of the key.

'I am certain it wasn't our dear friend Rupert's doing.'

'I may have some breakfast after all.'

They sat together on the window ledge, soaking in the sun's light as it climbed above the trees and the day wore on. Although most of the road below was obscured by the chunky twisted branches, they could still glimpse sections of the path from the open window. They had decided it best to wait until after the Society members departed before escaping.

'If we are lucky,' began Betty, 'we will walk out of here without needing to cast a spell.'

'Not cast a spell?' questioned Naldy. 'But we must intercept them before the Corium is delivered to Maverick. He must not get his hands on it, Betty.'

'Following them will not be wise,' she said as the

afternoon sunlight caught her wrinkled face. 'They will have the magic of the Devante with them—something we do not currently have on our side.'

'We must at least try.'

'They are Society members,' said Betty, fiddling with the white pearl on her necklace. 'We must not underestimate their ability. I believe our chances of success might best lie in finding my sister.'

'You want to abandon the Corium?' said Naldy.

'Barbra must be warned that she is being hunted. We should try to convince her to reunite the magic of H.'

'If that's even possible,' replied Naldy.

'We know it is,' said Betty. 'The Society has managed to extract the Corium from you.'

'Yes, but we've no idea if only one half can be extracted. I'd wager not, as the Society probably would have already taken your half if it could be done.'

'Regardless,' said Betty, 'we must at least warn my sister of the power that resides within her.'

'We ought to fight,' said Naldy passionately. 'We mustn't allow Maverick to take control of such magic. We'd have more luck battling Mortous than convincing your sister to come to an agreement.'

'The time for duelling may come,' said Betty. 'The Society is highly skilled at wielding magic, so let us hope today is not that day—oh look, there they go now.'

Naldy peered down. Through the trees, she spotted Mason, Rupert, Mortous, Deslong, and

Getergrin all making their way along the road. She felt disappointed to see so many familiar faces she'd once trusted. Each carried a broom, except for Getergrin and Rupert. While the others mounted their broomsticks, Getergrin pulled a magical carpet from his cloak pocket, and Rupert climbed on behind him.

'That's Ralph's old carpet,' said Naldy sadly. 'Maverick flew off with it when we were in Edengar. I created a replacement for Ralph when we set out from the abandoned dragon cave.'

'I have been cooped up in this room for far too long,' said Betty, standing. 'I think now is a good time for us to be going.'

They went to the door, listening for any movement outside before Betty inserted the key into the lock. The passageway was clear, and together, they silently made their way along until they stood at the top of the stairs. Naldy could hear her own heartbeat as they nervously descended the steps.

Betty stopped at the bottom of the stairs, holding up a warning finger to instruct her to wait. Naldy strained her ears to listen. Over the pattering of her heartbeat, she could hear someone flitting about in a chamber that led from the main passage.

'I'm to stay behind,' grumbled Grace to herself. The chamber door was wide open, and there was no way for them to pass without being seen. 'The founding member is given guard duty while the two non-magical dullards escort the most coveted power to The Great City.'

Betty glanced at Naldy nervously. Though the large stone passage was dark, walking past the open door was too risky. Betty's face was stern, her eyes narrowing as she weighed their options.

'Someone magical must watch them,' declared Grace in a mocking tone, clearly imitating something Mortous had said to her. 'It's an important job you have, Grace.'

They heard her laugh to herself before continuing—'So important, is it? Well, why don't you do it yourself, then?'

Without warning, Grace entered the passage from the chamber, but she was in such an irritable state that she didn't notice them in the shadows at the foot of the stairs. By sheer luck, she turned in the opposite direction, entered an adjacent room, and slammed the door behind her in frustration. Betty nodded at Naldy, and they hurried across the passage.

Naldy was relieved when they reached the front door.

'Let's not celebrate just yet,' said Betty. 'We have some way to go until we are clear of this castle.'

They made their way out into the afternoon glare. There was no sign of the Society members who had departed. They hurried along the road, leaving Mortous's castle behind them.

'We need to find broomsticks,' said Naldy.

'I do not think we should risk flying,' said Betty. 'We mustn't risk being captured by townsfolk eager to see witches burnt at the stake. We should travel on foot.'

'On foot,' said Naldy, shocked. 'It will take us days to reach the nearest town.'

Naldy could see Betty making a great effort to walk quickly, but her old legs would only move so fast.

'We should get off the path,' suggested Naldy. 'If anybody notices we're gone, it won't take long for them to catch up.'

'Yes, agreed,' said Betty. 'Let's head into the thicket.'

Before they could head into the cover of the trees, Naldy glimpsed Mortous gliding calmly on a broomstick towards them from up ahead.

'Betty,' called Naldy in alarm as Mortous approached.

'Go, Naldy,' said Betty. 'I'll keep the old witch occupied.'

Naldy made her way underneath the cover of the trees, but she did not venture far, wanting to keep sight of Betty, who steadfastly faced Mortous. Betty stood with her chin lifted high, undaunted by the approaching witch. He soon landed only a few metres from her.

'Go back to your Society, Mortous,' said Betty sternly.

'Betty, my old friend,' said Mortous, shaking his head and pouting. 'You would not think to leave without saying goodbye to your dear host, would you?'

'Stay back, Mortous,' said Betty. 'I will not let you

drag me back to your prison.'

'We have known each other for some time,' said Mortous, hurt by Betty's coldness. 'I know being locked in the upstairs chamber has not been ideal, but it is for the best. The Society is working to ensure magic is reserved for those who deserve it.'

'You are not protecting magic,' said Betty. 'You are destroying it. You are delivering it to the wizard, who will see it brought to ruin.'

With a swift motion of his hand, Mortous threw something small to Betty, who caught it. She lifted the object to her eyes. Naldy noticed it was a colourless moonstone.

'The chamber,' said Betty.

'Yes,' replied Mortous. 'The moonstone shows the room you have come from. It is where you and the girl must now return. I knew we could not rely on Grace to keep proper watch. You hold something immensely important—well, at least half of it. I saw you both sitting by the window, watching us as we departed. We must escort you back to keep you safe.'

'Safe,' spat Betty, 'you mean imprisoned.'

'They've escaped, Mortous!' cried Grace, hurrying out from the castle, her brunette hair in a messy bun.

'They are here, Grace,' said Mortous. 'Go back to the castle, I have this under control.'

'You do not appear in control,' screeched Grace, tensing her fingers into claw-like shapes as she approached. 'You seem to have lost the girl.'

'She is watching from the bushes,' retorted

Mortous, turning his head. Naldy got the impression he was looking directly at her.

'I'll fetch her,' said Grace.

'You'll do no such thing,' said Betty fiercely, and a flash of red shot from the old woman's palms.

Grace deflected Betty's spell, and the brunette woman sent a dangerous blue ball of light whizzing towards Betty.

'We need them both alive,' cried Mortous as a purple spark shot from his palms in Betty's direction.

Naldy could not simply sit, watching from the trees, and she rushed out to help Betty. At first, the old woman seemed frustrated that Naldy had come to assist her in the duel.

'You silly, girl,' said Betty, dodging an oncoming spell. 'You must go at once.'

'I won't leave you,' said Naldy stubbornly, sending a fireball hurtling at Grace, who skilfully jumped out of its way. 'Not when it's two against one.'

Flashes of light were flying in every direction, and Naldy spent most of her efforts casting spells to deflect the oncoming assault.

'You must get out of here, Naldy,' called Betty.

'You are the one that must go,' replied Naldy, dodging one of Grace's *Prosterno* spells. 'You have half the magic of H dormant within you.'

Betty shot a blue light that moved at an alarmingly rapid speed, colliding with Grace's right arm. Naldy heard the crunch of bones as the woman's arm bent backwards, and she knew that Betty's spell had broken something. Grace cried out in pain.

'Naldy, you must go,' called Betty.

'I won't leave you.'

A purple light was released from Mortous's outstretched palm, colliding with Betty. Her body went limp, and she fell to the ground, paralysed by Mortous's *Prosterno* spell.

Then, to Naldy's horror, a second black spell produced by Grace struck Betty's immobilised body. Naldy watched the life drain from her friend's face.

One moment, there was colour in her cheeks and life behind her eyes. The next, the pink flush vanished, and her stare turned cold—it was as if her soul had left her.

'No,' cried Naldy, kneeling beside Betty.

'You fool,' shouted Mortous, pivoting to confront Grace, who whimpered, clutching her broken arm. 'We needed them both alive! What have you done?'

'You need the girl alive,' replied Grace sourly. 'Now that the old woman is dead, we need only her sister living. The magic of H will be whole again.'

Naldy felt numb. She held Betty's shoulders, tears streaming down her face. How could this be real? How could Betty be dead?

'You, clod!' exclaimed Mortous furiously. 'We don't have any clue where her sister is hiding. That is why we have been keeping her here all this time. With one spell, you've gone and killed her.'

Grace took a few sheepish steps back, unsettled

by Mortous's anger.

'Look what you have done?' said Mortous.

Naldy felt as if the blood were draining from her body. She shook Betty's hand, but the grey-haired woman did not move, and Naldy's heart seemed to splinter in her chest from the pain.

Mortous shot a spell at Naldy, who fell limply beside Betty. She didn't care that she was captured. All she cared about was Betty.

'The old woman broke my arm,' snivelled Grace. 'Her death is deserved.'

'Your arm can be fixed,' said Mortous heatedly. 'The magic has been invented with the Devante.'

'You can bring her back with the Devante if you need her so badly,' retorted Grace. 'We have the Corium with us, Mortous.'

Naldy felt more tears trickling along her cheeks. *Yes,* she thought, *bring her back to life again.*

'There would be no point,' said Mortous to Grace, a hint of anguish in his voice. He spoke slowly, in a low tone. 'Now Betty is dead, the magic of H would have passed from her to Barbra. There would be no point in bringing her back.'

'If Barbra is anything like this old dithering woman,' said Grace, holding her arm, 'she will be easy to hunt.'

'Her sister, Barbra, does not know about the magic of H,' said Mortous. 'She will be shocked to suddenly have such power thrust upon her.'

'Can you fix my arm?'

'Maverick will not be pleased with you, Grace. I

will leave it up to you to tell him what you have done. Take Naldy back to the castle, and I'll deal with the body.'

Naldy saw Mortous approach, standing over Betty and her, looking down with a sad expression.

'You say the magic to fix broken bones exists,' whimpered Grace. 'Fix my arm so I can carry the girl.'

'As punishment,' said Mortous, bending low to gently touch Betty's cheek. 'You deserve to feel the pain for a while, Grace. Carry the girl back, then I will consider healing your broken bones.'

'You are not the leader of the Seagull Society,' Naldy heard Grace mutter. 'Do not make the same mistake Hannah made. Thinking she was the leader. Your castle may be our temporary base, Mortous, but do not falsely believe you are superior to me.'

'I will make sure she has a grand burial,' said Mortous softly, ignoring Grace's muttering. His eyes were wet and filled with remorse. 'With the finest flowers from my garden. She was a wonderful woman, and I have always been fond of her.'

An unexpected flash of green light burst nearby, accompanied by a resounding thunderclap. Naldy could not swivel her head to see what had caused the sound, but then she heard a familiar voice.

'Step away,' called Ralph firmly.

Ralph's magical carpet swooped into view, and Mortous stumbled backwards in surprise. Grace sent a purple spell soaring at Ralph, but he nimbly deflected it, and instead it collided with Mortous's bristly broomstick, snapping it in two places. Ralph returned two flashes of brilliant orange—one that knocked Grace to the ground, and the other that Mortous narrowly avoided.

Naldy found herself being pulled onto Ralph's carpet, and then together, they were lifted higher and higher. Flashes of light whizzed over their heads as Ralph swerved the carpet, deftly avoiding Mortous's onslaught of spells.

Ralph's strawberry-blonde hair was flapping in the wind, and he squinted in concentration as he steered the carpet towards safety.

Naldy should have felt pleased to be with Ralph now, but any happiness at being reunited with him —at having been saved—was clouded by an internal ache. She wanted to be with Betty, but their dear friend was gone.

—Chapter Thirteen—

GRACE, GRIEF, AND THE GUARDS

When Naldy awoke, the air was scented with a salted smokiness. She lifted her head from the soft pillow, rubbing her eyes, still sore from all the tears she had shed over the past few weeks. Climbing out of bed, she made her way through the draped linen curtain and into the main living space of the old dragon's cave. The entrance was flooded with sunlight as the screen of watergrass had been pulled back.

'The bacon smells delicious,' said Naldy, watching Ralph place it on top of thick slices of toast.

'I thought I heard you stir,' said Ralph, cracking an egg into a pan. 'I got up early and walked to the nearest town to fetch supplies. It was further than I thought.'

Naldy sat at the dining table in the ornate green chair, helping herself to the pot of brew.

Over a fortnight had passed since Grace's fatal spell had claimed Betty's life. Following their narrow escape from Mortous's castle, the two of them had travelled on Ralph's carpet until they reached the edge of Kirkwood Forest. They hadn't risked flying any further, knowing that Maverick's edicts were being enforced, and they had continued on foot until they reached the cave. Neither had spoken much during that time.

'How are you feeling?' Ralph asked gently.

She didn't want to talk about how she felt, partly because she wasn't sure how to describe the strange ambivalence that oscillated between pain and numbness.

She pretended to be distracted by the local newspaper. Ralph must have purchased it in town.

When she had the power of the Corium, Naldy had invented a spell to conjure food. Pulling the newspaper closer, she now realised the real reason Ralph had made the long journey to the nearest town was to gather news on the progress of Maverick's edicts—not to fetch bacon.

'There's at least some good news in the paper,' he said, bringing two laden breakfast plates to the table. Naldy noticed his eyes looked a painful red.

'I don't think any news in the world could cheer me up.'

'It's Grace,' said Ralph. 'She was sentenced to the stake last night. Declared dead. It's printed on page forty-two.'

Naldy could tell from Ralph's delivery that the news of Betty's murderer being sentenced to death was meant to bring her a sense of closure. Yet, the news of another public burning only made her more miserable.

'We don't have to make any decisions today,' said Ralph reassuringly, 'or tomorrow, or even this week.'

Naldy knew what Ralph was referring to, as he had made the same statement every day since Betty's death. Ralph thought she would want to cease the search for the Devante now that she no longer possessed its power. Each day, he delicately hinted but stopped short of actually saying it.

'Now you're no longer the Corium's guardian,' Ralph continued delicately, 'I thought perhaps you'd want to...'

He trailed off, leaving his sentence unfinished.

'Abandon the quest?' Naldy suggested, agitated by Ralph's words. 'Betty lost her life trying to protect magic. And so did many others. I should have broken the *Banned Spell of Death* and ended it when we had the chance.'

'I thought after everything that has happened, you would want it all to be over.'

'I do want it all over,' Naldy replied. 'But that won't happen unless we defeat Maverick. It's a brutal thing for him to do, sentencing one of his own to death.'

'Grace deserved her death,' said Ralph as he bit into his toast.

'Where would we even start, Ralph?' she asked glumly. 'We don't have a Devante to help us.'

'Hear me out,' said Ralph, occupying himself by tearing the bacon into strips with his fingers. 'We ought to find Barbra. I know it's not ideal—but she has the magic of H. If we're to have any chance of defeating Maverick, we're going to have to work alongside her.'

'She may not want to work with us,' Naldy said. 'Have you forgotten what she's like?'

'We have no chance of defeating Maverick without a Devante.'

'She may not be alive. The Society may have already captured her.'

'I know she is still alive,' said Ralph, looking across the table with a sheepish gaze.

'How can you be certain?'

'When I landed next to you and Betty on the carpet,' he said, using a napkin to clean the bacon grease from his hands, 'I didn't realise Betty was gone. I tried to pull her on with you.'

'I wish you had of. I would have liked to have given her a proper burial.'

When they had returned, they spent one overcast afternoon giving a memorial in honour of Betty's life. They lit many candles and shared some memories they had of the kind and warm-hearted woman.

'Ah, here it is,' said Ralph, removing a thin gold chain with a shiny white pearl from his cloak pocket. He passed it to her.

'Betty's necklace,' said Naldy, surprised. 'If the pearl turns black, we will know Barbra has passed.'

'The chain broke as I tried to pull her onto the carpet,' said Ralph. 'Unfortunately, the necklace won't help us find Barbra. She could be anywhere. I thought perhaps we could start in Heatherton?'

'*Restituo*,' said Naldy, as the break in the chain repaired itself. She put the necklace on, tucking it underneath her clothes. 'I doubt she's foolish enough to remain in her hometown.'

'What should we do?' asked Ralph.

'Let's make a list of places we think she may have gone.'

'Alright,' said Ralph. 'But before we do that, something has been bothering me.'

'What is it?'

'The Corium presumably reached Maverick weeks ago,' he said. 'I don't understand why he hasn't destroyed magic. I keep waiting for the day when I cannot cast spells.'

'I've had the same thought lately,' replied Naldy. 'There must be some reason why he hasn't done it. Come on, let's make this list.'

As they finished their breakfast, they compiled a list of locations where Barbra might be hiding. The list was much shorter than they'd hoped, and they realised how little they knew about Betty's twin sister.

'Perhaps starting at her home is a good idea after all,' said Naldy. 'Although I also like your suggestion of beginning in the towns where her books are most well-received.'

'It seems we don't have any obvious destination,' said Ralph, pulling out his journal and a feather quill. He occupied himself with his writing.

Naldy poured herself another cup of brew. Her thoughts returned to Betty's death, and she wondered if the empty feeling inside would ever leave her. She wished they had a clear place to set out to. She longed to be taking action instead of sitting around waiting once again.

Naldy picked up the newspaper to distract herself from her own thoughts. She was surprised to find the first quarter of the paper taken up by a comprehensive listing of Maverick's edicts, and she wondered if Ralph had bought it so they could familiarise themselves with the new laws.

'Edict Twenty-Seven,' read Naldy, 'all dwellings must report the arrival of any witch or wizard to The Establishment within no more than one hour from the time of check-in.'

Naldy shook her head and tossed the newspaper aside. She didn't want to think about Maverick or his edicts. She wished Smookers were with them, as he had always been good company when she was feeling low. Sadly, they couldn't risk returning to The Academy to collect him. However, she knew he could look after himself for the time being, as he was good at catching his own food.

Naldy leant back in the dining chair. She ran the small pearl between her fingers, wondering how they would ever find Barbra. Even if they did manage to find the old woman, Naldy doubted she would readily accept their help. Their history with Betty's sister wasn't exactly friendly. But Naldy knew that working alongside her was the only way to defeat the Seagull Society, who now controlled the Corium. They needed a power equal to it.

She caught sight of a familiar name printed on the back page of the paper.

'Diamone,' said Naldy, curiously reaching for the newspaper and unfolding it. She noticed the fortune teller's name was marked amongst six others, which she did not recognise. 'Ralph, look.'

'It's a list of upcoming burnings,' said Ralph, exhaling. He was displeased to be distracted from his writing. 'We can't save every witch and wizard that Maverick decides to set fire to. He holds a burning in The Great City every night.'

'Diamone is on the list,' Naldy replied irritably.

'I'll admit, it's sad,' muttered Ralph. 'I don't like seeing the nutty fortune teller marked to be killed, but we can't risk saving Diamone just because we met her a couple of times.'

'She may have seemed nutty,' said Naldy. 'But you have to admit she has talent.'

'She should have been more careful and obeyed Maverick's edicts if she didn't want to be captured and sentenced to the stake.'

'She predicted that Oak would be burnt. She may be able to help us.'

'Naldy, please. We can't risk being captured again. We must stay far away from The Great City. You don't have the magic of the Corium to help protect us.'

'I think Diamone is our answer to finding Barbra,' she said, standing. 'I'm going to The Great City. With or without you.'

'We can't risk flying because of Edict Twenty-

Two. Guards will be patrolling the skies, and we don't have a permit. We'll never make it in time on foot.'

'You're right,' said Naldy, leaning on the dining table. 'Unless... stand up, Ralph.'

'What for?'

'I have an idea.'

He reluctantly stood, and Naldy approached him, holding out her palms. His strawberry-blonde hair turned jet black, while his green cloak transformed into a blue cotton blazer with golden buttons. Ralph's hands moved to his head to remove the blue felt porkpie hat that had appeared there.

'We may not have the Corium,' said Naldy, pleased with the work of her spell. 'But unless Maverick undoes the spells I have created with the Devante, we can still perform the magic we invented.'

'Are you sure about this?' asked Ralph, returning the hat to his head.

Naldy's black woollen jumper reshaped into a military-style guards' blazer, and her hair shortened into a layered bob.

'I know you dislike travelling by broom,' said Naldy, approaching the cave's entrance, 'but I haven't seen any guards travelling by magical carpet. Are you coming? We should set out if we're to make it by sundown.'

Naldy made her way outside into the sunshine, collecting the broomstick from the entrance.

'*Frangere,*' said Naldy, as the broom snapped clean

in two.

'Why did you do that?' asked Ralph, appalled, as she passed him the two pieces.

'Because I've never seen two Establishment guards travelling on the same broom,' replied Naldy.

She held out her palm, and a sleek wooden broom—the type the Establishment guards flew—materialised from thin air.

'Although the disguises are good,' said Ralph, nervously, 'we should take some time to think about this. The Great City is far from safe.'

Naldy climbed onto the broom, positioning herself near the front.

'You can stay here if you wish,' said Naldy.

Ralph sighed and climbed on behind her. They shot up into the sky, rising high above the tops of the pine trees. Naldy leant forward to increase their speed. Flying helped ease her troubled thoughts as the cool air washed over her face.

They had been in the air for less than an hour when up ahead she saw two guards flying towards them. Naldy's arms tensed at the sight.

'We have our uniforms,' said Ralph. 'We mustn't panic.'

She kept her focus ahead, taking a deep breath as the guards approached. Ralph, perched behind her, held up the two pieces of the broomstick. One of the guards lifted an arm to his head, tipping his hat cordially as they passed.

'Our plan works,' said Naldy once the guards had flown out of earshot. 'They believe we're one of them

—and they think you've broken your broom.'

They passed at least thirty guards during the rest of their flight before landing their broomstick in the streets of The Great City at sundown.

'It's good to have my legs on solid ground again,' said Ralph, leaning back to stretch his spine.

'Come,' said Naldy, making her way along the busy street. 'The sun has already begun setting, and the burnings will begin soon. They won't wait for us.'

They walked briskly along the narrow cobblestone road, passing the many stone and brick shopfronts. People averted their gaze as they passed, afraid to make eye contact with them, and some even anxiously crossed the street. It didn't take them long to realise it was because they were dressed to look like Establishment guards.

The sky was a pastel orange when they reached the wide street that the Bleckdale Witchery Museum overlooked. The crowd was about half the size of the attendance at Sallandra's burning, and those who had gathered at the bottom of the steps seemed eager for the burning to begin. Some held rocks, ready to throw at the captives once the flames had been lit.

Maverick was seated in an ornate golden chair at the top of the museum steps. Further down, seven stakes had been erected, and a terrified person was fastened to each wooden pole. Diamone, the frizzy brown-haired fortune teller, was the only prisoner without a tear-streaked face. She stood bizarrely calm, seeming disinterested in the events unfolding around her.

'We could join them on the steps,' suggested Ralph, pointing to the forty-odd guards who had formed two neat rows on either side of the prisoners, starting at the top step and finishing at the bottom.

The crowd parted as Naldy and Ralph crossed the wide street. When they mounted the museum steps, Naldy noticed the building had been renamed. The large stone sign above the grand wooden doors no longer read 'The Bleckdale Witchery Museum.' It had been replaced with the words 'The Establishment'.

'Do you think Maverick has turned it into his palace?' asked Naldy.

'It appears that way,' replied Ralph. 'He looks pretty comfortable in that throne.'

The guards on the stairs were positioned neatly in a line, and once they climbed to the step where Diamone was situated, they had no choice but to stand awkwardly in front.

From this view, Naldy could see the public clearly. They were beginning to get impatient, eager to see the prisoners burn. She glanced up at Maverick, who was occupied with sipping from a silver goblet. He appeared to be waiting for someone. The wizard wasn't dressed in his usual black clothes but wore an intricate golden blazer with matching trousers. A long burgundy mantle with a white inner lining was draped over his shoulders.

'We have this section covered,' said a guard

gruffly. He pointed to the rowdy crowd. 'You might be better served down there. They're getting restless.'

Naldy saw Ralph's skin turning pale as he nodded at the guard.

'The head of the Establishment wants extra security around this witch,' stated Naldy confidently. She nodded towards Diamone, who was gazing absentmindedly at the darkening sky. 'She's known to be dangerous and unpredictable.'

The questioning guard scrutinised Diamone.

'Stand on either side of her, then,' said the guard. 'You know he expects us to be kept in even lines.'

Ralph and Naldy shuffled closer to the fortune teller. At her feet lay a stack of chopped dry wood and clumps of straw.

The crowd cheered, and Naldy glanced behind her. Getergrin, Mason, Deslong, Mortous, and Rupert had emerged from the grand double doors. All five were wearing matching regal red coats. Getergrin awkwardly approached Maverick and whispered something into the wizard's ear.

'I could kill Rupert,' muttered Ralph under his breath. There was grief in his voice. 'How could he betray us like this? I want to confront him.'

Naldy pretended to adjust the wood at Diamone's feet so she could watch Maverick. Betty's pearl necklace swung forward on the chain around her neck as she did so. Seeing the necklace ignited a familiar anger within her. Betty was dead because of the Seagull Society's greed, and she knew Maverick was the group's unofficial leader. She wanted him to pay for what he had done. The pearl on the necklace was still white, which meant Barbra was out there somewhere, still alive.

'Diamone,' said Naldy, noticing the fortune teller's hands had been bound by leather straps.

'Oh, yes, I know those eyes,' said Diamone in a faraway voice.

Naldy knew the leather straps were designed to prevent the wearer from performing magic. She knew the thick handcuffs would not come off without the key.

'Ralph, stop staring at your cousin,' said Naldy, noticing his gaze was still fixed sadly on Rupert. 'Diamone, we've come because we need your help.'

'What a divine evening it is,' said Diamone vacantly. She was peering at the moon. The last rays of light disappeared, and Naldy knew the burnings would begin any moment.

'I need to undo your handcuffs,' said Naldy. 'We need your help to find a woman named Barbra. It's extremely important. If we get the handcuffs off, can you help us?'

'There is no point,' said Diamone, exhaling softly. 'Danger on every side. Now is not the time to be going.'

'Diamone, please,' said Ralph. 'We need you to tell us where we can find Barbra. Can you please do that?'

'Too late,' said Diamone, and she smiled calmly. 'Just like you were too late to save the oak tree.'

'You really do know who we are,' said Naldy, a

little surprised.

'I warned you both,' said Diamone. 'Death awaits if you take the path to Edengar. Much death has been suffered. And there is more death to come. But you did not listen.'

'Naldy,' said Ralph anxiously. Maverick had risen from his throne.

'We are running out of time,' said Naldy. 'I'll try to burn through the leather cuffs.'

'Second chances are not often given,' said Diamone, widening her brown eyes. 'When they come for you, do not struggle too much—for she is old, and he is young. It would be wise not to fight.'

'You are not listening to us,' pleaded Naldy impatiently. 'We need to find Barbra.'

'Welcome,' called Maverick, addressing the crowd. 'What another wonderful evening. The witches you see before you have disobeyed the edicts and must be punished. But first, there is something we must attend to. It has come to our attention that amongst us are two impostors. These impostors are masquerading as guards.'

—*Chapter Fourteen*—

THE SEVENTH STAKE

Anyone standing close to a guard took several steps backwards. The guards themselves appeared uneasy.

'But how does he know it's us,' said Ralph, moving closer to Naldy. 'What do we do?'

'You must do nothing,' said the fortune teller, still fastened to the stake. Despite Naldy's attempts, she could not undo Diamone's restraints.

'There is no need to fear,' called Maverick, raising his arms to quell the audience's panic. 'These pretenders have no way out, and it has become obvious who these traitors are. For they are not stood in line.'

Maverick glanced in their direction, his black stare lingering on them and his lips curling into a smirk.

'Naldy, should we run?' asked Ralph.

'But how does he know it's us?' said Naldy, stumped. 'We don't look anything like ourselves.'

Before either could move, two nearby guards grabbed them, forcing Naldy and Ralph into thick leather handcuffs. Diamone watched with an absent smile.

Naldy struggled, trying to free herself from the young female guard's grip. The woman narrowed her grey eyes coldly, sneering as she held Naldy's hands tightly.

Naldy attempted to cast the spell she had invented with the Corium to make the guards topple over—but it was too late. The leather handcuffs restricted all magic.

Ralph's guard, a burly man with reddish-brown hair poking out from beneath his porkpie hat, laughed gruffly, as if he knew Naldy had tried to cast magic and failed.

'If you keep wriggling,' the female guard said snappishly, as the crowd applauded, 'you will regret it.'

Naldy stopped moving. She felt ill. She had foolishly led them directly into danger—once again, they were imprisoned.

'The Establishment is here to protect you,' said Maverick to the crowd, a thin smile emerging on his lips. 'It must be noted that we believe in second chances, at least for those who prove they are repentant for their ill-doings. One of our lawbreakers tonight has shown they deserve a second chance.'

The crowd groaned, displeased by Maverick's generosity. The guard behind Naldy tightened her grip.

She wished they had stayed in the dragon cave. Oak had once cursed Naldy to teach her the importance of caring for others, yet she had put herself first and impatiently led them into trouble.

'Diamone,' continued Maverick, gesturing to the fortune teller, 'has been convicted for breaking Edict Number Forty-Seven: predicting the future without first obtaining written permission from The Establishment is prohibited. For this crime, she has been sentenced to burn.'

The crowd cheered loudly. Some even shouted insults at Diamone.

'However,' said Maverick, raising his cane to silence the excitable crowd. 'She has redeemed herself by demonstrating her loyalty to The Establishment. She has done this by making a prediction in our favour. The fortune teller forewarned us that two guards planned to harm The Establishment. She told us these two impostors would arrive just before the burnings began tonight.'

Naldy saw Mortous whispering to Rupert, as Mason exchanged a concerned look with Deslong. She felt an agony within her, watching the men who had once helped her now standing faithfully behind her enemy.

'These two impostors,' continued Maverick, as the crowd watched with concern. 'They may be wearing the uniforms of The Establishment, but they do not belong in them. The fortune teller has proven her loyalty by warning us. Diamone, you are free to go.'

Diamone's leather restraints broke free, and she

lowered herself from the stake, making her way down the stone steps rather clumsily. The crowd were disappointed.

The woman whom Naldy had hoped would assist them had also betrayed them.

'Do not grumble now,' said Maverick to the unhappy crowd as six more guards emerged from the grand wooden doors behind them. 'I have promised you seven burnings, and I shall give you what you have come to witness.'

'They're going to burn us,' said Ralph, panicking. He tried to break free from the guard holding him.

'You'll regret trying to run,' snarled the guard, tightening his grasp.

'If they burn us,' said Naldy, 'that would make eight.'

'They won't burn you today,' grunted Naldy's guard.

'Who are they burning then?'

Naldy saw the six guards who had emerged from the museum approach Mason. They surrounded the Boat Builder.

'The key was covered in sticky plum jam,' said Maverick. 'It took us some time to realise you were on breakfast duty that day.'

The onlookers were confused by Maverick's words. Mason tried to dodge out of the way, but it was too late. He was outnumbered. They captured him and began escorting him towards the unoccupied stake.

'The man before you,' stated Maverick, 'was

welcomed into The Establishment. He showed much promise. But we have since discovered that he secretly assisted criminals with their escape. Tonight, he must pay the price for his disloyalty. He will be your seventh.'

The crowd whistled and celebrated as the Boat Builder was fastened to Diamone's stake. He was writhing, desperately trying to free himself from the leather handcuffs.

Naldy blinked back tears as she watched him. She thought of the jar of jam in which Mason had hidden the key. She wanted to call out to him but was too distraught to speak.

'Let this night be a lesson to all,' said Maverick coldly. 'Disobeying the edicts will come with consequences. Tonight, Mason will burn. The two guards Diamone warned us about will be taken below to the prison for questioning. They will be given a brief opportunity to prove their loyalty. If they fail to accomplish this, they too shall burn at the stake.'

'No,' said Naldy, her lip quivering. 'You cannot burn him. Please.'

Her words were drowned out by the crowd's cheering. Naldy caught Mason's dark brown eyes and thought they held a glimmer of recognition. He nodded at her before facing the crowd. There was nothing Naldy could do.

Their captors forced them up the steps towards what was once the Bleckdale Witchery Museum, but now displayed the words: The Establishment.

The female guard, who had a firm grip on Naldy, led them through the grand wooden doors. Once the doors closed, the sound of the unruly crowd was muffled.

'Well, that was an eventful evening,' said the guard behind Ralph.

'Let's take them down,' said the female guard, pushing Naldy forward.

Naldy was stunned to see that the inside of the museum didn't bear any resemblance to how she remembered it. The security barriers had been entirely removed, and as they made their way through the second set of doors and into the large chamber beyond, both Naldy and Ralph gasped at the transformation.

The monstrous display of dragon bones that once hung from the ceiling had been replaced by an enormous gaudy chandelier. The chamber had been redecorated with large freestanding alabaster columns, their surfaces carved with coiling dragons. Antique carpets had been rolled out, and many chaise lounges were dotted around the large room. Freshly cut flowers had been beautifully arranged in numerous huge golden vases resting on the floor. The museum's entrance hall was unrecognisable.

The most peculiar thing was the absence of other people. The enormous chamber, which was usually bustling with patrons marvelling at the dragon bones, was empty despite the many places for sitting. Naldy felt enraged that Maverick had the nerve to gut the museum—a public place—turning it into his private palace.

'This way,' said Naldy's captor, leading them along one of the side passageways.

These stone hallways were once occupied by countless artefacts. Now, all the display cabinets and their contents were nowhere to be seen. As they passed the rooms leading from the passage, Naldy saw that each chamber had also been stripped of its exhibits—all the witch and wizard history had been removed. However, the large chambers were not empty. Each room had been fashioned into a grand parlour, a kingly bedroom, or another opulent living quarter for Maverick to enjoy.

'But where has he put everything?' asked Ralph, staggered by the change.

'It's been destroyed,' replied Naldy's guard. 'It took months for them to burn it all. People initially liked the bonfires but grew tired of them by the time everything was finally reduced to ash.'

'They say the black smoke could be seen as far as Heatherton,' added Ralph's guard. 'They may have grown tired of the bonfires, but they still enjoy the burnings of witches. They don't seem to grow tired of those.'

'And they relish it when a wizard is caught and sentenced,' said Naldy's guard.

Naldy's stomach churned at the harsh realisation that these irreplaceable items could not be recovered and had been turned to ash.

They were led down numerous flights of stairs and along many stone passageways until they came to a small stone room the size of a closet. It took Naldy a moment to realise that it was, indeed, a cleaning cupboard. A stone shelf hosted tall glass jars half-filled with liquid chemicals. A couple of battered broomsticks leant against one stone wall, and against the opposite wall stood a wooden cleaning cart on rickety wheels, holding an array of cleaning brushes, small buckets, and bars of strong-smelling soap.

Naldy's guard reached for the cart and swivelled it out of the way, revealing a discreet doorway with stone steps leading steeply downward. Naldy guessed that the prison must be deep beneath the museum.

The guards led them into the gloomy, cavernous corridor. Tapered candles interspersed along the walls flickered ominously in their brass holders.

The slope eventually levelled, and Naldy was reminded of the tunnel they had once journeyed through that led them to the Edengar Mountains. It felt like they walked some distance before being escorted up an almost vertical stone staircase.

Naldy bumped her head on a trap door, and Ralph's guard came forward to use his free hand to force it open.

As they climbed out, Naldy expected to see a dingy prison cell. Instead, they stood in the middle of *Hereto's broomsticks.* The long, clean, narrow shop had numerous brooms mounted on the walls, each made with different woods and twigs. Naldy had been in this shop once before, when Betty had pretended to be her sister, Barbra.

'This doesn't look like a prison,' said Ralph, rubbing his eyes.

Naldy was shocked to see Hereto—the same boy who had once sold them two new broomsticks—standing directly behind Ralph. The guard who had been there moments ago had vanished. The young witch, no older than ten, smiled at them with a toothy grin, his curly reddish-brown hair framing his freckled face.

'Why did you change us back?' asked Hereto, addressing Naldy's captor standing behind her.

'Because I have some questions for these two,' said a familiar voice.

Naldy spun, jolted to see Betty's wrinkled face, her choppy grey hair tousled. She must have been dreaming or hallucinating—Betty had died.

'I felt strong and tough,' said Hereto, flexing a small bicep as he held up Ralph's leather restraints, which he had just unfastened.

'Barbra?' asked Ralph, his eyebrows skewed.

'Do not undo their handcuffs yet,' snapped the woman, fastening the leather straps back around Ralph's wrists.

Ralph's words made Naldy realise that the woman standing near her was not Betty's ghost, but her twin sister, Barbra. She wore a tatty black travelling cloak. The guards who had led them through the underground corridor were nowhere in sight.

'How did you come by that pearl?' demanded

Barbra.

Naldy hesitated—she couldn't believe they had found the person they'd been looking for. As she considered Barbra's question, she realised they would need to tell the old woman that her sister had died. She felt guilt-ridden, unsure how to impart the horrible news.

'I have known for some time that she is gone,' said Barbra delicately, as if she had gleaned the truth from Naldy's expression.

Barbra reached into the neck of her woollen garment and retrieved a golden necklace. A small black pearl hung from the chain.

'You have one too,' remarked Naldy, as her hand reached to the white pearl dangling around her own neck.

'We each had one,' said Barbra sombrely, her eyes clouding with tears. She fussed with the chain, tucking it back into her woolly garment as though trying to distract herself from painful thoughts. When she spoke again, her tone was sour. 'But I didn't need the pearl to know my sister had passed.'

Naldy understood the wrinkled woman was referring to the Devante. She, too, had felt the intense surge of energy when the Corium's magic transferred from her mother to her.

'We didn't kill her, if that's what you think,' said Ralph quickly.

'There's always trouble with you two,' remarked Barbra tetchily. 'Why are you both dressed as guards? What were you doing?'

'Could you at least free us from these handcuffs?' pleaded Ralph. 'We'll answer your questions, but we're on the same side. We've come to help you.'

'Help,' Barbra cackled. 'What makes you think I require any help?'

'What were you both doing there?' pressed Naldy. 'We were there to seek Diamone's guidance, but why on earth were you both dressed like guards?'

'I'll ask the questions,' grumbled Barbra.

'We were looking for you,' explained Naldy. 'We know you hold the magic of H.'

'Come to steal it from me, have you?' Barbra barked. 'Just as you've chased after the other Devante—all of which have perished.'

'We want to help you protect it,' said Naldy. 'The power you hold, Barbra, must be kept safe. It cannot not fall into Maverick's hands. He wants to eradicate magic. We only want to assist you.'

Barbra squinted, her wrinkled skin shifting as she stared at them. Naldy felt her handcuffs release and knew Barbra must have freed them. 'When I saw the necklace, I assumed it must be the two of you. One thing was certainly obvious—neither of you was a guard.'

Ralph rubbed his wrists.

'Hereto,' ordered Barbra, 'would you fetch us some chairs?'

Hereto sauntered further into his shop. Naldy waved her palm, and their blue-blazered uniforms were replaced with their usual cloaks. Her layered bob lengthened, returning to its original state.

Ralph's jet-black hair returned to its strawberry-blonde.

'It's nice to have my cloak back,' said Ralph. 'But how did you and Hereto transform into guards?'

'The magic of H,' interrupted Naldy, knowing Barbra and Hereto must have used its power to disguise themselves as guards—not just with uniforms, as Naldy and Ralph had done, but by changing their entire appearance, including their facial structure, height, and age.

'Take one each,' said Hereto, returning with four polished brooms made of dark red wood.

'I said to fetch chairs, Hereto,' groaned Barbra.

'These are more comfortable than any chair you'll encounter in this city,' replied Hereto, passing Naldy one of the brooms. She could almost see her reflection in the wood's polished gleam. 'And if you'd prefer a chair, you could conjure one yourself.'

'What was your plan, then?' asked Barbra, turning to Naldy with an interrogative stare as Hereto passed Ralph a broomstick. 'You thought you could casually stroll up the palace steps?'

'Diamone didn't help us at all,' said Ralph, perching himself in the comfortable bend of the hovering broom. 'She exposed us.'

'Perhaps it was us,' said Hereto, 'that Diamone intended to unmask. By appearing this evening, you may have saved our skin.'

'We were going to put a stop to Maverick's wicked burnings,' said Barbra once they were all settled. 'That was before you both interfered with our plan.'

'We might have succeeded if you hadn't shown up,' added Hereto. 'We just needed a little more time.'

'Time for what?' asked Naldy.

'We were going to condemn him to the stake,' said Barbra. 'We tried breaking the *Banned Spell of Death,* hoping to kill him from afar, but...'

'But what?' asked Naldy.

Barbra shifted uncomfortably on her broomstick.

'She has been unable to break it,' said Hereto. 'That's why we went in person tonight.'

'We've seen Maverick break through the *Banned Spell* before,' said Ralph.

'Well, we have tried,' said Barbra irritably. 'The *Banned Spell* will not be broken. But at any rate, tonight has made one thing clear—we won't get close to him disguised as guards.'

An awkwardness settled between them, as neither party knew what to say. They needed to gain Barbra's trust, because working alongside her was the only way to stay close to the magic of H.

'I know we've had our differences,' said Naldy, shifting on the broom, 'but we share the same goal—to defeat Maverick. Will you let us help you?'

'No,' said Barbra curtly. 'I don't think we require your *help.*'

She emphasised the word help in a mocking tone.

'Why did you save us, then?' asked Naldy.

'Because I've heard you possess the power of the Corium,' remarked Barbra.

A pang of guilt struck Naldy, and she glanced remorsefully at the floor. Once again, Barbra must have deciphered the truth from her expression, as she jumped from the broom and began to pace.

'You've lost another Devante, it seems,' said Barbra, twiddling her fingers in thought.

'We didn't lose it,' retorted Ralph, 'Maverick and the Society stole it.'

At the mention of the wizard's name, Barbra stopped pacing and fixed her concerned gaze on Naldy.

'How can he possess the Corium?' Barbra mumbled. 'He has not used its power.'

'If Maverick does have it,' added Hereto, troubled, 'as you say he does, why has he not undone magic? You say that is his goal?'

'I do not know,' answered Naldy. 'But we know he has it. The Society extracted its power from me, and we saw them heading towards The Great City weeks ago. Perhaps he fears you will undo his spells.'

'You believe he wants me dead first—out of the equation?' asked Barbra, her tone serious.

Naldy did not answer but offered a hesitant look. Barbra narrowed her gaze before speaking again.

'It is late, and you should both be on your way.'

'On our way?' echoed Ralph, his voice rising in outrage. 'But we've come to help you.'

'Help me?' laughed Barbra piercingly. 'You keep throwing that word around as if it is your right—but we do not need your help. Go and meddle elsewhere. You don't have the power of the Corium, so what use are you to us?'

'I can help you break the *Banned Spells*,' lied

Naldy. Ralph glanced at her puzzlingly, but Naldy returned a firm stare. 'You say you've had trouble breaking them. If you let us stay, I can help you.'

A flicker of enthusiasm lit up Barbra's face. Naldy had never broken the *Banned Spells,* but she knew her promise to help would entice the wrinkled witch.

'You have an insider,' said Barbra, her tone softening.

'An insider?' Naldy repeated, confused.

'The strawberry-blonde one,' continued Barbra, 'he is working with you, is he not? I have seen you all together before.'

'You mean Rupert,' said Naldy sadly. 'He has betrayed us.'

'Pity,' said Barbra as Ralph's eyes welled. 'It is getting late. We can decide tomorrow if you're useful.'

'I will have the spare beds made up,' said Hereto.

'How does this place still exist?' asked Naldy, glancing around at the pristine broomsticks mounted on the wall. 'Maverick has emptied the museum's display cabinets and burnt every artefact, yet in the middle of the city, *Hereto's Broomsticks* remains untouched.'

'Rupert may not be an insider,' said Barbra, passing her broom to the young witch, 'but Hereto, here, is.'

Chapter Fifteen

INSIDER'S TRICKS

The sound of a delicate tap woke Naldy early the following morning. She was accustomed to Ralph's heavy-handed knocking and could tell from the gentle noise that it must have been either Hereto or Barbra beyond the eight-panel door.

Naldy placed her tired head into her hands. The curtains were open, but the sun had not yet risen, and it was still dark outside.

Months ago, a faint knock wouldn't have roused Naldy, and nothing less than Ralph's pummelling knuckles would have caused her to stir from sleep. However, since Betty's death, Naldy had been sleeping lightly. These days, the feathery rustle of lace curtains suspended over open windows was enough to propel her eyelids open.

The gentle knock came again.

'I'm up,' Naldy called sleepily.

'Maverick will be arriving within the hour,' returned Hereto's boyish voice. 'You'd best come to the kitchen if you'd like breakfast.'

Naldy sleepily propped herself up in bed. She glanced at the darkened window, then at the unlit candle in its brass holder on the bedside table. For a fleeting moment, she wondered if magic still existed or if Maverick had eradicated it while she slept.

'*Comburite,*' whispered Naldy, and the candle flickered to life. She let out a sigh of relief.

Forcing herself out of bed, she changed out of the robin's-egg-blue nightdress Barbra had fashioned for her using the magic of H. As Naldy dressed, she remembered her promise to Barbra—to help break the *Banned Spells*. But she had no clue how and wondered if Barbra would send them away once she discovered the truth.

Hereto's modest living quarters were situated directly above the broom store. Though the Hereto lineage was known for constructing and maintaining high-quality broomsticks, the residence above stood in stark contrast to the impeccably clean business below. Upstairs, the tired floorboards needed repair, and the moth-eaten soft furnishings had collected many years of undisturbed dust.

By the time Naldy entered the neglected kitchen at the end of the hallway, the grubby round windows let in a dull navy-tinged light.

Naldy joined Ralph, who was sitting sleepy-eyed at the table, clutching a mug of warm brew. Hereto was busy at the stove, and Barbra was seated at the head of the table, pursed-lipped as she perused the morning newspaper.

'There's disappointment that the two guard traitors have escaped,' said Barbra, wincing. 'News travels fast. Come and sit, Hereto, I will do the rest.'

'Again, with respect, Miss Hexogg,' said Hereto, pouring a mug of brew for Naldy, 'I find preparing breakfast to be calming. How do you like your eggs, Naldy? I can do scrambled or fried, but I haven't the knack for poached.'

'Scrambled, please,' replied Naldy. The brew's nutty smell was helping to drive away her drowsiness.

'Maverick will want a large burning tonight as compensation,' said Barbra, putting down the paper. 'More death.'

'Once Naldy helps you break these *Banned Spells*,' said Hereto, cracking eggs into a sizzling pan, 'we'll be able to take them all down effortlessly. I think we should create an army—make a show of it.'

Barbra winced, and Naldy had the distinct impression that she doubted her ability to break the *Banned Spells.*

'After last night's display,' mumbled Barbra, 'it's clear that more than a few guards will be necessary. Now then, let's undo these *Banned Spells.*'

Naldy felt her face flush as all eyes turned to her expectantly. Ralph bit his lip awkwardly, knowing Naldy had never accomplished the thing she'd promised to help them do.

'She's never broken them,' said Hereto from the stove.

'Evidently,' remarked Barbra. 'You can remove the pan from the hob, Hereto, dear. Naldy won't be staying long enough to enjoy her breakfast.'

'We have to work together,' said Ralph passionately.

'It seems,' Barbra began irritably, 'you've nothing useful to contribute—only blatant lies.'

'We want to see Maverick defeated,' said Ralph, 'just as much as you do.'

'There is something that might help us,' said Naldy.

Barbra straightened her posture, and Naldy exchanged a glance with Ralph.

Naldy wondered whether they could trust the old woman—but realised they had little choice. Barbra had the magic of H, and her plan depended on it. She needed to rebuild trust with the old witch.

'Killing Maverick may make him a martyr,' said Naldy. 'Not only do the public love him, but The Seagull Society has made him their leader. Maverick does have a secret.'

'Alright, then what do you suggest?' asked Hereto, passing Naldy her breakfast of fluffy yellow eggs. 'What is this secret of his?'

'I don't know what it is,' said Naldy, staring at her plate.

Barbra nodded at Hereto and the young witch removed Naldy's plate of eggs.

'But I know he has something he doesn't want known. When we were staying at *The Golden Opulent,* I undid one of Maverick's spells. It allowed me to see his memory. In it, Maverick was going to murder Audry to protect this secret of his. If we can find out what it is...'

'If he was willing to kill to keep it hidden,' said Barbra, squinting thoughtfully, 'then it must be something deeply incriminating.'

'There is a way we might be able to uncover it,' said Naldy.

Barbra nodded at Hereto again, and he returned her plate to the table.

'Don't tell them any more,' stated Ralph flatly. 'Not unless they agree to work with us.'

Having finished his own breakfast, Ralph picked up his fork and helped himself to some egg from Naldy's plate.

'The Society blindly trusts Maverick,' muttered Barbra, her lips pursed as if tasting something sour. 'I must admit, if we cannot break the *Banned Spells*, then breaking the Society's trust in their leader is an apt proposal. You're convinced this secret of his is weighty enough to strip him of power?'

'You say he wants to destroy magic,' said Hereto, settling at the table. 'We don't need to chase after forgotten secrets—his intention to eradicate magic seems incriminating enough. We just need a way to prove that is his end goal.'

'People already know he wants magic destroyed,' said Naldy, swatting away Ralph's fork as he tried to steal more egg. 'His edicts are no secret—they're printed in every newspaper throughout Kirkwood. We need something more.'

'Tell us your plan,' Barbra croaked, 'and we'll allow you to stay... for the time being.'

'How do we trust you?' demanded Ralph through

a mouthful of Naldy's breakfast, which he had managed to steal without her noticing. 'After we tell you, how do we know you won't just throw us out?'

'Rich of you to lecture us on trust,' said Barbra.

Though Naldy was hesitant to open up to them about the plan, she knew she and Ralph couldn't carry it out without the magic of H—without Barbra.

'By undoing the spells Maverick has invented with the Devante, I was taken into his memories,' said Naldy. 'That's how I first learnt about his secret.'

Ralph dropped his fork childishly onto his empty plate, shaking his head.

'Yes, but how do you know which memory you'll see when you undo his spells?' asked Hereto. 'Do you choose?'

Naldy hesitated and Barbra was quick to jump in.

'Also,' Barbra interjected moodily, 'we would need to know which spells he invented using the Devante in order to undo them.'

'You're right,' said Naldy. 'There's no guarantee we'll see anything of value, and we'd need to find out which spells he's created with the Devante—but I believe that if we come upon this secret, it could help bring the wizard down.'

'We'll have to decide our path later,' said Hereto. 'Look at the time—we'd best get downstairs before the wizard arrives.'

They followed Hereto into the hallway and took the spiralling iron staircase down into the broom store. Hereto guided them to a large storage cupboard with wooden slats near the front of the shop. He slid the door open, revealing shelves neatly stacked with broom cleaners and maintenance supplies.

To Naldy's and Ralph's shock, Barbra climbed inside. She had ample space to stand but filled out most of the cupboard's depth.

'You don't expect us to squeeze in there together?' asked Ralph.

'You can stay out here with me and greet Maverick if you prefer,' said Hereto, smiling cheekily. 'Or go back upstairs. The floors above creak, though, so you'll have to remain still as a statue. And you'd better make up your mind, quick now, because I think I can—yes, that is him—coming up the street.'

Naldy and Ralph shuffled into the storage cupboard. Hereto slid the cabinet door shut just as the bell above the entry tinkled.

'Welcome back, Mr Gadswell, sir,' chimed Hereto, almost in tune with his shop's bell. 'I see you've brought Mr Bomtayle.'

Peering through the slats from her cramped position inside the cupboard, Naldy could not see Maverick or Getergrin, but she had a clear view of Hereto bowing low.

'We have had quite the morning,' replied Maverick sourly. 'Quite the mess to clean up after last night. I'm sure you've seen the papers. Do you have the list?'

'Let me fetch it for you, sir,' said Hereto, skipping further into the store.

Maverick stepped into view. His tall, slender frame carried a tension she wasn't accustomed to seeing, as he leant on his black cane, waiting for Hereto to return.

'You were saying something about a cave as we entered,' muttered Maverick, only half curious.

'Yes,' replied Getergrin, his round shape moving into Naldy's line of sight. 'It was reported late yesterday evening by some townsfolk picking blueberries near a river down south.'

Naldy felt the hairs on her neck prickle at Getergrin's words.

'Is it another unregistered residence?' asked Maverick, picking up his Imporiom and turning. He seemed only vaguely interested.

'It was empty,' replied Getergrin.

'Then we have no culprit to burn,' replied Maverick. 'Have the district guards keep it under surveillance.'

'I've had Deslong inspect it,' said Getergrin, puffing his porky chest, causing the buttons on his floral waistcoat to strain.

'Why would you send a Society member?' said Maverick, appalled at Getergrin's actions. 'You silly man. I'm sure Deslong's time is better spent elsewhere.'

'Deslong lives south and was passing through— it was no bother to him,' said Getergrin, though he looked shame-faced at his shoes. 'I sent him because of the description the berry pickers gave of the cave's interior. The craftsmanship was said to be so detailed that I suspected it might be the work of the Devante.'

'What did Deslong think?' asked Maverick, his frustration switching to inquisitiveness.

'He suspects it could be,' replied Getergrin, 'although he couldn't be certain. The detail impressed him. At the least, he was confident it was the home of a witch, and better still, he was adamant whoever resided there didn't want to be found.'

'It's not surprising the inhabitants want to remain unknown,' said Maverick coldly. 'We are burning law-breakers, after all. You must consult me in the future, Getergrin, before dispatching Society members on pursuits founded on your inklings.'

Getergrin lowered his head even further until his chin met his bulky neck. Evidently, this was not the reaction he'd hoped for from Maverick.

Naldy felt as though another disappointment had been added to their growing pile of misfortunes. From Getergrin's description, she knew it was their cave that had been discovered. It had been a comfortable shelter, and she was saddened they could no longer return safely.

Hereto came bounding from the rear of the store, brandishing a yellow parchment.

'I apologise for the delay, sir,' said Hereto, passing Maverick the paper. 'For a moment, I thought I had misplaced it.'

'Twelve names,' remarked Maverick, pleased, inspecting the list. 'Yes, this will do nicely.

Getergrin, will you ensure the violators are arrested before the evening burnings? News has spread fast that the two guards have escaped, and we must put on a good performance tonight.'

'You'd think people would learn,' said Getergrin, taking the list. 'We've burnt so many for violating Edict Twenty-Two, yet they still arrive here without permits, wanting to purchase broomsticks.'

'Yes,' said Maverick, 'you've done a wonderful job, Hereto, of documenting the names of any who have tried to obtain broomsticks without first being issued a permit from The Establishment.'

Naldy's head felt light. Had she heard correctly? Were Hereto and Barbra betraying witches and wizards who had come to seek their help?

She glanced sideways at Barbra, cramped against the cupboard's interior shelf. Her wiry grey hair was almost touching a glass bottle of broom polish. Unlike Ralph, whose mouth was also open in shock, Barbra was plainly unperturbed by what Maverick had said.

'I'm glad I can be of service,' said Hereto, bowing his head again.

The tiny hairs on Naldy's arms stood on end, joining those on her neck. It was clear that Barbra and Hereto were snitching on magical folk who had come to *Hereto's Broomsticks,* hoping to secure a means of transport. Those who had turned to him for help would now be burnt at the stake.

'I hope the hunt for the witch they call the Corium is going well,' said Hereto before Maverick could turn to leave. 'Knowing someone is in control of such power frightens me.'

'We momentarily had her imprisoned,' replied Getergrin, his fist clenched tight.

'The Establishment is doing a wonderful job,' said Hereto, revealing a toothy smile.

'We must be going,' said Maverick. 'There is much for us to do, thank you kindly.'

'I can assist with addresses,' added Hereto, bouncing on the balls of his feet. 'I keep a ledger of all previous purchases. Some of the names on the list have bought broomsticks from *Hereto's* during Sallandra's rule. I can provide you with their home addresses to ensure they are arrested before this evening's events.'

'A grand idea,' said Maverick, sounding weary and eager to depart. 'Getergrin, I will leave you to look after that, can I? Good. I will see you next week, Hereto.'

Maverick moved out of Naldy's sight, and she heard the bell tinkle as the wizard left the store. Naldy knew Hereto was an insider—pretending to be one of Maverick's allies—but she hadn't realised that, to stay in the wizard's good graces, he was throwing other witches to the fire. Hereto retrieved a hefty leather book with frayed pages from a nearby drawer.

'Let us get this done,' pressed Getergrin. 'I've quite the day's work ahead of me.'

'I believe the first name is Abbey Sellingstone,' said Hereto, flipping through the pages of the ledger.

'Her application for a flying permit was denied by The Establishment, and she came by last week, pleading that I take her currents in exchange for a broomstick. She offered triple. Yes, here it is. Her home address was last recorded as Unit Seven, Fourteen Greenbone Lane, The Great City.'

Hereto dipped a feather quill into an inkwell and passed it to Getergrin, who scribbled the address onto the list of names.

'Jackson Vinerey,' read Getergrin from the parchment.

'I don't ever recall seeing Jackson before last week,' said Hereto, rubbing his hairless chin. 'I'm certain it was the first time I had met the young man. He said his broomstick had been confiscated by the district guards, and he urgently required one to fly south so he could visit his sick grandmother. I told him he must wait for his application to be reviewed. I suppose you'll find him somewhere south of Kirkwood. Oh, this next name, Somdevi Gualder, I do have an address for him somewhere in this ledger. Moody chap. Tried to take off with an anglewood broom.'

Naldy felt her back muscles stiffening. She was beginning to find the confined cupboard intolerable, mostly because she couldn't bear to witness Hereto aiding with the capture of more witches.

Name by name, Hereto made his way down the list, seeming in no hurry. She wondered if he'd forgotten they were still squished together in the stock cupboard. Ralph's face drooped, revealing his regret at ever having chosen to enter the narrow space. Barbra, on the other hand, remained unflustered, as if the discomfort of standing stiffly amongst the bottles of broom oils and cleaners was something she was accustomed to.

Through the slats, Naldy watched with growing weariness as Hereto announced each name, each followed by a personal anecdote. She was sure the stories were increasing in length as they progressed further down Hereto's list.

'Eric Fault had the most peculiar ideas,' said Hereto dramatically. 'He seemed to believe Maverick had once owned the power of these magical Devante.'

The mention of the Devante instantly distracted Naldy from the ache of her lower back muscles.

'Where did Eric Fault hear that?' asked Getergrin, unsettled by Hereto's words.

'I told Mr Fault that if Maverick possessed one of these rumoured Devante, then I should be pleased to hear it.'

'We have three names left,' said Getergrin, anxious to move on. 'I'll need to send out the guards, so let's get this done.'

'The magic intrigues me,' said Hereto, his eyes glistening. 'Come, Bomtayle. Although you cannot produce spells yourself, I know you are as fascinated by new magic as I am. You have been Maverick's indispensable ally and must be privy to some marvellous creations.'

'I may have seen a thing or two on our travels,'

said Getergrin, a hint of a smile appearing as the portly man retreated momentarily into his own memories.

'I always believed Maverick was destined to be a great leader,' said Hereto. 'I respect you, Mr Bomtayle, for you have earned the privilege of being in this distinguished man's inner circle.'

'Maverick always said to me that I remind him of himself.'

Naldy almost sniggered at Getergrin's statement. She had to pinch her lips tightly to stop herself from laughing out loud. Maverick and Getergrin couldn't be more opposite: one was slim, the other round; one held potent magic, the other could produce none; one effortlessly garnered admiration, the other could be easily overlooked in a quiet room.

'You are lucky, Mr Bomtayle,' said Hereto.

'Lucky?'

'You must have seen wonders during your time with him.'

'Maverick once produced a wall of water,' said Getergrin, his eyes darting to the ceiling, as if the unbelievable magic that he'd once witnessed had been borrowed from some great power above.

At that moment, Naldy realised she already knew many of the spells Maverick had invented—she had witnessed them firsthand. She and Ralph had been there when Maverick conjured the mesmerising wall of water Getergrin was referencing. Naldy also recalled a spell that had once trapped a night heron in a pocket of air as she and Ralph tried to flee on his magic carpet. There had been the smoky orb in Edengar, too, which the wizard had summoned to detect if they were lying. Spell after spell from their encounters with Maverick was rising to the forefront of Naldy's mind—undoubtedly, each one had been crafted using the Devante's power.

'I'd love to hear about other magic that Maverick has invented,' said Hereto. 'Could you tell me?'

After the young boy asked the question, Naldy realised Hereto was fishing for spells they could undo—spells that would help them access the wizard's memories, spells that might uncover Maverick's secret.

'We should finish the list,' said Getergrin, peering around nervously as if he had already said too much, 'the next name on it is Regina Nithsdale.'

'I know you're interested in broomsticks,' said Hereto. The young witch took a breath, as if what he was about to say would be painful. 'I hear you are fascinated by magical artefacts, and I could show you a few of our finest before you depart.'

Getergrin's face lit up with delight at the young witch's offer. Hereto's jaw twitched. It was clear to Naldy that, despite having suggested it, he was reluctant to allow the portly non-magical man a private perusal of his prized inventory. Naldy had once seen Hereto react similarly when Betty handed Rupert—who had no magical ability—the broomsticks they had purchased from him.

She felt a moment of warmth for the young witch, who was setting aside his firm dislike of non-magical people to help their quest.

'Well, I would quite enjoy that,' said Getergrin, swallowing air, 'but the orders for arrest must be sent out. Maverick has entrusted the task to me. Enough chitchat. We have three names left.'

'These last three names, yes, I don't know any of them,' said Hereto somewhat bluntly.

'Another time,' replied Getergrin. 'I'd love to see your finest brooms. Duty calls, though. Oh—before I depart, I just remembered Deslong would like me to purchase some broom polish for him. I owe him a favour.'

Without warning, Getergrin approached the cupboard where they were squished and began sliding open the door before Hereto could stop him.

—*Chapter Sixteen*—

THE CHEERFUL WITCHES

Naldy's brain faltered, her knowledge of spells abandoning her.

'*Nihil Videre,*' whispered Barbra.

Curiously, Getergrin appeared not to notice them. Ralph's mouth was agape as Getergrin's hand calmly reached into the cupboard towards Naldy's head, which she tilted to avoid colliding with the man's sausage-like fingers. From the shelf behind her, he seized a short glass pot labelled *Hereto's Wax-Based Broom Polish.*

'This should do it,' said Getergrin, pointing to the handwritten label. 'How much is it?'

'For you, sir,' replied Hereto, trying to mask his bewilderment that the three of them seemed to have vanished from the cupboard, 'it is complimentary.'

'Wonderful,' said Getergrin, approaching the exit. 'I must be going.'

'Thank you, Mr Bomtayle, for stopping by on this fine morning,' said Hereto, bowing low as the bell above the door tinkled. Getergrin had left the store.

'Miss Hexogg?' croaked Hereto nervously, approaching the stock cupboard. He gingerly peered inside.

Then, with a sudden jump, Hereto started backwards.

'You're still there,' said Hereto, his hand clutching his chest. 'I can see you again.'

'But how did you do that?' asked Ralph, as Barbra climbed out of the cupboard. 'How did Getergrin not see us?'

'I couldn't see you either,' added Hereto. 'Gave me quite the fright.'

'I made the three of us invisible,' said Barbra casually. 'Using the magic of H, of course.'

'If you could make us invisible,' said Ralph, 'why did we have to squish into the storage cupboard?'

'It just came to me on the spot,' said Barbra airily.

As Naldy exited their hiding place, she was momentarily impressed by the old witch's quick thinking. However, her fleeting admiration faded as she remembered their hosts were helping Maverick capture victims to be burnt.

'You sentenced those innocent people to be killed,' said Naldy, unable to contain her outrage any longer.

'A sorry affair,' said Hereto dryly. 'But to remain within the inner circle, we must make sacrifices.'

'You are sacrificing others,' said Naldy heatedly, her forehead creased with anger. 'It is no sacrifice for you when you clearly have no regard for these people's safety in the first place. A sacrifice would be giving up something you cherish.'

'We need to be trusted by our enemy,' said Barbra,

rolling her eyes. 'We must keep them close.'

'I refuse to work alongside either of you,' said Naldy, her heart racing. 'Not when you are both delivering innocent people into Maverick's hands.'

'We saved you from the stake,' Barbra began indifferently, 'because we noticed my sister's pearl necklace. I wanted to know how it came into your possession. We thought you had the magic of the Corium. There is no obligation for you to stay here with us. We can handle Maverick without your help.'

The bell above the door jingled. Naldy assumed a customer had entered the shop but soon realised the old bell had chimed because Hereto had opened the door for her—should she wish to leave.

Naldy's emotions carried her through the open doorway and out into the sunlit street. She refused to stay, unable to bear the thought of Barbra and Hereto betraying other witches just to remain close to The Establishment.

It was still early morning, and the road was quiet. She could feel her heart racing with anger. From where she stood, Naldy could see the tops of the tall pines in the Kirkwood Forest. A great crested flycatcher with grey and yellow plumage was perched peacefully in the trees' higher branches. The sight of the bird, with its untroubled manner, made Naldy long for the tranquillity of the Witch House. She took a deep breath of the crisp morning air, trying to forget that there was no home to return to—the Witch House had burnt down, and the cave had been discovered.

'Naldy, wait,' called Ralph's voice. He had followed her outside. 'You can't go. Please, stay.'

'We can find another way,' said Naldy, facing her friend.

'You don't have a broomstick,' said Ralph. 'Or a permit, for that matter. Where are you going to go on foot?'

'They made it clear they don't want our help,' said Naldy. 'They are selling out other witches.'

'Naldy,' said Ralph, softening his voice. 'I don't like the way Hereto and Barbra are behaving either, but the truth is, we no longer have possession of the Corium. To stand any chance of defeating Maverick, we need to work alongside them. Barbra has the magic of H. We must be here. To protect it. And to keep an eye on them.'

Naldy glanced up at the pine trees again. The bird that had been resting in the branches was gone.

'I don't like admitting it,' said Naldy. 'But I know you are right, Ralph.'

'Let's go inside.'

'You go,' said Naldy. 'I'll be inside in a moment.'

Ralph gave Naldy a consoling half-smile before turning and making his way back indoors.

Alone again, Naldy's thoughts drifted to the idea of fleeing beneath the trees of Kirkwood Forest. She longed to be far away from the Devante and everyone connected to it. She wanted to run, but knew it would do no good. It wouldn't bring back what had already been lost.

Though Naldy made her way back inside, she

was too upset to speak to Barbra and Hereto for the entire day, her mind troubled by what she had seen them do. It wasn't until after the sun had set that they regrouped in the kitchen. Naldy busied herself tidying the sink and benchtop.

A few pillar candles, with pendant-like drips of white wax, were positioned in the wooden table's centre, casting long shadows over Hereto, Barbra, and Ralph, who were seated around it. Every time Naldy looked at them, she tried to keep her mind from imagining the poor victims who would be tied to the stake—all because of Hereto and Barbra's double-dealing that very morning.

'Shall we begin?' asked Hereto, indicating for Naldy to stop fussing over the cleanliness of the room.

'What are we looking for?' asked Barbra, thoughtfully running her index finger along her chin.

'I don't know exactly,' said Naldy, accepting the wooden chair that Hereto had pulled out for her. 'A secret of some kind.'

'This secret,' Hereto said sceptically, 'can it really be something strong enough to dismantle Maverick's influence over the Society?'

'I saw Audry,' said Naldy, thinking of the remote cottage where the woman had waited for the wizard's arrival. 'She was the last living person who knew the information. Maverick hunted her down —along with others. He wanted them dead so the secret would remain hidden.'

'I imagine Maverick to be the sort of wizard with many secrets,' quipped Barbra. 'Hereto, would you boil the cauldron? I would like some more brew before bed.'

'*Arcesso,*' said Hereto, and a small cauldron filled itself with water from the kitchen tap before gliding over to hover above the flames of the pillar candles on the table.

'We shall soon know,' said Barbra, 'if any of these secrets are weighty enough to disempower him. Naldy, you said he created a spell to produce a wall of water. Let's begin by undoing that, shall we?'

Barbra closed her eyes. Her left cheek twitched, and her eyes snapped open after mere seconds.

'Has the brew gone cold?' asked Barbra, concerned.

'You cannot have done it already?' said Naldy, doubting that Barbra could have witnessed any of the wizard's memories in the brief time that had passed—she had barely blinked.

'Visiting these memories is exhausting work,' said Barbra.

'But how can you have seen any memory?' remarked Naldy.

'At The Academy,' said Ralph, 'when you undid Maverick's spell, Naldy, no time passed. Not for us, anyway.'

Naldy recalled the moments she'd ventured into Maverick's past. To her, it had felt as though she'd been gone a long while.

'I'm in dire need of some hot brew before

continuing,' huffed Barbra, gingerly dipping a finger into the cauldron to confirm her suspicion that the water was still cold. 'I'll say this—I think the chances of us stumbling upon a memory that discloses the wizard's secrets are incredibly slim. Has the bark even been added?'

'No time—,' repeated Ralph.

'Has passed,' said Barbra impatiently. 'Yes, yes, you keep saying.'

'Will you tell us what you saw, Miss Hexogg?' asked Hereto.

'Nothing meaningful,' said Barbra. 'I was transported to some grubby little town. It was noisy and crowded. I could barely hear myself think. A horrendous band was playing ghastly music. Maverick was shaking hands with a dishevelled bunch, forcing a smile. Big, ugly tents were everywhere.'

'A town fair,' said Ralph.

'He seemed determined to make a good impression,' continued Barbra. 'From an outsider's perspective, it was obvious that he held contempt for the hands he was grasping. Suddenly, I was taken to a small office. Getergrin was there. I believe it must have been his office, for it was decorated with the most hideous magical contraptions. They both stood whispering by the door.'

'What were they whispering about?' asked Naldy eagerly.

'Nothing of use to us,' replied Barbra. 'I had to get so close to hear them that I almost walked through them.'

'If they were speaking in whispers,' said Hereto, 'well, it must have been something they wanted kept secret.'

'Yes, I think it was,' said Barbra, delicately touching the metal cauldron with her hand, impatiently testing its temperature again. 'They'd discovered a scandal involving the mayor of Valingfield. Getergrin reassured Maverick he was tipped as the favourite to replace the disgraced official.'

'But did they say anything else?' asked Naldy, concerned Barbra might have missed some crucial information. 'Were the Devante mentioned?'

'The brew will be ready by the end of the week at this rate,' groaned Barbra, directing her wrinkled palms at the cauldron. The water instantly boiled, sending hot steam rising.

'Did they maybe hint—' began Naldy.

'The Devante were not mentioned. Nor anything that will help us loosen Maverick's grip on power. Hereto, would you add the bark?'

Hereto went to the cupboard to retrieve a jar of violet-coloured bark. He sprinkled a large handful into the cauldron, and purple steam billowed.

'Are you certain you didn't hear anything?' pressed Naldy.

'Frankly, I doubt we'll come across anything of use,' said Barbra, prickly. 'It appears the memories we may witness span the wizard's entire lifetime. It is improbable that we'll discover his secret. We should drink our brew and go to bed. Tomorrow, we can come up with a different plan.'

'Perhaps there was something implied that you may have missed,' said Naldy.

'I've told you what I've seen,' said Barbra, scowling. 'Now, I'd like to have my brew in peace.'

'Please, Barbra,' said Naldy, 'we must uncover his secret. We know plenty of spells for you to undo. Could you try again?'

'Not this evening,' said Barbra curtly.

Hereto ladled brew into ceramic cups. An unpleasant silence grew between them, as if their tongues had all frozen.

Naldy knew there was no point in persistently pleading, as the pinched expression on Barbra's face clearly conveyed that the old woman's patience wouldn't tolerate any more pestering questions.

An awkward silence settled while Barbra and Hereto sipped at their Kineleek brew. Ralph scrunched his nose up at the purple liquid. Immediately after emptying her cup, Barbra lifted herself out of her chair, mumbled a quick 'goodnight,' and departed the kitchen.

'This secret,' declared Hereto, rising to his feet, 'I know you believe it's the best way to turn the Society against Maverick, but personally, I think we should take them all down with magic.'

The young witch yawned and also bid them goodnight, leaving Ralph and Naldy alone at the dining table.

'Barbra doesn't trust us,' said Ralph.

'I don't trust her either,' replied Naldy. 'But what choice do we have? She has the one power that could save magic. We need to stay on her good side.'

'I think Barbra has a fair point,' said Ralph, the candlelight reflecting off his pale face. 'We know Maverick has created a limited number of spells using the Devante. The chances of us witnessing a memory that incriminates him are extremely slim.'

'We should at least try,' said Naldy, lifting herself from her chair.

'What about Hereto's suggestion?'

'Attacking the entire Seagull Society will probably see ourselves killed. They've been around a long time. They're highly skilled.'

Naldy noticed Ralph had flinched at the mention of the Society. She realised they had not spoken much about his cousin swearing allegiance to their rival.

'What if we talk to Rupert?' asked Ralph timidly.

Naldy lowered herself back into the wooden dining chair, leaning across the table to take Ralph's hand.

'He is not himself,' she said gently. 'I'm sorry, Ralph, but we can't trust Rupert anymore.'

'We could disguise ourselves as guards again,' suggested Ralph, averting his gaze, unable to face the truth of Naldy's words. 'I think if I spoke to him, he would realise he is helping the wrong side.'

'Your cousin can no longer be trusted.'

Ralph pulled his hands away from Naldy's and stood. 'I think I'll go to bed.'

He left her sitting alone in the kitchen. Guilt gnawed at her, and she tried to distract herself by watching the candles cast dancing shadows on the old walls. She wasn't tired and felt bad for upsetting Ralph, so she sat for another hour before retiring, pondering Barbra's reluctance to journey into Maverick's memory. She wondered if the old witch intended to explore them alone.

Early the next morning, she woke to light pouring in through the bedroom windows. The rest of the house was still asleep, and sitting alone in the kitchen did not appeal to her. She decided to make her way downstairs to the shop instead.

Naldy ran her fingers over a few brooms, feeling their polished, smooth wood. She felt a strong desire to take one from its display on the wall and escape south to Edengar, as she'd always planned. She doubted Maverick's edicts had reached that remote corner of the world.

To avoid the temptation of taking flight, Naldy went out into the cold street. She didn't bother with disguising spells but instead pulled the hood of her travelling cloak low over her head. The morning air was crisp, and she knew that to an onlooker, it would simply appear as if she were trying to keep warm.

Although it was a cold morning, there wasn't a wisp of cloud in the sky, and a brilliant baby blue stretched above. Naldy walked along the wide cobbled streets, passing the doors of many shopfronts that had yet to open for business.

Through the glass windows, she glimpsed the occasional shopkeeper preparing for a day of trade, stocking shelves or wielding a feather duster.

She soon found herself standing in the broad street where the burnings occurred each evening. The old museum, now rechristened 'The Establishment,' loomed large atop the many stone steps. The remnants of the previous night's burnings had been left behind. Naldy counted twelve piles of black ash.

Something small and deep red wrapped in brown paper caught her eye. It was placed at the bottom of the steps. As Naldy approached, she realised the lovingly prepared crimson package was a bouquet of red roses, plainly left as a tribute to the deceased. The flowers were the only evidence that someone had been brazen enough to openly honour the victims, and Naldy wondered if the defiant display had gone without punishment.

At that moment, two guards emerged from the grand wooden doors of the stone building above. They were chatting casually to each other in a carefree manner. Naldy knew that despite appearing friendly, the guards would relish the chance to question her for lingering near The Establishment's quarters. She continued across the road and took refuge inside *The Mortismor.*

The bistro was quiet, with only two other elderly patrons. Naldy settled into one of the booths by the window, overlooking the wide cobbled road. She ordered a smoked Highland brew and some poached eggs.

She sat with her thoughts, watching the street outside gradually become more active. The bistro became busier and noisier as people stopped in for their breakfast and a morning brew.

Naldy couldn't help but feel more despondent. It seemed people were going about their day as if no burnings had ever occurred—and as if no future burnings were planned. The newspaper on the table suggested otherwise, with nine more condemned to die that evening.

To Naldy's surprise and horror, she soon noticed a group of four cheerful witches. Their broomsticks were leaning against the table—clearly approved by The Establishment—and the witches were deep in a gossipy exchange. Naldy wondered how they could be so openly cheerful, knowing that many other witches and wizards were being sentenced to the stake.

She left currents on the table to settle her bill, including a tip, before returning to the broom store. She found Hereto sitting at the service desk amongst his brooms. He barely looked up when the bell tinkled, busy dipping a feather quill into an inkwell before scrawling something on a piece of parchment.

'Barbra wondered if you had left,' said Hereto, his tongue poking between his teeth as he concentrated on his handwriting. 'I think she had hoped you had.'

'How can any witch endure Maverick's edicts?' said Naldy irritably, throwing back the hood of her cloak. She was frustrated by the residents of The Great City, all going about their day as if the edicts didn't exist.

'There are many witches and wizards who welcome the edicts,' said Hereto, untroubled by Naldy's passion.

'But how could they!' exclaimed Naldy. 'He wants magic destroyed.'

'He wants magic controlled,' corrected Hereto, raising his eyes to meet hers.

'He is killing people, Hereto,' said Naldy. 'Why are they not more afraid?'

'I hope you wore a disguise when you ventured out,' said Hereto, placing down his quill. 'It is upsetting, but it shouldn't surprise you that some witches favour the edicts. Many themselves are frightened by the prospect of new magic. It has been years since the ability to create new spells was possible. They believe they are being protected.'

'Their ignorance and fear is enabling Maverick to kill,' said Naldy. 'And you're wrong, he wants magic destroyed, not controlled.'

Hereto returned an empathetic expression before holding up the parchment he'd been working on.

'What do you think of my sign?'

'*Always Open, by Appointment Only,*' read Naldy aloud.

'I'll just fix it to the window, and we should head upstairs,' said Hereto, making his way to the front of the shop.

'I've already eaten,' said Naldy.

'As have the rest of the household,' said Hereto. 'Barbra has agreed to try again this morning.'

'Try again?' asked Naldy, surprised. 'You mean travel into Maverick's memories?'

'On one condition,' added Hereto, turning to face her now that the sign was secured in the shop's window. 'We are to go with her this time.'

'Go with her?'

'Yes,' said Hereto, beaming happily. 'I had the idea myself. Barbra has the rare power to create new magic. She's produced a spell to take us into his memories with her. We should head upstairs.'

As she climbed the spiral staircase behind the young witch, Naldy could hardly feel excited that they wouldn't need to rely on Barbra's ability to recount Maverick's memories. Her thoughts clung to the image of the cheerful witches in the bistro. She felt unsettled by the recollection of their bright, carefree smiles.

They found Barbra and Ralph at the table in tense conversation when they entered the kitchen.

'You should ask Maverick for a position within The Establishment,' said Ralph, his arms rigidly crossed over his chest.

'Are you both still at it?' asked Hereto, helping himself to brew from the hot cauldron.

'I don't support Maverick's oppressive edicts,' croaked Barbra. 'But magic ought to be reserved for those with the ability to wield it.'

'How can you believe that?' said Ralph passionately. 'It is beliefs like that which strengthen support for his edicts. Magic should not be restricted for the sole benefit of those privileged enough to wield it.'

'You will not change my mind,' said Barbra, frowning. 'Those without magic have always treated us like dirt. Even now, they rally behind Maverick, crying for us to be burnt. They do not deserve the advantages that magic affords.'

'It is not just townsfolk that support Maverick's burnings,' said Naldy, taking a seat. 'I've just learnt many witches support them too.'

'We did not ask for your opinion,' said Barbra stubbornly. 'Where have you been?'

Ralph pinched his lips together and slumped back into his dining chair.

'It's not as simple as them versus us,' said Naldy. 'If our travels have taught me anything, it is that good and bad operate on both sides. Are we ready, then?'

'*Ready?*' repeated Barbra waspishly. '*We* have been waiting for *you*.'

Ralph rolled his eyes. Naldy struggled to stay tight-lipped, knowing that if she upset Barbra, she might change her mind and refuse to take them into Maverick's memories.

'I have little faith,' continued Barbra, 'but I've agreed to give it one last shot. To begin, we must hold hands.'

Ralph limply took hold of the woman's outstretched, wrinkled hand, and the others followed suit, linking their fingers.

As an Effangale witch, Barbra didn't give them the courtesy of uttering the spell aloud as a warning. Naldy felt her body drop through the floor.

Chapter Seventeen

THE GOLDEN CROWN

Although the feeling of free-falling had begun abruptly, it also came to a jarring stop.

They found themselves in a large stone building that seemed both unfamiliar and strangely familiar. The ceiling was high, with decorative carved edges beautifully gilded. At least twenty life-sized golden statues depicting winged gargoyles lined the spacious room, each solid gold gargoyle clasped a hefty crystal candelabra. The roof supported twelve grand chandeliers fashioned from the same crystal. The centre of the room, with its clean stone floor, was left empty.

'I don't see Maverick,' said Barbra, disinterested in the grandeur surrounding them.

'I recognise this place,' said Naldy. 'At least I think I do. I feel as if I've been in here before.'

'Yes, we are just up the road,' said Hereto, resting a hand on his stomach. 'I think I would have rather walked than lurched across town like that.'

'But where are we?' asked Ralph, clearly as confused as Naldy in identifying their location. 'And isn't this supposed to be Maverick's memory? Where is the evil brute?'

'We may be a short walk from *Hereto's*,' said Barbra, swivelling on the balls of her feet in the hope of spotting Maverick, 'but we are a long way back in time.'

'I recognise those doors,' said Naldy, noticing the sizable wooden entrance looming at one end of the chamber.

'Yes, you do,' confirmed Barbra. 'We are standing in the foyer of The Bleckdale Witchery Museum. An inner wall was eventually built to separate the entrance doors from the rest of the chamber for security purposes. It seems we have arrived long before this building was converted.'

'If it's not a museum,' asked Ralph, 'whatever is it now?'

'It is the palace of The Establishment,' answered Hereto.

'Well, whoever designed this place,' noted Ralph, 'they have the same expensive taste of Maverick. It reminds me of the horrid decorating he has recently done with the museum.'

No sooner had Ralph finished talking than the double doors opened. A handsome young man, no older than sixteen, entered, sauntering across the chamber. The young man was tall for his age and had youthful pale skin. His wavy black hair hung loosely over his forehead in a boyish, unkempt way. He wore an elegant sage green robe that shimmered as he walked. His dark eyes seemed to be scanning the room for something.

'Who is that?' asked Ralph in a tentative whisper, afraid the young man approaching might hear him.

'That is Titus,' replied Barbra. 'What I'm more interested in knowing is where we can find Maverick?'

As if to answer Barbra's question, Maverick appeared out of thin air, less than a metre from them. They all jumped, including the young man crossing the grand room.

Naldy suspected Maverick had used some sort of spell to make himself temporarily invisible, just as Barbra had done when Getergrin had opened the store cupboard.

'I didn't see you there,' said Titus, recovering from the fright and flashing an endearing smile at the wizard.

'I am told last night's burnings were quite something,' said Maverick, leaning smugly on his black cane. The wizard was the same middle-aged man Naldy had always known him to be, frozen in time by the regular consumption of Veserum.

'It is a pity you couldn't make it,' said Titus. 'I'd hoped you would.'

'Yes, I am disappointed myself,' replied Maverick. 'But I cannot be seen openly supporting the burnings.'

'You would be welcomed within The Establishment,' expressed Titus with casual charm. 'I have said it before. You would be well looked after.'

Naldy thought she saw Maverick wince slightly.

'What is it that you are hiding from?' asked Titus, cocking his head to one side.

'The reason I have come,' said Maverick, taking a few steps closer to the boy. 'Is to warn you, Titus.'

'Warn me?'

'You must listen to me. It is not safe for you to continue. You are the one that now must go into hiding.'

'You show up out of nowhere,' said Titus, placing a hand on Maverick's shoulder, 'offering your support. Now you come to tell me I must give it all up. I control The Establishment, Maverick. I am safe here.'

'I can no longer continue assisting you,' said Maverick, and using his cane, he gently pushed away Titus's hand resting on his shoulder. 'Your charisma will not disarm me.'

The two men were almost the same height, with Maverick only slightly taller than the young man. Naldy thought they could easily be mistaken for father and son.

'If you believe I should go into hiding,' said Titus, 'you must tell me why.'

'I cannot.'

'Why have you helped me? Why won't you tell me who you really are?'

'You wanted to avenge the injustice your father imposed on you,' said Maverick. 'You've achieved that. Now, it is time for you to stop. You must head to the mountains or the woods where you will be safe.'

'Safe,' replied Titus, turning away from the

wizard. 'If you must go, then you may leave. But how dare you tell me I must hide. I will not quit.'

'All those years of not being good enough because you hold no magical ability,' replied Maverick. 'I have helped you achieve much, Titus, more than you may ever truly understand.'

'And I have repaid your service,' said Titus, meeting the wizard's gaze, 'with an offer that any sensible person would have accepted: join the Establishment. If you refuse, it is an offer that will not be repeated.'

'The burnings must stop,' said Maverick. 'It is too dangerous to continue.'

'I will do as I please,' said Titus, his face twisting into a sneer.

The boy had tight, fresh skin and was still attractive while making such an ugly expression. In contrast, Maverick's skin was etched with lines and had a greyness, giving the wizard a wearied appearance.

'It will not end well,' said Maverick, reaching into the pockets of his black cloak. 'I have told you how you can save yourself the embarrassment. But if you will not listen, you must learn the hard way. Before I depart, I want to leave you with a gift.'

Titus's expression softened as the wizard pulled a golden crown from his pocket. Naldy felt awestruck by the crown's beauty. The rich gold gleamed in the black irises of Titus's eyes as the young man admired the exquisite metal. Naldy had seen this alluring gold once before, while she and Ralph were in Edengar, and on that occasion, it had also been in Maverick's hands.

'The Aurum,' said Ralph, with a look suggesting he wanted to snatch it from the wizard's grasp. 'I always knew it was Maverick who gave it to Titus. Didn't I say so?'

'Where did you find such a thing?' asked the boy, eagerly holding out his hands, desiring the crown.

'Here,' said Maverick, delicately placing the gold onto Titus's head. It was a perfect fit. 'You have everything you need.'

Titus looked resplendent in the golden adornment. It gave the young man a formidable appearance.

'You must stay,' said Titus boldly, tears pooling in his eyelids. 'I command it. I will not allow you to leave.'

Before Maverick responded, Naldy felt her body lurch forward. The scene before them vanished into blackness, accompanied by an intense vibration. Then, they found themselves in another room—one that Naldy also recognised.

They were beneath The Academy, in the chamber where the Devante were created. The room was remarkably similar to when Professor Deslong Piggett first escorted Naldy and Ralph into the chamber. It was crowded with magical and ordinary objects, just as it had been when Naldy was last inside the space. The *Forever Flame* was ablaze within the grand fireplace at the end of the room.

'As I said, Maverick, even I will not know its

location,' said a familiar husky voice.

Naldy's heart ballooned. Standing by the large stone table, her wrinkled face set in stony disapproval, was a witch she was glad to see.

'Odorf,' exclaimed Ralph, teary-eyed.

As Maverick approached the stone bench, where Odorf had turned her attention to a small bubbling cauldron resting on a portable burner, Naldy recalled the journey she and Ralph had made through the Edengar Mountains with the wrinkled witch. She remembered the piglinns they'd flown and how, when they'd reached the ravine with the dragons, the old woman had duelled Maverick to protect the beasts.

It was this same wizard, now approaching her bench as she stirred the bubbling cauldron, who had cast a horrible spell that claimed her life. Naldy and Ralph had buried the old woman beside the river, while the dragons had watched on sadly from the caves.

She did not raise her head as Maverick drew nearer.

'Do you not trust me?' asked Maverick coldly, picking up a small crystal phial filled with a sticky dark red liquid. Naldy recognised the potion to be Veserum.

'Nobody is to know where the store of potion will be kept,' said Odorf. 'It is not a matter of trust.'

Although they had been transported to a new memory, Maverick's appearance was unchanged. Even his long black cloak was the same one he'd worn when he gifted Titus the golden crown. Naldy guessed the two memories must have occurred close together in time.

'I don't see the point in having an undisclosed location,' said Maverick. 'The phials should be kept closer to Kirkwood, and all members ought to be made aware of the chosen site.'

'When the invention of the Devante was finally successful, I recall you telling me potions like Veserum had been made redundant,' said Odorf. She clipped a thin green leaf from a severed branch resting on the benchtop. Then, using a pair of brass forceps, she dropped the leaf into the cauldron—the liquid inside let off a hiss and a swirl of grey vapour. 'Of course, then you came to realise that spells invented with the Devante could be undone. You've gone from showing no interest in potion-making to being intensely curious.'

Maverick held the small phial up to the candlelight, squinting, before removing the bottle's stopper and drinking the liquid.

'It's almost peppery, but there's a subtle sweetness,' said Maverick. 'Must it be so thick?'

'That'll be the dragon's blood,' replied Odorf, picking up a wooden ladle and stirring the potion in a circular motion. 'Nothing I add will be able to thin that.'

The secret door leading into the chamber opened, and Naldy swivelled to see who had entered. Ralph's puzzled expression revealed that he likely had the same thought as Naldy—the tall woman with angular features and long black hair bore a striking resemblance to Naldy's mother, Tarren.

'Look at you both, working away,' said the woman in a carefree way as she approached the stone bench. 'The sun is out. A rare occurrence this far south.'

'Maverick is displeased with the potion,' said Odorf, raising an eyebrow.

'It is not the potion that is my concern,' replied Maverick, 'it is its safety, Hannah.'

Naldy felt a sense of awe as it dawned on her that she was staring at her great-great-grandmother. This was the woman who had assembled the team to create the grandest spellbooks ever to exist. This was Hannah Hale.

Chapter Eighteen

GULLS

'The others have suggested a game of lawn bowls,' said Hannah. Although her tone was friendly, there was also a firmness. 'The break in the wind won't last long. I suggest you leave your work for later. We're playing in pairs. Would you like to be a team?'

'Was a game of lawn bowls Deslong's idea?' asked Maverick.

'Will you join us, then?' asked Hannah. 'We should be able to finish the game before the weather turns.'

'This will need to steep overnight,' said Odorf, turning off the burner's flame and placing a lid over the cauldron. 'A game of lawn bowls sounds like a marvellous idea.'

'I am in no mood for games,' said Maverick. 'Deslong also has his reservations regarding this potion. How are we to know it won't be tampered with?'

'It will be kept in Edengar,' said Hannah. 'You needn't worry, Maverick. Enough is being made to last us a thousand years.'

'What happens when the shipment is depleted?' queried Maverick.

'We will need to reconvene,' said Hannah. 'Odorf has decided the shipment will be delivered by seagulls. The birds can travel long distances. They can navigate land and sea.'

'Gulls do not live long,' said Maverick. 'One or two decades, usually. I will invent a spell that has the potion magically delivered—without the need for birds.'

'The seagulls will deliver the potion,' said Odorf sternly. 'The birds can be trusted—more than any magic created by someone in society.'

Maverick and Odorf glowered at each other as Hannah rested a hand on the stone bench, observing them intently.

'We are a team, Odorf,' sneered Maverick. 'The decisions should not solely be made by you.'

'No spell will touch this potion,' said Odorf tensely. 'I do not trust your spells.'

'I do not trust your sea birds,' replied Maverick with quiet menace. 'It's clear you would rather place your trust in a society of seagulls than in people. It is unwise.'

'Let us not argue with each other,' said Hannah as she made her way back towards the door. She stopped halfway, turned, and thrust out her hand as if tossing something. In mid-air, two small silver objects materialised and flew towards Maverick and Odorf. Both were quick to catch them.

Maverick held the solid object up to the light, and

Naldy saw that it was a silver brooch shaped like a seagull.

'We should give ourselves a name,' said Hannah with a smile. 'The Seagull Society is fitting. I've heard that some witches wear pins depicting insects to secretly show their allegiance to magic. We can wear a seagull brooch instead. I'll make sure to give one to the others as well.'

Maverick was not impressed. Odorf was securing the brooch to the breast of her cloak.

'We will outlive any sea bird,' said Maverick dryly.

'Their offspring will carry on the duties,' said Hannah. 'It is Odorf's invention, and let that be the end of it. Come now, the others are waiting.'

The chamber door opened, and a beautiful woman entered. She had piercing green eyes and a mane of red hair.

'The wind has returned,' said the green-eyed woman. 'It carries ominous clouds, so we've had to abandon the fun. How is the batch coming along?'

'It needs to stew,' replied Odorf.

'Deslong won't allow me to banish the clouds,' said the red-haired woman, stepping further into the room. She hoisted herself onto one of the stone benches, plucked a piglinn feather from a vase, and twirled it between her fingers.

'Rightly so, Audry,' replied Hannah, watching her fondly. 'We mustn't do anything that draws Titus's attention.'

Naldy realised it was the same Audry who knew Maverick's secret—only she was at least three or four decades younger. Her smooth skin was free of wrinkles, and not a single grey strand marked her bushy red hair.

'Hiding will not stop him,' said Audry. 'We are the most equipped group to see him removed from his throne, yet we are determined to remain in the shadows.'

'We are not ready,' replied Hannah.

'If you'll excuse me,' said Odorf. 'I must change into my hunting gear.'

'The Devante can take care of dinner,' said Maverick. 'There is no need to go hunting.'

'I have a new potion to attract rabbit I'd like to put to the test,' said Odorf, slowly making her way to the exit.

'What are your thoughts on the matter?' Audry asked Maverick, pointing at him with the piglinn feather. 'Should we attack Titus?'

'We ought not to underestimate Titus's power,' said Maverick. 'We may each have a Devante, but Titus has an entire army of guards protecting him and the strength of The Establishment behind him. When we act, it must be done with caution.'

'You've warned us against taking his life,' said Hannah.

'Titus may appear to be an autocrat, but I'm certain others are waiting to take his place. His death will make him a martyr. It will only instil more fear in his followers, and the Establishment will hunt the Devante more ruthlessly. We must be careful.'

'Yes,' said Hannah. 'I fear you are right, and murder may not be sufficient to end his madness. We have not had the Devante long, and we must be wise with how we use our new invention.'

'I might go out for some air before this rain comes,' said Maverick. 'I can't bear the smell of bubbling dragon's blood.'

Maverick made his way to the exit with his black cane in one hand.

'We must remember why we invented the Devante,' said Audry, dropping the feather back into the vase. 'With every day that passes, more witches are burnt. I fear we may have lost sight of what we initially set out to do.'

Naldy desperately wanted to stay with her family and learn more about her past—about Hannah and Audry. But as Maverick departed the chamber, the scene dissolved into blackness, and the women's voices dimmed.

'Are you coming, Naldy?' called Ralph from behind her.

Naldy could see the image of Maverick walking through the underground library as darkness enveloped her.

Audry and Hannah had faded completely, and Naldy could no longer witness their exchange—it was not part of Maverick's memory. With no other choice, she followed Barbra, Hereto, and Ralph through the hidden door into the library beyond as they pursued Maverick.

The wizard made his way up the stone steps and

into The Academy's circular entrance hall. Naldy half expected Maverick's excuse for departure to be a lie, but true to his word, the wizard made his way out into the windy landscape. Coloured bowls lay strewn across the grass, but there was no sign of any other Society members, who had taken shelter indoors.

Maverick's black travelling cloak flapped around his feet as he walked. The wizard used the cane to steady himself in the harsh wind.

Naldy felt an intense trembling—a horrible jolt —and then found herself again seated in Hereto's grimy kitchen, gripping Hereto and Ralph's hands.

'Another waste of time,' said Barbra, lifting herself from the dining chair.

'I don't think it was a complete waste,' replied Ralph, the morning sun streaming through the window and catching the red tones in his hair.

'We already know Maverick is a member of the Society,' grumbled Hereto, 'and it is hardly surprising that Maverick supports the burnings.'

'Yes, but now we know for certain that he was conspiring with Titus,' replied Naldy. 'We saw him give Titus the Aurum. The crown was unmistakably a Devante. He knew he couldn't hold back the Society forever—he was warning Titus that they were coming for him, now that the Devante had been invented.'

'Did nobody else notice the striking resemblance?' asked Ralph, exasperated. He looked at them all intently, as if they'd missed a crucial part of the memory. 'It's obvious why Maverick wanted to save Titus. They would be the right ages—didn't you all see it? Maverick must be Titus's father.'

Barbra could not contain her amusement, breaking into an unrestrained cackle.

'What's so humorous?' asked Ralph, hurt by Barbra's response to his theory. 'They had the same eyes and the same hair colour.'

'It is widely known that Grigory was Titus's father,' said Hereto, grimacing at Ralph.

'Perhaps Grigory changed his name?' suggested Ralph.

'Grigory was killed by Titus,' said Barbra, recovering from laughter and wiping her wet cheeks on the sleeve of her cloak. 'He sentenced his father to death early on in The Great Witch Hunt.'

'And the event has been well documented,' added Hereto. 'There were many pages and sculptures in the museum that depicted the burning of Grigory —before Maverick burnt it all. He does not share a likeness to Grigory. Titus got his features from his mother.'

'Maverick could be an uncle or a cousin?' suggested Ralph, clinging stubbornly to his idea. 'You can't deny they share similarities, not only in appearance. That must be his secret.'

'For argument's sake,' said Hereto, 'let's assume you're right—that Maverick is somehow related to Titus. But how does such a secret help us defeat him? We have no proof, and even if we did, how would it stop the burnings?'

Ralph bit his lip, struggling to answer how a closer connection between the wizard and the previous ruler would help them bring down Maverick.

'These expeditions into Maverick's memories,' said Barbra, making her way to the sink to fill up a glass with water, 'they have been a waste of our precious time.'

'We may not have discovered his secret yet,' said Naldy passionately. 'But can't you feel that we are close?'

'At any rate,' replied Barbra. 'Chances of us stumbling upon this supposed secret are rather unlikely. These expeditions have tired me, and I want you to listen to me as I say this: we *won't* be travelling together into Maverick's past again.'

'It may be the only shot we have at defeating him,' said Ralph dryly.

'That is your opinion,' returned Barbra icily. 'We must find another way. Such serious matters should not be left foolishly to chance. Let us call it a day.'

'I must place my solidarity alongside Barbra,' added Hereto, before the two of them left the room, leaving Ralph and Naldy alone in the kitchen.

'Now what?' asked Ralph miserably. 'Barbra has control of the Devante's magic. We can't undo spells without it.'

'Unless...' replied Naldy.

'It won't work.'

'What won't?'

'I know what you're thinking,' replied Ralph,

staring at the grimy window above the sink. 'Stealing the Devante's magic—that's what you're suggesting, isn't it?'

'The Society was able to manage to extract it from me. There is some way to do it. We need to work out how.'

'The Seagull Society have an intricate understanding of how the Devante works. They created it. We don't have the slightest clue how to transfer magic from one being to another.'

'You're right,' conceded Naldy, slumping her elbows onto the table. 'But there must be more we can do.'

Seeing her ancestors had stirred something within her—a deeper sense of responsibility to protect magic had taken hold. They had sacrificed so much to create it. Her own parents, too, had given up a great deal.

'We can't let it be up to Barbra,' said Naldy. 'We must try something.'

'I spent many nights,' began Ralph timidly, guiltily diverting his gaze, 'trying to use the magic of the Corium. Every attempt I made to bring back my cousin failed.'

'Betty managed it, though,' said Naldy, feeling wounded by the reminder that the pair had "borrowed" her power without her permission to resurrect Rupert.

'Yes, but I've no idea how she did it, and she's not here to help us. I doubt we'll succeed in using the Devante's power without Barbra's approval.'

'That's enough for one day,' said Naldy, uncomfortable with his remorseful stare.

She felt a rush of emotion creeping up behind her eyes and exited the kitchen before the tears fell.

When Naldy entered the small, dusty room where she was staying, she sat on the edge of the shabby bed. It wasn't just Ralph's apologetic look that had upset her; it was the trip into Maverick's memory where she'd seen her great-great-grandparents. Naldy felt responsible for saving the Devante, which her ancestors had worked tirelessly to create. To date, all she'd accomplished were failures—many Devante and many loved ones had died.

Sunlight was coming in through the closed window, and the air in the room felt humid. Naldy stood to try and pry it open, but the lower sash was stuck to the sill. The window casing, sealed from years of disuse, wouldn't budge.

Outside, on an adjacent tiled roof, Naldy caught sight of a grey tabby cat lazily licking its paws. She instantly longed for the companionship of her cat. Sadly, she knew it would be too dangerous to venture south to find him and had no option but to hope Smookers had found somewhere safe to shelter until they could be reunited.

The grey tabby on the opposite roof ambled across the slats. As the cat passed out of sight, she wondered whom she could rely on. Even Oak and her parents had hidden the truth about the Devante —and Betty and Ralph had borrowed her power without permission.

Was taking Barbra's Devante the wrong path? What other choice did they have if Barbra refused to collaborate?

If only she still had the magic of the Corium— then she wouldn't need to rely on the old witch. A wave of guilt washed over her. She had failed to protect it. She wished she'd done more while she still possessed it.

But why wasn't Maverick using the Corium's magic to his advantage? He had the highest-ranking Devante—he could break the *Banned Spell of Knowledge* and find every witch and wizard in Kirkwood. So why wasn't he wielding its power?

A soft knock at the bedroom door startled Naldy.

'It's me,' came Ralph's voice from the other side.

'I'm not in the mood for talking, Ralph,' she replied.

'I think you might want to see this,' said Ralph.

When Naldy opened the door, nobody was there. She found herself staring at the ugly oil painting hanging crookedly on the wall in the hallway. It depicted an old bearded man holding a broomstick. She leant her head out of the bedroom door and spotted Ralph bounding down the long hall lined with portraits. Ralph turned into his own room, which adjoined the long corridor.

'Where are you going?' called Naldy.

His urgency intrigued her, and she followed him. Ralph's room was much like the one Naldy occupied, but it was slightly smaller. The plastered walls had cracks, and dust had settled on every surface.

'Come,' said Ralph, standing by the window and peering into the street below.

'What am I looking at, Ralph?' asked Naldy, approaching the window.

'Barbra and Hereto,' replied Ralph, gesturing with his hands. 'And keep your voice down.'

'Yes,' whispered Naldy irritably. 'I can *see* Barbra and Hereto in the street, but why should they be of any interest to me?'

'I don't want you to see them,' said Ralph. 'I want you to *listen* to them.'

Both Barbra and Hereto appeared to be heading somewhere. They were dressed in their travelling cloaks, each holding a broomstick. Barbra anxiously swivelled her head, glancing left and right as if afraid they might be noticed. The faint sound of their voices carried on the breeze.

'I still believe we should ask them to leave,' suggested Hereto. 'Or we could simply turn them in —it would strengthen Maverick's trust in us. I don't see why you've changed your mind and now think it's best to keep them here.'

'It is best we keep them close,' said Barbra. 'The two of them have caused much trouble, and I'd like to keep an eye on them.'

'I think our new plan,' said the young witch, drumming his fingers on the sleek broomstick, 'is far superior to visiting the wizard's memories.'

'Our new plan is good,' agreed Barbra, mounting her broomstick, 'but we ought not to abandon

Naldy's idea. Though I doubt our luck in stumbling upon the wizard's secret, I shall continue to visit Maverick's past—but I don't plan on sharing what we discover with the others.'

'I worry they will interfere. Do you think they'll try to steal your power?'

'They will try,' replied Barbra, straightening her back defiantly atop her broom. 'But I've created many protections using H. Any attempt would be in vain—and they'll learn the true meaning of regret.'

'We'd best get going,' said Hereto. 'Everyone will be waiting for us, and they can't start without us.'

Barbra, along with her broom, vanished. They watched as Hereto flew along the street towards Kirkwood Forest, and Naldy knew Barbra was flying invisibly beside him. She felt aggravated—there were now more secrets.

'Where do you think they're off to?' asked Ralph. 'Don't you find it curious?'

'They don't trust us,' said Naldy, turning away from the window. She noticed a leather notebook and feather quill lying on the bed.

'They ought to work alongside us,' insisted Ralph. 'We all want the same thing.'

'It's understandable, Ralph, considering our shared history with Barbra.'

Any distrust she had felt towards Ralph earlier seemed to vanish as she met his blue eyes. She could sense his care for both the quest and her.

'We could follow them,' suggested Naldy.

'There's no knowing where they've gone now,'

replied Ralph. 'But if they venture out again tomorrow, I like that idea.'

Naldy turned to depart, but before leaving, a question entered her mind.

'Ralph, what are you writing about? I don't imagine you're expecting to return to The Academy?'

'I know Professor Piggett has turned out to be our opponent,' he said, 'but I still want to continue my paper on wizards, even if it must be done without his help.'

Naldy gave Ralph a warm smile, and she sat on the edge of the bed.

'Do you want to read me some of what you've got?'

'Really? You want to hear it?'

'We can't tail Barbra and Hereto today, and a distraction right now might be good. I know you've worked hard on the paper.'

Ralph picked up his journal, beaming. Naldy thought about the cheerful witches she'd seen that morning in the bistro—after journeying into Maverick's past, it now felt like some time ago. She wondered if they had the right idea in permitting themselves to enjoy each other's company. Allowing Maverick's reign of terror to overshadow every aspect of their lives wouldn't end the ongoing horror. Had they simply been trying to find some small light in the dark?

'What do you think of the opening?' asked Ralph, glancing up from his journal. Naldy had been too distracted with her own thoughts to hear any of the words he had spoken.

'It's wonderful,' said Naldy. 'Excellent, Ralph. Keep going.'

Chapter Nineteen

PUMPKIN PIE

Tailing Barbra and Hereto proved more difficult than expected. On numerous occasions, Ralph and Naldy had spotted the pair leaving the broomstick store and hurried to covertly pursue them, pulling on their black boots as they rushed out. They managed to follow Hereto until they reached the edge of the Kirkwood Forest, knowing that the old witch was gliding invisibly beside him. Then the boy vanished as well.

'They are using the magic of H,' said Ralph after one of their failed attempts. He slumped into one of Hereto's old dining chairs, defeated.

'Whatever they are up to,' replied Naldy, passing Ralph a goblet of water, 'they seem eager for their secret not to be discovered.'

'We need to get closer,' said Ralph.

'If we get any closer,' stated Naldy, 'they'll be certain to see us.'

Indeed, on their next attempt, Naldy thought she had caught sight of Hereto looking directly at her with a cheeky grin.

They tried using the invisibility spell Barbra

had used when they'd hidden in Hereto's broom cupboard—*Nihil Videre*—but it was no help. Naldy and Ralph were always left stumped as to where they had gone.

'They must be using the same spell,' said Ralph.

'Evidently,' added Naldy. 'Where do you think they are going?'

'Do you think they're sneaking off to see Maverick?' Ralph asked.

'It's the opposite way to The Establishment's palace,' replied Naldy. 'Besides, Maverick is hunting for Barbra. It won't be anybody in the Society.'

'Well, then who are they sneaking off to see?'

A few more days passed, and Naldy was beginning to doubt they'd ever discover what the duo was up to. It didn't help that each evening, as the sun set, she could see a plume of dark smoke trailing across the sky through the windows of Hereto's living quarters—knowing more witches had been burnt.

'They were there moments ago,' said Ralph, peeking over a thick log. 'Did you see which direction they went?'

'It's no good,' said Naldy, standing and brushing the debris from her cloak.

'Stay down, Naldy, they might see you.'

'They know we're following them, Ralph. They've seen us. I swear I saw Hereto wink in our direction even while we were using the invisibility spell.'

'Should we return to plan A?'

'What is plan A?' questioned Naldy.

'Convincing Barbra to venture into Maverick's memories.'

'She *is* venturing into Maverick's memories,' she replied. 'Just without us.'

Ralph sighed as dappled light filtered through the pine trees, casting shifting shadows across his face, which was creased in thought.

'There's got to be a better way,' said Naldy, watching a line of black ants marching across the top of the log. 'We're spending all this time pursuing secrets, hoping it'll help end the burnings.'

'Let's return to the store,' said Ralph, continuing ahead of her towards The Great City.

On the way back, Naldy spotted a hand-painted sign above a green shop door reading *Ander's Fruit & Vegetable.* Without telling Ralph, she entered the store.

Upon returning to *Hereto's Broomsticks,* arms full of paper bags, she found Ralph outside with his arms crossed.

'Where did you go?' asked Ralph, his nostrils flaring. 'You worried me. I thought you were just behind me.'

'I have plan C,' said Naldy, holding up her bags. As she did so, the bottom of one tore open, and a heavy pumpkin rolled across the ground. Ralph bent and picked up the slightly bruised gourd.

'Where did you get the currents for all of this?' asked Ralph.

'It's the last I had in my drawstring pouch,'

replied Naldy. 'Don't worry, I'm not foolish enough to visit the local Treasury to retrieve more currents. Maverick will no doubt have it under surveillance.'

'What's plan C, then?' asked Ralph. 'Are we going to clobber Maverick with a pumpkin?'

'Comforting food can bring people together,' said Naldy as Ralph opened the door for her to enter the shop. 'It's for Barbra and Hereto.'

'Persuasion with pumpkin pie,' said Ralph.

After many hours of baking and fussing over the table setting, Naldy placed the butternut pumpkin and potato pie into the wood-fired oven to keep it hot before taking a seat. The white tablecloth, embroidered with pink and red garden roses, had been found languishing at the rear of one of the kitchen cabinets. The fragile dinner plates, each embellished with a hand-painted golden broomstick, had also been salvaged from their long-forgotten place in a cupboard in the hall. Ralph drummed his fingers restlessly on the table while the comforting, spiced scent of the pie caused his stomach to grumble.

'Can I just have a small slice?' asked Ralph, looking at Naldy across the table with pleading eyes.

'They don't usually return this late,' said Naldy. 'I'll make us some brew while we wait.'

It was past midnight by the time Hereto and Barbra returned.

'What's all this?' asked Barbra, entering the kitchen and fidgeting with her fingers as if trying to conceal her delight at the decorated dining table.

'It smells delicious,' said Hereto, eagerly sitting beside Ralph.

The setting was perfect. Naldy took a breath, admiring her efforts.

'We won't be convinced with pie,' said Barbra bitingly.

'Convinced?' repeated Naldy, pretending to be unaware of the meaning of the old woman's blunt comment.

'Bribed,' said Barbra stonily. 'I have already told you—I won't be venturing back into Maverick's memories. It may have seemed like a good idea at first, but the stakes are too high to leave such matters to chance.'

Naldy wanted to say she knew Barbra was venturing into Maverick's memories without them, that the old woman was intentionally excluding them—but she bit her tongue and smiled.

'You have given us lodging,' said Naldy, using a tea towel to remove the pie from the wood-fired oven. 'It is not a bribe. It is a thank you.'

'We've had a long day,' said Hereto. 'The food and drink will be a pleasant way to end it.'

'Yes, it's past midnight,' noted Naldy. 'You're back so late. A long day doing what?'

Barbra reluctantly took a seat, ignoring Naldy's probing question. Naldy served them each a generous slice of pie and filled their glasses with apple cider.

'This is delicious,' said Hereto, savouring each bite.

'My grandmother's recipe,' said Naldy, glad the boy appreciated it.

In her imagination, Naldy had pictured the four of them merrily eating and conversing—but nobody was speaking. Barbra and Hereto were occupied with nourishing themselves with food and drink, showing little interest in engaging in conversation.

Naldy eyed Ralph—hoping to enlist his help in breaking the silence—but he, too, was busy savouring his meal.

'That was lovely,' said Hereto, placing his cutlery on his empty plate.

'There's seconds,' said Naldy quickly.

'Go on then,' replied Hereto eagerly.

'Me too, please,' said Ralph, holding out his plate.

Naldy served Hereto and Ralph a second slice of the pie.

'More for you, Barbra?' asked Naldy.

'You will have to give me the recipe,' replied Barbra, dabbing the napkin at the corners of her mouth before placing her wrinkled hands on the table to support herself as she stood. 'It is late, and I must go to bed. I have a big day tomorrow.'

'Another big day?' asked Naldy. 'What have you both been so busy with?'

The old woman remained still, pursing her thin lips.

'Perhaps it's something we could help with,' Naldy continued. 'Whatever it is, we want to help. We should work together.'

'Together,' said Barbra, returning an icy smile. 'It

seems, dear, anyone who works alongside you winds up dead.'

Naldy felt a sharp pang of guilt at Barbra's words. She knew the old witch was referring to her sister—Betty.

'That isn't fair,' said Ralph, appalled by the woman's assertion. 'We have both spent our time trying to protect the Devante. Naldy wants to save magic.'

'Little saving has been achieved,' replied Barbra sourly. 'Before you both turned up at my front door in Heatherton, the Devante were almost all still in existence. Every Devante you have tried to protect has fallen into Maverick's hands.'

'How can you say that so indifferently,' said Ralph, 'when you unquestioningly handed Maverick Metallum?'

'Let me ask you this in return, boy,' said Barbra hoarsely, 'how can you stand so loyally beside her when even your own cousin finished up at the bottom of a lake.'

'Rupert is alive,' said Ralph.

'With little thanks to Naldy,' said Barbra. 'I believe I am right in saying that when she possessed the power to bring Rupert back—she refused to. Those who are closest to her seem destined for a bitter end.'

'You have the power to resurrect your sister,' challenged Ralph.

'My sister made it extremely clear that she had no desire to live forever,' said Barbra, her eyes pooling with tears.

'We want to help,' said Naldy softly.

'Your help is not wanted—not here,' said Barbra. With those final words, she smiled, winked at Hereto, and tottered out of the kitchen.

Naldy's guilt felt raw, as if an old stitched wound had been re-opened.

'She doesn't mean it,' said Hereto with a tenderness.

'But she has a fair point,' said Naldy, tears trickling down her cheeks. 'The Devante are mostly gone, and so many who helped me are gone too.'

'Those who died trying to protect the Devante,' said Hereto, 'did so because they believed in saving the magic. You mustn't blame yourself.'

'All this time,' said Naldy, dabbing her cheeks with a napkin, 'I have achieved nothing. Barbra is right.'

'Barbra has made many foolish decisions herself along the way,' said Hereto. 'Choices which have directly led to Maverick getting hold of the Devante. She seeks someone else to take the blame for the part she has played. She is still grieving the death of her sister.'

'Maverick has the Corium,' said Naldy, matter-of-factly. 'If Barbra doesn't want my help, perhaps it is time for me to make my way to Edengar, as I had always planned.'

'Go fetch your travelling cloaks,' said Hereto.

'Whatever for?' asked Ralph. 'No, we're not leaving.'

'Barbra may believe you both to be a troublesome

burden,' said Hereto, 'but it's obvious that you care about defeating Maverick. I will show you what we have been working on.'

'You will?' asked Ralph, surprised. 'When?'

'Now,' said Hereto. 'Barbra has retired for the evening. There may not be another chance. Perhaps showing you will provide you with some peace.'

'Must we venture into the forest this late?' asked Ralph. 'Can't you simply tell us? If there are thirds, I'd quite like another slice.'

'I'll fetch our cloaks,' said Naldy, ignoring Ralph as she made for the door.

A short while later, they assembled at the entrance to the broomstick shop. It was a warm night, and the sky above was clear, twinkling with bright stars.

'This way,' instructed Hereto, leading them through the quiet street towards the forest.

'Well, we didn't need our cloaks,' said Ralph, draping it over his shoulders, the arms of the outer garment hanging loosely.

Naldy walked with her black cloak over her arm. She still felt bruised by Barbra's cruel words.

'Do you trust him?' asked Naldy.

'Hereto?' said Ralph. 'He's showing us the secret, isn't he?'

'Yes,' she replied, 'and I know that was the goal, but I'm not sure whose side Hereto is truly on. Barbra's or ours?'

'Neither, I'd say,' Ralph said, stepping from the cobbled stones onto the dirt path leading beneath the tall pines. 'I think Hereto just wants to protect magic. Besides, we're on the same side—remember?'

'What does it matter, Ralph,' replied Naldy, drooping her head so that her long black hair fell over her cheekbones. 'Barbra won't allow us to help them. The pie failed to bring us all together.'

'Don't allow the old woman's words to dig in,' said Ralph. 'The death and the destruction—all that is not your fault. It belongs to Maverick, and deep down, Barbra knows it.'

'This way,' called Hereto from up ahead.

'Look,' said Ralph, nodding towards Hereto, who was guiding them away from the winding path and deeper into the forest. 'Our goal was to find out what they've been up to. Your grandmother's pumpkin pie has successfully helped achieve that objective.'

Naldy felt her lips curve into a smile.

As there was no longer any path to follow, they needed to stay close to Hereto to keep track of him. They wound through the endless pine trees, with the moonlight shining silver above.

'Where did he go?' asked Ralph, as they'd lost sight of the young witch. 'Is he trying to get us lost?'

'I'm here,' called Hereto, somehow now behind them.

They spun around to find the young witch standing before a large, circular portal. It hovered just above the ground, nearly as tall as Naldy. The rim of the portal glimmered gold, and the centre appeared to be made from an opaque, shimmering glass.

'What is that?' asked Ralph, his blue eyes wide with a mix of fear and wonder.

'This is our plan to see Maverick defeated,' said Hereto proudly.

Naldy gazed curiously at the glass. Something shifted behind it, and as she stepped closer, a faint humming emanated from the mysterious circle.

'What does it do?' asked Ralph, taking a cautionary step backwards.

'It looks like some sort of portal,' said Naldy, trying to perceive what was moving behind the glass.

'A portal that leads to where?' asked Ralph suspiciously. 'I'm not stepping foot inside that thing.'

Hereto gestured at the glass circle, inviting them to walk through it. Ralph appeared disinclined to draw any nearer. Naldy, on the other hand, eagerly moved closer until her slanted nose was mere inches from it.

'How does it work?' asked Naldy, close enough to see the blurred reflection of her face in the shimmering surface.

'You just step through,' said Hereto.

'Why couldn't we see this before? We followed you both so many times,' asked Naldy. 'And what's on the other side?'

'To answer your first question,' said Hereto, 'the portal must be summoned. As for your second, take a look for yourself.'

As she lifted her hands, the glass seemed to

transform into a gas-like substance. She stepped through, expecting some secret weapon—some machine or contraption—to be waiting on the other side, but she wasn't prepared for what she encountered.

—Chapter Twenty—

THE ARMOUR OF HEXOGG & HERETO

Naldy found herself standing on a sloped hill. Far below, moonlight illuminated a large clearing in the pine forest where the trees appeared to have recently been felled and stacked at one end. An army of about four hundred people clad in metal armour moved about a camp. Many circular pavilion tents had been pitched, and scattered between them were outdoor fire pits, their flames crackling as soldiers warmed their hands.

'What do you think?' asked Hereto, who had stepped through the portal after Naldy, his young face beaming proudly.

'Where did you find all these people?' she asked, astounded by the number of armoured men and women.

'Lieutenant,' said a large man approaching, addressing Hereto. He offered Hereto a rigid salute. Like the others in the camp, the man was clad in heavy armour. He had a head of thick, dark, wavy hair and a long scar running down his left cheek—a deep wound that had healed long ago.

'How are things coming along, General?' asked

Hereto.

'We are well prepared for battle,' reported the Lieutenant, bowing his head so that his black hair fell over his broad forehead. 'We await your command.'

'This is Lieutenant Naldy,' said Hereto, nodding towards her. 'Meet General Huegon.'

The brawny man straightened his posture again and raised an arm in salute to her. Naldy nodded somewhat awkwardly.

'Inform the armourer we will require two suits,' said Hereto. 'And have a tent prepared with two beds.'

'Will you be spending the night?' asked Huegon in a gruff voice.

'Not I,' said Hereto, looking over his shoulder at the portal. 'Lieutenant Naldy and our dear friend Ralph will be.'

'As you wish,' saluted Huegon, before marching down the slope.

'We don't intend on staying here,' said Naldy.

'If you want to offer your help, then staying is your only option. Barbra will not accept your assistance—certainly not after the argument at dinner. You'll need to stay here and out of Barbra's sight. She mustn't know you're here if you want to be involved.'

'Involved with what?' asked Naldy. 'And where is Ralph?'

'Working up the courage to step through, I suppose,' said Hereto. 'Any day now, we march to

The Establishment's palace.'

'You're going to start a war with Maverick,' said Naldy.

'It is Maverick that has started the war on magic,' replied Hereto. 'We intend to finish it.'

'Maverick has the guards on his side—they are all witches. Your army is impressive, but you won't defeat Maverick with townsfolk dressed in armour.'

'They are not townsfolk,' said Hereto smiling.

'Witches?' asked Naldy, noticing that none of the members of the camp carried any weapons. 'But where did you find all of these witches to fight? People are afraid to stand up against The Establishment. There must be hundreds of people down there.'

'Over four hundred,' said Hereto. He paused, somewhat nervously, and took a breath. 'They are not quite witches, though. And not quite people either.'

'Not people?' repeated Naldy. 'What have you done? Have you resurrected an army of the dead?'

'That was our initial plan, yes,' said Hereto. 'But we weren't able to achieve it. You see, to revive the dead, one must first break the *Banned Spell of Death*. We've failed to break those spells.'

'We brought back Rupert,' came Ralph's voice from behind them. Hereto and Naldy both jumped at the sound of his concerned voice. Ralph had, at some unknown point, come through the portal and had been listening to them. 'The *Banned Spell of Death* prevents resurrecting those you do not know.

However, you can still bring back those known to you without breaking the *Banned Spells*.'

'You made it through,' said Naldy.

'Yes,' said Ralph, his voice cracking with anxiety, 'and we should return to the other side. Away from those soulless creatures Hereto and Barbra have created.'

'Soulless?' questioned Naldy.

'I suspect Hereto and Barbra do not personally know this many who have died,' said Ralph.

'What are you getting at?' asked Naldy, unsettled by the fear on his face.

'If they have failed to break the *Banned Spell of Death,* they would not have been able to resurrect people they didn't personally know. The ban wouldn't allow it. This means the army below us is not made up of acquaintances of Barbra or Hereto— the army below us is not human.'

'You are right, Ralph,' said Hereto, smiling at the camp. 'The army are creatures of our own invention.'

'What do you mean creatures?' asked Naldy. 'They all *seem* human.'

'Before a few days ago, they were neither living nor dead,' explained Hereto. 'They did not exist. They have never been human. Ralph is right, we have created them.'

'Created them?' asked Naldy. 'But from what?'

'From the magic of H,' Ralph said, his voice cracking nervously again.

'The ghouls are creations of our own

imagination,' Hereto said proudly, nodding to confirm that Ralph had guessed correctly.

'They look real enough,' said Naldy.

'They are here but not quite as real as you or I. They are made of flesh and blood, and have free will. They think and feel, yes, but they lack a history. They are good fighters—exceptional, even—but they don't have souls.'

'I wouldn't have guessed that Barbra had the creativity,' remarked Ralph.

'I come from a long line of Heretos,' said the young boy, lifting his chin. 'Imagination courses through my veins.'

'So, this was your idea,' said Naldy. 'Creating these human-like things without any souls?'

'I have said it all along, we must attack with force.'

'Why haven't you already stormed the palace then?' asked Naldy. 'You appear to have everything you need. What's been the delay?'

'Maverick's guards cannot be defeated without magic,' said Ralph.

Naldy recalled the time The Establishment guards had chased them through the museum. They were indeed skilled with magic, and she agreed that no army could defeat them unless they too possessed powers.

'Hereto said they were witches,' she pressed. 'So, can't they perform witchcraft?'

'The ghouls are not quite witches,' replied Hereto, frowning. 'At least, not yet.'

Naldy raised an eyebrow as the young boy bounced back and forth on the balls of his feet. She didn't understand what Hereto meant by *not quite witches.*

'The Devante,' said Ralph, answering her bewildered look, 'can give or take life without breaking the *Banned Spell,* just as we did with Rupert, but—'

'—But the caveat is that you must *know* the person,' said Naldy, beginning to realise the issue. Barbra couldn't use the magic of H to grant permanent magical ability because she didn't know the ghouls.

Naldy watched a soldier in a white linen shirt, buttons half undone, cross the clearing and disappear into one of the tents, evidently heading to bed. She found it odd that these creatures needed sleep.

Hereto had found a loophole: they were able to create these four hundred soldiers precisely because they were not truly people, but soulless creatures. Yet even this workaround couldn't grant them lasting magical power.

'If you don't know them,' added Ralph, clearly mulling over the same thoughts as Naldy, 'they must be within sight for you to give them power. But it's temporary—only while you're present.'

Naldy stared at the busy camp. The low hum of soldiers conversing around the crackle of campfires reached them at the top of the hill. The occasional throaty laugh rose above the murmur of the soldiers. They sounded like real people.

'Barbra has been able to use the magic of H,' continued Hereto, 'to temporarily gift members of the army magical abilities. If Barbra is here and focused—well, you should see them—they are exceptional at duelling. I've never witnessed such skill in battle before. We've practised on the ground and on brooms.'

'And when Barbra is not with the army?' asked Naldy.

'They are stripped of their power. They are as useful in warfare as the twigs beneath our feet.'

Naldy squinted, mulling over their dilemma. She knew it would be far too risky to go to war with The Establishment if the army's ability to defend itself depended on one witch's presence at the battle.

'You're still trying to break the *Banned Spell of Death,*' said Naldy, putting the pieces together. 'Which would allow you to gift each soldier permanent magical ability. Barbra would not need to be with them.'

'Yes,' admitted Hereto. 'Then, Barbra can remain safely at a distance while the army does their work.'

'But you created them,' said Naldy, wrinkling her forehead. 'They are all here now, so you can get to know them. That way, you won't have to break the *Banned Spell of Death.* If you know them personally, you can grant them magic of their own.'

'They don't have histories,' said Hereto sadly. 'We have tried, believe me. They may act and look like people, but Ralph is right—they have no souls. We can never truly know them, for they do not possess a past. The only way forward is to break the *Banned Spell* or for Barbra to fight alongside them.'

'Well,' said Ralph. 'Thank you for showing us. We wish you all the best. Let us head back to the city.'

'Hereto has ordered a tent to be prepared,' said Naldy.

'We are not staying,' said Ralph, his eyes darting uneasily towards the moonlit camp below.

'You'll find the tents quite comfortable,' said Hereto. 'If you wish to help, you must stay here. Barbra will not allow you to be involved, and I may have little chance to inform you of our progress. From here, you can witness everything. That said, the portal is open if you would rather return.'

Hereto made his way down the hill towards the bustle of the campsite. Naldy eagerly went after him, while Ralph reluctantly trudged behind.

Although it was a warm night, the soldiers gathered around the outdoor fires, drinking from metal mugs. Some were still clad in shiny metal armour, while others had changed into loose linen shirts. Those who noticed Hereto passing halted their conversations to salute the young boy. Hereto occasionally returned a courteous nod in their direction.

'Barbra and I will be back early tomorrow morning,' said Hereto. 'You must stay out of sight.'

'What is happening tomorrow morning?' asked Ralph, staring at the soldiers suspiciously.

'Training,' replied the young witch. 'You'll need

to be dressed in armour to avoid attention. She'll be furious with me if she knows you're hiding out here. This is yours.'

Hereto stopped in front of a large circular pavilion tent.

'Why are you allowing us to stay?' asked Naldy. 'Why help us?'

'Because,' said Hereto, 'although Barbra would never admit it, we are all on the same side.'

The bulky man, Huegon, emerged from the tent's opening. Seeing Hereto, he straightened his posture and offered another enthusiastic salute.

'I hope you'll find your quarters comfortable, Lieutenant Naldy,' said Huegon.

'It's much appreciated,' replied Naldy.

'We will let you both settle in,' said Hereto. 'Come, General Huegon, allow me to show you tomorrow's training plans. We require more practice on the ground.'

Hereto and Huegon departed, making their way through the camp.

'We're not seriously spending the night?' said Ralph. 'I don't like the idea of living alongside these ghouls.'

'Ralph, if we want to take part in the final battle,' said Naldy, pulling back the tent's opening, 'we don't have any other option.'

'We could return to *Hereto's*,' suggested Ralph, 'we could focus our efforts on convincing Barbra to revisit Maverick's memories.'

'Barbra's distrust of us runs deep,' said Naldy,

gesturing for him to enter the tent. Ralph did not move. 'They may manage to break the *Banned Spell* any day now. We don't have the time to earn her trust.'

'You think storming The Establishment is going to work?'

'I don't know, Ralph. But if they are going to war with Maverick, I'd like to be there.'

'It goes against everything Betty believed in,' said Ralph. 'Bringing a war may not end the witch hunt—not if we lose.'

'What other options do we have?' said Naldy. 'Are you staying or making your way back up the hill?'

Ralph sighed and entered the pavilion tent. Naldy followed, letting the canvas opening drop closed.

The tent was large enough for them to stand comfortably inside. Various cowhide rugs had been laid across the ground. There were two comfortable beds, their wooden frames carved from the forest's pine trees. Near the entrance was a circular table with two dining chairs displaying elegant carvings of acorns and grapevines. Three large candelabras cast a soft glow over the space.

Naldy settled into one of the dining chairs, slumping her elbows onto the table. She pondered if Ralph was right—was an army the wrong way to go about defeating Maverick? Betty had seemed to think fighting would make matters worse. Then again, if they didn't fight alongside the others, they might miss their last opportunity to help protect the magic of H.

Ralph sat opposite Naldy.

'The room is cosy,' said Ralph. 'Still, I don't know how I'll sleep knowing the camp is full of ghouls.'

Naldy listened to the fading hum of the camp filtering through the tent's canvas as the soldiers retired for the night. The deep breaths of a noisy snorer could be heard from a nearby tent. Once again, she was astounded by how human-like the ghouls were.

'Do you think they'll really go to war?' asked Ralph.

'If Barbra can manage to break the *Banned Spells*,' replied Naldy. 'I can't see the Seagull Society standing much of a chance against Barbra's ghouls once she grants them all powers. Maverick and his followers will finally get what they deserve.'

Ralph fiddled with the corner of the pinewood table, his expression glazed. Naldy knew by this look that he was thinking of his cousin.

'He made up his mind,' said Naldy, running her fingers over Betty's white pearl necklace. 'Nobody forced him to take the Society's side, and if Rupert chooses to fight alongside Maverick, then whatever happens to him is his own doing.'

Ralph scowled as he stood. He took a few flustered steps before stopping, his lips stretched thin with displeasure. He opened his mouth to speak, but changed his mind and settled on one of the twin beds.

Though Naldy knew she wasn't to blame for Rupert's betrayal, guilt still rose inside her. Neither spoke, allowing a few quiet moments to pass between them.

'We should get some rest,' mumbled Naldy, making her way to the other twin bed.

'If there is a war,' said Ralph softly, 'nothing good will come of it.'

Chapter Twenty-One

TRAINING THE OFFENSIVE

The high-pitched wail of a bugle woke them early the following day. Naldy pulled her pillow over her head to dampen the sound of the brass instrument until it stopped.

'These must be for us,' said Ralph excitedly, climbing out of bed and approaching two beautifully crafted suits of armour displayed on upright stands near the tent's entrance. 'Someone must have brought these in during the night. There are freshly laundered shirts and trousers, too.'

Naldy sat upright, rubbing her sleepy eyes. The sounds of a busy campsite penetrated through the tent's canvas.

'The armour is surprisingly light,' said Ralph as he finished changing into the uniform.

The metal armour gave Ralph a dignified appearance.

'There's a note on the table,' he said, unfolding the parchment. 'It says breakfast is served in the dining hall at a quarter past six sharp. You'd better get up and get ready then. I'll wait for you outside.'

Ralph departed the sleeping quarters to give

Naldy some privacy. The shiny metal suit was expertly crafted and was—as Ralph had said—unexpectedly lightweight. When Naldy made her way outside, Ralph's mouth dropped open upon seeing her.

'You look like a warrior,' said Ralph, the campsite bustling around them.

'You look a little too excited,' replied Naldy. 'Last night, you were frightened of the ghouls.'

'I realised something,' said Ralph as they set off through the crowded camp. 'The ghouls can't perform magic without Barbra's presence. And if she manages to break the *Banned Spells,* then there won't be any need to go to war—Barbra could simply do away with Maverick from afar. Come, one of them told me the dining hall was this way.'

They wove their way through the humming camp, the golden sun reflecting off the many suits of armour teeming around them. The tall pine trees surrounded the large clearing.

The dining hall was at the edge of the encampment, an enormous pavilion tent with five rows of long wooden tables. It was extremely noisy underneath the tent's canopy as the many men and women in battle attire conversed while eating breakfast. Ralph and Naldy made their way along the rows until they found two empty seats together. Each place at the table had a deep metal bowl filled with cooked oats waiting to be eaten. The gloopy meal reminded Naldy of the congealed oats they'd once been served when locked in the bird cages of the Greenswood prison.

'They have the magic of H,' said Ralph, tilting his spoon so the sloppy oats fell back into his bowl with an unappetising plop. 'You'd think they could invent a more appealing breakfast for their soldiers?'

'Something keeps playing on my mind,' said Naldy, as Ralph reached for a jar of honey. 'All that talk of *Banned Spells* yesterday—I keep wondering why Maverick still hasn't cast a spell to undo magic. What if he doesn't have the Corium.'

'Naldy,' replied Ralph, spooning large amounts of honey onto his oats. 'You said you saw the Seagull Society leaving Mortous's castle, heading for The Great City.'

'Yes, but how can we be certain they made it there with the magic? Perhaps the Corium never reached The Great City. What if it never reached Maverick?'

'Maverick has the Corium,' said Ralph flatly, placing his spoon down and facing her. 'I know you don't want to believe it, but the fact is, he does.'

She returned his gaze for a moment but glanced away irritably. As she observed the many soldiers finishing their breakfast, Naldy marvelled at the powers of the Devante.

During their time at Hereto's, she had often wondered why Maverick hadn't appeared to be using the powers of the Corium. Something must be preventing him from breaking the *Banned Spells*— but what was it?

'Barbra and Hereto have managed all this,' Naldy mumbled aloud, turning back to Ralph. 'What has

Maverick done?'

'Furnished his palace,' replied Ralph.

'Something must be stopping him from doing more, though.'

'Do you want some honey?' he asked, almost knocking over his bowl of mushy breakfast, which now contained as much honey as oats. He leant closer to her, his expression animated. 'What if the reason Maverick hasn't broken the *Banned Spells*... is because he can't?'

'If he has the Corium,' replied Naldy, rolling her eyes, 'then he has the highest-ranking Devante.'

'H was born four minutes before Corium,' continued Ralph.

A few noisy soldiers passed the table. Naldy considered Ralph's words. H was the elder twin by only a few minutes—but then she remembered that Maverick had briefly undone magic while they were on the ship, and doing so would have required him to undo the *Banned Spells*.

'He used the Corium in Arkus Day,' said Naldy.

'At that stage,' said Ralph, 'perhaps the Corium was temporarily the highest-ranking Devante.'

'What do you mean, *temporarily?*'

'When we were in Arkus Day, Naldy, the magic of H was inactive: half resided in Betty, the other half in Barbra. When Betty died, the two halves reunited. What if, from that moment, H became the highest-ranking Devante?'

'That would also explain why Grace was sentenced to the stake,' said Naldy. 'Remember the newspaper? We wondered why Maverick would sentence one of his own to death—Grace had interfered with his plans.'

'He needs to find H,' said Ralph, growing excited as they pieced things together. 'Maverick cannot undo the *Banned Spells* with the Corium since it no longer holds the highest-ranking status. He needs H to break them.'

'He needs Barbra,' replied Naldy, 'but it seems that even with the magic of H, she still cannot break the spells.'

'She'll manage it eventually,' said Ralph.

'That's right, Lieutenant,' said a gruff voice behind them. Naldy and Ralph turned to see Huegon. In the light, she could more clearly see the deep scar on his cheek. 'Which means the Field Marshal should be able to grant us permanent powers.'

'Field Marshal?' queried Ralph.

'He means Barbra,' said Naldy.

'She will be arriving shortly,' said Huegon with a serious tone. 'Training will begin on the field, and I've been instructed by Lieutenant Hereto to advise you both that it would be wise to stay out of sight.'

'Of course,' agreed Naldy.

Huegon gave them a suspicious glance before saluting them and making his way from the tent.

'Should we head to the field?' asked Ralph, pushing his unfinished breakfast aside.

'I guess,' said Naldy, lifting herself from the wooden bench. 'I wonder why Barbra has had so much trouble breaking these *Banned Spells?*'

'Perhaps,' said Ralph, standing and stretching his back, 'for the same reason you had so much trouble breaking it.'

'I never tried to break them.'

'When we stayed at *The Golden Opulent* with Betty in The Great City,' said Ralph. 'You wanted Maverick dead, remember.'

'Yes, but I barely tried, and it's fair to say Barbra has less of a conscience than I do. It sounds as if she has spent much time attempting and yet, for some reason, is still failing.'

'Let's get to the field to see what these ghouls are capable of,' said Ralph as they made their way along the rows of soldiers still finishing their breakfast.

They continued through the campsite with its many tents. A few soldiers stood to attention and saluted as they passed.

'How do they know we're lieutenants?' asked Ralph, waving awkwardly at a stern male soldier who had stopped and held his hand rigidly to his forehead.

'You're not a lieutenant,' replied Naldy.

'What do you mean?' asked Ralph. 'If you're a lieutenant, I'm obviously a lieutenant.'

'You're not,' said Naldy dryly.

'If you are. I certainly am, too.'

'The soldiers know I'm a lieutenant because of my armour,' said Naldy. 'The shape is different in the shoulders, see, it points out. Yours is more rounded.'

'Must have been an oversight,' said Ralph,

chewing his lip and staring at his shoulders, displeased. 'Why would Hereto grant you the privilege of being a lieutenant but not myself?'

'Maybe you could ask him when we see him,' said Naldy as they headed in the direction the rest of the soldiers were moving.

The field, as Huegon had called it, turned out to be more of an arena. Long benches of raked wooden seating surrounded a large rectangular area of dry dirt. Soldiers filled the seats and chatted noisily with each other.

'There's Barbra,' said Ralph, pointing across the stadium to a private seating area where Barbra was positioned on an oversized, almost throne-like chair. 'Where do you think Hereto is?'

'Hereto told you to stay out of sight,' said the young witch himself, standing behind them. Hereto was dressed in gleaming silver armour. 'You're both seated opposite Barbra. Move across so you're not in her direct line of sight.'

Naldy and Ralph wove their way between the rows of benches, Hereto trailing behind.

'This should do,' said Hereto. 'I'd best be getting to the other side. Training will commence soon, and Barbra will wonder where I've gone. It's a pity they're doing groundwork today, for the ghouls' true talents are in the air.'

'Before you go,' said Ralph, making himself comfortable on the bench. 'I think there may have been a mistake. They seem to have issued me the incorrect armour.'

'It looks fine to me,' noted Hereto.

'But you see, I have the rounded shoulders,' said Ralph.

'And a fine job they have done,' said Hereto, admiring the craftsmanship of the uniform.

'But ought they not to be pointed like Naldy's?' asked Ralph.

'Naldy comes from the bloodline of Hale,' said Hereto, matter-of-factly. 'She is related to the Field Marshal. You were born to simple townsfolk in the east, and you happen to have recently had the rare luck of being united with an Imporiom.'

Ralph returned a sour smile as Hereto nodded cheekily before departing, weaving through the rows of chatting soldiers who stood and saluted as he passed.

'Simple townsfolk,' grumbled Ralph, 'and after all I've done in service of protecting the Devante.'

'Don't let it bother you,' said Naldy. 'In my opinion, it was foolish of Hereto to make me a lieutenant, especially if he meant for us to stay out of sight. Everyone keeps stopping to salute me. Hardly helps us to remain unnoticed by Barbra.'

They expected Hereto to join Barbra in the private booth, but several minutes later, the young witch marched into the arena's centre. The ghouls fell silent, standing to attention. Hereto saluted, and everyone returned their bottoms to their seats.

'Rows E through F,' called Hereto.

The soldiers from the two rows Hereto had announced began entering the arena—one of them the very row where they had first taken their seats. Naldy counted fifteen soldiers, both men and women, all wearing stern expressions.

The young witch made his way into the private booth to sit beside Barbra. The soldiers from rows E through F stood rigidly in the arena, their metal plates reflecting the hot sun. They appeared to be waiting for something.

'When does the training begin?' asked Ralph.

Just as he had finished asking the question, fifty guards appeared magically in the arena, all neatly dressed in The Establishment-issued blazers, complete with blue porkpie hats. The soldiers were outnumbered.

'Where did they come from?' asked Ralph, rubbing his eyes.

'Barbra,' said Naldy, nodding in the old woman's direction.

Calmly seated in her ostentatious chair, Barbra appeared entirely untroubled by the arrival of Maverick's guards. Naldy knew she must have created them using the magic of H.

They both jumped in fright as a loud bang erupted. It soon became clear that the boom signalled the start of training—a duel between the guards and the soldiers. The whizzing and whirring of many colourful spells were joined by a thunderous roar from the excitable onlookers as they cheered and shouted across the field.

Naldy and Ralph ducked as a jet of brilliant purple flew in their direction. As it turned out, the spell evaporated before it even reached them, and Naldy realised the arena had been hexed so that no spells could travel beyond an invisible border surrounding the inner field. Still, whenever a ball of blazing light hurtled towards them, Naldy and Ralph instinctively recoiled in fear.

Hereto's account of the ghouls' impressive ability to wield magic in combat was entirely truthful. They moved across the field with quick steps, twisting and twirling to avoid the many spells streaking across the arena like shooting stars. Coloured jets of light burst from their outstretched palms with astonishing speed, seeking out the blue-blazered guards with surprising accuracy. While Naldy was impressed by the soldiers' skill in casting spells, it was clear that their true strength lay in deflecting them.

'It will be over quickly,' remarked Ralph, wincing as one of the soldier's brilliant green spells collided with the chest of one of the guards.

In a matter of minutes, the majority of The Establishment guards had been forced out of the duel, having been met with one of the ghouls' spells. The defeated lay either paralysed or unconscious in the dirt. Only three Establishment guards were still in the fight, and they had all but one of Barbra's fifteen armoured ghouls to contend with.

'Look,' said Ralph, pointing to the booth where Barbra and Hereto were seated.

A circular portal had emerged in the booth beside Barbra's grand chair. It was similar to the one they'd climbed through in the Kirkwood Forest to reach the hidden army camp. It had a shimmering glass-like appearance and a shiny golden rim.

'Where do you think she's going?' asked Ralph, as a whirling ball of amber struck another guard, knocking him out of the fight. His blue porkpie hat toppled into the dry dirt.

'Do you think she's broken the *Banned Spell?*' asked Naldy. 'Has she gifted them power?'

They watched as Barbra climbed through the portal and vanished. Below, in the dirt field, the answer to Naldy's question became clear. The fourteen upright soldiers thrust their palms forward into the air—but no magic was expelled.

The two remaining blue-blazered guards glanced at each other, and their cowardly expressions turned to grins. In unison, they immediately discharged a deluge of bloodthirsty spells. Clangs vibrated across the arena as high-speed flashes of light from the two remaining guards collided with the soldiers' metal armour. Howls of agony rang out over the shouting from the crowd as each soldier in the arena, one by one, was wounded by a guard's unforgiving spell.

'Do ghouls feel pain?' asked Ralph, wincing.

'Judging by those horrible cries, I believe they might.'

It was all over. The fifteen soldiers from rows E through F lay injured in the dirt, unable to stand. The crowd fell silent.

Barbra re-emerged from the portal. Seeing the

beaten soldiers, her face became stony, and her eyes narrowed. The crowd remained still, waiting for their next instruction. She had once again failed to break the *Banned Spell*.

From their position, Naldy could see Barbra and Hereto engaged in a tense conversation. After a brief moment, Barbra broke away, approaching the edge of the private booth to address the crowd.

'The time has come,' called Barbra, as the soldiers exchanged whispers. 'Prepare for battle. Today, we march.'

Barbra turned and walked through the portal, with Hereto following after her. Once they stepped through the circular floating glass threshold, the portal vanished.

'Battle?' said Ralph as the soldiers exited the field. 'What does she mean, *battle?* We just witnessed her fail to break the *Banned Spell*. They can't go to war.'

'She's impatient,' said Naldy, standing. 'She plans on marching with them.'

'But she mustn't,' exclaimed Ralph. 'If Maverick captures her, he will take the magic of H. We cannot let him get his hands on the highest-ranking Devante.'

'We won't,' said Naldy, making her way along the row of wooden seats, Ralph trailing after her. 'We must talk her out of it.'

The camp was soon alive with the sound of soldiers readying for combat. There was excitement and nervousness as the ghouls prepared: polishing their armour, stretching, and packing large wicker baskets with supplies.

'Where are we going?' asked Ralph, pursuing Naldy as she marched through the noisy crowd. The sun was still shining hot.

'I told you already,' said Naldy. 'We need to speak with Barbra. She'll be at *Hereto's*.'

She led them up the hill to the edge of the army camp, where they had first entered through the portal. They were surprised to discover there was no floating glass circle. Instead, Huegon stood, leaning casually on a pine tree.

'General Huegon,' said Naldy. 'We need to get through the portal. Where has it gone?'

'There is no portal, Lieutenant,' replied the General with an odd smile.

'The portal we came through yesterday,' said Naldy insistently. 'Where has it gone?'

'Hereto and Barbra have ordered the portal to be sealed off for now,' declared Huegon.

'Well, then we will simply walk,' said Ralph.

'Walk?' chortled Huegon. 'You are no longer in the Kirkwood Forest. The walk will take you many months.'

'We came through the portal from Kirkwood Forest,' said Naldy.

'Yes,' said Huegon. 'It has transported you here.'

'Here?' asked Ralph

'This pine forest is deep within the Edengar Mountains.'

'Edengar?' repeated Ralph, his voice cracking with nervousness.

They both turned to take in the view from the hill. When they'd first arrived, it had been night, but now, in the sunlight, they could see the vast snow-capped mountains encircling them. The bustling camp below was surrounded by tall pine trees, which looked much like the ones that grew in the Kirkwood Forest.

'You must allow us through the portal, Huegon,' demanded Ralph, his face creased with worry. 'We need to get back to The Great City. We must warn Barbra.'

'The Field Marshal has given me strict instructions,' said Huegon. 'You will both be staying here.'

'Instructions from Barbra?' repeated Naldy. 'Does she know we are here?'

'It was her idea to bring you here,' said Huegon.

'Her idea?' asked Ralph. 'Hereto brought us here.'

'On the Field Marshal's instructions, yes. She wants you kept here in Edengar while the battle commences.'

'Kept here!' exclaimed Naldy.

'Yes, they believe you both to be a liability. The plan was to bring you here and to keep you here, where you cannot interfere.'

'You don't understand, Huegon,' pleaded Naldy. 'Barbra is planning on storming the steps of The Establishment. She is going to risk the Devante's magic.'

'Marching alongside us is the only way,' said Huegon calmly. He acknowledged someone behind them with a nod. 'Ah, good, just in time.'

Naldy felt her shoulders and arms held firmly by soldiers who had approached from behind them. She saw that Ralph had also been restrained.

'Listen to me, Huegon,' said Naldy desperately. 'Maverick needs the magic of H because it is the highest-ranking Devante. Barbra must not risk being present at the battle. She must focus on breaking the *Banned Spell* so she can gift the army powers without needing to be there herself.'

'She cannot break the *Banned Spell*,' said Huegon.

'She must continue to try,' pleaded Naldy.

'Take them to the hold,' instructed Huegon, wiping beads of sweat from his brow.

'H was born four minutes before Corium,' said Ralph, glowering at Huegon. 'Betty's half has been reunited with Barbra's.'

'Take them,' instructed Huegon.

'Naldy is a lieutenant,' shouted Ralph. 'She outranks you, General.'

Huegon raised his hand to inform the soldiers to wait a moment. He took a step closer to Naldy.

'Yes, she is a lieutenant,' said Huegon, running his hand over the shoulder of Naldy's pointed armour. 'The reason you were granted such a privileged status wasn't because you earned it. No, it was to make it easy for us to monitor your whereabouts. Barbra and Hereto, together, planned to bring you here. She knew all along Hereto was bringing you here last night. Do you think Barbra failed to see the saluting crowds as you moved through them? I'm not sure if you've noticed, but Hereto is the only lieutenant of this army. Though you may outrank us, the order to detain you has come directly from someone higher: the Field Marshal.'

'You're making a mistake,' said Naldy, trying to shake herself free from the firm hold of the soldiers.

'You are mistaken,' said Huegon, the scar on his left cheek wrinkling as he smirked. 'H is not the highest-ranking Devante. When Hannah Hale gave birth to twins, the magic of the Devante was split. The two halves must be rejoined to break the *Banned Spells*.'

Naldy felt a lump form in her throat as she listened to Huegon's words—they had been wrong. They had believed that with H's power united, it had become the highest-ranking Devante. But now, Naldy understood: neither half was the highest-ranking.

'The Corium and H were never meant to function separately,' continued Huegon. 'They were one entity, two halves that need to be reunited to break the *Banned Spells*.'

'But we've seen Maverick use the Corium,' said Ralph. 'He used it when we were on the ship, returning from Arkus Day.'

'At that time,' said Naldy, 'the magic of H was inactive, its power split between the Hexogg twins.'

'Yes,' Huegon replied, eyeing Naldy. 'While H's power was inactive, it granted temporary highest-ranking status to the Corium. But now that the magic of H is whole again, both halves—the Corium and H—must be reunited to break any of the *Banned Spells.* Both must be joined to become the highest-ranking Devante. And so, you see, Barbra cannot break them—she has known this for some time. Take them to the hold.'

'Wait,' said Naldy. 'You are overlooking one important detail.'

'What is that?' asked Huegon curiously.

'Without Barbra being present,' said Naldy, 'you ghouls cannot perform magic.'

Naldy kicked hard behind her, forcing the two soldiers holding her arms to release their grip. She sent an electric ball of red light whirring towards Huegon, knocking him backwards with its force.

'But *we* can,' she called.

She conjured a jet of green light, directing it at the soldiers restraining Ralph. Naldy and Ralph found themselves free.

'We've got to go,' shouted Naldy, bounding downhill.

She could hear the metallic whoosh of spells, knowing Ralph was casting more magic to fend off Huegon's soldiers as he followed her into the crowded campsite.

'We need to hide,' said Naldy, leading them into a nearby tent.

She pulled the canvas opening closed and peered out, watching as Huegon's comrades ran past.

Inside, the shelves were lined with medical supplies. A few large wicker baskets were filled with bandages and glass bottles of antiseptic liquid, ready to be taken to the battlefield.

'What now?' asked Ralph, catching his breath.

'Huegon will sound the alarm,' said Naldy. 'The ghouls may be unable to perform spells without Barbra being present, but soon, the whole camp will be looking for us. Even with the advantage of magic, I doubt we can defend ourselves against the entire army.'

'Should we head into the mountains?' suggested Ralph. 'They won't be able to find us there.'

Naldy closed the lid of one of the large baskets and sat. She placed her head in her hands. They had journeyed through the Edengar Mountains before, but they'd had the aid of Odorf and a map to help guide them safely through. Naldy also knew luck had played a pivotal role in their survival when they last trekked through the dangerous terrain of Edengar.

'If we head to the mountains,' said Naldy, 'we may never find our way back to the Kirkwood Forest.'

'We can't stay here,' said Ralph, peeking through the gap in the tent's entrance. Naldy heard more soldiers running past and knew they must be searching for them. 'They'll catch us soon enough.'

'The only way back is through the portal,' said Naldy, gripping the sides of the basket.

'The portal is gone.'

'Yes, but it will return. The ghouls will need to use it to get to The Great City if they plan on storming The Establishment. We need to find some way through it.'

'My vote is for the mountains,' said Ralph, facing her with a concerned expression. 'We need to get far away from this camp. We cannot fight against hundreds of ghouls, Naldy.'

'The baskets,' said Naldy, feeling the intertwined bamboo underneath her fingers. 'We could hide in the baskets. They are planning on taking these to the battlefield. I think this one is large enough to fit us both. Quick, help me empty it.'

Naldy removed the bandages and bottles of antiseptic. Ralph shook his head.

'At least place them neatly,' said Ralph, bending to help. 'We need to arrange them carefully to avoid suspicion.'

The basket was three-quarters empty when they decided there was enough room to climb inside. They crouched low, barely fitting with the remaining medical stock. Naldy pulled the lid shut.

'My leg has cramped already,' said Ralph after being squashed into the confined area for a moment. 'Shouldn't we empty the basket to give us more room?'

'If we take everything out,' said Naldy, 'it may draw suspicion.'

'But it could be ages before the ghouls march to war.'

Naldy opened her mouth to respond, but the sound of someone entering the tent cut her off.

'Clear,' called a gruff soldier's voice. 'Take these supplies to Huegon.'

'Medical supplies?' questioned a female soldier with a stern voice. 'We may have needed these at the camp, but we won't require them once we get to the battle. The Field Marshal is going to grant us permanent powers.'

'No,' replied the gruff soldier. 'They say she didn't manage the breaking of these *Banned Spells*.'

'You mean she'll fight alongside us?' the woman replied.

'Now you see why we must take these,' said the man gravely. 'If something happens to our Field Marshal during the battle, we'll be fighting without magic.'

Naldy's heart pounded in her chest as she felt the basket they were in being lifted from the ground.

The camp was so noisy with soldiers preparing for war that Naldy doubted anyone would hear them if they accidentally coughed or sneezed. Still, they refrained from even whispering. Through the gaps in the wicker basket, Naldy could see the grim faces of the soldiers preparing for battle.

After some time, they felt the movement of the basket come to a halt.

'Medical supplies for the fifth unit,' said the female soldier.

'Open it,' they heard Huegon reply.

Ralph's eyes widened with fear. Naldy reached out and placed her hand over his mouth. The lid of the basket opened, and they felt the sun streaming onto their backs.

The same spell Barbra had used when they were

hiding in the broom cupboard entered Naldy's mind. She wondered why she hadn't thought of the spell sooner to make them invisible.

'The fifth unit, did you say?' asked Huegon.

'Yes,' replied the woman.

'There's space for plenty more,' said Huegon, 'take it back down and fill it up.'

'It's quite heavy to carry up that hill,' replied the woman. 'There's scant time to be adding more and plenty more empty baskets that need filling.'

'Make sure the next ones are filled,' said Huegon. 'Through the portal and follow the others.'

The basket was lifted, and they were moving again. Through its gaps, Naldy watched as they crossed the glass-like portal. Her nostrils were filled with the earthy scent of pine, unmistakably belonging to the trees of the Kirkwood Forest. The familiar smell comforted her until the troubling reality sank in: they were being carried towards the battlefield. They were going to war.

Chapter Twenty-Two

CRY OF THE FIELD MARSHAL

Nervous soldiers clunked noisily in their metal armour. Ralph and Naldy felt the basket lower onto the cobbled stones, but neither dared lift the bamboo lid. Naldy's muscles ached from terrible cramping, and she pressed her eye against a small gap in the woven wicker, catching a glimpse of soldiers hurrying back and forth.

'They all have broomsticks,' whispered Ralph.

'Hereto's contribution, no doubt,' said Naldy, noticing that every soldier held a broomstick with its bristles pointed to the ground.

'We can't hide in here forever,' said Ralph.

The ghouls appeared to be organising themselves into rows in front of the stone steps leading to Maverick's new palace. The afternoon sun was still high in the sky and reflected from their metal breastplates.

Maverick and the Seagull Society were nowhere to be seen, but Naldy glimpsed two distressed Establishment guards retreating through the grand wooden doors of the old museum.

'The ghouls seem distracted enough,' said Naldy.

'Can't you make us invisible again?' pleaded Ralph.

'There are too many people moving about,' said Naldy. 'They'll bump into us, which will only cause more trouble and confusion. It's best we stay visible. Our armour should help us blend in.'

Naldy cautiously lifted the lid of the basket. She was concerned that her pointed armour would draw attention, as it had at the camp, but the soldiers were too anxious preparing for the oncoming battle, and nobody seemed to pay them any attention while they stiffly climbed out of their hiding place. The task of capturing them seemed to have been quickly forgotten as the imminent battle became the ghouls' priority.

'We need to find Barbra,' said Naldy, 'and we better be quick.'

The wide cobbled street was filled with hundreds of soldiers. The basket had been placed near *The Mortismor.* A frightened waiter urgently ushered patrons out of the bistro, while another anxious worker in a black apron locked the windows and drew the blinds.

They wove through the soldiers, who were busy forming rows facing the vacant steps, but could not find the old woman or Hereto amongst all the gleaming armour.

The piercing sound of a bugle rose above the gathering, and the soldiers turned to create a centre parting along their neat military rows.

Barbra, perched sideways on a hovering broomstick, glided along the central aisle. Unlike the others clad in solid silver, Barbra wore a long black shimmering cloak and had a black pointed witch hat. Her back was straight, one wrinkled hand extended to hold the broom's handle, giving her a steely and noble appearance.

'There she is,' remarked Ralph before waving his arms and calling out. 'Barbra!'

The shrill note of the bugle drowned out his voice, and the ghouls nearest them glared distrustfully as they passed.

'Ralph, we are drawing too much attention,' said Naldy, pulling him closer. 'Let's just make our way quietly down this row.'

They hurried along, keeping their faces angled towards the cobbled stones. The soldiers looked puzzled as they shuffled past. Barbra had stopped at the bottom of the steps, hovering a few inches off the ground. She remained focused on Maverick's palace, her posture fearless and heroic.

As Naldy and Ralph approached the centre aisle, the bugle's call came to an echoing finish. Before either could step out into the aisle, the rounded wooden end of a broomstick was thrust out, obstructing them from going further.

'Where do you think you're both off to?' asked a gruff voice belonging to Huegon. 'We thought you had fled into the mountains.'

Ralph seized Naldy's hand and led her back the way they had come. Naldy glanced over her shoulder to see Huegon smirking, but he wasn't pursuing them.

'We are going the wrong way, Ralph,' said Naldy. 'We must get Barbra to safety.'

'Maverick,' rang Barbra's voice above the army. 'You coward! Come out, and let us finish the madness you have unleashed.'

'Let me go, Ralph,' said Naldy, freeing her hand.

'It's too late, Naldy,' said Ralph desperately. 'We have to get out of here.'

'We have to get Barbra to safety before Maverick gets hold of her, and with her, the magic of H. We cannot let Huegon stop us.'

'Don't you see,' replied Ralph anxiously, his blue eyes watering. 'We are too late.'

The grand wooden doors creaked open. Maverick emerged, dressed elegantly in a long, embroidered green cloak, holding his stylish black cane. He was alone, with no sign of any of The Establishment's guards.

'What a pleasant surprise,' said Maverick coldly, stepping calmly down a few steps. 'I have spent much time thinking of you, Barbra—oh, and look— you've brought along some of your friends.'

'It is time for you to relinquish the Corium,' said Barbra sternly, her broomstick rising higher so she floated above the soldiers' heads. 'You have exhausted my patience, and if you know what's good for you, you'll do as I've instructed.'

'Why don't you come inside,' suggested Maverick, gesturing to the wooden doors of the old museum.

'I will have some Kineleek brew made up—I know how much you adore it. We can reach a suitable agreement—a valued position within The Establishment?'

'You cannot win this fight, Maverick,' returned Barbra snappily. 'I suggest a quiet surrender.'

From where they stood, Naldy had a clear view of Barbra's back. She looked formidable atop her broom, valiantly opposing the wizard in her shimmering cloak and black pointed witch hat. There was no sign of the young witch, Hereto.

Maverick held out his free hand that wasn't clasped around his cane. A loud whooshing sound accompanied the rush of black flame surging from the ground through Maverick's outstretched hand. The ferocious fire almost immediately vanished, leaving thick, billowing black smoke. As the haze cleared, it became evident that Maverick now held a long, elegant black broomstick. The beautifully polished broom reflected the sunlight, its dark wood curved elegantly at the handle, and its tail was made from fine, long black twigs.

Barbra rose higher on her old, battered broom. She refused to let Maverick intimidate her.

'I believe you have something I require,' said Maverick, smirking. 'And if you refuse to settle this over brew, we will simply have to do it your way—let's settle it with war.'

Maverick leapt onto his stylish broomstick. Barbra shot a fiery white spell at the approaching wizard, who swerved skilfully, sending a jet of purple hurtling back towards the old woman. Barbra flew higher, narrowly dodging Maverick's spell.

'Naldy,' called Ralph in terror, his face angled towards the blue sky.

Before glancing up, Naldy noticed countless shadows on the ground, each one growing in size. She lifted her head to find the source—hundreds of Establishment guards were approaching from above on brooms. They swept into the street from every direction, dressed in blue military-style blazers, their faces tense with concentration as they soared over the rooftops.

The ghouls, clad in their metal armour, broke formation and leapt onto their brooms to meet them in the sky. Many colourful flashes broke out overhead as Maverick's guards and the ghouls engaged in battle. Each side sent violent spells charging at the other.

Ralph and Naldy sprinted towards the nearby buildings as loud cracks and bangs split the air. The deafening sounds of battle surrounded them.

'Stop!' shouted Naldy as one of Maverick's guards fell to the ground from above, narrowly missing them. Fresh blood trickled across the cobblestones. The guard's broken broomstick lay splintered beside him. 'We need to get indoors, Ralph.'

Naldy took his hand, and they continued towards *The Mortismor*—but it proved difficult as more bodies fell from the sky, landing with heavy thuds on the hard street. Howls of agony rang out from the few who survived the fall. Flickering shadows blanketed the wide road as the battle intensified beneath the sun.

Naldy felt nauseous as she stepped into a shallow puddle of crimson blood. The path to the bistro was becoming more treacherous.

Explosions of colour crackled above their heads as relentless spells collided with their targets.

The injured guards and ghouls, whose brooms were damaged, clambered to their feet to continue the fight. They sent flashes of wild spells speeding across the street. The ground soon became as busy as the sky above.

Ralph and Naldy ducked as more fiery balls of light tore through the air in their direction. She pulled him out of the way of an approaching spell, and they fell to the ground. One of Barbra's armoured soldiers landed beside them with a thunderous clang. His broad face was covered in sweat, and he winced in pain before jumping to his feet and running towards a nearby guard, shooting spells and crying as he went.

Sitting up, Naldy took in the violence and chaos around her. The surrounding buildings no longer appeared safe—spells shattered their windows, their drawn coverings burned, and fiery tongues of flame licked at the wooden frames. Those who had chosen to take shelter indoors peered out in horror at the unfolding conflict.

'I think we may be winning,' said Ralph.

Naldy noticed nearly three times as many fallen Establishment guards as soldiers—but she struggled to agree with Ralph's description of 'winning.' There were many deaths and injuries on both sides.

While surveying the battlefield, she saw a guard wearing a blue porkpie hat shoot an orange ball of light that struck Ralph's armour, knocking him to the ground. He wasn't moving.

The guard raised his palms in the direction of Ralph's motionless body. Instinctively, Naldy returned a purple spell, sending it whizzing towards the guard. It collided with his chest, and he collapsed with a loud crack. It only took her a moment to realise she had killed him.

A river of blood trickled from the guard's body, and Naldy's heart raced. Though she had acted in self-defence, guilt surged within her.

'Ralph,' called Naldy, rushing to his side. He gingerly lifted his strawberry-blonde head, and she was relieved to see he was still alive—the spell hadn't been fatal.

'We need to get away from this battle,' said Ralph weakly.

She helped him to his feet, lifting him by the arm of his metal armour. A rush of adrenaline overwhelmed her as she took in the guard she had killed. A strange mix of exhilaration and triumph coursed through her—she had never killed anyone before and hadn't expected to feel this way.

'I have my magical carpet in my pocket,' said Ralph, leaning on her shoulder. 'It's underneath my armour.'

Naldy felt frozen to the spot. The elation she had

briefly felt was once again replaced by guilt. She shook her head, trying to remind herself that it had been in self-defence—to save Ralph—but it was no good; the wretched feeling of having taken a life engulfed her.

'If we don't move,' said Ralph, spells erupting around them, 'we'll die here, Naldy.'

'It's not safe to fly,' she said, taking a deep breath. 'Let's go on foot.'

She focused on supporting Ralph across the road. They tried to stay as low as possible, deflecting spells.

Naldy stepped onto a black, pointed witch's hat. Her chest tightened as she picked it up—there was no sign of Barbra.

'It probably fell off,' said Ralph. 'The ghouls are still casting magic. She must be alive—but we won't be if we don't get to safety.'

'We can go inside *The Golden Opulent*,' suggested Naldy.

'No building is safe,' said Ralph. 'We need to get far away from here. We may need to risk flying.'

'Okay,' conceded Naldy, discarding the hat and beginning to search for a broomstick that was still intact. 'Let's not use your carpet, though—it'll draw too much attention. We need to find a broom.'

Ralph held out his palm, and with a puff of smoke, a wooden broomstick materialised.

'You invented the spell, remember,' said Ralph, passing the broom to her. 'You'll have to fly—I haven't the knack.'

She climbed on, with Ralph clambering on behind her. Together, they kicked off the ground, rising above the street littered with bodies. She swerved around ghouls and guards attacking each other, focused on steering them away from the battlefield. Being in the air proved more hazardous than remaining on the ground, as those still airborne were skilled fighters who had not been knocked from their brooms. The unpredictability of rogue spells was frightening, so she decided it was safer for them to fly nearer to the cobbled street.

Out of nowhere, Naldy heard the wood snap beneath her fingers as a white spell struck the broomstick, sending them toppling. Her armour slid across the ground as Ralph let out a cry of pain.

Then, out of nowhere, the fighting stopped. Naldy could hear her own breathing. There were no exploding spells, no clanging armour, and no whirring broomsticks darting across the sky.

She breathed deeply, listening to the moans of the injured. Glancing around the street from the ground, she tried to find Ralph amidst the chaos. Blue military blazers were strewn, bloody, across the cobbled stones—something didn't feel right.

She peered up into the sky where the sun had begun its descent. Many of Maverick's guards hovered on broomsticks, their bloodstained faces twisted in confusion.

'Naldy?' said Ralph, limping closer to her. 'Are you okay? We need to leave. We lost the battle.'

Naldy realised what didn't feel right: no other

metal uniforms, apart from their own, glinted in the afternoon sun. Not a single ghoul was in sight—they had all vanished.

'It's over,' said Ralph, helping Naldy to her feet.

'Indeed it is,' came a cold, familiar voice.

Maverick landed his sleek black broom only metres from them, his long, green cloak glistening. Compared to the other guards, Maverick appeared to be unscathed. Naldy desperately scanned her surroundings for an undamaged broomstick.

'There is no point in trying to flee,' said the wizard, gesturing to the guards in the sky. 'We have you surrounded.'

'What have you done with them?' asked Naldy.

'With Barbra's ghouls,' sniggered Maverick, taking a few steps closer before stopping to lean on his black cane. 'It was an intelligent plan, I'll admit that. It took me some time to realise the fiends were not human.'

'Where are they?' asked Naldy. 'What have you done with them?'

'Magic created with the Devante can be undone,' remarked Maverick.

'And where is Barbra?' added Ralph. 'And Hereto?'

'I had a pleasant little trip,' continued Maverick icily. 'When I undid the old woman's spell, it took me to her memory, and I was surprised to find Hereto had aided her in creating the army of ghouls. Particularly surprised because our young Hereto did not show up for the battle.'

'He didn't show?' said Ralph.

'He fled the city before it even began.'

'What have you done with Barbra?' asked Naldy, pulling the chain around her neck to retrieve the necklace with the singular pearl from beneath the metal breastplate. The white pearl had turned black.

'You have murdered her,' said Ralph, his voice choking with emotion.

'I believe you have something I require,' said Maverick, lifting his cane from the floor. 'If you are wise, you shall give it to me without fuss.'

'I don't have what you need,' said Naldy, her angular jaw jutting out defiantly.

'Very well,' said Maverick, pointing his cane at them.

Naldy kept her stony gaze on Maverick's dark eyes. She heard a shrill pulsing sound and saw a flash of golden light. Maverick's expression changed from icy calmness to confusion, and Naldy felt her body pull backwards. In her periphery, she saw a glass-like sphere with a golden rim, realising she was being sucked backwards into a portal.

Maverick jabbed his cane forward, sending a jet of vibrant red towards her. She landed on soft green grass. The sphere was closing, and she saw Maverick's vicious red spell hurtling from the other side. The magic struck the sphere and exploded in a brilliant shattering of red light.

'Are you okay?' asked Ralph from behind her.

'How did you create the portal?' asked Naldy from the grass, feeling tender as she sat upright. 'The portal must have been made with a Devante, but Barbra never shared the spell with us, Ralph.'

'I used you,' said Ralph, wincing with pain.

'Me?' said Naldy, taking in the comforting sight of the tall pine trees before her. They were on the edge of a forest. She knew they weren't Edengar pines but those of the Kirkwood Forest.

'You have the magic of H,' mumbled Ralph, still behind her. 'That is what Maverick was requesting you to give him. It was transferred from Barbra to you when she was killed.'

Naldy gingerly twisted to face him, stunned first by the information he had conveyed, and then by the sight she glimpsed behind him.

'It was the first place I could think of,' he explained.

Behind Ralph was the burnt skeleton of the Witch House. The ash-covered rubble and blackened stones looked eerie in the evening light.

'Why would the magic of H have been transferred to me?' asked Naldy.

'Isn't it obvious,' he replied, delicately repositioning his leg. 'We should have realised it sooner. Both you, Betty, and Barbra are descendants of Hannah Hale. Barbra didn't have any children, and neither did Betty. You are the next descendant in the bloodline.'

Naldy should have been happier to hear that the power of H had been transferred to her, but instead, she was filled with dread.

'Let's fix our injuries, Ralph, and then let's get ourselves out of this armour,' said Naldy, trying to ignore the reality that she had once again been burdened with the responsibility of protecting the magic Maverick was seeking. '*Sanitatem Restituere.*'

—Chapter Twenty-Three—

MAVERICK'S MEMORY

Silver stars twinkled peacefully above as Naldy watched the grey curling smoke drift into the night sky. She had used the magic of the Devante to fashion a modest campsite for them, complete with a small leather tent for sleeping and a pleasant fire. They knew that the magic of H could be used to rebuild the Witch House—even an exact replica, just as they had seen her mother do in Arkus Day—but they had decided it would be far too risky. Maverick's edicts required all places of residence to be registered, and rewards were being offered to those who reported law-breakers, so the tent was created to be inconspicuous, akin to the simple shelter they had used during their travels through Edengar with Odorf.

'I know Barbra has caused us some grief,' said Ralph, warming his bum by the crackling fire. 'But I can't help but feel sad she is gone. I'll really miss the old bat.'

'None of it feels real,' said Naldy, twiddling the black pearl between her fingers.

Her thoughts kept returning to the guard she

had killed in the heat of combat and to the strange feeling of exhilaration she'd felt. She wanted to believe the surging adrenaline had come when the magic of H had been transferred to her, at the time of Barbra's death—and not from dealing the final blow to the guard who had attacked them.

'Killing felt too easy,' said Naldy, tears falling onto her cloak.

'I wouldn't be here if you hadn't,' replied Ralph softly.

'I should have taken Maverick's life when I had the chance,' said Naldy. 'Now H is whole again, the *Banned Spell of Death* cannot be broken unless we have both the Corium and H. To take his life without both, we'd have to be close to him.'

'We need to disband the entire Seagull Society,' said Ralph gently. A small silence passed between them. They listened to the fire's crackling. 'Are you still thinking about the guard?'

'I killed him, Ralph. I'm no different to Maverick.'

'You did it to save me,' said Ralph. 'Maverick kills in cold blood.'

'An entire army, and yet it still failed to take him down,' she said, staring at the yellow flames licking the charred logs. 'I fear we'll never be strong enough to stop him.'

'Edengar?' suggested Ralph. 'You did want to go there. We could take the magic of H and set up a quiet life for ourselves. Your mother hid the Devante, and perhaps we should do the same?'

'Maverick would find us eventually,' said Naldy.

'Rupert might even tip him off. He knows I am fond of the place.'

Ralph shifted uncomfortably, and Naldy regretted mentioning his cousin's name—she knew Rupert's betrayal still troubled him.

'I was surprised Hereto abandoned Barbra,' remarked Naldy. 'After advocating so passionately for the fight.'

'Let's never go to war again,' said Ralph, stretching his back.

'Sadly,' she mumbled, 'we may not have a choice.'

'We should get some rest,' said Ralph. 'We'll come up with a new plan tomorrow.'

Ralph retired to the tent, and Naldy sat alone for almost an hour, staring out at the shadows of the tall pines. The familiar shapes comforted her until she realised they couldn't stay at the edge of the Kirkwood Forest forever—not while Maverick's edicts were still being enforced.

Lifting her tired body from the log, Naldy entered the tent, where Ralph snored softly. She climbed into her hammock, wrapping the covers tightly around her weary body.

The next morning brought another bright day with a clear blue sky. After finishing their breakfast of scrambled eggs and hot brew, which Naldy had conjured using the magic of the Devante, Ralph suggested they search the rubble of the Witch House to see if anything had survived the fire.

'It's just ancestral junk,' insisted Naldy, reluctantly following Ralph to the ruins. 'You already know I can conjure a replica of it all with the help of H. There's no need for us to go searching through it.'

'It wasn't all junk,' protested Ralph, making his way towards the blackened remains, 'my Imporiom was hiding in the Witch House.'

'Have you forgotten that we already did search through it all?' said Naldy, kicking the longer blades of grass as she walked. 'Every trunk and neglected drawer. There was nothing worth saving. Why do you want to go looking through the ruins?'

Ralph stopped to face her, cocking his head and raising his blonde eyebrows.

'It's your family home,' he said affectionately. 'I think we should see if anything has survived.'

Naldy shrugged, fiddling with the sleeve of her cloak in an attempt to hide her feelings. She didn't want to forage through the remnants—she wanted to pretend it had never happened.

Although scorched a charcoal black, parts of the frame were still intact, standing eerily. They entered where the front door had once been, walking between two blackened beams. All of the furnishings and items had been reduced to ash.

As they continued through the wreckage, Naldy could make out where some of the rooms had been situated, and she instantly felt a pang of emotion—a strange mixture of sadness and anger.

The large stone chimney, standing in what had once been the comfortable lounge, had survived the fire. Naldy's mind was flooded with memories of her time in the house.

'It was just stuff,' said Naldy, walking over the soot-covered ground.

'I'm sorry, Naldy,' said Ralph, tears welling in his eyes.

They continued walking in silence, treading carefully over the charred debris.

'What's that?' he asked curiously, bending to pick up something small, glinting amongst the dark ash. 'Oh, look, it's a seagull pin.'

'You can throw that back into the fire,' said Naldy. 'The Seagull Society is the reason we're in this mess.'

'Maybe it belonged to your great-great-grandmother,' suggested Ralph warmly. 'This could be the very pin Hannah Hale wore.'

'Keep it if you want,' said Naldy. 'I don't want anything to do with the Seagull Society.'

'They aren't all bad,' said Ralph, exhaling deeply. He gently took her hand and placed the silver seagull brooch into it. 'Odorf and Mason were good. They tried to help us save magic.'

'They also helped to create it,' said Naldy, clenching her fist around the brooch. 'I'm starting to wish it had never been invented.'

'The Society created it to try and protect the art of inventing new spells.'

'Yes, well, most of those who helped to invent it, Ralph, are now aiding Maverick in his quest to destroy all magic.'

'I can't help pity those working with him,' said Ralph. 'I don't think they understand Maverick's real goal.'

'We need to find out his secret,' said Naldy, holding out her hand. 'Shall we?'

'We're running out of spells to undo,' said Ralph nervously. 'Let's hope we find something soon.'

Naldy focused all her energy on undoing one of Maverick's spells—a spell that had been intended for her and Ralph but had instead ensnared a night heron in a pocket of air.

She felt her body lurch forward, and the sounds of nearby birds were replaced by the cacophonous noise of a violent battle. They had returned to the recent fight between the soldiers and the guards. Ralph squeezed her hand in panic.

'It's okay,' said Naldy. 'They can't harm us.'

'It's not their spells I'm concerned with,' his voice cracked.

Naldy realised they were floating mid-air at a great height—without the help of a broomstick.

'It's just a memory,' said Naldy, trying not to let the altitude concern her.

Lethal spells whizzed by in many directions. Streaking past them on all sides were blue military blazers and the shine of silver metal.

'Where is Maverick?' asked Ralph over the deafening sounds of combat.

A jet of green light sped through Naldy's chest, but she felt nothing. The fighting was occurring at various heights and in every direction. Naldy was unable to see any sign of the wizard in the chaos.

'Hopefully, we will move on soon,' said Ralph.

'I don't think we'll discover anything useful here, certainly not Maverick's secret. Floating this high without a magical carpet is making me queasy.'

The air around them cleared slightly as the nearby fighters dipped lower on their brooms. Then, a wave of anger rose in Naldy's chest as she caught sight of Maverick. There was a calm smirk on his pale lips as he skilfully weaved his sleek black broom out of the way of an onslaught of brilliant pink spells. Naldy turned to see the magic had been delivered from Barbra's outstretched palm. The woman's wrinkled face was pinched in intense concentration as she pulled on the handle of her broom, climbing higher.

Maverick hovered in one place, keeping his eye on the old woman, dressed in her black cloak and pointed witch hat, as she rose above him. Several blue spells came tearing towards the wizard, but he dodged each one. Barbra leant forward and, at an impressive speed, flew in a wide circular motion.

Maverick shot after her with one spindly hand grasping his broom's handle, the other clutching his black cane. The wizard closed the distance between them before thrusting his cane forward and sending a bolt of black electricity chasing the tail of Barbra's broom. She swerved out of its path, and the black spell collided with one of The Establishment guards.

'Where did Maverick go?' asked Ralph, peering up.

Naldy had also lost sight of the wizard, but kept her eye on Barbra, who pulled her broomstick to a halt just metres away. Anxiety clouded the woman's expression as she scanned the sky. Then, a blue ball of hurtling light collided with Barbra's hands, binding them together with black leather handcuffs. Naldy knew Barbra couldn't perform magic while wearing them.

Barbra's broomstick no longer responded to her commands, and she was forced to hover in place.

'We have to undo the handcuffs,' called Naldy desperately as Maverick approached Barbra.

'It's just a memory,' said Ralph sadly.

She realised that although wild spells were shooting dangerously through the air, they were only being cast by Maverick's guards. Barbra's inability to cast magic due to the leather bounds had affected the ghouls' capabilities.

Maverick had only left them the power to fly, and many fled towards the Kirkwood Forest. Others, stripped of magic, tried to fight back, lunging at the guards and grabbing for their brooms.

Maverick stopped his broomstick less than a metre from the old witch, her broom fixed in place.

The sun's reflection bounced off silver armour, briefly depriving Naldy of sight. Huegon, clad in his armour, was flying determinedly towards the wizard. The ghoul let out an angry cry, his palm outstretched—but no spell emerged. The ghoul's eyes widened in terror as Maverick flicked his cane, and a brutal black spell collided with Huegon. The ghoul was knocked from his broom.

Naldy watched sadly as Huegon fell.

'You ought to have accepted my proposal,' Maverick said with steely calm. 'This could all have been resolved over brew. You've always been a vocal advocate for the restriction of magic.'

'You have taken it too far,' replied Barbra sternly. 'Murdering our kind.'

'I believe you have something I need,' said Maverick, untroubled by her accusation. 'Let's get this over with, shall we?'

'Let's,' replied Barbra with an iciness in her voice.

Before Maverick could wield his cane, Barbra threw the weight of her body sideways and slid from her broom. Maverick gasped, steering his broom downward, but there was no point trying to follow Barbra's falling body because she could no longer be seen—the commotion of the airborne battle blocked the old woman's descent from view. Maverick was unable to fly fast enough to save her.

A few seconds later, the ghouls' magic was restored, and Naldy knew Barbra had died—that the magic of H had been transferred to her in that moment. The soldiers retaliated against the guards. Maverick was stunned to see their powers returned.

Naldy felt her body fall, initially believing that whatever magic kept them airborne had worn off. But she quickly realised they weren't falling from the sky—they were being pulled into another memory.

Naldy didn't need to see anything more from the battle, for she knew what happened next. She knew Maverick would work out that the ghouls could all be destroyed by undoing Barbra's spell.

Naldy and Ralph found themselves in a tastefully decorated dining room with an impressively high ceiling. In the centre was a long wooden table laden with breakfast items. Soft light filtered through large ornate windows. The walls were lined with a rich, deep blue wallpaper. Establishment guards stood statuesque beside the three doorways that led into the room. Each guard was dressed in the same blue uniform and porkpie hat that Naldy had always known them to wear.

'There is no point in you wasting your time with such a book,' said a man with a deep voice from one end of the table.

Naldy and Ralph stood a few metres from the middle-aged man who had spoken. He was dressed lavishly in a teal cloak embroidered with yellow florets, his thick brown hair framing solemn, dark brown eyes. Naldy glanced around, wondering who the middle-aged man was addressing.

'You will answer when spoken to,' said the brown-eyed man.

'You said I could pick any book from the library, Father,' said a small, somewhat nervous voice.

Naldy and Ralph had to turn their heads multiple times before they noticed the young boy sitting midway along the table. He held open a small blue leather book and ate a golden apricot pastry. The boy must have been about seven or eight years old, with straight black hair and dark eyes.

'What use is a spellbook to you?' probed the

middle-aged man irritably.

'This is the book I want to read,' said the boy's small voice.

'You are not a witch,' said the older man, frowning.

The young boy did not respond but turned his attention back to his book. This greatly displeased the older man, who stared at the young boy with resentment.

Naldy and Ralph glanced at each other.

'Who is that?' asked Ralph. 'Is it young Maverick?'

'I think it may be Titus,' replied Naldy, as the older man rose from his chair and marched towards the boy. 'Maverick must be here somewhere.'

'He is probably lurking in the shadows somewhere,' mumbled Ralph.

The boy appeared not to notice his father approaching, too preoccupied with the contents of his spellbook. When the older man reached him, he snatched the book from the boy's hands and held it up. The book burst into blue flame, leaving nothing but a grey-blue smoke.

'*Prosterno,*' cried the boy, thrusting his trembling palms towards his father. No spell emerged.

The older man grimaced, and the boy sank back into his chair.

'I instructed you to pick a book,' snapped the man, 'and you have chosen one useless to you.'

'I mightn't be a witch,' said the boy stubbornly, 'but maybe I am a wizard.'

The old man laughed amusedly, making his way

back along the table. He did not sit but leant one hand on the table, picking up his goblet of brew with the other.

'It is a horrible thing that has happened, Titus,' said the man, seeming repulsed by his own words. 'Two witches birthing someone like you, without any power. It has never happened before. We must accept the reality and learn to live with it.'

'Anyone could become a wizard,' replied the boy hopefully.

'An extraordinarily rare occurrence,' said the man, sneering. 'You will not become a wizard, Titus.'

'I could find an Imporiom,' said the boy optimistically, 'and when I do, I'd like to be ready.'

'There will be no Imporiom!' shouted the man, slamming his goblet of brew onto the breakfast table. The nearby guards flinched. However, the boy sat still, unblinking. 'You must give up this foolish obsession—you are not a witch or wizard, Titus, and you never will be! You do not have any power, and we must all learn to accept this.'

One of the doors opened, and a tall Establishment guard entered.

'I am sorry to interrupt your breakfast, Grigory,' said the guard, bowing his head. 'The board is expecting you.'

'I will be there shortly,' said the man, waving the guard away.

The guard bowed again but hesitated to leave without Grigory accompanying him. Realising he had no choice, he made his exit alone. Titus sat slumped in his chair, arms crossed. Grigory turned to him, as if about to say something, but changed his mind and merely said, 'I will see you at dinner.'

'You do not know what the future holds,' whispered Titus under his breath. 'I will be greater than you ever were.'

'What was that?' asked the man, scowling at the boy.

'Nothing,' mumbled Titus.

'You are banned from the library,' said Grigory. 'You cannot be trusted to choose books that are useful to you, and so there will be none.'

'You can't!' protested the boy.

'It is done,' stated Grigory sternly. He nodded to the nearest guard standing by the doorway, instructing him to see that his order was carried out. 'It is for your own good. I do not want my son entertaining these ridiculous sentiments.'

'You cannot ban me from reading books,' replied Titus.

'Fools must learn their lessons the hard way,' said Grigory dryly. 'You will not read any more books, magical or otherwise. I must be going. I am expected in the Establishment's chamber.'

The guards swiftly opened the nearest doors for Grigory to pass through. Titus was left alone with his apricot pastry and tears. His fists were clenched tight, his fingernails digging into his skin. Naldy thought she saw blood being drawn.

'Where is Maverick?' asked Ralph, scanning the large room. 'Isn't this supposed to be his memory?'

'I'm not sure,' said Naldy. 'The memory appears to be years before the two of them would have met.'

'Do you think Grigory created the spell we have undone?' asked Ralph. 'Perhaps this is his memory?'

'I don't see how Grigory could have invented it,' replied Naldy. 'He was burnt at the stake before the creation of the Devante.'

Before either of them could see any sign of Maverick, they were sent lurching forward into another memory. It was a memory that Naldy instantly recognised, for she had seen it before.

'If you've murdered Lampard,' said Audry, her kind green eyes meeting Maverick's across the table. 'Then, yes, I am the last who knows of your secret.'

A warm fire crackled in the corner of the cosy cottage. The windows outside were dark. The two sat opposite each other at the kitchen table, with steam drifting from their cups of brew. Audry brushed a greying hair from her wrinkled face.

'You will not survive because you pity me,' said Maverick. He stood, directing his cane at Audry, who did not flinch.

'Your secret may follow me to the grave,' said Audry, unbothered by Maverick's threat, 'but many others still in the Society uphold the oath to protect magic.'

Maverick grimaced at her words.

'They may never understand the true reason you are hell-bent on seeing it destroyed, Maverick,' continued Audry, her fingers reaching for her cup. 'But they will stop you, nonetheless. Cutting the tongue off your secret will not help you win this fight.'

Maverick seemed to have a change of heart, placing his cane on the table and lowering himself back into the chair.

'You must be hungry after your journey here?' said Audry.

The pantry door behind her opened. A glass jar of shortbread biscuits floated down to the table, but the inner shelves of the pantry from where the shortbread had come grabbed Naldy's attention. Maverick also glanced curiously at the shelves, filled with hundreds of small potion phials, each containing a sticky blood-red liquid.

'It took me some time to realise you had stopped drinking your Veserum,' said Maverick. 'You have allowed yourself to grow old. I have spent a great deal of time looking for someone younger.'

'Odorf's creation was too beautiful to destroy,' said Audry. 'Although I did not consume the shipments of Veserum, I have kept each bottle.'

'Little good they'll do you now,' said Maverick, helping himself to a shortbread from the jar.

'When we asked you to join the Society, Maverick, we thought we were doing the right thing. You are a great wizard—that is certain—but we made the foolish mistake of thinking you were a good wizard.'

Maverick did not respond but took a nibble of the shortbread he was holding.

'The very thing we invited you to create with us,' continued Audry, her voice low and heavy, 'was the exact thing that has given you this power.'

'Time is a dangerous thing,' said Maverick. 'You should have told the Society what you knew while you had the chance.'

'I told some of the Society members,' said Audry. 'Those you have killed. Those I trusted. It took even them some convincing of the truth. At first, they did not believe me. They did not want to believe that you were not really Maverick. That you are, in fact, Titus.'

Chapter Twenty-Four

THE WIZARD'S SHAME

Neither spoke, afraid they'd miss crucial information if they did. Naldy squeezed Ralph's arm in disbelief. She was still determining if she had heard Audry correctly. How could the wizard be Titus?

Maverick ran his finger along the cane resting on the table.

'Is it true that your father, Grigory, used to call you a maverick?' asked Audry. 'The rumour is that you adopted the name he once used to ridicule you.'

'Rebel, maverick, fool,' said Maverick, sinking back into his chair. 'My father had many names for me.'

Audry looked at the wizard with pity. He shifted uncomfortably under her gaze before picking up his black cane.

'I am surprised to see you travelling without your assistant,' said Audry. 'You have often relied on him to do your dirty work.'

'Getergrin has business in The Great City to attend to,' replied Maverick. 'There are some things I don't want even him to know.'

'I had always wondered what you saw in him,' said Audry, helping herself to a biscuit from the jar on the table. She dunked it into the brew. 'I often wondered why you kept him close to you. It took me some time to realise you were fond of him because he was just like you.'

'I think it's time we got this over with,' said Maverick with disdain.

'When you were born,' said Audry, in a low and somewhat sympathetic voice, 'what happened to you was—well, it was unheard of. Witches giving birth to someone unmagical. Your father was deeply ashamed of you. Your existence made him feel ashamed of himself. Your mother died in labour.'

'And his only son had no power,' said Maverick, finishing her train of thought. Audry's brow wrinkled with sorrow. Maverick continued, 'There were times he couldn't even bear to be in the same room as me.'

'And then all of those years later, you meet Getergrin,' said Audry, settling the rest of her shortbread on the table. 'Suddenly, you weren't the only one. You had discovered someone else, born to magical parents, who could not cast magic. I suppose Getergrin's existence comforts you. You were no longer alone. You decided to take him under your wing.'

'We have talked for long enough,' said Maverick.

'The brewpot is still half-full,' said Audry. 'I will not fight you Maverick, for I know it would be a duel that I would have little chance of winning. Let us finish the brew. I'd like to hear how you did it—and to have another shortbread—then you may kill me.'

'How I did what?' queried Maverick.

'How you went back in time,' said Audry, her eyes twinkling in the candlelight. 'The Devante were created to stop you. How did you go back when they had not yet been invented?'

'Time is a troublesome thing,' replied Maverick. 'I did not realise the seriousness of what would happen when I entered the past.'

'It is why my beloved Hannah eventually decided to mark *Time* as a *Banned Spell*,' said Audry. 'But too late, it seems.'

'Time,' said Maverick, setting his cane back onto the table, 'is intricate and delicate. Time is not one shared thing. Each individual has their own timeline.'

'*Arcesso,*' Audry whispered calmly. The brewpot rose and filled Maverick's cup with more amber brew.

'Going back is treacherous,' continued Maverick. 'The past can be reshaped, altered, and even erased.'

'You were burnt at the stake as a young man. I was there. I saw it happen, and yet here you sit. You died, Maverick.'

'A painful thing to watch,' said Maverick, wincing.

Audry raised her chin, staring at the wizard curiously, trying to decipher his words.

'You see,' continued Maverick, 'I was there. In the crowd.'

'How did you survive the fire?'

'You invited me into the Society,' said Maverick, a hint of a smile on his lips. 'So I will grant you the rare privilege of knowing what happened.'

'Alright,' said Audry, speaking in a low voice, a trace of fear on her face.

'We have covered how I was born,' said Maverick, leaning back in his chair and grimacing. 'Son, to the esteemed Grigory. Born without magical ability and a mother who died in childbirth. My father despised me. It was a miserable childhood, and there was little love. But things changed when I turned fourteen. One ordinary day, I was paid a visit by a wizard. He was much older than me. He promised to help me.'

'Who was this wizard?' asked Audry curiously.

'It was me,' replied Maverick. 'Although I did not know it at the time. This wizard, he called himself Maverick, and he promised to help me gain influence with members of the Establishment. He promised me great power, and he fulfilled his promise.'

'He helped you by using his magical ability,' remarked Audry, as the silhouettes of the pine trees outside the window shifted in the night breeze. 'Something you did not have.'

'Yes. He was a skilled wizard and gradually aided me in becoming favoured amongst my father's associates. I become head of The Establishment at only fourteen.'

'You wanted revenge, and so you sentenced your father to death,' said Audry.

'I had no other choice,' remarked Maverick, the candlelight reflecting in his watery eyes. 'I wanted my father to witness me as I gained influence within The Establishment. I wanted him to see me with great power. I did not want him to die. But the older wizard who came to me, the one who helped me gain this power—'

'Yourself.'

'Yes. My older self convinced my younger self that my father had to die. If I let him live, he would regain power, and he would make sure I suffered for stripping him of his influence. Townsfolk everywhere adored me, for I promised to ensure magic was controlled and regulated, and that rule-breakers were punished. My father had to die so that people would witness firsthand that I valued them over everything else—even family bonds.'

'You killed your biggest opponent,' said Audry sadly. 'Your own father.'

'My father neglected the needs of those without magical power. But no more. I was my father's successor, and things were going exceptionally well with him out of the equation. But then something happened. It was just before I turned sixteen that Maverick returned. He came to me and gave me a golden crown, a parting gift, and insisted that I go into hiding.'

'The Aurum,' said Audry. 'You were trying to protect yourself.'

'I did not listen to this older wizard,' said Maverick. 'I was stubborn. I thought I could do it without his help. I accepted the crown and continued with my grand witch hunt.'

'But you were wrong.'

'Yes, how wrong I was. Soon after the wizard Maverick departed, Hannah Hale was captured and sentenced to the stake. But before her death, her actions had an alarming effect.'

Tears welled in Audry's eyes, and Naldy knew the old woman was recalling Hannah and that very day she died.

'I had never seen anything like it,' continued Maverick. 'Hannah's performance before her death frightened even me.'

'She could have easily freed herself,' said Audry softly. 'She had the power of the Devante. Hannah knew people—including many witches—tolerated and at times praised the burnings, for they too feared the dark sorcerer. You and I both know there was never any such sorcerer. The idea was merely a fabrication, a justification for the horror.'

Naldy thought about the night Maverick declared the Witch Hunt and announced to the crowd that a dark witch wielded the Corium's power. He had painted Naldy as a dangerous sorcerer.

'Hannah was bound to the stake on the palace steps,' said Maverick. 'A large crowd had gathered as rumours spread that the sorcerer had been captured. But before the burning commenced, green smoke rose from nowhere around her stake, twisting into the shape of a mighty dragon. The beast of smoke swooped over the crowd, opening its jaws and sending a jet of hot flame just above their heads, narrowly missing them. Hundreds of seagulls landed on the buildings overhead, filling the air with a cacophony of wailing cries. Then, the dragon circled.'

'The guards with the flaming torches were too scared to act,' remarked Audry. 'I saw you, young Titus, snatch a torch from one of their hands and hurl it at Hannah's feet. She let herself die because she knew that, with her death, people would no longer fear the imaginary sorcerer you had convinced them to believe in. She could have saved herself, but she didn't.'

'It was her death,' said Maverick bitterly, 'that became my undoing. Soon after she died, people grew restless with the ongoing witch hunt. I was declared a tyrant for continuing the burnings, and those who had once supported me soon ordered that I be tied to the stake. I had no magical ability. Without the help of the older wizard, who had warned me to go into hiding and had then abandoned me, I was powerless.'

'I witnessed your burning,' said Audry, the flickering candlelight reflected in her wet eyes. 'Just as I watched Hannah die. You were not yet a wizard. You could not use the golden crown to save yourself —yet, remarkably, here you are.'

Maverick hesitated, his face pained; there was a deep sadness in his expression. Naldy felt sympathy for him.

'I narrowly escaped death,' said Maverick timidly.

'At the time, I did not understand how I had survived. It was only much later that I realised older Maverick had saved me by casting a spell on the Aurum. When the flames licked the golden crown, I was suddenly transported to safety. The straw beneath my feet ignited in a rush of fire—one moment, I saw the flames in front of my face, and the next, I found myself lying in a muddy marsh on the outskirts of a dilapidated town. It was far south, and the town was poor—its inhabitants had little interest in the goings-on of The Great City. I went into hiding for a long time. One of my father's allies became head of The Establishment. Though the rule of magical folk never returned to the heights it had reached before The Great Witch Hunt, it began to spread again. It was all around me, mocking me.'

'Magic,' said Audry.

'Yes, magic,' repeated Maverick weakly. 'The very thing I could not do. Meanwhile, I lived in the shadows, growing older as the decades turned. Then, years later, I discovered my Imporiom. You think I would be happy.'

'Were you not?' asked Audry. 'You were finally granted the one thing you had always desired. You were a wizard, Titus, as you had always wished.'

'Do not call me that,' said Maverick. 'It is a name I wish to forget.'

Audry pursed her lips and waited for the wizard to continue.

'How could I have been happy? I had spent most of my life loathing magic. My father had loved it more than he had ever loved me.'

Maverick took a black silk handkerchief from his pocket and blew his nose. Audry did not interrupt but patiently waited for him to continue.

'I learnt that I had great skill in wielding it—magic, that is. I had spent my childhood with my nose in many books concerning the craft. My father banned me from reading magical books at a young age, but this only increased my appetite for them. I would sneak into the library at night to immerse myself in books about spells, charms, curses, and hexes.'

There was a glint of excitement as he recalled his childhood memory of secretly devouring spellbooks.

'When I discovered my Imporiom, I realised I was incredibly gifted. I had practised my whole childhood without ever having produced any actual magic. But the fact I was talented made me loathe my father—and magic—even more.'

'When did you understand you needed to go back in time?'

'After being united with my black cane, my Imporiom, I soon noticed the resemblance between myself and the stranger who had once appeared to me as a young man. I had spent so long in hiding —and then, there he was in the mirror. The wizard had never been a stranger—I was Maverick. Going back in time was the most logical explanation for how I had appeared to my younger self. The one thing Maverick had gifted me was the crown. I soon discovered its importance. That is when I first travelled time.'

'You returned to your younger self,' said Audry. She stood and moved to the window, peering out at the dark forest in thought. 'To set in motion The Great Witch Hunt.'

'No,' replied Maverick, staring at her back. 'Not at first. I didn't go back. Instead, I went forward.'

Audry turned from the window, her lips parting in silent question.

'It was going forward in time,' said Maverick, 'that made me realise I had to go back. I needed to start The Great Witch Hunt.'

'What did you see?' she asked.

'I saw magic,' replied Maverick. 'Everywhere, magic was celebrated. Those who wielded it were glorified. The Establishment was solely run by those with magic, and anyone without it was treated as lesser. I had to go back to change that.'

'You say you went back using the Devante, but the Devante only existed, Maverick, because we created them to defeat Titus—we created them to defeat you.'

'I am not the inventor of time,' said Maverick, picking up his cane again. 'I have merely travelled it.'

'You went back and gave yourself the crown,' said Audry, as fear washed over her wrinkled face. 'Are you saying that if we had never invented the Devante, the person you are today would not exist?'

'I believe so,' said Maverick, gesturing with his cane for Audry to sit. Once she had returned to her chair, he continued. 'If the Devante had never existed, I would not have been able to save my younger self. I realised I had to gift the crown to young Titus, for that was what I had done. With the Devante, I created a spell—so when I was whisked away, a boy of similar age and appearance from the dilapidated town took my place at the stake.'

'Why did you join the Seagull Society when you returned?' asked Audry. 'You already had a Devante —the Aurum. Why did you help us create the others?'

'Firstly,' said Maverick, 'I needed to ensure they were invented. Although I had the crown, I feared it might cease to exist if I didn't help bring the Devante into being—they had been forged in the past. I also knew I had to relinquish the Aurum to Titus. My plan, initially, was to return to the future— but Hannah did something that I had not expected. Something she had not done previously.'

'She created the *Banned Spells*,' said Audry.

'Yes,' replied Maverick, as horror crept across his face. 'She discovered that I was Titus and had travelled back in time. She wanted to ensure I couldn't travel through it again, and so she created the *Banned Spells*. I was trapped in the past. I went into hiding again—in the Edengar Mountains. For many years, I mulled over what to do. Veserum kept me alive.'

'What is it you want?' asked Audry. 'Why do you seek to destroy the Devante?'

'I have always had one goal,' said Maverick

bitterly. 'I will not stop, Audry, until they are all destroyed—along with the thing my father loved most. All magic must die.'

'Don't you see, Maverick,' said Audry, her voice cracking. 'You are a wizard. You do not have to fear your father's hatred anymore.'

Maverick stood abruptly, raising his cane and pointing it threateningly towards her. Audry's words had infuriated him.

Before any flash of light emerged, Naldy and Ralph were pulled forward and found themselves standing amongst the sunlit ruins of the burnt Witch House.

Naldy felt prickles of sweat on her forehead, her heart racing. She still clutched the small silver seagull pin.

'He is Titus,' said Ralph breathlessly. 'He travelled time. He is destroying magic because he has a vendetta against his father.'

'It's shocking, I agree,' replied Naldy, stepping carefully over a blackened wooden beam. 'But, Ralph, I'm failing to see how this secret will help us thwart Maverick. If we walk around claiming he is actually Titus, who will believe us?'

'We tell the Seagull Society,' said Ralph. 'It will surely turn them against him.'

'Titus's death is well documented,' said Naldy, disheartened. 'Even if they believe us, I can imagine Mortous being impressed by it.'

'Maverick thought the information was incriminating enough to warrant killing those who knew the secret.'

'Don't you see, Ralph, what we've seen is the past,' said Naldy, panicked. She quickened her pace through the burnt house. 'The Seagull Society support Maverick. They know he is burning witches. They don't care because he has promised them power.'

'We tell the people then,' said Ralph, refusing to give up hope. 'The public burnt Titus once before.'

'Centuries ago,' said Naldy, heading towards the tent. 'The people who lived back then aren't alive today—unless they've consumed Veserum. They probably won't know who Titus is, since they weren't around during his reign. It may be too late.'

As Naldy marched back to the small tent, she felt more anxious than ever. Had they known this information much earlier, perhaps it could have prevented Maverick from gaining control of The Establishment. But she couldn't help but feel it was too late now—Maverick's influence had grown too strong.

They barely spoke for the remainder of the day. Ralph decided to go for a long walk through the forest to clear his thoughts, leaving Naldy alone with her own. The black, skeletal house in front of their campsite was a constant reminder of all they had failed to save.

When Ralph returned, it was late afternoon. With the aid of magic, he prepared a dinner of roasted venison and vegetables. They sat on the log in front of the fire. One by one, stars appeared, glimmering in the cloudless night sky.

'We'll come up with something,' said Ralph. 'You have the highest-ranking Devante, Naldy.'

'Part of it,' she replied. 'Thank you for dinner.'

'What if we convince enough witches to fight alongside us,' suggested Ralph. 'Not ghouls, actual witches. We could travel from town to town. Enlist support.'

'It could take us months,' said Naldy. 'Maverick is a mastermind. He has made witches afraid—even of each other—nobody knows who to trust.'

'The witch commune down south,' said Ralph. 'They could help us. They may be old, but Odorf was stronger than any witch I've known. They would make a grand army.'

'They don't care for saving Devante, Ralph,' said Naldy. 'Potion making is their sole concern.'

'Well,' he replied, 'if Maverick undoes magic, it will undo the power residing in the ingredients they use. Potions may become as useless as spellbooks.'

'Perhaps,' replied Naldy. 'I think we'd have a hard time convincing them, but maybe you're right—it could be a good place to go next.'

'I might head to bed,' said Ralph, lifting himself from the log.

He bid Naldy goodnight and made his way into the tent. Candlelight penetrated the tent's fabric, and Naldy knew Ralph was probably writing in his journal. She stared into the flames, wondering if the witches of the commune would help them. She doubted they'd be convinced to sign up for battle.

She mulled over the memory they'd seen, feeling as though they'd wasted so much time chasing an old secret. Audry's final words to Maverick echoed in her mind—*you do not have to fear your father's hatred anymore*—and Naldy couldn't help but feel pity for the wizard.

'No—it's horrible,' called Ralph in alarm. He emerged from the tent holding a newspaper.

'Where did you get a newspaper?' asked Naldy curiously.

'It doesn't matter,' replied Ralph, shaking the paper.

'It *does* matter,' said Naldy irritably. 'We must be careful, Ralph. If you walked into Frubry, you might have been seen. We need to stay out of sight.'

'Nobody saw me,' said Ralph, panicked. 'Take the newspaper, Naldy. Look—they have Smookers.'

'What do you mean?'

'They must have captured him down south,' said Ralph. 'They are planning on burning him tomorrow night.'

Naldy snatched the paper from him. Her mouth felt dry as she stared in horror at a black-and-white picture of Smookers trapped in a small iron cage. The heading read: *Wicked Witch's Feral Feline Found.* The image made Naldy feel ill. Smookers' black eyes were filled with fear as he cowered in the corner of the small iron cage. She recognised the tip of Maverick's black cane resting threateningly against the enclosure. The pity she'd felt moments ago had vanished.

Chapter Twenty-Five

THE COST OF COURAGE

'It's a trap,' said Ralph, pleading for the umpteenth time.

'You won't talk me out of it,' said Naldy, firm and resolute. 'Trap or not.'

They had spent the last hour arguing around the campfire. Neither had replenished the logs on the smouldering fire.

'They'll take the magic of H,' replied Ralph, exasperated. 'If you go, magic will be destroyed, Naldy. It's not worth risking.'

'I'm not going to let them murder Smookers,' said Naldy, tossing the newspaper onto the dwindling embers. The paper ignited into a hot flame. 'He has taken enough from us.'

Naldy lifted her hand, and a white tapered candle appeared. To light it, she held the wick to the flames of the burning newspaper, then brought the candle a few inches from her mouth. She whispered something—so quietly that it was inaudible even to Ralph, who was standing close by—before blowing out the flame. Although he hadn't heard the words Naldy had uttered, the expression on Ralph's face made it clear he knew it was no ordinary candle.

'Who was the message for?' he asked, concerned. 'Don't pretend that wasn't a candle from the Tebellos.'

Naldy didn't answer him but turned to face the tall shadows of the nearby pine trees.

'*Locultra*,' said Naldy, her palms raised.

A circular glass portal appeared. Its shimmering surface reflected the flickering orange glow of the burning newspaper.

'Please, don't rush into anything,' pleaded Ralph.

Naldy turned away from the portal to meet his blue eyes. The green emerald dangling from his right ear caught the glimmering portal's light. She reached into her pocket and retrieved the small silver seagull pin they'd recovered earlier from the ruin. She secured it to the breast of her cloak.

'If that's a pledge to protect magic,' said Ralph, 'then you best steer clear of The Great City.'

'The portal doesn't lead to The Great City.'

'Maverick doesn't play fair, Naldy. You may have the magic of H, but don't forget that he has the magic of the Corium.'

'Magic is not safe, Ralph. If the surviving Seagull Society members won't help protect it, then I need to. It's time to put an end to his madness.'

She made her way to the humming glass-like circle, ignoring Ralph's protests. Glancing back, she offered him a last apologetic look before stepping through the portal.

On the other side lay a wide circular clearing,

encircled by tall pine trees and bathed in moonlight. At its centre, small green blades of grass pushed through the scattered dry ash—the cold, black remnants of a burnt tree.

Naldy heard someone emerge from the portal behind her, and without turning, she knew Ralph had followed.

'You should go back,' said Naldy, staring painfully at the jagged stump positioned in the centre of the clearing. 'I don't want to be responsible for your safety.'

'I know this place,' said Ralph sadly, recognising their location. 'This is where Oak once stood. I'm not leaving you to face Maverick alone. That is what you're planning to do, isn't it?'

'I asked him to meet me here,' said Naldy as the glass portal diminished before vanishing entirely.

'Why here? What's your plan, Naldy?'

'To make a trade,' came Maverick's voice from the darkness of the forbidding trees. 'A Devante for the feline.'

Although they had heard the wizard's voice, they could not see him. Then, stepping out of the shadows, Establishment guards encircled the entire perimeter of the clearing. Naldy and Ralph stepped closer to the charred stump in the middle. There must have been at least one hundred guards.

'Naldy,' whispered Ralph, 'we are outnumbered. Let's go.'

She did not respond to him but watched as the blue-blazered guards made a small gap. The tall wizard entered, dressed in an elegant black cloak. Behind Maverick came Getergrin, Mortous, Deslong, and Rupert. They were all dressed as elegantly as Maverick, each in a different coloured cloak.

'It took us some time to capture your little friend,' said Maverick.

'He hasn't brought Smookers,' said Ralph quietly. 'We must go, Naldy.'

'We sent Rupert south,' continued Maverick, leaning on his cane. Rupert's expression remained stern and rigid as the wizard spoke. 'The creature was quite fond of him.'

'How could you,' spat Ralph at his cousin. Rupert glared stonily.

'Now, now,' said Maverick, 'let's not start another fight. You are far outnumbered. Your lucurn candle mentioned a trade. Shall we get on with it so we can all go home? Guards!'

Two guards entered the circle carrying an iron cage. Smookers had just enough room to pace anxiously back and forth. The guards placed the cage on the ground next to Maverick.

'We can't trust him, Naldy,' said Ralph bitterly. 'None of you should trust him. We know who you really are. You aren't *really* Maverick—you're Titus. We saw how your father treated you. You want to punish him by destroying all magic—the thing he always loved more than you.'

Ralph's words wiped the sneer from Maverick's face. The wizard's posture changed, and he seemed uncomfortable.

'But he isn't here to witness it,' continued Ralph. 'You had your father killed. When you destroy all magic, it won't be him who suffers.'

Standing loyally behind Maverick, the Seagull Society members appeared unbothered by Ralph's words—if anything, they seemed amused by Ralph's accusations.

'Titus was killed,' said Deslong, chuckling. 'Many centuries ago.'

'It is the truth,' said Ralph. 'He went back in time.'

'Audry's lies have found you somehow,' groaned Mortous. 'She had a penchant for peddling falsehoods.'

'They are not lies,' said Ralph, taken aback by what Mortous had said.

'Audry was always jealous,' said Mortous. 'Especially of those who achieved success. It is a lie that we have all heard.'

'Tell them what we saw, Naldy,' said Ralph.

Naldy remained silent. Although she knew it to be the truth, it was obvious that Maverick's supporters would not believe them.

'Hannah always had the spotlight,' said Deslong. 'Audry—oh, she was beautiful, yes—but she lacked Hannah's charisma. Together, they created the highest-ranking Devante. There's no denying her intelligence. But after Hannah's death, Audry sadly became increasingly envious. Hannah's name was somewhat synonymous with the Devante. Hannah sacrificed herself, and history remembers her for it. They do not remember Audry.'

'Audry,' added Mortous, 'went batty after her dear Hannah passed. Poor thing. They say she even stopped taking her Veserum. A death wish, some say. Unable to bear the loss.'

'Rumours became the only way that she could remain relevant,' said the Professor.

'That is enough history, Deslong,' said Maverick.

'Yes, we are not here for a history lesson,' said Naldy. 'I am here for Smookers.'

Maverick and Naldy shared a look of momentary understanding. The wizard unlatched the cage door and reached in, picking up Smookers by the scruff. Smookers dangled from his grasp, intense distrust on his little furry face. Maverick held him away from his torso so Smookers' desperate claws couldn't swipe at him.

'The Devante,' said Maverick, a bitter sneer on his face.

'Let him go first,' demanded Naldy. 'Then, I will give you what you have come for.'

Maverick placed the cat on the ground, and Smookers scurried to Naldy. She bent and lovingly picked him up. He rubbed his furry face fondly against her cheek.

Naldy focused on trying to create another portal —but none would emerge.

'Smookers,' whispered Naldy in the cat's ear, 'make for the safety of the trees and do not return.'

'What a heartfelt reunion,' said Maverick. 'I hate to interrupt, but we have unfinished business. The magic of H, if you please.'

Naldy gently placed Smookers on the ground, and he scampered away, weaving between the legs of the nearby guards before making for the cover of the forest.

'*Locultra*,' said Ralph, thrusting his palm forward. Nothing happened.

Maverick and the Seagull Society members sniggered in amusement.

'I've already tried,' said Naldy to Ralph. 'I'm an Effangale, Ralph. I thought we'd be able to escape through a portal. He must have undone the spell.'

'You can recreate it,' said Ralph frantically.

'What makes someone great,' interrupted Maverick, taking a few long strides forward, gripping his black cane, 'is a good balance of imagination and sheer cunning.'

'You have the magic of H,' said Ralph urgently to Naldy. 'You can create any spell. Recreate the spell to form a portal.'

'It's not working, Ralph, nothing is working.'

In one swift movement, Ralph reached into his pocket and pulled out his magical carpet. The blue material unfurled with a majestic shimmer. He took Naldy's hand, and they leapt onto the carpet. It lifted barely off the ground before vanishing beneath them. They fell, landing hard on the cold, ash-covered dirt.

'You will not escape,' she heard Maverick's voice, but when Naldy glanced up, the wizard's lips were not moving. She could hear his voice in her head. 'Any spell you create, I will undo. You will not escape me. I can hear every thought in your head.'

Naldy felt as if her heart had plunged into ice-cold water. Maverick was reading her mind.

'I should have listened to you,' said Naldy to Ralph. 'I don't know what to do.'

'Alright, Titus,' said Ralph, raising his palms, his blue eyes squinted in concentration. 'You want the magic of H? Well, you shan't get it without a good duel.'

A jet of brilliant green shot from Ralph's palms, and Maverick skilfully leapt out of the spell's way. The rest of the Seagull Society stood back, watching as the two wizards engaged in a magical battle. The guards watched on, stubbornly maintaining their circle—ducking only when a spell whizzed violently in their direction.

As coloured light soared recklessly across the clearing, Naldy stood motionless, feeling numb and frozen to the ground. It wasn't a spell keeping her in place, but her own inner thoughts. Oak had once cursed her—in this very spot—to teach her to put others first. Now, she feared that saving Smookers had been selfish, and magical folk everywhere would pay the price for her foolishness. Despite Ralph's warnings, she had walked right into the wizard's trap.

'Naldy,' warned Ralph—but it was too late. She felt her body drop to the ground as a spell collided with her. A second darting ball of orange flew noisily overhead.

Naldy realised the first spell to strike her had

been Ralph's—he had knocked her to the ground to protect her from Maverick's whirring orange spell.

She sat up. They were surrounded by at least one hundred guards, possibly more, with the experienced Seagull Society members standing by. Naldy knew there was no conceivable way for them to win. It was clear that if Ralph had the fortune of injuring Maverick, the others would quickly intervene.

She watched Ralph and Maverick move about the clearing with light steps, evading attacks and adeptly retaliating with quick spells. Naldy was astonished by Ralph's ability to duel. She took a deep breath, telling herself she needed to stand. She mustn't give up, despite the improbable odds. She had to help Ralph.

Lifting herself from the ground and holding out her palms, she sent a lightning-like spell hurtling towards Maverick. The spell missed the wizard.

'No, you don't,' said Mortous, using magic to bind Naldy's feet. She fell back to the ground.

Naldy shifted the weight of her body, lifting an arm, ready to cast another spell. She felt someone grip her forearm. Mortous attached black leather cuffs to her wrists. It was too late—she had been too slow to join the fight and was now unable to produce magic.

'It'll be better for you if you don't resist,' said Mortous, nodding. 'Just wait here until Maverick is done with your companion.'

Out of nowhere, Smookers leapt onto Mortous's

chest, clawing at his face.

'Get off me!' shrieked Mortous, failing to pry Smookers' claws from his skin.

Mortous finally managed to pull the cat from his body. Smookers had drawn blood. The witch cupped his bloody cheek and returned to the other Society members, whimpering. Smookers climbed onto Naldy's chest and anxiously pressed his paws against her, urging her to get up.

'I told you to go, Smookers,' said Naldy sadly. 'It's no good, we're outnumbered. You have to leave before it's too late.'

He chewed at the leather cuffs, but Naldy could see that even the cat's sharp teeth couldn't pierce the thick leather.

Naldy heard Ralph cry out in pain. Maverick had sent a deep purple electric bolt from the end of his cane, and the ruthless spell had struck him, lifting him inches from the ground. Ralph's face twisted in concentration as he struggled to break free.

Maverick calmly approached Ralph and reached for his right ear. The wizard ripped the emerald earring from his earlobe, and blood spilt down Ralph's neck. The earring must have burned Maverick's hand—he winced in pain before flinging the emerald to the ground.

Maverick lifted his cane, and the force of his purple spell vanished, causing Ralph to drop to the floor, cupping his bloody ear. He crawled across the ground, reaching for his Imporiom, but Maverick speared the end of his black cane into the earth to obstruct his path.

'I won't deny you are good with a spell,' said Maverick, smiling. 'You are a quick learner, like myself.'

'I am nothing like you,' snapped Ralph, disgusted by Maverick's words.

The guards lining the circle appeared relieved that the duel had ended. The Society members showed no surprise that Maverick had emerged the winner. The wizard pointed his cane at Ralph's chest, but before magic could emerge, Smookers—having had no luck with Naldy's leather cuffs—vaulted at Maverick.

The wizard's reflexes were quick, and a spell collided with Smookers. The cat let out a distressing wail, falling limply to the ground.

'Smookers,' cried Naldy, her vision blurred from her watery eyes.

She crawled towards Smookers—but felt a hand grip her ankle, pulling her to a halt.

'You shouldn't move,' said Mortous, holding her still.

Naldy was too far from Smookers to tell whether he was still breathing.

'Let us get on with things,' said Maverick, spinning to face Ralph once more.

He pointed his cane at Ralph's chest. Ralph closed his eyes, wincing in fear and bracing for the spell—but the wizard seemed to change his mind. Instead of casting something lethal, leather cuffs materialised around Ralph's wrists.

Maverick's black embroidered cloak rippled as he turned and stepped towards Naldy. A pang of guilt and shame gripped her as she stared up at his gaunt face. Everything they had lost on their quest to save magic, all they had been through, seemed pointless now. Naldy could see no way out.

Maverick directed his cane at her, the corner of his mouth raised in a satisfied smirk. But then, a suppressed sneeze distracted him. Maverick turned, wincing. One of the guards had sneezed.

'Who was that?' asked Maverick, his forehead creased in agitation.

Nobody answered. Maverick raised his head with deliberate sternness.

'He's allergic to cats,' muttered one of the guards, nearly swallowing his words.

'Guards,' ordered Maverick, as a shimmering portal appeared. 'You are to make your way back to The Great City.'

'They ought to stay,' said Mortous. 'You have yet to make the extraction, Maverick. They may still be of use—for our protection.'

Maverick looked offended by the remark—it was clear from his expression that he considered himself protection enough.

The wizard stood with his chin held high. The guards took it as their cue and immediately shuffled through the portal, one by one.

'Is that wise, Maverick?' asked Getergrin, nervously watching the blue-blazered guards stepping through the portal. 'Perhaps we oughtn't send them away.'

'All my life, they have stood by,' mumbled Maverick to himself. Of everyone present, Naldy was close enough to hear him. 'Little good they have ever done for me.'

Once the last guard disappeared through the humming glass circle, the portal closed and vanished. The wizard took a deep breath, lifting his black cane once more.

'Why did you want them sent away?' asked Deslong.

'Only the worthy shall bear witness,' said Maverick confidently. 'The two halves of the Devante will be united—it is a sight only Society members should be privileged to behold.'

Maverick's words pleased the Society members. However, Naldy knew he had dismissed the guards before they could discover the sudden loss of magic that was about to occur.

'I know you have felt great pain,' said Naldy softly, meeting Maverick's black eyes. 'Your father unfairly hurt you. But this will not fix it, Titus.'

A ray of light erupted from the wizard's cane, and Naldy felt something attempting to lift out of her body. It felt as if a part of her soul was trying to tear itself away. It wasn't a painful feeling—there was something strangely spiritual about the sensation. A kaleidoscopic light lifted from her, humming softly as the ground vibrated. The light coursed through Maverick's cane, travelling up his hand.

Then, it was gone. The humming stopped, and

the pine trees' gentle sway could be heard.

Ralph was cupping his torn earlobe, blood trickling down his arm, his pale face fixed on Maverick with a frightened expression. The members of the Seagull Society struggled to mask their own fear. Naldy had never seen Mortous this troubled as the witch gazed nervously at the tall wizard.

They all knew the Corium and H had been united. They all waited with bated breath.

Maverick raised his eyes to the moon above, smiling serenely.

'The things we will be able to achieve,' muttered Deslong anxiously, stepping forward. 'The Establishment will be ours to control for many centuries. Congratulations, Maverick, my dear friend.'

Maverick glanced sourly at Deslong before turning away. He lifted his cane, and shades of green light—almost gas-like—poured from his Imporiom, travelling in wavelike patterns across the sky. A faint, thunderous rumbling echoed around them.

When the vibrations stopped, the wizard lowered his cane, and with his back still turned to them, he gently laughed. It was the happy laugh of someone who had spent many years trying to achieve something and had finally done so. It was both triumphant and a laugh of great relief.

'Shall the prisoners be taken to The Great City then?' asked Getergrin. 'You will be celebrated, Maverick, for capturing the feared witch.'

Getergrin was the only one who appeared unaware of the immense change. He looked at Mortous and Deslong, who both had concerned expressions.

'What have you done?' asked Mortous, all colour had drained from his face.

Naldy knew Getergrin had no magical ability and hadn't felt the shift. But like the others, she had sensed it. She knew she would not be able to produce magic. Rupert seemed to have realised the situation from his companions' troubled expressions.

'Should we summon the guards,' suggested Getergrin. 'They can help escort the prisoners.'

'You have destroyed it,' said Deslong softly. 'But why? Why would you do such a thing?'

The latch on Naldy and Ralph's leather cuffs slipped free. She knew it had been magic keeping them secured.

'The girl has undone her restraints,' said Getergrin, panicked. 'The boy, too.'

'Do not fear,' said Maverick. 'They will not harm you, Getergrin. You needn't worry. I will not harm you either.'

Maverick scrutinised Deslong, Mortous and Rupert.

'*Prosterno,*' called Deslong, raising his palms.

No spell was produced.

'The girl was right,' said Mortous, his mouth open in awe. 'Audry had spoken the truth all along. It is you, isn't it? Titus.'

Mortous dropped to his knees, lowering his head

in a reverent bow. Rupert followed his lead, also falling to his knees.

'But you helped us to create the Devante,' said Deslong, taking an anxious step backwards. 'Why would you want to destroy the very thing you helped make, Maverick?'

'He is not Maverick, Deslong,' said Mortous from the ground. 'You are standing before the greatest wizard to have ever lived. Bow before him. He is in control of great power. He carries the highest-ranking Devante, and it is complete. It will be my pleasure to serve alongside you, Titus.'

Maverick turned his nose up at Mortous as if he was a bad smell.

'Why have you undone magic?' asked Deslong, tensely. 'You must cast a spell to bring back our power.'

'Get on your knees, Deslong,' said Mortous. 'Show some respect. It is not Maverick who stands before you but our new leader. We must pledge our loyalty.'

'My next spell,' said the wizard, raising his cane, 'will be the last.'

The wizard tapped his cane on the ground. A mesmerising ball of kaleidoscopic light emerged from the tip. Naldy knew it was the power of the final surviving Devante—H and Corium united. Maverick was preparing to destroy it to ensure magic could never be restored. In one swift motion, the wizard drove his cane through the kaleidoscopic ball.

'No,' shouted Naldy and Ralph in unison, hurling

their bodies towards him.

Naldy seized Maverick's foot, and Ralph grabbed the wizard's arm.

The cane pierced the multicoloured orb, fracturing it into millions of tiny beams of light. Naldy felt like the ground was swallowing her.

Magic had been destroyed.

Chapter Twenty-Six

BLOODLINE

The scent of sweet roasting butternut pumpkin filled Naldy's nostrils, and there was a soothing warmth on her cheek as she lifted her head from the wooden floor. Orange flames crackled in the nearby hearth of the familiar stone fireplace. Naldy knew she was inside the Witch House.

'Is this a memory?' asked Ralph. He was standing beside Maverick, who leant casually on his cane.

'It will all be over soon,' said Maverick.

She raised her body from the floorboards to take in the living room. Everything was almost exactly as it had been when Naldy had lived at the Witch House. The same comfortable clutter filled the shelves. Soft candlelight and the glow from the fireplace created a cosy atmosphere.

It was dark outside the windows, and the pattering rain obscured her view of the nearby pine trees. Naldy knew that by destroying the final Devante, Maverick had been thrust into the memory of the person who had invented it. When they had grabbed onto the wizard's body, they too were pulled into the memory.

'Whose memory is this?' asked Ralph.

'Hers,' replied Maverick, nodding towards the sofa.

Amongst all the items, Naldy had failed to notice Hannah Hale slumped on the sofa with a swollen pregnant abdomen.

The woman reminded Naldy so much of her mother, Tarren, with her long black hair and angular jaw. Hannah sat peacefully, a hand resting on her stomach.

Naldy faced Maverick. There was no point in trying to fight the wizard; the two could not harm each other in this space.

'You've destroyed the last Devante,' said Naldy, feeling the first twinge of grief.

'And with it, he has destroyed all magic,' added Ralph. His face held no trace of hope.

'It cannot be undone,' said Maverick, his eyes fixed on the pregnant woman. 'The invention that so many have coveted, the power many have sought their entire lives, no longer exists.'

'But why?' asked Naldy. 'You spent your whole childhood longing for magic. So why have you spent your whole adulthood trying to destroy it? Your father is not here to witness any of it.'

'I know you have glimpsed some of my memories,' said Maverick, shifting with noticeable discomfort. 'I have known of this quirk Mason introduced to the Devante for a long time. I have seen some of yours, too.'

'Some of my memories?'

'Your parents abandoned you,' said Maverick. 'I saw you, a young girl, waiting by the door. The truth is, they prioritised the safety of the Devante over their relationship with you, their one daughter. They left you alone, fleeing to Arkus Day. They prioritised magic.'

She felt her chest tighten. Naldy had despised the wizard for so long, but as she returned his gaze, a sadness overcame her.

'They left for my protection,' replied Naldy timidly. 'They knew the Devante were being hunted.'

In that moment, she couldn't help but feel a wave of pity for the wizard. Maverick had been loathed by his father through no fault of his own—and as she stared at the bitter sneer on his face, she could see he might never fully heal from his father's lack of love.

The front door creaked open—bringing Naldy out of her thoughts.

'Dinner smells delicious,' called a young Audry from the hallway. Naldy could hear the woman removing her shoes and hanging her coat. When Audry entered the room, Naldy hadn't expected another pregnant belly.

'Always my favourite on a cold winter's night,' said Audry, approaching Hannah and lowering herself onto the sofa. Her red hair and youthful face were wet.

'How was your walk?' asked Hannah. 'You didn't wear your hood, I see.'

'I love walking in this weather,' replied Audry,

placing both hands on her stomach. 'You'd think we were both having twins judging from our size.'

'We are having twins,' replied Hannah, taking one of Audry's hands.

'Just one twin each,' said Audry. Her relaxed expression changed to concern. 'What is it? You look troubled?'

'There is something we need to discuss.'

'If it is about the Society, Hannah, I do not want to discuss it. Our work is done. We cannot be held responsible for how the other members conduct themselves with the Devante they have been given.'

'Maverick has handed the Aurum to Titus,' replied Hannah, letting go of Audry's hand.

'Why would he do that?' asked Audry. 'Titus, famously, has no magical ability.'

From the corner of her eye, Naldy caught Maverick wince.

'That is what I want to discuss with you,' said Hannah, unsettled.

'We moved here to start a family,' said Audry, frowning. 'Look at us. Any day now. Let us focus on this. You promised we'd put the Society work behind us. It is not our fault that Odorf refused a Devante and retreated south to the commune, or that Mortous has preoccupied himself with becoming ruler of The Mortous Woods, contending with the Great Fairy Queen. Mason has secluded himself in the east with his boats, Grace went to the plains, and Deslong, well, he won't leave The Academy. And now, you tell me Maverick has given the Aurum to

Titus.'

'And disappeared.'

'You must not blame yourself, Hannah. We have done what we could and must get on with things.'

'Let us have dinner,' said Hannah, slowly lifting herself from the sofa. She made her way through to the kitchen.

Audry appeared bothered by Hannah, and after a quiet moment of sitting, she lifted her pregnant body from the sofa with some effort before following her. Maverick, Ralph and Naldy went with them. When they entered, Hannah was lifting a pumpkin pie from the wood-fired oven.

'You are not to blame,' said Audry, sitting at the table, which had been laid with plates and cutlery. 'The Society is afraid of losing the creation they spent so long making. You must not blame yourself for how they have chosen to use their power.'

'There is something I need to tell you, Audry,' said Hannah, turning with a sad expression. Hannah placed the pie onto a wooden board in the centre of the kitchen table. She took a seat next to Audry.

'Maverick is Titus,' said Hannah.

'What do you mean?'

'We should never have created the Devante. He has gone back in time, Audry, and he will hunt the Devante until they are all destroyed. We handed him the power to ruin everything we set out to protect. This is our fault.'

'Maverick helped create the Devante,' said Audry, shaking her head in disbelief.

'We have made something great,' said Hannah, pouring brew into her metal goblet. 'I'm not denying that—but I fear what we've created may be too great. That is why the *Banned Spells* must exist. We cannot be trusted to wield such power.'

'*Banned spells?* What are you talking about?'

'The twins,' said Hannah, looking sheepishly into her goblet.

'What have you done?' asked Audry, her voice suddenly desperate. 'What have you done with the twins, Hannah?'

'Together, they will make two halves of the same power.'

'Devante,' said Audry, lifting herself out of the chair. 'You haven't. Please, tell me you haven't made the children Devante. What have you done?'

'A bloodline,' replied Hannah, her voice solemn. 'Don't you see? It is the only way magic can be protected. Each twin will hold tremendous power —a power strong enough to rule over the other Devante.'

'We are giving birth to prey,' said Audry, crossing towards the kitchen window where she peered at the pattering rain against the glass. 'I feel ill. You have made our children targets. They will be hunted.'

'They will protect the magic,' said Hannah. 'Believing we will always be around to do so is foolish, Audry. Even with Odorf's invention of Veserum, we cannot rely on ourselves to always be there. Titus has used its power to go back in time. We have a responsibility not to allow such things to happen again. I have ensured the twins hold a magic that somewhat restrains the others. They contain *Banned Spells*, preventing anyone from casting certain magic using the other Devante.'

'Do you hear yourself?' said Audry, gazing out at the dark, wet night. 'You are talking about our children. You told me we were having twins.'

'We are,' said Hannah.

'You lied to me.'

'They will be our daughters,' said Hannah delicately.

'But they will also be two halves of... what?'

'The highest-ranking Devante,' answered Hannah. 'They will protect magic. The power is split to give it the best chance.'

Naldy felt a pang of guilt at Hannah's words. She had failed to fulfil what she was born to do—protect the Devante.

From where Naldy stood, she could see Audry's reflection in the window, but she could not discern if it was Audry's cheeks that were wet with tears or if it was just the raindrops running down the glass outside.

'Did you ever really want to have a family with me?' asked Audry coldly.

'Of course I did,' said Hannah. 'Come and eat. It's your favourite.'

'You should have told me,' said Audry.

'I'm telling you now.'

'It's too late now,' replied Audry painfully,

turning and placing both hands on her round abdomen.

'Nobody will be able to destroy the magic,' said Hannah. 'If someone tries to erase the power, it will always return to the youngest female in the bloodline. Our children will always be the most powerful in existence. It will protect them.'

'The power will be a mark on their backs,' said Audry dryly.

The floor seemed to drop from beneath Naldy's feet, and a whirl of blurred colour surrounded her momentarily before being replaced by the darkness of night.

A strong, chill wind blew against her face.

They were standing high on the edge of a cliff overlooking a tumultuous sea, its choppy waves roaring below as they crashed against jagged rocks.

'It is the only way,' said Audry, as her mane of red hair whipped wildly around her tear-streaked face.

She stood a few metres from the cliff, watching the silhouette of a woman dangerously close to the edge, her back to them as she faced the sea. The woman didn't reply.

'The *Banned Spells* will be at risk of being undone,' Audry called over the howling wind. 'We cannot allow that to happen. This is the sole way to lock them in place.'

A sound came from the direction of the woman by the cliff, carried over the roar of the wind and waves. It was a squeaky wail—then another little wail joined in.

The woman facing the sea turned, and Naldy saw Hannah Hale holding two small, crying babies—one in each arm, both wrapped snugly in black knitted blankets.

'This is not how it's meant to be,' said Hannah sternly, framed by the stormy night sky.

'If they live,' began Audry, but she didn't finish her sentence, trailing off into silence.

'There, there,' said Hannah, rocking each swaddled baby gently in her arms. Their tiny voices stopped, soothed by the gentle motion of their mother.

'If they live,' said Audry, pained, 'the *Banned Spells* will be able to be undone.'

'If they live,' replied Hannah, approaching Audry with a tender expression, 'they will grow old, and they will protect the magic.'

'And who will protect them?' asked Audry.

'We will,' said Hannah, passing Audry one of the fragile bundles. 'Where is your broomstick? Let's return to the Witch House and never speak of this again.'

Naldy felt her body lurch forward. She found herself lying in the dirt of the moonlit clearing, gripping Maverick's black shoe. Ralph was clutching the wizard's arm. They had returned from the memory.

She felt the familiar rush of exhilaration coursing through her entire body. It was the same intense sensation she'd experienced on the battlefield and when on the boat from Arkus Day.

Naldy knew it was the combined power of H and the Corium—the power of the last surviving Devante—coursing through her body. Maverick had tried to destroy it, but as the bloodline still existed, it had come to her.

She glanced up to see Ralph tugging at Maverick's arm, trying to hold him back. Naldy released the wizard's foot and crawled backwards in desperation.

Mortous and Rupert were still on their knees, watching nearby with concerned faces, while Getergrin stood dumbfounded as he watched on. Deslong retreated cowardly into the cover of the forest.

From her great-great-grandmother's memory, Naldy knew the Devante's power could not be destroyed as long as the bloodline existed. But Maverick had seen the same memory, and she knew this meant the wizard would try to take her life—to end the bloodline and ensure magic could never be restored.

Naldy propped herself up, watching as Ralph struggled to hold back Maverick, whose face was twisted into an intense, determined sneer.

Though the wizard had succeeded in destroying all magic, Naldy knew she held the only source of power that could restore it—the combined magic of H and Corium. It had the power to create any spell, and she knew she had to re-invent magic.

She had to act fast. With a look of firm resolve, Naldy cast a spell, reigniting the power of magic —sending a thunderous boom reverberating across the atmosphere, emanating from her and rippling outward. Naldy saw Mortous's hair wisp upwards as the spell quivered over him. The branches of the pine trees trembled.

Freeing himself from Ralph's grasp, Maverick knocked the younger wizard with his cane. Ralph hit the ground.

Now that Naldy had restored magic—there was one more spell she knew she must cast to protect it— and she had little time. Maverick had lifted his sleek black cane and, with a swift movement, pointed it at her. She focused her energy inward, casting a final spell she hoped would protect the last surviving Devante.

The wizard's cane issued a surge of blue electricity, knocking Naldy to the ground. Her body flashed with pain.

Behind Maverick, Naldy glimpsed Ralph's hand reaching for his emerald earring in the dirt before another of Maverick's spells entered her body.

Shades of gas-like green rippled across the night sky. Though Naldy had just restored magic, Maverick had once again used the Devante—still within her—to undo it. Maverick lowered his cane as the moonlight illuminated his joyful smirk, knowing he was closer to attaining his goal. Naldy caught a glimpse of the lifeless, jagged stump behind him, where Oak had once stood tall. Anger bubbled within her as she tried to summon the strength to restore magic again.

'There is no point in fighting it,' the wizard said,

the folds of his black cloak draping from his body as he held himself in a smug posture. 'I have made you weak, and you do not have the strength to restore magic a second time. There is only one thing left for me to do.'

She felt lightheaded, as though she might faint at any moment. She tried to focus, but Maverick's earlier spell still sent waves of pain through her, making it hard to concentrate. The last Devante remained within her. She knew she had to restore magic—before the wizard took her life, before the Devante were lost forever.

'*Comburite*,' shouted Ralph, holding his earring. But there was no flame as his palms thrust towards the tall wizard.

'You think you can win?' said Maverick. He laughed coldly. 'Your Imporiom will not help you now, boy. She is too weak to bring magic back.'

Hasty footfalls could be heard on the ground. Maverick's collaborators must have been fleeing into the pine forest.

'My Imporiom may not be able to help,' said Ralph. 'But neither will yours. You cannot use it, Maverick—not unless magic is brought back.'

'I do not require magic,' said Maverick, sneering, 'for what I intend to accomplish next.'

The wizard pulled the tip of his cane, revealing a concealed silver longsword. Maverick turned away from Ralph and approached Naldy.

'Watch out,' called Ralph.

Before she could cast a spell, her whole body

turned ice cold. She heard Ralph's cry of anguish—a sound she'd never heard from him before—and it sent a shiver down her spine.

She caught sight of a long glint of silver protruding from her chest. Ralph's cry had come from sheer terror—Maverick had driven the sword into her flesh. The wizard stood over her, his black eyes squinting in concentration. He gripped the sword with one hand, while the other held the body of his black cane, which acted as a sheath.

'*Comburite*,' cried Ralph. Again, there was no flame.

'Grab the boy, Getergrin,' demanded Maverick, lifting his gaunt face. But even Getergrin—his most trusted ally—had deserted him. The Seagull Society had already fled into the forest.

The betrayal hurt Maverick, and for a fleeting moment, Naldy saw the disappointment in his expression. He winced before driving the sword deeper into her chest.

'Stop,' pleaded Ralph, rushing angrily towards him.

'You won't come any closer, Ralph,' said a familiar voice. It was Rupert's voice.

From the ground, Naldy saw Ralph's broad-shouldered cousin step between him and Maverick. He held a small silver blade with floral engravings in his outstretched arm, indicating he was ready to fight if his cousin came any closer.

'Carry on with your work, Maverick,' said Rupert dryly. 'Aim for the heart if you want it to stop beating.'

'She's going to die if we don't do anything,' said Ralph, his voice pained. 'It's me, Rupert. Get out of the way.'

'Take one step further, and you will regret it. Maverick is right, Ralph. It is unfair that some should hold power while others go without. This will create a fairer world.'

'What have they done to you?' asked Ralph, stunned.

Naldy was too weak to restore magic—she could feel herself dying. Her chest felt warm, blood seeping from it.

'Step out of the way,' said Ralph furiously.

'No,' replied Rupert, gripping his knife tighter.

Ralph leapt forward, seizing Rupert's arm. Naldy could see the two cousins struggling, each trying to get hold of the blade.

Maverick was too preoccupied watching the life drain from Naldy to care about the fight behind him. Naldy stared up into Maverick's face and into his black eyes. A flicker of pride passed over him.

The two cousins fell to the ground, out of sight, and Naldy couldn't tell who was winning the scuffle as she listened to them roll across the ash-covered dirt. But it didn't matter—she knew it was too late to be saved.

'It was a fight you were never going to win,' said Maverick, pressing down on the end of his cane.

Then, Naldy saw the younger wizard lift himself up, and with the blade in one hand, Ralph drove it deep into Maverick's neck.

'There is no magic to save you,' said Ralph, letting go of the blade, leaving it lodged in Maverick's flesh. 'You've undone it, you fool.'

Rivers of blood poured from the wizard's pierced skin. Maverick's expression changed from triumph to placid acceptance.

To Naldy's surprise, Maverick did not attempt to remove the blade. Nor did he try to fight or save himself. As the blood soaked through his embroidered cloak, he simply smiled peacefully. Maverick gently laid his weakening body on the ground next to her. She could hear the wizard wheezing, gasping for air, as the trickle of liquid filled his lungs.

'Naldy,' said Ralph, rushing to her side. He pulled out the longsword from her chest, casting it aside. 'You cannot leave. I'm going to bring back magic. Don't go anywhere. If you go, magic cannot be restored, and I won't be able to save you.'

Naldy's body was numb, and she could not speak. Rotating her head, she glanced at Maverick resting beside her. The wizard was dead. Naldy knew she, too, would die soon.

Ralph was mumbling something, but she could not hear him. He waved his palms over her body, trying to cast a spell, but Naldy knew it was too late to save her. It was too late to save magic.

Then, over Ralph's shoulders, she noticed Rupert rising up. He rose higher and higher—so high that his feet were no longer touching the ground. She wondered if she was hallucinating. Naldy tried to speak, to warn Ralph that his cousin was floating behind him, but her mouth would not move.

Behind Rupert's broad shoulders, large, translucent, glass-like wings stretched out.

Rupert looked patiently down at her—had he died and become an angel? Was he waiting for Naldy to join him?

As her consciousness faded, Naldy realised the end had come.

Chapter Twenty-Seven

THE DEPARTURE

Under Ralph's touch, her skin felt cold, but it was Naldy's unmoving hazel eyes—devoid of all hope—that revealed to him she had died.

'You cannot go,' cried Ralph. 'You cannot, Naldy.'

The emotional ache growing inside him became so strong that it seemed to numb any physical pain in his body. His bloody ear was still dripping onto his cloak, but he could not feel the injury.

Glancing around the clearing, Ralph took a moment to absorb the sinister sight. The black, broken stump stood jagged and burnt, like an ominous centrepiece.

Near the edge, marked by forbidding pine trees, Maverick's body lay motionless on its side. Resting beside him, lifeless, Naldy's pale skin caught the moon's soft light. Between them, a deep-coloured pool of blood merged, seeping into the dirt.

Ralph caught sight of a black ball of fur lying nearby. He made his way over to Smookers. There was no movement from their furry companion, and Ralph knew that Smookers had also been a victim of

Maverick. More tears trickled down his cheeks.

Mortous, Deslong and Getergrin had disappeared into the forest, and he knew they'd be halfway to the nearest town.

Naldy's death also meant magic had been lost. They had failed, and Maverick had won. Ralph stood, clenching his emerald earring. He would give up all the magic in the world to bring back his friends.

But wait, thought Ralph. *A body was missing.*

He took in the clearing a second time, his vision blurred from tears.

'It is sad to see your friends die,' came Rupert's voice behind him.

Ralph's cousin hovered above the ground with two enormous outstretched wings emerging from his shoulders. Rupert smiled calmly.

'I've seen those wings before,' said Ralph.

'You have, yes,' said Rupert. 'I'm sorry to see them die.'

'You could have helped save her,' spat Ralph. 'You could have helped to save Betty, too. You betrayed us.'

'Sacrifices sometimes have to be made.'

'Those wings,' said Ralph, taking in their glass-like appearance. 'They belong to the Great Fairy Queen.'

Rupert lowered his body closer to Naldy's. He reached out an arm and gently stroked her cheek.

'She was strong,' remarked Rupert.

'It's you, isn't it?' said Ralph, watching fearfully as Rupert rose higher. 'You are the Great Fairy

Queen.'

'When Rupert dived into the lake,' continued his cousin, folding his wings a little. 'He sacrificed his life. That was the bargain he made. It belongs to me. He has tried to fight me at times, but it is a battle he cannot win. For he willingly gave his life when he went into the water.'

'What is it that you want?'

'What everybody else so desperately desires,' said Rupert, his wings stretching out again. 'I desire the highest power. Many have crossed the lake, seeking it, and all have failed. But when you three came, I saw the hope and determination in your eyes. It was unmatched by any who had crossed the lake before.'

'I knew something was wrong when we revived Rupert in The Great City. He would never betray us the way you have. He gave his life to save us.'

'And I possess it now,' said Rupert, crossing the clearing. 'Until you revived him, I have been restricted to the water of the lake. I will use his life to take what I have always longed for—what I have always feared. It will be mine to control.'

'It is too late,' said Ralph, fearlessly. 'You are too late. Naldy is dead. The magic of the Devante ends with the bloodline.'

'Yes,' said Rupert, facing him from the other side of the clearing. He raised his palms towards Naldy. 'We must act fast, or the bloodline will end.'

A great boom thundered across the Kirkwood Forest, frightening Ralph and making him shudder. Ralph knew that magic had—somehow—been restored.

'How did you do that? Is she still alive?'

'Naldy is dead,' said Rupert, slowly gliding towards her lifeless body. 'But the fetus within her is alive, and the little heart still beats.'

'The fetus?' said Ralph, confused. 'She is with child? But how?'

'Just as Hannah and Audry were impregnated with twins, your beloved Naldy used the Devante's power to cast a final spell, giving herself a daughter.'

'The magic has been transferred to her child,' said Ralph, rushing to Naldy's side. 'She kept the bloodline alive. We must revive her, or the baby will die.'

Ralph held his trembling hands over Naldy's body. He had tried using the Devante's power within Naldy to raise the dead before, but he had failed without Betty's assistance. Ralph's breathing was unsteady. He struggled to keep his hands still as he attempted to cast a spell to bring back Naldy from death.

'It is not working,' said Ralph, panicked, glancing at his cousin. 'You must help me.'

Ralph focused all his energy and attention on Naldy, willing her back to the world, but she remained lifeless.

'The power will be mine,' said a voice. But it was not Ralph's cousin's voice that had spoken—it was the husky voice of the Great Fairy Queen.

Ralph turned to see Rupert's strawberry-blonde hair lengthening and turning blue. His skin was beginning to glow. The blue hair stretched down the side of his whole body like a beautiful garment. His clothes vanished, and his broad shoulders narrowed. Rupert was transforming into the graceful figure of the Great Fairy Queen. The translucent wings stretched out, framing her formidable appearance.

It wasn't just the emergence of the Great Fairy Queen that startled him. Floating towards the woman was an amniotic sac, an unborn baby resting peacefully inside the fluid. The Fairy Queen had her arms outstretched, beckoning the unborn child towards her. Naldy lay motionless.

'I will raise you as my own,' said the woman. 'Together, we will accomplish great things.'

'What are you doing?' called Ralph. 'You must revive, Naldy.'

There was a flash of blinding light, and Ralph lifted an arm to shield his eyes. When the light retracted, he saw the Great Fairy Queen resting her hand on her slightly protruding belly. Ralph knew the child was within her.

'I will not only oversee the lake within the wood,' said the woman, rising higher. 'I will hold power enough to be the majesty of all corners of the world. All shall tremble in my presence.'

'You must revive her,' pleaded Ralph. 'Please... bring Naldy back to life.'

Something fast shot through the air, reflecting the Fairy Queen's glow as it spun towards her. Ralph recognised it as Rupert's small floral blade—

the same one he had driven into Maverick's neck. But how was it flying across the clearing towards the Fairy Queen? His gaze flicked to Maverick's body, and tears choked him.

'Not while the Hale line exists, you won't,' said Naldy, sitting upright as Ralph heard the blade embed itself deep into the Great Fairy Queen's chest.

Ralph cried out in relief—Naldy was alive. He realised she must have taken the blade from Maverick's neck and sent it spinning towards the Great Fairy Queen. His spell to bring her back from death had worked.

The Great Fairy Queen stared in horror at the blood seeping from her chest before dropping to the ground with a thud. Upon impact, another blinding flash of light erupted, and her appearance transformed back to that of his broad-shouldered cousin.

'Ralph,' said Rupert from the ground. He had no wings, and his own floral blade was still embedded in his chest. 'Please, cousin. You must help me.'

Ignoring his cousin, Ralph rushed to Naldy's side. Her chest was still covered in blood from the wound caused by Maverick's longsword.

'*Sanitatem Restituere*,' said Ralph. The wound on her chest began healing. 'You're alive, Naldy. I'm so happy you're alive.'

From the ground, he pulled her into a comforting hug. It was the most pleasant hug he'd ever had. There was life in her.

'Where is your Imporiom?' asked Naldy, letting

Ralph go.

'Here,' said Ralph, opening his clenched palm.

Naldy held the earring to his ear, which healed at her touch.

'Good as new,' she said.

'I thought I lost you,' said Ralph, feeling an ache of sadness wash over him again. 'The Devante. We need to save it. The Great Fairy Queen has it.'

Naldy placed her hand on her abdomen.

'The child is inside you?'

Naldy nodded. Ralph noticed the familiar glint of hope returning to her hazel eyes.

'You must help me,' whimpered Rupert from the ground.

Ralph stood and walked over to his cousin, looking down at Rupert with a sad expression.

'We can try to save him if you want?' said Naldy gently. 'I owe you at least that for bringing me back from death.'

'No,' said Ralph, shaking his head tearfully. 'His life belongs to the Fairy Queen. He decided to jump from the rowboat. I think we need to let him rest.'

Ralph held out his palm, and Maverick's Imporiom glided over to him. He caught the end of the silver sword.

'Please, cousin,' pleaded Rupert. 'I did not mean to betray you. If you help me, I can get you in good favour with Mortous and The Establishment.'

The floral blade was still embedded in his chest, and Ralph positioned the sharp tip of the longsword close to it. He pushed the blade deep into his cousin's body. The light from Rupert's blue eyes faded.

'Who'd have believed it,' said Naldy sadly, 'the fight for the Devante would end, not with spells and hexes, but with swords and gardening daggers.'

'The other Society members,' said Ralph, helping Naldy to her feet. 'They fled into the forest.'

'Let them go,' said Naldy. 'Without Maverick they do not have the courage to be leaders. History has proven that to be true.'

'The burnings. We need to stop The Great Witch Hunt.'

'The wizard's edicts,' said Naldy, 'I don't think they will survive. Not after tonight's events. Not with Maverick gone. And they do not have a Devante on their side. If Mortous, Deslong or Getergrin erect a single stake on the steps, they'll have us to deal with.'

'What do we do now, then?' asked Ralph.

'We bury the dead,' said Naldy softly.

'And afterwards?'

'Edengar,' said Naldy, looking at Ralph. 'You can come with me if you like?'

'Maybe,' said Ralph, catching himself admiring her bravery. 'What will you do in Edengar?'

'Before long,' said Naldy, 'I'll have a young one to raise. I'll have to teach her how to stay out of trouble.'

'Well,' replied Ralph, 'we are both well practised at that, aren't we.'

'I'd like to build a house by the river,' said Naldy. 'Set up a home there, in the ravine, near the dragons.

There will be a beautiful garden by Odorf's grave. It'll be peaceful, and I'll teach the little one all about her family and the Devante's long history as she grows up.'

'All about everything we've been through to save them,' said Ralph, smiling tearfully.

'Of course,' said Naldy. 'She'll know about you, and Oak, Betty and Barbra, Hereto, Odorf, and Mason —even Maverick.'

'Did we really stop him?' asked Ralph, staring at Maverick's lifeless body.

'The Devante will always be hunted,' replied Naldy, her hazel eyes reflecting the moonlight. Ralph noticed the seagull pin still attached to the breast of her travelling cloak. 'Others may come hunting it. Maybe even those still in the Seagull Society. But so long as the Hale line exists, you can always count on us to do our best to protect the magic.'

'Well, you needn't do it alone,' said Ralph. 'Which way to Edengar?'

They exchanged a tender look, one shared only by the most genuine of friendships.

Then, together, they set about burying Rupert and Maverick. By the time they'd completed the task, the sun was rising. Beside Oak's stump, they laid fresh flowers.

'I think it's time to go,' said Naldy.

'We have one more to bury,' he said with a heavy heart, turning towards Smookers.

'Come on, Ralph,' called Naldy, already making her way into the forest. 'It's a long journey to

Edengar. Let's stop by Greenswood for some brew.'

Ralph jolted as the black furball jumped to his feet and arched his back in a stretch. Ralph knew that she had revived him using the power of the Devante. Smookers tottered happily after Naldy.

Ralph pulled out his leather journal from the inside of his cloak pocket. So much had happened that he felt compelled to begin scribbling it all down so he didn't forget any of it.

'Ralph,' came Naldy's voice from up ahead. 'You better not be writing about me in that journal of yours.'

Ralph smiled, tucked his journal into his pocket, and followed Naldy under the cover of the pine trees of the Kirkwood Forest.